# MAP OF BONES

## BONES

A Σ Sigma Force novel

## JAMES ROLLINS

Printed and bound in Great Britain by Clays Ltd, St Ives plc

The Orion Publishing Group's policy is to use papers that
are natural, renewable and recyclable products and
made from wood grown in sustainable forests. The logging
and manufacturing processes are expected to conform to
the environmental regulations of the country of origin.

An Orion paperback

First published in the United States in 2005
by William Morrow
an imprint of HarperCollins*Publishers*
This paperback edition published in 2006
by Orion Books Ltd,
Orion House, 5 Upper St Martin's Lane,
London WC2H 9EA

An Hachette UK company

11  13  15  17  19  20  18  16  14  12

Reissued 2010

A CIP catalogue record for this book
is available from the British Library.

ISBN  978-1-4091-1752-0

To
Alexandra and Alexander.
May both your lives shine as
brightly as all the stars

# ACKNOWLEDGMENTS

In a book of this scope, I needed a legion of supporters: friends, family, critics, librarians, curators, travel agents, dishwashers, and pet-sitters. First, thanks to Carolyn McCray, who red-inked every page before anybody else, and Steve Prey, for his thoughts and insights that evolved into the artwork within these pages. Then, of course, I'm honored to acknowledge my posse of friends who meet every other week at Coco's Restaurant: Judy Prey, Chris Crowe, Michael Gallowglas, David Murray, Dennis Grayson, Dave Meek, Royale Adams, Jane O'Riva, Dan Needles, Zach Watkins, and Caroline Williams. And for all help with languages, my heartfelt appreciation to my friend from the Great White North, Diane Daigle. A special thanks to David Sylvian for his boundless energy, support, and enthusiasm and to Susan Tunis for her fact-checking of all manner and substance. For the inspiration for this story, I must credit the books by Sir Laurence Gardner and the pioneering research of David Hudson. Finally, the four people whom I respect for their friendship as much as their counsel: my editor, Lyssa Keusch, and her colleague May Chen, and my agents Russ Galen and Danny Baror. And as always, I must stress any and all errors of fact or detail fall squarely on my own shoulders.

The precision of any fiction is a reflection of the facts presented. As such, while truth may sometimes be stranger than fiction, fiction must always have a foundation of truth. To that end, all the artwork, relics, catacombs, and treasures described in this story are real. The historical trail revealed within these pages is accurate. The science at the heart of the novel is based on current research and discoveries.

# THE MEDITERRANEAN

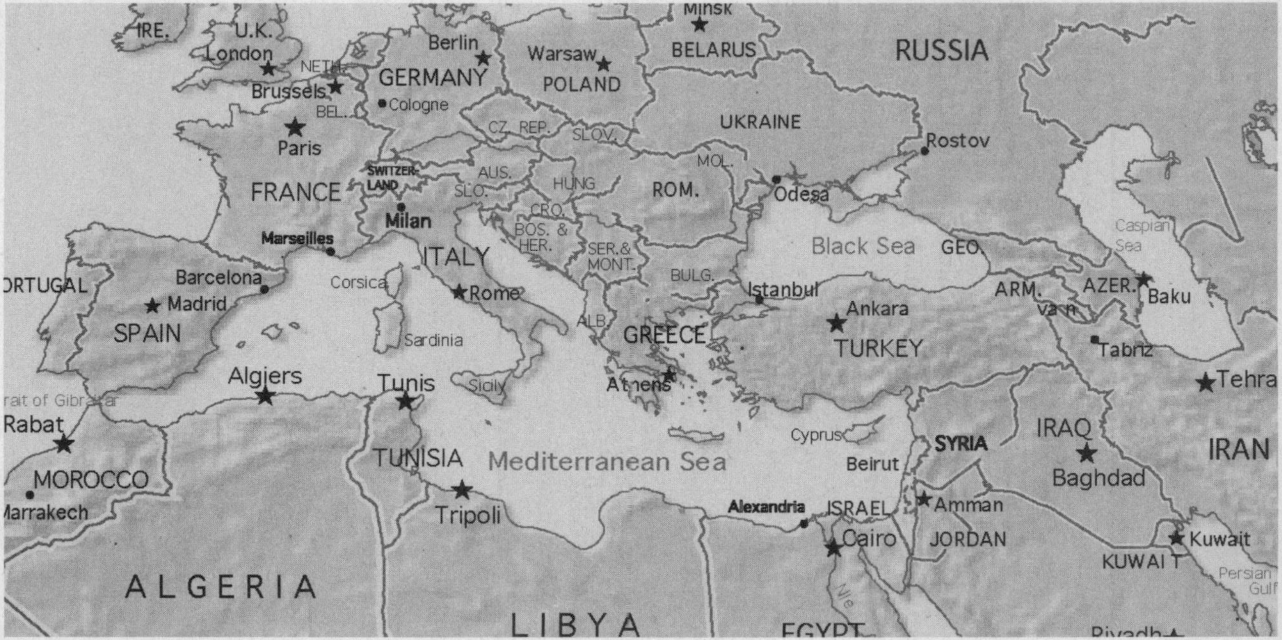

# THE VATICAN

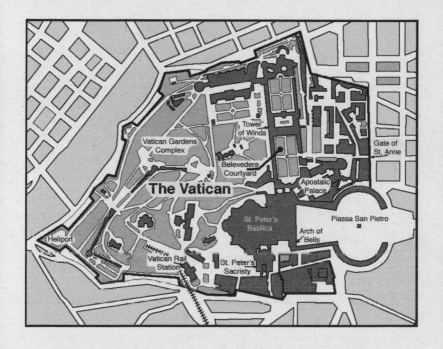

Tower
of Winds

Gate of
St. Anne

Vatican Gardens
Complex

Belevedere
Courtyard

**The Vatican**

Apostalic
Palace

St. Peter's
Basilica

Piassa San Pietro

Arch of
Bells

Heliport

Vatican Rail
Station

St. Peter's
Sacristy

The holy relics were granted to Rainald von Dassel, Archbishop of Cologne (1159–67), following Emperor Barbarossa's sacking of the city of Milan. Such a treasure was granted to the German Archbishop for his aid and chancellorship in service to the current Emperor. Not all were content to see such a treasure leave Italy . . . not without a struggle.

From *L'histoire de la Sainte Empire Romaine* (The History of the Holy Roman Empire), 1845, HISTOIRES LITTÉRAIRES

# PROLOGUE

The archbishop's men fled into the shadows of the lower valley. Behind them, atop the winter pass, horses screamed, arrow-bit and cleaved. Men shouted, cried, and roared. The clash of steel rang as silvery as a chapel's bells.

But it was not God's work being done here.

*The rear guard must hold.*

Friar Joachim clutched the reins of his horse as his mount slid on its haunches down the steep slope. The loaded wagon had reached the bottom of the valley safely. But true escape still lay another league away.

If only they could reach it . . .

With his hands clenched on the reins, Joachim urged his stumbling mare down to the valley's bottom. He splashed across an icy brook and risked a glance behind him.

Though spring beckoned, winter still ruled the heights. The peaks shone brilliantly in the setting sun. Snow reflected the light, while a billow of rime-frost flagged off the peaks' razored tips. But here in the shadowed gorges, snowmelt had turned the forest floor into a muddy bog. The horses slogged up to their fetlocks and threatened to break a bone with every step. Ahead the wagon was mired just shy of its axles.

Joachim kicked his mare to join the soldiers at the wagon.

Another team of horses had been hitched to the front.

1

Men pushed from behind. They must reach the trail coursing along the next ridgeline.

'Ey-ya!' yelled the wagon master, snapping a whip.

The lead horse threw its head back and then heaved against the yoke. Nothing happened. Chains strained, horses chuffed white into the cold air, and men swore most foully.

Slowly, too slowly, the wagon dragged free of the mud with the sucking sound of an open chest wound. But it was moving again at last. Each delay had cost blood. The dying wailed from the pass behind them.

*The rear guard must hold a little longer.*

The wagon continued, climbing again. The three large stone sarcophagi in the open wagon bed slid against the ropes that lashed them in place.

If any should break . . .

Friar Joachim reached the foundering wagon.

His fellow brother, Franz, moved his horse closer. 'The trail ahead scouts clear.'

'The relics cannot be taken back to Rome. We must reach the German border.'

Franz nodded, understanding. The relics were no longer safe upon Italian soil, not with the true pope exiled to France and the false pope residing in Rome.

The wagon climbed more quickly now, finding firmer footing with each step. Still, it trundled no faster than a man could walk. Joachim continued watching the far ridge, staring over his mount's rump.

The sounds of battle had settled to groans and sobbing, echoing eerily across the valley. The ring of swords had died completely, signaling the defeat of the rear guard.

Joachim searched, but heavy shadows steeped the heights. The bower of black pines hid all.

Then Joachim spotted a flash of silver.

A lone figure appeared, limned in a patch of sunlight, armor glinting.

Joachim did not need to see the red dragon sigil painted on the man's chestplate to recognize the black pope's lieutenant. The profane Saracen had taken the Christian name Fierabras, after one of Charlemagne's paladins. He stood a full head taller than all his men. A true giant. More Christian blood stained his hands than any other man's. But baptized this past year, the Saracen now stood beside Cardinal Octavius, the black pope who took the name Victor IV.

Fierabras stood in the patch of sunlight, making no attempt to chase.

The Saracen knew he was too late.

The wagon crested the ridge at last and reached the rutted, dry trail atop it. They would make good speed now. German soil lay only a league from here. The Saracen's ambush had failed.

Movement drew Joachim's attention.

Fierabras drew a great bow from over a shoulder, black as the shadows. He slowly set arrow to string, notched it, and then leaned back and drew a full pull.

Joachim frowned. *What did he hope to win with one feathered bolt?*

The bow sprang, and the arrow flew, arching over the valley, lost for a moment in the sunlight above the ridgeline. Joachim searched the skies, tense. Then, as silent as a diving falcon, the arrow struck, shattering into the centermost casket.

Impossibly, the sarcophagus's lid cracked with the sound of a thunderbolt. Ropes broke free as the crate split, scattering open. Loosed now, all three crates slid toward the open rear of the wagon.

Men ran forward, attempting to stop the stone sarcophagi from crashing to the ground. Hands reached. The wagon was halted. Still, one of the crates tilted too far. It toppled and crushed a soldier beneath, breaking leg and pelvis. The poor man's scream christened the air.

Franz hurried, dropping from his saddle. He joined the men in attempting to lift the stone crate off the soldier . . . and more importantly back into the wagon.

The sarcophagus was lifted, the man dragged free, but the crate was too heavy to raise to the wagon's height.

'Ropes!' Franz yelled. 'We need ropes!'

One of the bearers slipped. The sarcophagus fell again, on its side. Its stone lid fell open.

The sound of hoofbeats rose behind them. On the trail. Coming fast. Joachim turned, knowing what he'd find. Horses, lathered and shining in the sun, bore down on them. Though a quarter league off, it was plain all the riders were dressed in black. More of the Saracen's men. It was a second ambush.

Joachim merely sat his horse. There would be no escape.

Franz gasped – not at their predicament, but at the contents of the spilled sarcophagus. *Or rather the lack thereof.*

'Empty!' the young friar exclaimed. 'It's empty.'

Shock drove Franz back to his feet. He climbed atop the wagon's bed and stared into the crate shattered by the Saracen's arrow.

'Nothing again,' Franz said, falling to his knees. 'The relics? What ruin is this?' The young friar found Joachim's eyes and read the lack of surprise. 'You knew.'

Joachim stared back at the rushing horses. Their caravan had all been a ruse, a ploy to draw off the black pope's men. The true courier had left a day ahead, with a mule team, bearing the true relics wrapped in rough-spun cloth and hidden inside a hay bundle.

Joachim turned to stare across the vale at Fierabras. The Saracen might have his blood this day, but the black pope would never have the relics.

Never.

As midnight approached, Jason passed his iPod to Mandy. 'Listen. It's Godsmack's new single. It's not even released in the States yet. How cool is that?'

The reaction was less than Jason hoped. Mandy shrugged, expressionless, but she still took the proffered earphones. She brushed back the pink-dyed tips of her black hair and settled the phones to her ears. The movement opened her jacket enough to reveal the press of her apple-sized breasts against her black Pixies T-shirt.

Jason stared.

'I don't hear anything,' Mandy said with a tired sigh, arching an eyebrow at him.

*Oh.* Jason turned his attention back to his iPod and pressed Play.

He leaned back on his hands. The two were seated on a thin grass sward that framed the open pedestrian plaza, called the Domvorplatz. It surrounded the massive gothic cathedral, the Kölner Dom. Perched on Cathedral Hill, it commanded a view over the entire city.

Jason gazed up the length of the twin spires, decorated with stone figures, carved in tiers of marble reliefs that ranged from the religious to the arcane. Now, lit up at night, it held an eerie sense of something ancient risen from deep underground, something not of this world.

Listening to the music leaking from the iPod, Jason watched Mandy. Both were on summer holiday from Boston College, backpacking through Germany and Austria. They were traveling with two other friends, Brenda and Karl, but the other two were more interested in the local pubs than attending tonight's midnight mass. Mandy, though, had been raised Roman Catholic. Midnight masses at the cathedral were limited to a few select

5

holidays, each attended by the Archbishop of Cologne himself, like tonight's Feast of the Three Kings. Mandy had not wanted to miss it.

And while Jason was Protestant, he had agreed to accompany her.

As they waited for the approach of midnight, Mandy's head bopped slightly to the music. Jason liked the way her bangs swept back and forth, the way her lower lip pouted out as she concentrated on the music. Suddenly he felt a touch on his hand. Mandy had shifted her arm closer, brushing her hand atop his. Her eyes, though, remained fixed on the cathedral.

Jason held his breath.

For the past ten days, the two had found themselves thrown together more and more often. Before the trip, they had been no more than acquaintances. Mandy had been Brenda's best friend since high school, and Karl was Jason's roommate. Their two respective friends, new lovers, hadn't wanted to travel alone, in case their budding relationship soured while traveling.

It hadn't.

So Jason and Mandy often ended up sightseeing alone.

Not that Jason minded. He had been studying art history back at college. Mandy was majoring in European studies. Here their dry academic textbooks were given flesh and girth, weight and substance. Sharing a similar thrill of discovery, the two found each other easy traveling companions.

Jason kept his own eyes averted from her touch, but he did move one finger closer to hers. Had the night just gotten a tad brighter?

Unfortunately the song ended too soon. Mandy sat straighter, pulling away her hand to remove the earphones.

'We should be getting inside,' she whispered, and nodded toward the line of people flowing through the open door of the cathedral. She stood up and buttoned her

jacket, a conservative black suit coat, over her flamboy-
ant T-shirt.

Jason joined her as she smoothed her ankle-length skirt
and combed the pink tips of her hair behind her ears. In
a breath, she transformed from a slightly punk college
student into a staid Catholic schoolgirl.

Jason gaped at the sudden transformation. In black jeans
and a light jacket, he felt suddenly underdressed to attend
a religious service.

'You look fine,' Mandy said, seeming to read his worry.

'Thanks,' he mumbled.

They gathered their things, threw their empty Coke
cans into a nearby trashcan, and crossed the paved
Domvorplatz.

'*Guten Abend,*' a black-frocked deacon greeted them
at the door. '*Willkommen.*'

'*Danke,*' Mandy mumbled as they climbed the stairs.

Ahead, candlelight flowed through the cathedral's open
doorway, flickering down the stone steps. It enhanced the
feeling of age and ancientness. Earlier in the day, while
taking a cathedral tour, Jason had learned that the cathedral's cornerstone had been laid back in the thirteenth
century. It was hard to fathom such a breadth of time.

Bathed in candlelight, Jason reached the massive carved
doors and followed Mandy into the front foyer. She
dabbed holy water from a basin and made the sign of the
cross. Jason felt suddenly awkward, acutely aware that
this was not his faith. He was an interloper, a trespasser.
He feared a misstep, embarrassing himself and in turn
Mandy.

'Follow me,' Mandy said. 'I want to get a good seat,
but not too close.'

Jason stepped after her. As he entered the church proper,
awe quickly overwhelmed unease. Though he had already
been inside and learned much about the history and art of
the structure, he was again struck by the simple majesty

of the space. The long central nave stretched four hundred feet ahead of him, bisected by a three-hundred-foot transept, forming a cross with the altar at the center.

Yet it was not the length and breadth of the cathedral that captured his attention, but its impossible *height*. His eyes were drawn up and up, guided by pointed archways, long columns, and the vaulted roof. A thousand candles trailed thin spirals of smoke, sailing heavenward, flickering off the walls, redolent with incense.

Mandy led him toward the altar. Ahead, the transept areas to either side of the altar had been roped off, but there were plenty of empty seats in the central nave.

'How about here?' she said, stopping midway up the aisle. She offered a small smile, half thanks, half shyness.

He nodded, struck dumb by her plain beauty, a Madonna in black.

Mandy took his hand and pulled Jason down to the end of the pew, by the wall. He settled to his seat, glad for the relative privacy.

Mandy kept her hand in his. He felt the heat of her palm.

The night certainly *was* brightening.

Finally, a bell sounded and a choir began to sing. The Mass was beginning. Jason took his cues from Mandy: standing, kneeling, and sitting in an elaborate ballet of faith. He followed none of it, but found himself intrigued, becoming lost in the pageantry: the robed priests swinging smoking globes of incense, the processional that accompanied the arrival of the archbishop with his tall miter hat and gold-trimmed vestments, the songs sung by both choir and parishioners, the lighting of the Feast candles.

And everywhere the art became as much a part of the ceremony as the participants. A wooden sculpture of Mary and baby Jesus, called the Milan Madonna, glowed with age and grace. And across the way, a marble statue of Saint Christopher bore a small child in his arms with a beatific smile. And overlooking all were the massive Bavarian stained-glass windows, dark now, but still resplendent with reflected candlelight, creating jewels out of ordinary glass.

But no piece of art was more spectacular than the golden sarcophagus behind the altar, locked inside glass and metal. While only the size of a large trunk and constructed in the shape of a miniature church, the reliquary was the centerpiece of the cathedral, the reason for the construction of such a massive house of worship, the focal point of faith and art. It protected the church's most holy relics. Constructed of solid gold, the reliquary had been forged before the cathedral had even broken ground. Designed by Nicolas of Verdun in the thirteenth century, the sarcophagus was considered to be the best example of medieval goldwork in existence.

As Jason continued his study, the service wound slowly toward the end of the Mass, marked by bells and prayers. At last, it came time for Communion, the breaking of the Eucharistic bread. Parishioners slowly filed from their pews, traveling up the aisles to accept the body and blood of Jesus Christ.

When her time came, Mandy rose along with the others in her pew, slipping her hand from his. 'I'll be right back,' she whispered.

Jason watched his pew empty and the slow procession continue toward the altar. Anxious for Mandy's return, he rose to stretch his legs. He used the moment to study the statuary that flanked a confessional booth. Now standing, he also regretted that third can of Coke he had consumed. He glanced back toward the cathedral's vestibule. There was a public restroom outside the nave.

Glancing longingly back there, Jason was the first to spot a group of monks entering the rear of the cathedral, filing through all the back doors. Though in full-length black robes, hooded and belted at the waist, something immediately struck Jason as odd. They moved too quickly, with an assured military precision, slipping into shadows.

Was this some final bit of pageantry?

A glance around the cathedral revealed more cloaked figures at other doors, even beyond the roped transept beside the altar. While keeping their heads bowed piously down, they also seemed to be standing guard.

What was going on?

He spotted Mandy near the altar. She was just accepting her Communion. There were only a handful of parishioners behind her. *Body and blood of Christ,* Jason could almost lip-read.

*Amen,* he answered himself.

The Communion finished. The last parishioners returned to their seats, including Mandy. Jason waved her into the pew, then sat next to her.

'What's with all the monks?' he asked, leaning forward.

She had knelt down with her head bowed. Her only answer was a shushing sound. He sat back. Most of the parishioners were also kneeling, heads bowed. Only a few like Jason, those who had not taken Communion, remained seated. Ahead, the priest finished tidying up, while the elderly archbishop sat atop his raised dais, chin to chest, half dozing.

The mystery and pageantry had died to embers in Jason's heart. Maybe it was just the pressure of his bladder, but all he wanted to do was get out of here. He even reached to Mandy's elbow, ready to urge her to leave.

Motion ahead stopped him. The monks on either side of the altar pulled weapons from beneath folds of cloth. Gunmetal shone with oil in the candlelight, snub-nosed Uzis, mounted with long black silencers.

A chatter of gunfire, no louder than a chain-smoker's staccato cough, spat across the altar. Heads rose along the pews. Behind the altar, the priest, garbed in white, danced with the impacts. It appeared as if he were being pelted with paintballs – crimson paintballs. He fell atop the altar, spilling the chalice of wine along with his own blood.

After a stunned silence, cries rose from the parishioners. People sprang up. The elderly archbishop stumbled from his dais, drawing to his feet in horror. The sudden motion knocked his miter hat to the floor.

Monks swept up the aisles . . . from the rear and the sides. Orders were shouted and barked in German, French, and English.

*Bleiben Sie in Ihren Sitzen . . . Ne bouge pas . . .*

The voices were muffled, the faces beneath the hoods obscured by half-masks of black silk. But the raised weapons punctuated their orders.

*Stay seated or die!*

Mandy sat back with Jason. Her hand reached for his. He clutched her fingers and glanced around, unable to blink. All the doors were closed, guarded.

What was going on?

From the pack of armed monks near the main entrance, a figure appeared, dressed like the others, only taller, seeming to rise as if called forth. His cloak was more like a cape. Clearly some leader, he carried no weapon as he strode boldly down the central aisle of the nave.

He met the archbishop at the altar. A heated argument ensued. It took Jason a moment to realize they were speaking in Latin. The archbishop suddenly fell back in horror.

The leader stepped aside. Two men came forward. Guns blazed. The aim was not murder. They fired upon the faceplate that sealed the golden reliquary. Glass etched and pocked, but held. Bulletproof.

'Thieves . . .' Jason mumbled. This was all an elaborate robbery.

11

The archbishop seemed to draw strength from the stubbornness of the glass, standing taller. The leader of the monks held out his hand, speaking still in Latin. The archbishop shook his head.

'*Lassen Sie dann das Blut Ihrer Schafe Ihre Hände beflecke,*' the man said, speaking German now.

*Let your sheep's blood be upon your hands.*

The leader waved another two monks to the front. They flanked the sealed vault and lifted large metal disks to either side of the casement. The effect was instantaneous.

The weakened bulletproof glass exploded outward as if shoved by some unseen wind. In the flickering candle-light, the sarcophagus shimmered. Jason felt a sudden pressure, an internal popping of his ears, as if the walls of the cathedral had suddenly pushed inward, squashing all. The pressure deafened his ears; his vision squeezed.

He turned to Mandy.

Her hand was still clasped tightly to his, but her neck was arched back, her mouth stretched open.

'Mandy . . .'

From the corner of his eye, he saw other parishioners fixed in the same wracked poses. Mandy's hand began to tremble in his, vibrating like a speaker's tweeter. Tears ran down her face, turning bloody as he watched. She did not breathe. Her body then jerked and stiffened, knocking his hand free, but not before he felt the bite of an electrical shock arc from her fingertips to his.

He stood up, too horrified to sit.

A thin trail of smoke rose from Mandy's open mouth.

Her eyes were rolled back to white, but already they were smoldering black at the corners.

Dead.

Jason, muted by terror, searched the cathedral. The same was happening everywhere. Only a few were un-scathed: a pair of young children, pinned between their parents, cried and wailed. Jason recognized the unaffected.

Those who had not partaken of the Communion bread.

Like him.

He fell back into the shadows by the wall. His motion had gone momentarily unnoticed. His back found a door, one unguarded by the monks. Not a true door.

Jason pulled it open enough to slip inside the confessional booth.

He fell to his knees, crouching down, hugging himself. Prayers came to his lips.

Then, just as suddenly, it ended. He felt it in his head. A pop. A release of pressure. The walls of the cathedral sighing back.

He was crying. Tears ran cold over his cheeks.

He risked peeking out a hole in the confessional door.

Jason stared, finding a clear view of the nave and the altar. The air reeked of burnt hair. Cries and wails still echoed, but now the chorus came from only a handful of throats. Those still living. One figure, from his ragged garb apparently a homeless man, stumbled out of the pew and ran down a side aisle. Before taking ten steps, he was shot in the back of the head. One shot. His body sprawled.

*Oh God . . . oh God . . .*

Biting back sobs, Jason kept his eyes focused toward the altar.

Four monks lifted the golden sarcophagus from its shattered case. The slain priest's body was kicked from the altar and replaced by the reliquary. The leader slipped a large cloth sack from beneath his cloak. The monks opened the reliquary's lid and upended the contents into the bag. Once empty, the priceless sarcophagus was toppled to the floor and abandoned with a crash.

The leader shouldered his burden and headed back down the central aisle with the stolen relics.

The archbishop called to him. Again in Latin. It sounded like a curse.

The only response was a wave of the man's arm.

13

Another of the monks stepped behind the archbishop and raised a pistol to the back of the man's head.

Jason slunk down, wanting to see no more.

He closed his eyes. Other shots rang out across the cathedral. Sporadic. Cries suddenly silenced. Death stalked the cathedral as the monks slaughtered the few remaining survivors.

Jason kept his eyes closed and prayed.

A moment before, he had spotted the coat of arms upon the leader's surcoat. The man's black cloak had parted as he'd lifted his arm, revealing a crimson sigil beneath: a coiled dragon, the tail wrapped around its own neck. The symbol was unknown to Jason, but it had an exotic feel to it, more Persian than European.

Beyond the confessional door, the cathedral had grown stone silent.

The tread of booted footsteps approached his hiding place.

Jason squeezed his eyes tighter, against the horror, against the impossibility, against the sacrilege.

All for a sack of bones.

And though the cathedral had been built around those bones, and countless kings had bowed before them, even this very mass was a Feast to those long-dead men – the Feast of the Three Kings – one question rose foremost in Jason's mind.

Why?

Images of the Three Kings were found throughout the cathedral, done in stone, glass, and gold. In one panel, the Wise Men led camels across a desert, guided by the Star of Bethlehem. In another, the adoration of the Christ child was depicted, showing kneeling figures offering of the gifts of gold, frankincense, and myrrh.

But Jason closed his mind to all of this. All he could picture was Mandy's last smile. Her soft touch.

All gone.

The boots stopped outside his door.
He silently cried for an answer to all this bloodshed.
Why?
Why steal the bones of the Magi?

# DAY
# ONE

# 1

# BEHIND THE EIGHT BALL

The saboteur had arrived.

Grayson Pierce edged his motorcycle between the dark buildings that made up the heart of Fort Detrick. He kept the bike idling. Its electric engine purred no louder than a refrigerator's motor. The black gloves he wore matched the bike's paint, a nickel-phosphorous compound called NPL Super Black. It absorbed more visible light, making ordinary black seem positively shiny. His cloth body suit and rigid helmet were equally shaded.

Hunched over the bike, he neared the end of the alley. A courtyard opened ahead, a dark chasm framed by the brick-and-mortar buildings that composed the National Cancer Institute, an adjunct to USAMRIID, the U.S. Army Medical Research Institute of Infectious Diseases. Here the country's war on bioterrorism was waged across sixty thousand square feet of maximum-containment labs.

Gray cut the engine but stayed seated. His left knee rested against the satchel. It held the seventy thousand dollars. He remained in the alley, avoiding the open courtyard. He preferred the dark. The moon had long set, and the sun would not rise for another twenty-two minutes. Even the stars remained clouded by the shredding tail of last night's summer storm.

Would his ruse hold?

19

He subvocalized into his throat mike. 'Mule to Eagle, I've reached the rendezvous. Proceeding on foot.'

'Roger that. We've got you on satellite.'

Gray resisted the urge to look up and wave. He hated to be watched, scrutinized, but the deal here was too big. He did manage to gain a concession: to take the meeting alone. His contact was skittish. It had taken six months to groom this contact, brokering connections in Libya and the Sudan. It hadn't been easy. Money did not buy much trust. Especially in this business.

He reached down to the satchel and shouldered the money bag. Wary, he walked his bike over to a shadowed alcove, parked it, and hooked a leg over the seat.

He crossed down the alley.

There were few eyes awake at this hour, and most of those were only electronic. All of his identification had passed inspection at the Old Farm Gate, the service entrance to the base. And now he had to trust that his subterfuge held out long enough to evade electronic surveillance.

He glanced to the glowing dial on his Breitling diver's watch: 4:45. The meeting was set for fifteen minutes from now. So much depended on his success here.

Gray reached his destination. Building 470. It was deserted at this hour, due for demolition next month. Poorly secured, the building was perfect for the rendezvous, yet the choice of venue was also oddly ironic. In the sixties, spores of anthrax had been brewed inside the building, in giant vats and tanks, fermenting strains of bacterial death, until the toxic brewery had been decommissioned back in 1971. Since then, the building had been left fallow, becoming a giant storage closet for the National Cancer Institute.

But once again, the business of anthrax would be conducted under this roof. He glanced up. The windows were all dark. He was to meet the seller on the fourth floor.

20

Reaching the side door, he swiped the lock with an electronic keycard supplied by his contact at the base. He carried the second half of the man's payment over his shoulder, having wired the first half a month before. Gray also bore a foot-long plastic, carbonized dagger in a concealed wrist sheath.

His only weapon.

He couldn't risk bringing anything else through the security gate.

Gray closed the door and crossed to the stairwell on the right. The only light on the stairs came from the red EXIT sign. He reached to his motorcycle helmet and toggled on the night-vision mode. The world brightened in tones of green and silver. He mounted the stairs and climbed quickly to the fourth floor.

At the top, he pushed through the landing's door.

He had no idea where he was supposed to meet his contact. Only that he was to await the man's signal. He paused for a breath at the door, surveying the space before him. He didn't like it.

The stairwell opened at the corner of the building. One corridor stretched straight ahead; the other ran to the left. Frosted glass office doors lined the inner walls; windows slitted the other. He proceeded directly ahead at a slow pace, alert for any sign of movement.

A flood of light swept through one of the windows, washing over him.

Dazzled through his night-vision, he rolled against one wall, back into darkness. Had he been spotted? The sweep of light pierced the other windows, one after the other, passing down the hall ahead of him.

Leaning out, he peered through one of the windows. It faced the wide courtyard that fronted the building. Across the way, he watched a Humvee trundle slowly down the street. Its searchlight swept through the courtyard.

A patrol.

Would the attention spook his contact?

Cursing silently, Gray waited for the truck to finish its round. The patrol vanished momentarily, crossing behind a hulking structure that rose from the middle of the courtyard below. It looked like some rusting spaceship, but was in fact a million-liter steel containment sphere, three stories tall, mounted on a dozen pedestal legs. Ladders and scaffolding surrounded the structure as it underwent a renovation, an attempt to return it to its former glory when it was a Cold War research facility. Even the steel catwalk that had once circumnavigated the globe's equator had been replaced.

Gray knew the giant globe's nickname at the base.

The Eight Ball.

A humorless smile creased his lips as he realized his unlucky position.

*Trapped behind the eight ball . . .*

The patrol finally reappeared beyond the structure, slowly crossed the front of the courtyard, and rolled away.

Satisfied, Gray continued to the end of the corridor. A set of swinging double doors blocked the passage, but their narrow windows revealed a larger room beyond. He spotted a few tall, slender metal and glass tanks. One of the old labs. Windowless and dark.

His approach must have been noted.

A new light flared inside, incandescent, bright enough to require Gray to flick off his night-vision. A flashlight. It blinked three times.

A signal.

He stepped to the door and used a toe to push open one of the swinging sides. He slid through the narrow opening.

'Over here,' a voice said calmly. It was the first time Gray had heard his contact's voice. Prior to this moment, it had always been electronically muffled, a paranoid level of anonymity.

It was a *woman's* voice. The revelation piqued his wariness. He didn't like surprises.

He followed through a maze of tables with chairs stacked on top. She sat at one of the tables. Its other chairs were still stacked atop it. Except for one. On the opposite side of the table. It shifted as she kicked one of the legs.

'Sit.'

Gray had expected to find a nervous scientist, someone out for an extra paycheck. Treason for hire was becoming more and more commonplace among the top research facilities.

USAMRIID was no exception . . . only a thousandfold more deadly. Each vial for sale had the capability, if properly aerosolized in a subway or bus station, to kill thousands.

And she was selling fifteen of them.

He settled into his seat, placing the satchel of money on the table.

The woman was Asian . . . no, *Eur*asian. Her eyes were more open, her skin deeply tanned to a handsome bronze. She wore a black turtlenecked bodysuit, not unlike the one he wore, hugging a slim, lithe frame. A silver pendant dangled from her neck, bright against her suit, bearing a tiny curled-dragon charm. Gray studied her. The Dragon Lady's features, rather than taut and wary like his own, appeared bored.

Of course, the 9mm Sig Sauer pointed at his chest and equipped with a silencer might be the source of her confidence. But it was her next words that truly iced his blood.

'Good evening, Commander Pierce.'

He was startled to hear his name.

*If she knew that . . .*

He was already moving . . . and already too late.

The gun fired at near-point-blank range.

The impact kicked his body backward, taking the chair with him. He landed on his back, tangled in the chair legs. Pain flattened his chest, making it impossible to breathe. He tasted blood on his tongue.

Betrayed . . .

She stepped around the table and leaned over his sprawled form, gun still pointing, taking no chances. The silver dragon pendant dangled and flashed brightly. 'I suspect you're recording all this through your helmet, Commander Pierce. Perhaps even transmitting to Washington . . . to Sigma. You won't mind if I borrow a little airtime, will you?'

He was in no position to object.

The woman leaned closer over him. 'In the next ten minutes, the Guild will shut down all of Fort Detrick. Contaminate the entire base with anthrax. Payback for Sigma's interference with our operation in Oman. But I owe your director, Painter Crowe, something more. Something personal. This is for my sister in the field, Cassandra Sanchez.'

The gun shifted to his faceplate.

'Blood for blood.'

She pulled the trigger.


5:02 a.m.
WASHINGTON, D.C.

Forty-two miles away, the satellite feed went dead.

'Where's his backup?' Painter Crowe kept his voice firm, biting back a litany of curses. Panic would not serve them.

'Still ten minutes out.'

'Can you re-establish the link?'

The technician shook his head. 'We've lost main feed

24

from his helmet cam. But we still have the bird's-eye of the base from the NRO sat.' The young man indicated another monitor. It showed a black-and-white overshot of Fort Detrick, centered on a courtyard of buildings.

Painter paced before the array of monitors. It had all been a trap, one directed at Sigma and aimed at him personally. 'Alert Fort Detrick's security.'

'Sir?' The question rose from his second-in-command, Logan Gregory.

Painter understood Logan's hesitation. Only a handful of those in power knew of Sigma and the agents it employed: the President, the Joint Chiefs, and his immediate supervisors over at DARPA. After last year's shake-up among the top brass, the organization was under intense scrutiny.

Mistakes would not be tolerated.

'I won't risk an agent,' Painter said. 'Call them in.'

'Yes, sir.' Logan crossed to a phone. The man appeared more a California surfer than a leading strategist: blond hair, tanned, fit but going a bit soft in the belly. Painter was his darker shadow, half Native American, black hair, blue eyes. But he had no tan. He didn't know the last time he had seen the sun.

Painter wanted to sit down, lower his head to his knees. He had assumed control of the organization only eight months ago. And most of that time had been spent restructuring and shoring up security after the infiltration of the group by an international cartel known as the Guild. There had been no telling what information had been gleaned, sold, or spread during this time, so everything had to be purged and rebuilt from scratch. Even their central command had been pulled out of Arlington and moved to a subterranean warren here in Washington.

In fact, Painter had come in early this morning to unpack boxes in his new office when he had received the emergency call from satellite recon.

He studied the monitor from the NRO satellite.

25

A trap.

He knew what the Guild was doing. Four weeks ago, Painter had begun to put operatives into the field again, the first in more than a year. It was a tentative test. Two teams. One over in Los Alamos investigating the loss of a nuclear database . . . and the other in his own backyard, over at Fort Detrick, only one hour from Washington.

The Guild's attack sought to shake Sigma and its leader. To prove that the Guild still had knowledge to undermine Sigma. It was a feint to force Sigma to pull back again, to regroup, possibly to disband. As long as Painter's group was out of commission, the Guild had a greater chance to operate with impunity.

That must not happen.

Painter stopped his pacing and turned to his second, the question plain on his face.

'I keep getting cut off,' Logan said, nodding to the earpiece. 'They're having intermittent communication blackouts throughout the base.'

Certainly the handiwork of the Guild too . . .

Frustrated, Painter leaned on the console and stared at the mission's dossier. Imprinted atop the manila file was a single Greek letter.

$$\Sigma$$

In mathematics, the letter, *sigma,* represented 'the sum of all parts,' the unification of disparate sets into a whole. It was also emblematic of the organization Painter directed: Sigma Force.

Operating under the auspices of DARPA – the Department of Defense's research and development wing – Sigma served as the agency's covert arm out in the world, sent forth to safeguard, acquire, or neutralize technologies vital to U.S. security. Its team members were an ultra-secret cadre of ex-Special Forces soldiers who had been handpicked and placed into rigorous fast-track doctoral programs, covering a wide range of scientific disciplines, forming a militarized team of technically trained operatives.

Or in plainer language, killer scientists.

Painter opened the dossier before him. The team leader's file fronted the record.

Dr. and Commander Grayson Pierce.

The agent's photograph stared up at him from the upper right corner. It was the man's mug shot from his year of incarceration at Leavenworth. Dark hair shaved to a stubble, blue eyes still angry. His Welsh heritage was evident in the sharp cheekbones, wide eyes, and strong jaw. But his ruddy complexion was all Texan, burnt by the sun over the dry hills of Brown County.

Painter didn't bother glancing over the inch-thick file. He knew the details. Gray Pierce had joined the Army at eighteen, the Rangers at twenty-one, and served to distinction off and on the field. Then, at twenty-three, he was court-martialed for striking a superior officer. Painter knew the details and the back history of the two in Bosnia. And considering the events, Painter might have done the same. Still, rules were codified in granite among the armed forces. The decorated soldier spent one year in Leavenworth.

But Gray Pierce was too valuable to be cast aside forever.

His training and skill could not be wasted.

Sigma had recruited him three years ago, right out of prison.

Now Gray was a pawn between the Guild and Sigma.

One about to be crushed.

'I've got base security!' Logan said, relief ringing in his voice.

'Get them over –'

'Sir!' The technician leapt to his feet, still tethered to his console by the headset's cord. He glanced to Painter. 'Director Crowe, I'm picking up a trace audio feed.'

'What – ?' Painter stepped closer to the technician. He raised a hand to hold off Logan.

The technician turned up the feed on the speakers.

A tinny voice reached them though the video feed remained fritzed.

One word formed.

*'Goddamnmotherfuckingpieceofshit . . .'*

## 5:07 a.m. FREDERICK, MARYLAND

Gray kicked out a heel, catching the woman in the midriff. He felt a satisfying thud of flesh, but heard nothing. His ears rang from the concussion of the slug against his Kevlar helmet. The shot had spiderwebbed his faceshield. His left ear burned as the electronic bay shorted with a burst of static.

He ignored it all.

Rolling to his feet, he slipped the carbonized dagger from its wrist sheath and dove under a neighboring row of tables. Another shot, sounding like a loud cough, penetrated the ring of his ears. Wood splintered from the edge of the table.

He cleared the far side and kept a wary crouch while searching the room. His kick had caused the woman to drop her flashlight, which rolled on the floor, skittering shadows everywhere. He fingered his chest. The body blow of the assassin's first shot still burned and ached.

But no blood.

The woman called to him from the shadows. 'Liquid body armor.'

Gray dropped lower, attempting to pinpoint the woman's location. The dive under the table had jarred his helmet's internal heads-up display. Its holographic images flickered incoherently across the inside of his faceshield, interfering with his sightlines, but he dared not abandon

28

the helmet. It offered the best protection against the weapon still in the woman's hand.

That and his body suit.

The assassin was right. *Liquid body armor.* Developed by U.S. Army Research Laboratory in 2003. The fabric of his body suit had been soaked with a shear-thickening fluid – hard microparticles of silica suspended in a poly-ethylene glycol solution. During normal movement, it acted like a liquid, but once a bullet struck, the material solidified into a rigid shield, preventing penetration. The suit had just saved his life.

At least for now.

The woman spoke again, coldly calm, as she slowly circled toward the door. 'I rigged the building with C4 and TNT. Easy enough since the structure's already scheduled for demolition. The Army was nice enough to have it all prewired. It just took a minor detonator modification to change the building's implosion to one that will cause an explosive *updraft.*'

Gray pictured the resulting plume of smoke and debris riding high into the early morning sky. 'The vials of anthrax . . .' he mumbled, but it was loud enough to be heard.

'It seemed fitting to use the base's own demolition as a toxic delivery system.'

*Christ, she had turned the entire building into a bio-logical bomb.*

With the strong winds, it was not only the base at risk, but the entire town of nearby Frederick.

Gray moved. She had to be stopped. But where was she?

He edged toward the door himself now, wary of her gun, but he couldn't let that stop him. Too much was at stake. He tried flicking on his night-vision mode, but all he earned was another snap of flame by his ear. The heads-up display continued its erratic flashing, dazzling and confusing to the eye.

Screw it.

He thumbed the catch and yanked the helmet off.

The fresh wash of air smelled moldy and antiseptic at the same time. Staying low, he carried the helmet in one hand, the dagger in the other. He reached the back wall and hurried toward the door. He could see well enough to tell the swinging door hadn't moved. The assassin was still in the room.

But where?

And what could he do to stop her? He squeezed the handle of his knife. Gun against dagger. Not good odds.

With his helmet off, he spotted a shift of shadows near the door. He stopped, going dead still. She was crouched three feet from the door, shielded by a table.

Watery light filtered from the hallway, glowing through the windows of the swinging doors. Dawn neared, brightening the passage beyond. The assassin would have to expose herself to make her escape. For the moment, she clung to the shadows of the windowless lab, unsure if her opponent was armed or not.

Gray had to stop playing this Dragon Lady's game.

With a roundhouse swing, he threw his helmet toward the opposite side of the lab. It landed with a crash and tinkle of glass, shattering one of the old tanks.

He ran toward her position. He only had seconds.

She popped from her hiding place, swiveling to lay down fire in the direction of the noise. At the same time, she leaped gracefully toward the door, seeming to use the recoil from her gun to propel her.

Gray could not help but be impressed – but not enough to slow him.

With his arm already cocked, he whipped his dagger through the air. Weighted and balanced to perfection, the carbonized blade flew with unerring accuracy.

It struck the woman square in the hollow of her throat.

Gray continued his headlong rush.

Only then did he realize his mistake.

The dagger bounced harmlessly away and clattered to the floor.

*Liquid body armor.*

No wonder the Dragon Lady knew about his body suit. She was wearing the same.

The attack, though, threw off her leap. She landed in a half crash, plainly turning a knee. But ever the skilled assassin, she never lost sight of her target.

From a step away, she aimed the Sig Sauer at Gray's face.

And this time, he had no helmet.


5:09 a.m.
WASHINGTON, D.C.

'We've lost all contact again,' the technician said needlessly.

Painter had heard the loud crash a moment before, then all went deadly silent on the satellite feed.

'I still have base security,' his second said by the phone.

Painter tried to piece together the cacophony he had heard over the line. 'He tossed his helmet.'

The other two men stared at him.

Painter studied the open dossier in front of him. Grayson Pierce was no fool. Besides his military expertise, the man had first come to Sigma's attention because of his aptitude and intelligence tests. He was certainly above the norm, well above, but there were soldiers with even higher scores. What had been the final factor in the decision to recruit him had been his odd behavior while incarcerated at Leavenworth. Despite the hard labor of the camp, Grayson had taken up a rigorous regimen of study: in both advanced chemistry *and* Taoism. This disparity in his choice of study had intrigued Painter and Sigma's former director, Dr. Sean McKnight.

In many ways, he proved to be a walking contradiction:

a Welshman living in Texas, a student of Taoism who still carried a rosary, a soldier who studied chemistry in prison. It was this very uniqueness of his mind that had won him membership into Sigma.

But such distinctiveness came with a price.

Grayson Pierce did not play well with others. He had a profound distaste for working with a team.

Like now. Going in alone. Against protocol.

'Sir?' his second persisted.

Painter took a deep breath. 'Two more minutes.'

5:10 a.m.
FREDERICK, MARYLAND

The first shot whistled past his ear.

Gray was lucky. The assassin had shot too fast, before being properly set. Gray, still in motion from his lunge, just managed to duck out of the way. A head shot was not as easy as the movies made it seem.

He tackled the woman and pinned her gun between them. Even if she fired, he would still have a good chance of surviving.

Only it would hurt like hell.

She fired, proving this last point.

The slug slammed into his left thigh. It felt like a hammer blow, bruising to the marrow. He screamed. And why the hell not? It stung like a motherfucker. But he didn't let go. He used his anger to slam an elbow into her throat. But her body armor stiffened, protecting her.

Damn it.

She pulled the trigger again. He outweighed her, outmuscled her, but she didn't need the strength of fist and knee. She had the might of modern artillery at her disposal. The slug sucker-punched into his gut. Pounded all the way to his spine, his breath blew out of him. She was slowly maneuvering her gun upward.

The Sig Sauer had a fifteen-round magazine. How many shots had she fired? Surely she still had enough to pound him into a pulp.

He needed to end this.

He lifted his head back and slammed his forehead into her face. But she was no novice to brawling. She turned her head, taking the blow to the side of her skull. Still, it bought him enough time to kick out at a cord trailing from the nearby table. The library lamp attached to it came crashing to the floor. Its green glass shade shattered.

Bear-hugging the woman, he rolled her over the lamp. It was too much to hope that the glass would penetrate her body suit. But that wasn't his goal.

He heard the pop of the lamp's bulb under their combined weight.

Good enough.

Frogging his legs under him, Gray leaped outward. It was a gamble. He flew toward the light switch beside the swinging door.

A cough of a pistol accompanied a slam into his lower back.

His neck whiplashed. His body struck the wall. As he bounded off, his hand palmed the electrical box and flipped the switch. Lights flickered across the lab, unsteady. Bad wiring.

He fell back toward the assassin.

He couldn't hope to electrocute his nemesis. That only happened in the movies, too. That wasn't his goal. Instead, he hoped whoever had last used the desk had left the lamp switched *on*.

Keeping his feet, he pivoted around.

The Dragon Lady sat atop the broken lamp, arm outstretched toward him, gun pointing. She pulled the trigger, but her aim was off. One of the windows in the swinging door shattered.

Gray stepped around to the side, moving farther out of

range. The woman could not track him. She was frozen rigidly in place, unable to move.

'Liquid body armor,' he said, repeating her earlier words. 'The *liquid* does make for a flexible suit, but it also has a disadvantage.' He stalked up to her side and relieved her of her gun. 'Propylene glycol is an alcohol, a good conductor of electricity. Even a small charge, like from a broken lightbulb, will flow over a suit in seconds. And as with any assault, the suit reacts.'

He kicked her in the shin. The suit was as hard as a rock.

'Goes rigid on you.'

Her own suit had become her prison.

He searched her rapidly as she strained to move. With effort, she could make slow progress, but no more than the rusted Tin Man from *The Wizard of Oz.*

She gave up. Her face reddened from her strain. 'You won't find any detonator. It's all on a timer. Set for –' Her eyes glanced down to a wristwatch. 'Two minutes from now. You'll never deactivate all the charges.'

Gray noted the number on her watch drop below 02:00.

Her life was tied to that number, too. He saw the flicker of fear in her eyes – assassin or not, she was still human, afraid of her own mortality – but the rest of her face only hardened to match her rigid suit.

'Where did you stash the vials?'

He knew she wouldn't tell him. But he watched her eyes. For a moment, the pupils shifted slightly up, then centered on him.

The roof.

It made sense. He needed no other confirmation. Anthrax – *Bacillus anthracis* – was sensitive to heat. If she wanted the bloom of toxic spores to spread outward from the blast, the vials would have to be up high, caught in the initial concussive blast and jettisoned skyward. She couldn't risk the heat of the explosion incinerating the weaponized bacterium.

Before he could move, she spat at him, hitting him on the cheek.

He didn't bother wiping it off.

He didn't have the time.

01:48.

He straightened and ran for the door.

'You'll never make it!' she called after him. Somehow she knew he was going for the bio-bomb, not fleeing for his own life. And for some reason, that pissed him off. Like she knew him well enough to make that assumption.

He ran down the outer corridor and skidded into the stairwell. He pounded up the two flights to reach the roof door. The exit had been modified to meet OSHA standards. A panic bar gated the door, made for quick evacuation in case of a fire.

Panic pretty much defined this moment.

He struck the bar, initiating an alarm Klaxon, and pushed out into the dark gray of early dawn. The roof was tar and paper. Sand crunched underfoot. He scanned the area. There were too many places to hide the vials: air vents, exhaust pipes, satellite dishes.

Where?

He was running out of time.


5:13 a.m.
WASHINGTON, D.C.

'He's on the roof!' the technician said, jabbing a finger at the monitor from the NRO satellite.

Painter leaned closer and spotted a tiny figure stepping into view. What was Grayson doing on the roof? Painter searched the immediate area. 'Any sign of pursuit?'

'None that I can detect, sir.'

Logan spoke from the phone. 'Base security reports a

fire alarm going off in Building 470.'

'Must've tripped the exit alarm,' the tech interjected.

'Can you get us any closer?' Painter asked.

The technician nodded and toggled a switch. The image zoomed down atop Grayson Pierce. His helmet was gone. His left ear appeared stained, bloody. He continued to stand by the doorway.

'What is he doing?' the tech asked.

'Base security is responding,' Logan reported.

Painter shook his head, but a cold certainty iced through him. 'Tell base security to stay away. Have them evacuate anyone near that building.'

'Sir?'

'Do it.'

5:14 a.m.
FREDERICK, MARYLAND

Gray scanned the roof one more time. The emergency Klaxon continued to wail. He ignored it, drawing inward. He had to think like his quarry.

He crouched low. It had rained last night. He imagined the woman had only planted the vials recently, after the downpour. He looked carefully and noted where the sand washed smooth by the rain had been disturbed. It wasn't too difficult, as he knew she had to have passed through this door. It was the only roof access.

He trailed her steps.

They led across the roof to a hooded exhaust vent.

Of course.

The exhaust flume would serve as the perfect chimney to expel the spores as the lower levels of the building imploded, creating a toxic blowgun.

Kneeling, he spotted where she had tampered with the hood, disturbing an old layer of rust. He didn't have the time to check for booby traps. He yanked the vent off with a grunt.

The bomb rested inside the duct. The fifteen glass vials were arrayed in a starburst around a central pellet of C4, just enough to shatter the containers. He stared at the white powder filling each tube. Biting his lower lip, he reached down and carefully lifted the bomb out of the duct's throat. A timer counted down.

00:54.

00:53.

00:52.

Free of the ductwork, Gray straightened. He did a fast check of the bomb. It was rigged against tampering. He had no time to decipher the wires and electronics. The bomb was going to go off. He had to get it away from the building, away from the blast zone, preferably away from him.

00:41.

Only one chance.

He tucked the bomb into a nylon ditty pouch over one shoulder and stalked to the front of the building. Headlights aimed toward the building, drawn by the alarm. Base security would never reach here in time.

He had no choice.

He had to get clear . . . no matter his own life.

Retreating several steps from roof's edge, he took a deep breath, then sprinted back toward the front of the building. Reaching the roof's edge, he bounded up and leaped over the brick parapet.

He sailed out over the six-story drop.


5:15 a.m.
WASHINGTON, D.C.

'Christ almighty!' Logan exclaimed as Grayson made the leap off the roof.

'He's numb-nuts crazy,' the tech appended, jerking to his feet.

Painter simply watched the man's suicidal ploy. 'He's doing what he must.'

Gray kept his legs under him, arms out for balance. He plummeted earthward. He prayed the laws of physics, velocity, trajectory, and vector analysis didn't betray him.

He readied for the impact.

Two stories below and twenty yards out, the spherical roof of the Eight Ball rose up to meet him. The million-liter steel containment globe glistened with morning dew.

He twisted in midair, struggling to keep his plunge feet-first.

Then time sped up. Or he did.

His booted feet hit the surface of the sphere. The liquid body armor cemented around his ankles, protecting against a break. Momentum slammed him forward, facedown, spread-eagled. But he had not reached the center of the sphere's roof, only the curved shell closest to Building 470.

Fingers scrabbled, but there was no grip, no traction.

His body slid down the dew-slick steel, twisting slightly askew. He spread his legs, toes dragging for friction. Then he was past the point of no return, free-falling down the sheer side.

With his cheek pressed to the steel, he didn't see the catwalk until he struck it. His left leg hit, then his body tumbled after it. He landed on hands and knees atop the metal scaffolding that had been built around the equator of the steel globe. He shoved to his feet, legs wobbling from the strain and the terror.

He couldn't believe he was still alive.

He searched the curve of the sphere while freeing the bio-bomb from his ditty bag. The surface of the containment globe was pocked with portholes, once used by scientists to observe their biological experiments inside. In all the years of its regular use, no pathogen had ever escaped.

Gray prayed the same held true this morning.

He glanced to the bomb in his hand: 00:18.

With no time to curse, he ran along the exterior catwalk, searching for an entry hatch. He found it half a hemisphere away. A steel door with a porthole. He sprinted to it, grabbed the handle, and tugged.

It refused to budge.

Locked.

5:15 a.m.
WASHINGTON, D.C.

Painter watched Grayson tug at the hatch on the giant sphere. He noted the frantic strain, recognized and understood the urgency. Painter had seen the explosive device retrieved from the exhaust duct. He knew the mission objective of Grayson's team: to lure out a suspected trafficker in weaponized pathogens.

Painter had no doubt what form of death lay inside the bomb.

Anthrax.

Plainly, Grayson could not defuse the device and sought to safely dispose of it.

He was having no luck.

How much time did he have?

5:15 a.m.
FREDERICK, MARYLAND

00:18

Grayson ran again. Maybe there was another hatch. He clomped around the catwalk. He felt like he was running in ski boots, his ankles still cemented in his body suit.

He circled another half a hemisphere.

Another hatch appeared ahead.

'YOU! HOLD RIGHT THERE!'

Base security.

The fierceness and boom of the bullhorn almost made him obey.

Almost.

He kept running. A spotlight splayed over him.

'STOP OR WE'LL FIRE!'

He had no time to negotiate.

A deafening rattle of gunfire pelted the side of the sphere, a few rounds pinging off the catwalk. None were near. Warning shots.

He reached the second hatch, grabbed the handle, twisted, and tugged.

It stuck for a breath, then popped open. A sob of relief escaped him.

He pitched the device into the hollow interior of the sphere, slammed the door secure, and leaned his back against it. He slumped to his seat.

'YOU THERE! STAY WHERE YOU ARE!'

He had no intention of going anywhere. He was happy right where he was. He felt a small jolt on his back. The sphere rang like a struck bell. The device had blown inside, safely contained.

But it was only the primer cord of greater things to come.

Like the clash of titanic gods, a series of jarring explosions rocked the ground.

*Boom . . . boom . . . boom . . .*

Sequential, timed, engineered.

It was the wired demolitions of Building 470.

Even insulated on the far side of the sphere, Gray felt the slight suck of air, then a mighty whoosh of displacement as the building took its last deep breath and expelled it. A dense wall of dust and debris washed outward as the building collapsed. Gray glanced up in time to see a mighty plume of smoke and dust bloom upward, seeding high and spreading out with the wind.

But no death rode this breeze.

A final explosion thundered from the dying building. A rumble of brick and rock sounded, a stony avalanche. The ground bumped under him – then he heard a new sound.

The screech of metal.

Shoved by the explosion, its foundations shaken, two of the Eight Ball's support legs popped and bent, as if the sphere were attempting to kneel. The whole structure tilted away from the building, toward the street.

More legs popped.

And once started, there was no stopping it.

The million-liter containment sphere toppled toward the line of security trucks.

With Gray directly under it.

He shoved up and scrabbled along the tilting catwalk, struggling to get clear of the impact. He ran several steps, but the way quickly grew too steep as the sphere continued its plummet. Catwalk became ladder. He dug his fingers into the metal framework, kicked his legs at the support struts of the railings. He fought to get out from beneath the shadow of the crushing weight of the globe.

He made one final desperate lunge, grabbing a handhold and digging in his toes.

The Eight Ball struck the front lawn of the courtyard and pounded into the rain-soaked loam. The impact traveled up the catwalk, slamming Gray from his perch. He flew several yards and landed on his back on the soft lawn. He had only been a few yards from the ground.

Sitting up, he leaned on one elbow.

The line of security trucks had retreated as the ball fell toward them.

But they would not stay gone. And he must not get caught.

Gray gained his feet with a groan and stumbled back into the pall of smoke from the collapsed building. Only now did he hear the alarms ringing throughout the base. He shed out of his body suit as he moved, transferring his identification tags to his civilian clothes beneath. He hurried to the far side of the courtyard, to the next building, to where he had left his motorcycle.

He found it intact.

Throwing a leg over the seat, he keyed the ignition. The engine purred happily to life. He reached for the throttle, then paused. Something had been hooked around his handlebar. He freed it, stared at it for a moment, then shoved it in a pocket.

*Damn . . .*

He throttled up and edged his bike to a neighboring alleyway. The path appeared clear for the moment. He hunched down, gunned the engine, and shot between the dark buildings. Reaching Porter Street, he made a sharp left turn, coming around fast, leaning out his left knee for balance. Only a couple cars shared the street. None of them appeared to be MP vehicles.

He zigzagged around them and sped off toward the more rural section of the base that surrounded Nallin Pond, a parkland region of gently rolling hills and patches of hardwood forest.

He would wait out the worst of the commotion, then slip away. For now, he was safe. Still, he felt the weight of the object in his pocket, left as decoration on his bike.

A silver chain . . . with a dangling dragon pendant.

Painter stepped back from the satellite console. The technician had caught Grayson's escape by motorcycle as he appeared out of the cloud of smoke and dust. Logan was still on the phone, passing information down a series of covert channels, sounding the all-clear. Whitewashed from on high, the trouble at the base would be blamed on miscommunication, faulty wiring, decomposing munitions.

Sigma Force would never be mentioned.

The satellite tech held his earpiece in place. 'Sir, I have a telephone call from the director of DARPA.'

'Switch it over here.' Painter plucked up another receiver. He listened as the scrambled communication was routed.

The tech nodded to him as the dead air over the line seemed to breathe to life. Though no one spoke, Painter could almost sense his mentor and commander. 'Director McKnight?' he said, suspecting the man was calling to get a mission debrief.

His suspicion proved wrong.

He heard the stress in the other's voice. 'Painter, I just received some intel out of Germany. Strange deaths at a cathedral. We need a team on the ground there by nightfall.'

'So soon?'

'Details will follow within the quarter hour. But we're going to need your best agent to head this team.'

Painter stared over at the satellite monitor. He watched the motorcycle skim through the hills, flickering through the sparse canopy of trees.

'I may have just the man. But may I ask what the urgency is?'

'A call came in early this morning, requesting Sigma to

investigate the matter in Germany. Your group has been specifically summoned.'

'Summoned? By whom?'

To have Dr. McKnight this rattled, it had to be someone as high up as the President. But once again, Painter's supposition proved wrong.

The director explained, 'By the Vatican.'

# 2

# THE ETERNAL CITY

So much for making her lunch date.

Lieutenant Rachel Verona climbed down the narrow stairs that led deep under the Basilica of San Clemente. The excavation below the church had been under way for two months, overseen by a small team of archaeologists from the University of Naples.

*'Lasciate ogni speranza . . .'* Rachel muttered.

Her guide, Professor Lena Giovanna, the project leader, glanced back at her. She was a tall woman, mid-fifties, but the permanent crook in her back made her seem older and shorter. She offered Rachel a tired smile. 'So you know your Dante Alighieri. *Lasciate ogni speranza, voi ch'entrate!* Abandon all hope, ye who enter here.'

Rachel felt a twinge of embarrassment. According to Dante, those words were written on the gates of Hell. She had not meant her words to be heard, but the acoustics here left little privacy. 'No offense intended, *Professore*.'

A chuckle answered her. 'None taken, Lieutenant. I was just surprised to find someone in the military police with such fluency. Even someone working for the Carabinieri Tutela Patrimonio Culturale.'

Rachel understood the misconception. It was fairly typical to paint all the Carabinieri Corps with the same brush. Most civilians only saw the uniformed men and women guarding streets and buildings, armed with rifles.

45

But she had entered the Corps not as a military soldier, but with a graduate degree in psychology and art history. She had been recruited into the Carabinieri Corps right out of the university, spending an additional two years at the officers' training college studying international law. She had been handpicked by General Rende, who ran the special unit involved with the investigation of art and antiquity thefts, the Tutela Patrimonio Culturale.

Reaching the bottom of the stairs, Rachel stepped into a pool of dank water. The storm of the past few days had flooded the subterranean level. She glanced down sourly. At least it was only ankle-deep.

She wore a borrowed set of rubber boots that were too large, meant for a man. She carried her new Ferragamo pumps in her left hand, a birthday gift from her mother. She dared not leave them on the stairs. Thieves were always about. If she lost her shoes or got them soiled, she'd never hear the end of it from her mother.

Professor Giovanna, on the other hand, wore a utilitarian coverall, an attire more fitting for exploring water-logged ruins than Rachel's navy slacks and silk flowered blouse. But when Rachel's pager had gone off a quarter hour ago, she had been heading over to a lunch date with her mother and sister. She'd had no time to return to her apartment and change into her carabiniere uniform. Not if she was going to have any chance of still making that lunch.

So she had come directly here, meeting up with a pair of local carabinieri. Rachel had left the military police-men up in the basilica while she performed the initial investigation into the theft.

In some regards, Rachel was glad for the temporary reprieve. She had put off for too long letting her mother know that she and Gino had broken up. In fact, her ex-boyfriend had moved out more than a month ago. Rachel could already picture the knowing disappointment in her mother's eyes, accompanied by the usual noises that implied *I told you so* without coming out and actually saying it aloud. And her older sister, three years married, would be pointedly twisting that diamond wedding band on her finger and nodding her head sagely.

Neither had been pleased with Rachel's choice of profession.

'How are you to keep a husband, you crazy girl?' her mother had intoned, throwing her arms toward heaven. 'You cut your beautiful hair so short. You sleep with a gun. No man can compete with that.'

As a consequence, Rachel rarely left Rome to visit her family in rural Castel Gandolfo, where their family had settled after World War II, in the shadow of the pope's summer residence. Only her grandmother understood her. The two had shared a love of antiquities and firearms. While growing up, Rachel had listened avidly to her stories of the war: gruesome tales laced with graveyard humor. Her *nonna* even kept a Nazi P-08 Luger in her bedside table, oiled and polished, a relic stolen from a border guard during her family's flight. There was no knitting booties for that old woman.

'It's just up ahead,' the professor said. She splashed forward toward a glowing doorway. 'My students are keeping watch on the site.'

Rachel proceeded after her guide, reached the low doorway, and ducked through. She straightened into a cavelike room. Illuminated by carbide lanterns and flashlights, the vault of the roof arched overhead, constructed of hewn blocks of volcanic *tufa* sealed crudely with plaster. A man-made grotto. Plainly a Roman temple.

As Rachel waded into the room, she was all too conscious of the weight of the basilica overhead. Dedicated to Saint Clement in the twelfth century, the church had been built over an earlier basilica, one constructed back in the fourth century. But even this ancient church hid a deeper mystery: the ruins of a first-century courtyard of Roman buildings, including this pagan temple. Such overbuilding was not uncommon, one religion burying another, a stratification of Roman history.

Rachel felt a familiar thrill course through her, sensing the press of time as solidly as the weight of stone. Though one century buried another, it was still here. Mankind's earliest history preserved in stone and silence. Here was a cathedral as rich as the one above.

'These are my two students from the university,' the professor said. 'Tia and Roberto.'

In the semidarkness, Rachel followed the professor's gaze and looked down, discovering the crouching forms of the young man and woman, both dark haired and similarly attired in soiled coveralls. They had been tagging bits of broken pottery and now rose to greet them. Still grasping her shoes in one hand, Rachel shook their hands. While of university age, the two appeared no older than fifteen. Then again, maybe it was because she'd just celebrated her thirtieth birthday, and everyone seemed to be growing younger except her.

'Over here,' the professor said, and led Rachel to an alcove in the far wall. 'The thieves must have struck during last night's storm.'

Professor Giovanna pointed her flashlight at a marble figure standing in a far niche. It stood a meter tall – or would have if the head weren't missing. All that remained was a torso, legs, and a protruding stone phallus. A Roman fertility god.

The professor shook her head. 'A tragedy. It was the only piece of intact statuary discovered here.'

Rachel understood the woman's frustration. Reaching out, she ran her free hand over the stump of the statue's neck. Her fingers felt a familiar roughness. 'Hacksaw,' she mumbled.

It was the tool of the modern-day graverobber, easy to

conceal and wield. With just such a simple instrument, thieves had stolen, damaged, and vandalized artwork across Rome. It took only moments for the theft to occur, done many times in plain sight, often while a curator's back was turned. And the reward was well worth the risk. Trafficking in stolen antiquities had proved a lucrative business, surpassed only by narcotics, money laundering, and arms dealing. As such, the military had formed the Comando Carabinieri Tutela Patrimonio Culturale, the Cultural Heritage Police, back in 1992. Working alongside Interpol, they sought to stem this tide.

Rachel crouched before the statue and felt a familiar burn in the pit of her stomach. By bits and pieces, Roman history was being erased. It was a crime against time itself.

'*Ars longa, vita brevis,*' she whispered, a quote from Hippocrates. One of her favorites. *Life is short, art eternal.*

'Indeed,' the professor said in a pained voice. 'It was a magnificent find. The chisel work, the fine detail, the work of a master artisan. To mar it so savagely . . .'

'Why didn't the bastards just steal the whole statue?' asked Tia. 'At least it would've been preserved intact.'

Rachel tapped the statue's phallic protuberance with one of her shoes. 'Despite the convenient handle here, the artifact is too large. The thief must already have an international buyer. The bust alone would be easier to smuggle across the border.'

'Is there any hope of recovery?' Professor Giovanna asked.

Rachel did not offer any false promises. Of the six thousand pieces of antiquity stolen last year, only a handful had been recovered. 'I'll need photographs of the intact statue to post with Interpol, preferably concentrating on the bust.'

'We have a digital database,' Professor Giovanna said. 'I can forward pictures by e-mail.'

Rachel nodded and kept her focus on the beheaded statue. 'Or Roberto over there could just tell us what he did with the head.'

The professor's eyes darted to the young man.

Roberto took a step back. 'Wh-what?' His gaze traveled around the room, settling again on his teacher. '*Professore* . . . truly, I know nothing. This is crazy.'

Rachel kept staring at the beheaded statue – and at the one clue available to her. She had weighed the odds of playing her hand now or back at the station. But that would've meant interviewing everyone, taking statements, a mountain of paperwork. She closed her eyes, thinking of the lunch to which she was already late. Besides, if she had any hope of recovering the piece, speed could prove essential.

Opening her eyes, she spoke to the statue. 'Did you know that sixty-four percent of archaeological thefts are abetted by workers at the site?' She turned to the trio.

Professor Giovanna frowned. 'Truly you don't think Roberto –'

'When did you discover the statue?' Rachel asked.

'T-two days ago. But I posted our discovery on the University of Naples website. Many people knew.'

'But how many people knew the site would be unguarded during last night's storm?' Rachel kept her focus on one person. 'Roberto, do you have anything to say?'

His face was a frozen mask of disbelief. 'I . . . no . . . I had nothing to do with this.'

Rachel unsnapped her radio from her belt. 'Then you won't mind if we search your garret. Perhaps to turn up a hacksaw, something with enough trace marble in its teeth to match the statue here.'

A familiar wild look entered his eyes. 'I . . . I . . .'

'The minimum penalty is five years in prison,' she pressed. '*Obbligatorio.*'

In the lamplight, he visibly paled.

'That is, unless you cooperate. Leniency can be arranged.'

He shook his head, but it was unclear what he was denying.

'You had your chance.' She raised her radio to her lips. The squawk of static echoed loudly in the arched space as she pressed the button.

'No!' Roberto raised his hand, stopping her as she suspected he would. His gaze dropped to the floor.

A long silence stretched. Rachel did not break it. She let the weight build.

Roberto finally let out a soft sob. 'I . . . had debts . . . gambling debts. I had no choice.'

'*Dio mio,*' the professor swore, raising a hand to her forehead. 'Oh, Roberto, how could you?'

The student had no answer.

Rachel knew the pressure placed on the boy. It was not unusual. He was only a tiny tendril in a much larger organization, so widely spread and embedded that it could never be fully rooted out. The best Rachel could hope was to keep picking at the weeds.

She lifted the radio to her lips. 'Carabiniere Gerard, I'm heading up with someone who has additional information.'

' – *capitò, Tenente* – '

She clicked the radio off. Roberto stood with his hands over his face, his career ruined.

'How did you know?' the professor asked.

Rachel did not bother explaining that it was not uncommon for members of organized crime to ply, petition, or coerce cooperation among site workers. Such corruption was rampant, catching up the unsuspecting, the naive.

She turned away from Roberto. It was often only a matter of discerning who in the research team was the

weak spot. With the young man, she had made an edu-
cated guess, then applied pressure to see if she was correct. It had been a risk playing her hand too soon. What
if it had been Tia instead? By the time Rachel was done
chasing the wrong lead, Tia could have passed a warning
on to her buyers. Or what if it had been Professor
Giovanna, padding her university salary by selling her
own discovery? There were so many ways it could've all
gone sour. But Rachel had learned it took risk to win
reward.

Professor Giovanna continued staring at her, the same
question in her eyes. *How had she known to accuse
Roberto?*

Rachel glanced to the statue's stone phallus. It had
taken only one clue – but a prominent one at that. 'It's
not only the *top* head that sells well on the black market.
There's a huge demand for ancient art of the *erotic*
nature. It outsells more conservative pieces almost four-
fold. I suspect neither of you two women would've had
any problem sawing off that prominent appendage, but
for some reason, men are reluctant. They take it so
personally.'

Rachel shook her head and crossed to the stairs leading up to the basilica. 'They won't even neuter their own
dogs.'


1:34 p.m.

Still so very, very late . . .

Checking her watch, Rachel hurried across the stone
piazza in front of the San Clemente Basilica. She stumbled on a loose cobble, bobbled a few steps, but managed
to keep her feet. She glanced back at the stone, as if it
were at fault – then down to her toes.

*Merda!*

A wide scuff marred the outer edge of her shoe.

Rolling her eyes heavenward, she wondered which saint she had offended. By now, they must be lining up to take a number.

She continued across the plaza, avoiding a covey of bicyclists that scattered around her like frightened pigeons. She moved more cautiously, reminding herself of the wise words of Emperor Augustus.

*Festina lente.* Make haste slowly.

Then again, Emperor Augustus didn't have a mother who could nag the hide off a horse.

She finally reached her Mini Cooper parked at the edge of the plaza. The midday sun cast it in blinding silver. A smile formed, the first of the day. The car was another birthday present. One to herself. You only turned thirty once in your life. It was a bit extravagant, especially upgrading to leather and opting for the S-convertible model.

But it was the joy of her life.

That might be one of the reasons Gino left her a month ago. The car inspired her far more than the man sharing her bed. It had been a good trade. The car was more emotionally available.

And then again . . . it *was* a convertible. She was a woman who appreciated flexibility – if she couldn't get it from her man, she'd get it from her car.

Though today it was too hot to go topless.

A shame.

She unlocked the door, but before she climbed inside, her cell phone chimed at her belt.

Now what?

It was probably Carabiniere Gerard, into whose care she had just left Roberto. The student was on his way to be interrogated at Parioli Station. She squinted at the incoming phone number. She recognized the international telephone prefix – 39-06 – but not the number.

Why was someone from the Vatican calling her?

Rachel flipped her cell phone to her ear. 'Lieutenant Verona here.'

A familiar voice answered. 'How is my favorite niece doing today . . . besides aggravating her mother?'

'Uncle Vigor?' A smile formed. Her uncle, better known as Monsignor Vigor Verona, headed the Pontifical Institute of Christian Archaeology. But he was not calling from his university office.

'I called your mother, thinking you were with her. But it seems a carabiniere's work follows no clock. A fact, I think, that your dear mother does not appreciate.'

'I'm on my way to the restaurant right now.'

'Or you would be . . . if not for my call.'

Rachel leaned a hand against her car. 'Uncle Vigor, what are you –'

'I've already passed on your regrets to your mother. She and your sister will see you for an early dinner instead. At Il Matriciano. You'll be paying, of course, due to the inconvenience.'

No doubt Rachel would pay – and in more ways than just in euros. 'What's this all about, Uncle?'

'I need you to join me here at the Vatican. Immediately. I'll have a pass waiting for you at the St. Anne's Gate.'

She checked her watch. She would have to cross half of Rome. 'I'm supposed to meet with General Rende back at my station to follow up on an open investigation.'

'I've already spoken with your commander. He's approved your excursion here. In fact, I have you for a full week.'

'A week?'

'Or more. I'll explain all when you get here.' He gave her directions to where he wanted to meet. Her brow crinkled, but before she could ask more, her uncle signed off.

'*Ciao,* my *bambina.*'

Shaking her head, she climbed into her car.

*A week or more?*

It seemed when the Vatican spoke, even the military listened. Then again, General Rende was a family friend, going back two generations. He and Uncle Vigor were as close as brothers. It wasn't pure chance that Rachel had been brought to the general's attention and recruited from the University of Rome. Her uncle had been watching over her since her father had died in a bus accident fifteen years before.

Under his tutelage, she had spent many summers exploring Rome's museums, staying with the nuns of Saint Brigida, not far from the Gregorian University, better known as *il Greg*, where Uncle Vigor had studied and still taught. And while her uncle might have preferred she had entered the convent and followed in his footsteps, he had recognized she was too much of a hellion for such a pious profession and encouraged her to pursue her passion. He had also instilled in her one other gift during those long summers: the respect and love of history and art, where the greatest expressions of mankind were cemented in marble and granite, oil and canvas, glass and bronze.

And now it seemed her uncle was not done with her yet.

Slipping on a pair of blue-tinted Revo sunglasses, she pulled out onto Via Labicano and headed toward the massive Coliseum. Traffic congested around the landmark, but she crisscrossed through some backstreets, narrow and lined with crookedly parked vehicles. She zipped, slipping between the gears with the skill of a Grand Prix racer. She downshifted as she approached the entrance to a roundabout where five streets converged into a mad circle. Visitors considered Roman drivers illtempered, short of patience, and heavy of foot. Rachel found them sluggish.

She lunged between an overloaded flatbed and a boxy Mercedes G500 utility vehicle. Her Mini Cooper appeared to be no more than a sparrow flitting between two elephants. She flicked around the Mercedes, filled the tiny space in front of it, earned the blare of a car horn, but she was already gone. She whisked off the roundabout and onto the main thoroughfare that headed toward the Tiber River.

As she raced down the wide street, she kept an eye fixed to the flow of traffic on all sides. To move safely through Roman streets required not so much caution as it did strategic planning. As a result of such particular attention, Rachel noted her tail.

The black BMW sedan swung into position, five cars back.

Who was following her – and why?

**2:05 p.m.**

Fifteen minutes later, Rachel pulled into the entrance of an underground parking garage just outside the walls of the Vatican. As she descended, she searched the street behind her. The black BMW had vanished shortly after she had crossed the Tiber River. There was still no sign of it.

'Thank you,' she said into her cell phone. 'The car is gone.'

'Are you secure?' It was the warrant officer from her station house. She had called in the tail and kept the line open.

'It appears to be.'

'Do you want a patrol sent out?'

'No need. There are carabinieri on guard on the Square. I'll be fine from here. *Ciao*.'

She felt no embarrassment for calling in the false alarm. She would earn no ridicule. The Carabinieri Corps fostered a certain level of healthy paranoia among its men and women.

She found a parking space, climbed out, and locked her

car. Still, she kept her cell phone in hand. She would've preferred her 9mm.

At the top of the ramp, she stepped out of the car park and crossed toward St. Peter's Square. Though she approached one of the architectural masterpieces of the world, she kept a watch on the nearby streets and alleys.

There continued to be no sign of the BMW.

The car's occupants had probably just been tourists, surveying the city's landmarks in air-conditioned luxury rather than on foot in the blaze of the midday heat. Summer was high season, and all visitors eventually headed to the Vatican. It was most likely the very reason she thought she was being followed. Was it not said that all roads lead to Rome?

Or at least in this case, all traffic.

Satisfied, she pocketed her cell phone and crossed St. Peter's Square, heading toward the far side.

As usual, her eyes were drawn down the length of the piazza. Across the travertine square rose St. Peter's Basilica, built over the tomb of the martyred saint. Its dome, designed by Michelangelo, was the highest point in all of Rome. To either side, Bernini's double colonnade swept out in two wide arcs, framing the keyhole-shaped plaza between. According to Bernini, the colonnade was supposed to represent the arms of Saint Peter reaching out to embrace the faithful into the fold. Atop these arms, one hundred and forty stone saints perched and stared down upon the spectacle below.

And a spectacle it was.

What had once been Nero's circus continued to be a circus.

All around, voices babbled in French, Arabic, Polish, Hebrew, Dutch, Chinese. Tour groups congregated in islands around guides; sightseers stood with arms around shoulders, wearing false grins as photographs were taken; a few pious stood in the sun, Bibles open in hands, heads

57

bowed in prayers. A tiny cluster of Korean supplicants knelt on the stones, all dressed in yellow. Throughout the square, vendors worked the crowd, selling papal coins, scented rosaries, and blessed crucifixes.

She gratefully reached the far side of the square and approached one of the five entrances to the main complex. Porta Sant'Anna. The gate nearest to her destination.

She stepped to one of the Swiss Guards. As was traditional for this gate, he was dressed in a uniform of dark blue with a white collar, topped by a black beret. He took her name, checked her identification, and glanced up and down her slender frame as if disbelieving she was a Carabinieri lieutenant. Once satisfied, he perfunctorily directed her off to the side, to one of the Vigilanza, the Vatican Police, where a laminated pass was handed to her.

'Keep it with you at all times,' the policeman warned.

Armed with her pass, she followed the line of visitors through the gate and down Via del Pellegrino.

Most of the city-state was off-limits. The only public spaces were St. Peter's Basilica, the Vatican Museums, and the Gardens. The rest of the hundred acres were restricted without special permission.

But one section was truly forbidden territory to all but a few.

The Apostolic Palace, the home of the pope.

Her destination.

Rachel marched between the yellow-brick barracks of the Swiss Guard and the gray cliffs of St. Anne Church. Here was none of the majesty of the holiest of the holy states, just a crowded sidewalk and a congested line of cars, a gridlock inside Vatican City. Passing the papal printing office and post office, she crossed toward the entrance to the Apostolic Palace.

As she approached, she studied the gray-brick structure. It appeared more a utilitarian government building than the seat of the Holy See. But its looks were deceptive.

Even the roof. It appeared drab and flat, unremarkable. But she knew atop the Apostolic Palace lay a hidden garden, with fountains, trellis-lined paths, and neatly manicured shrubs. All was masked behind a false roof, sheltering His Holiness from the casual eye below and from any assassin's high-powered scope out in the city.

To her, it represented the Vatican at large: mysterious, secret, even slightly paranoid, but at its heart, a place of simple beauty and piety.

And perhaps the same could be said of her. While she was mostly a lapsed Catholic, only attending mass on holidays, she still had a core of faith that remained true.

Reaching the security station before the palace, Rachel showed her pass three more times to the Swiss Guards. As she did, she wondered if this was some nod back to Peter's thrice denial of Christ before the cock crowed.

At last, she gained admission to the palace proper. A guide awaited her, an American seminary student named Jacob. He was a wiry man in his mid-twenties, his blond hair already balding, dressed in black linen slacks and a white shirt, buttoned to the top.

'If you'll follow me, I've been directed to take you to Monsignor Verona.' He did a comical double take at her visitor's pass and stuttered with surprise. 'Lieutenant Verona? Are . . . are you related to the monsignor?'

'He's my uncle.'

A rapid nod as he collected himself. 'I'm sorry. I was only told to expect a Carabinieri officer.' He waved her to follow him. 'I am a student and aide for Monsignor Verona at the Greg.'

She nodded. Most of her uncle's students revered the man. He was deeply devoted to the Church but still maintained a strong scientific outlook. He even had a placard on the door to his university office, bearing the same inscription that once graced Plato's door: *Let no one enter who does not know geometry.*

Rachel was led through the entrance to the palace. She quickly lost her way. She had only been here once before, when her uncle was being promoted to the head of the Pontifical Institute of Christian Archaeology. She had attended the private papal audience. But the place was gigantic, with fifteen hundred rooms, a thousand staircases, and twenty courtyards. Even now, rather than heading up toward the pope's residence on the top floor, they were headed down.

She did not understand why her uncle asked her to meet him here, rather than at his university office. Had there been a theft? If so, why not tell her on the phone? Then again, she was well aware of the Vatican's strict Code of Silence. It was written into canon law. The Holy See knew how to keep its secrets.

At last they reached a small, nondescript door.

Jacob opened it for her.

Rachel stepped through into an odd Kafkaesque chamber. Sterilely lit, the chamber was long and narrow, but its ceilings were high. Against the walls, gray steel filing cabinets and drawers climbed from floor to ceiling. A tall library ladder leaned against one wall, necessary to reach the highest drawers. Though spotlessly clean, the space smelled dusty and old.

'Rachel!' her uncle called from a corner. He stood with a priest at a desk in a corner. She was waved over. 'You made good time, my dear. Then again, I've driven with you before. Any casualties?'

She smiled at him and crossed to the desk. She noted that her uncle was not wearing his usual outfit of jeans, T-shirt, and cardigan, but was dressed more formally, suiting his station, in a black cassock with purple piping and buttons. He'd even oiled the curls of his salt-and-pepper hair and trimmed his goatee tight to his face.

'This is Father Torres,' her uncle introduced. 'Official keeper of the bones.'

The elderly man stood. He was short and stocky, dressed all in black with a Roman collar. A hint of smile ghosted his face. 'I prefer the title "rector of the *reliquiae*."'

Rachel studied the towering wall of file cabinets. She had heard of this place, the Vatican's relic depository, but she had never been here before. She fought back a chill of revulsion. Catalogued and stored in all the drawers and shelves were bits and pieces of saints and martyrs: finger bones, snips of hair, vials of ash, scraps of garments, mummified skin, nail clippings, blood. Few people know that, by canon law, each and every Catholic altar must contain a holy relic. And with new churches or chapels being erected worldwide regularly, this priest's job was to box and FedEx bits of bone or other earthly remains of various saints.

Rachel had never understood the Church's obsession with relics. It simply gave her the creeps. But Rome was chock-full of them. Some of the most spectacular and unusual were found here: Mary Magdalene's foot, the vocal cords of Saint Anthony, the tongue of Saint John Nepomucene, the gallstones of Saint Clare. Even the entire body of Pope Saint Pius X lay up in St. Peter's, encased in bronze. The most disturbing, though, was a relic preserved in a shrine in Calcata: the supposed foreskin of Jesus Christ.

She found her voice. 'Was . . . was something stolen here?'

Uncle Vigor lifted an arm to his student. 'Jacob, perhaps you could fetch us some cappuccinos.'

'Certainly, Monsignor.'

Uncle Vigor waited until Jacob left, closing the door. His eyes then settled to Rachel. 'Have you heard of the massacre in Cologne?'

Rachel was taken off guard by his question. She had been running all day long and had had little chance to watch the news, but there had been no way to avoid hearing about the midnight murders up in Germany last night. The details remained sketchy.

'Only what's been reported on the radio,' she answered.

He nodded. 'The Curia here has been receiving intelligence in advance of what's being broadcasted. Eighty-four people were killed, including the Archbishop of Cologne. But it is the manner of their deaths that is being kept from the public for the moment.'

'What do you mean?'

'A handful were shot, but the greater majority seemed to have been electrocuted.'

'Electrocuted?'

'That is the tentative analysis. Autopsy reports are still pending. Some of the bodies were still smoking when authorities arrived.'

'Dear God. How . . . ?'

'That answer may have to wait. The cathedral is swarming with investigators of every ilk: criminologists, detectives, forensic scientists, even electricians. There are teams with the German BKA, terrorist experts from Interpol, and agents with Europol. But as the crime took place in a Roman Catholic cathedral, sanctified territory, the Vatican has invoked its Omerta.'

'Its Code of Silence.'

He grunted the affirmative. 'The Church is cooperating with German authorities, but it is also limiting access, trying to keep the scene from becoming a circus.'

Rachel shook her head. 'But what does all this have to do with you calling me here?'

'From the initial investigation, there seems to be only one motive. The golden reliquary at the cathedral was broken into.'

'They stole the reliquary.'

'No, that's just it. They left behind the solid gold box. A priceless artifact. They only stole its contents. Its relics.'

Father Torres interjected, 'And not just *any* relics, but the bones of the biblical Magi.'

'Magi . . . as in the Three Wise Men from the Bible?' Rachel couldn't keep the incredulity out of her voice. 'They steal the bones, but leave the gold box. Surely the reliquary would fetch a better price on the black market than the bones.'

Uncle Vigor sighed. 'At the secretary of state's request, I came down here to evaluate the provenance of those relics. They have an illustrious past. The bones came to Europe through the relic-collecting verve of Saint Helena, the mother of Emperor Constantine. As the first Christian emperor, Constantine had sent his mother on pilgrimages to collect holy relics. The most famous being, of course, the True Cross of Christ.'

Rachel had visited the Basilica of Santa Croce in Gerusalemme, out on Lateran Hill. In a back room, behind glass, were the most famous relics collected by Saint Helena: a beam of the True Cross, a nail used to crucify Christ, and two thorns from his painful crown. There persisted much controversy as to the authenticity of these relics. Most believed Saint Helena had been duped.

Her uncle continued, 'But it is not as well known that Queen Helena traveled further than Jerusalem, returning under mysterious circumstances with a large stone sarcophagus, claiming to have recovered the bodies of the Three Kings. The relics were kept in a church in Constantinople, but following the death of Constantine, they were transferred to Milan and interred in a basilica.'

'But I thought you said Germany –'

Uncle Vigor held up a hand. 'In the twelfth century, Emperor Frederick Barbarossa of Germany plundered Milan and stole the relics. The circumstances surrounding this are clouded with a mix of rumors. But all stories end with the relics in Cologne.'

'Until last night,' Rachel added.

Uncle Vigor nodded.

Rachel closed her eyes. No one spoke, leaving her to think. She heard the door open to the depository. She kept her eyes closed, not wanting to lose her train of thought.

'And the murders?' she said. 'Why not steal the bones when the church was empty? The act must have been meant also as a direct attack upon the Church. The violence against the congregation suggests a secondary motive of revenge – not just thievery.'

'Very good.' A new voice spoke from the doorway.

Startled, Rachel opened her eyes. She immediately recognized the robes worn by the newcomer: the black cassock with shoulder cape, the wide sash worn high around the hips, scarlet to match the skullcap. She also recognized the man inside the clothes. 'Cardinal Spera,' she said, offering a bow of her head.

He waved her up, his gold ring flashing. The ring marked him as a cardinal, but he also wore a second ring, a twin of the first, on his other hand, representative of his station as the Vatican's secretary of state. He was Sicilian, dark haired and complexioned. He was also young for such an esteemed position, not yet fifty years old.

He offered a warm smile. 'I see, Monsignor Verona, that you were not wrong about your niece.'

'It would've been improper of me to lie to a cardinal, especially one who happens to be the pope's right-hand man.' Her uncle crossed over, and rather than chastely kissing either of the man's two rings, he gave him a firm hug. 'How is His Holiness handling the news?'

The cardinal's face tightened with a shake of his head. 'After we met this morning, I contacted His Eminence in St. Petersburg. He will be flying back tomorrow morning.'

*After we met* . . . Rachel now understood her uncle's formal attire. He had been in consultation with the secretary of state.

Cardinal Spera continued, 'I'll be arranging for his official papal response with the Synod of Bishops and the College of Cardinals. Then I have to prepare for tomorrow's memorial service. It's to be held at sundown.'

Rachel felt overwhelmed. While the pope was the head of the Vatican, its absolute monarch, the true power of the state rested with this one man, its official prime minister. She noted the weary glaze to his eyes, the way he held his shoulders too tightly. He was plainly exhausted.

'And has your research turned up anything here?' the cardinal asked.

'It has,' Uncle Vigor said dourly. 'The thieves don't possess all the bones.'

Rachel stirred. 'There are more?'

Her uncle turned to her. 'That's what we came down here to ascertain. It seems the city of Milan, after the bones were plundered by Barbarossa, spent the past centuries clamoring for their return. To finally settle the matter, a few of the Magi bones were sent back to Milan in 1906, back to the Basilica of Saint Eustorgio.'

'Thank the Lord,' Cardinal Spera said. 'So they aren't entirely lost.'

Father Torres spoke up. 'We should arrange for them to be sent here immediately. Safeguarded at the depository.'

'Until that can be arranged, I'll have security tightened at the basilica,' the cardinal said. He motioned to Uncle Vigor. 'On your return trip from Cologne, I'll have you stop off and collect the bones in Milan.'

Uncle Vigor nodded.

'Oh, I was also able to arrange an earlier flight,' the cardinal continued. 'The helicopter will take you both to the airfield in three hours.'

*Both?*

'All the better.' Uncle Vigor turned to Rachel. 'It looks like we must disappoint your mother once again. No family dinner, it seems.'

'I'm . . . we're going to Cologne?'

'As Vatican nuncios,' her uncle said.

Rachel tried to keep pace in her head. Nuncios were the Vatican's ambassadors abroad.

'Emergency nuncios,' Cardinal Spera corrected. 'Temporary, covering this particular tragedy. You are being presented as passive observers, to represent Vatican interests and report back. I need keen eyes out there. Someone familiar with thefts of antiquities.' A nod to Rachel. 'And someone with a vast knowledge of those antiquities.'

'That is our cover, anyway,' Uncle Vigor said.

'Cover?'

Cardinal Spera frowned, a warning tone entering his voice. 'Vigor . . .'

Her uncle turned to the secretary of state. 'She has a right to know. I thought that had already been decided.'

'*You* decided.'

The two men stared each other down. Finally, Cardinal Spera sighed with a wave of an arm, relenting.

Uncle Vigor turned back to Rachel. 'The nuncio assignation is just a smoke screen.'

'Then what are we – ?'

He told her.


3:35 p.m.

Still stunned, Rachel waited for her uncle to finish a few private words with Cardinal Spera outside the doorway. Off to the side, Father Torres busied himself with shelving various volumes that had been piled on his desk.

Finally, her uncle returned. 'I had hoped to grab a brioche with you, but with the timetable accelerated, we must both get ready. You should grab an overnight bag, your passport, and whatever else you might need for a day or two abroad.'

Rachel stood her ground. 'Vatican spies? We're going in as Vatican *spies*?'

Uncle Vigor lifted his brows. 'Are you really that surprised? The Vatican, a sovereign country, has always had an intelligence service, with full-time employees and operatives. They've been used to infiltrate hate groups, secret societies, hostile countries, wherever the concerns of the Vatican are threatened. Walter Ciszek, a priest operating under the alias Vladimir Lipinski, played a cat-and-mouse game with the KGB for years, before being captured and spending over two decades in a Soviet prison.'

'And we've just been recruited into this service?'

'*You've* been recruited. I've worked with the intelligence service for over fifteen years.'

'What?' Rachel almost choked on the word.

'What better cover for an operative than as a well-respected and knowledgeable archaeologist in humble service to the Vatican?' Her uncle waved her out the door. 'Come. Let's see about getting everything in order.'

Rachel stumbled after her uncle, trying to see him with new eyes.

'We'll be meeting up with a party of American scientists. Like us, they'll be investigating the attack in secret, concentrating more on the deaths, leaving us to handle the theft of the relics.'

'I don't understand.' That was a vast understatement. 'Why all this subterfuge?'

Her uncle stopped and pulled her into a small side chapel. It was no larger than a closet, the air stagnant with old incense.

'Only a handful of people know this,' he said. 'But there was a survivor to the attack. A boy. He is still in shock, but slowly recovering. He is at a hospital in Cologne, under guard.'

'He witnessed the attack?'

A nod answered her. 'What he described sounded like

67

madness, but it could not be ignored. All the deaths – or rather those that succumbed to the electrocution – occurred in a single moment. The dying collapsed where they sat or knelt. The boy had no explanation for *how* it occurred, but he was adamant about the *who*.'

'Who killed the parishioners?'

'No, who succumbed, which members of the congregation died so horribly.'

Rachel waited for an answer.

'The ones who were electrocuted, for lack of a better word, were only those who took the Holy Eucharist during the Communion service.'

'What?'

'It was the Communion host that killed them.'

A chill passed through her. If word spread that the Communion wafers were somehow to blame, it could have repercussions around the world. The entire holy sacrament could be in jeopardy. 'Were the wafers poisoned, tainted somehow?'

'That's still unknown. But the Vatican wants answers immediately. And the Holy See wants them first. And without the resources necessary for this level of clandestine investigation, especially on foreign soil, I've called in a chit owed to me by a friend deep within U.S. military intelligence, someone I trust fully. He will have a team on site by tonight.'

Rachel could only nod, struck dumb by the last hour's revelations.

'I think you were right, Rachel,' Uncle Vigor said. 'The murders in Cologne were a direct attack against the Church. But I believe this is just an opening gambit in a much larger game. But what game is being played?'

Rachel nodded. 'And what do the bones of the Magi have to do with any of this?'

'Exactly. While you collect your things, I'm going off to the libraries and archives. I already have a team of scholars sifting through all references to the Three Kings. By the time the helicopter lifts off, I'll have a full dossier on the Magi.' Uncle Vigor reached to her, hugged her tight, and whispered in her ear. 'You can still refuse. I would think no less of you.'

Rachel shook her head, pulling back. 'As the saying goes, *fortes fortuna adiuvat.*'

'Fortune does indeed favor the brave.' He kissed her gently on her cheek. 'If I had a daughter like you –'

'You'd be excommunicated.' She kissed his other cheek. 'Now let's go.'

Her uncle led her out of the Apostolic Palace, then they parted ways, he toward the Libraries, she toward St. Anne's Gate.

Before long and with barely any note of the passage of time, Rachel reached her parked car and climbed into the Mini Cooper. She sped out of the underground car park and squealed around a tight corner into traffic. She ticked off all she would need, while trying to keep any speculation to a minimum.

She raced over the Tiber River and headed toward the center of town. With her mind on autopilot, she failed to note when she had regained her tail. Only that it was back there again.

Her heartbeat quickened.

The black BMW kept five car lengths behind her, matching her every move around slower cars and even-slower pedestrians. She made a couple of fast turns, not enough to alert her tail that he had been spotted, just her usual controlled recklessness. She needed to know for sure.

The BMW kept pace.

Now she knew.

*Damn.*

She fought her way into the narrower byways and alleys. The roads were congested. It became a slow-motion car chase.

She pulled up on a sidewalk to squeeze past a stall of traffic. Edging to the next cross street, a pedestrian alley, she turned into it. Startled strollers leaped out of her way. Shopping carts spilled. Obscenities flew. A loaf of bread hit her back window, thrown by a particularly irate matron.

At the next thoroughfare, she punched into second and sped a block, then made another turn, then another. This section of Rome was a maze of alleyways. There was no way for her tail to keep up with her.

Streaming out Via Aldrovandi, she raced around the edge of the Giardino Zoological Park. She kept a watch on her rearview mirrors. She had escaped her pursuit . . . at least for now.

Able to free up a hand, she snatched her cell phone. She hit the speed dial for Parioli Station. She needed backup.

As the connection dialed through, she left the main thoroughfare and ducked into the backstreets again, not taking any chances. Who had she pissed off? As a mcm ber of the Cultural Heritage Police, she had a number of enemies among the organized-crime families who trafficked in stolen antiquities.

The phone line clicked, buzzed, then all she heard was dead air. She checked the phone's screen. She had hit a patch of poor reception. The seven hills of Rome and its marble-and-brick canyons wreaked havoc on signal strength.

She hit the Redial button.

As she prayed to the patron saint of cell reception, she used the time to debate returning home and decided against it.

She would be safer at the Vatican until she left for Germany.

Merging onto Via Salaria, the old Salt Road, a main artery through Rome, she finally heard the line connect.

'Central desk.'

Before she could respond, Rachel spotted a blur of black.

The BMW whipped up alongside her Mini Cooper.

A second car appeared on her other side.

Identical, except this one was *white*.

She'd had not the one tail . . . but *two*. Fixed on the conspicuous black car, she had failed to spot the white one. A fatal mistake.

The two cars slammed into her, pinning her between them with a screech of metal and paint. Their back windows were already lowered. The blunt noses of submachine guns poked out.

She slammed on her brakes, metal screamed, but she was wedged tight. There was no escape.

# 3

# SECRETS

He had to get out of here.

In the gym locker room, Grayson Pierce pulled on a pair of black biker's shorts, then slipped a loose-fitting nylon soccer jersey over his head. He sat on the bench and tied on a pair of sneakers.

Behind him, the locker room door swung open. He glanced back as Monk Kokkalis entered, a basketball under one arm and a baseball cap on backward. Standing only three inches over five feet, Monk looked like a pit bull wearing sweats. Still, he proved to be a fierce and agile ballplayer. Most people underestimated him, but he had an uncanny talent to read an opponent, to outfox any guard, and few of his layups ever missed.

Monk tossed the basketball into the equipment bin – again making a perfect shot – then crossed to his locker. He stripped off his sweatshirt, balled it up, and shoved it inside.

He eyeballed Gray. 'That's what you're wearing to meet Commander Crowe?'

Gray stood. 'I'm heading over to my folks'.'

'I thought the ops manager told us to stick to campus?'

'Screw that.'

Monk raised an eyebrow. The bushy brows were the only hair on his shaved head. He preferred to stick to the look drilled into him by the Green Berets. The man carried

72

other physical attributes from his former military life: puckered bullet wound scars, three of them, shoulder, upper leg, and chest. He had been the only one of his team to survive an ambush in Afghanistan. During his recovery Stateside, Sigma had recruited him because of his genius-level IQ and retrained him through a doctoral program in forensic medicine.

'Have you already been cleared by medical?' Monk asked.

'Just contusions and a couple bruised ribs.' *Along with a wounded ego,* he added silently, fingering the tender spot below his seventh rib.

Gray had already given his videotaped debriefing. He had secured the bomb but not the Dragon Lady. The one lead into a major pipeline of bioweapons trafficking had escaped. He had sent her dragon-charm pendant down to forensics for any trace or fingerprint evidence. He didn't expect anything to be found.

He grabbed his backpack from the bench. 'I'll have my beeper with me. I'm only fifteen minutes away by Metro.'

'And you're going to leave the director waiting?'

Gray shrugged. He'd had enough: the postmission debriefing, the in-depth medical exam, and now this mysterious summons by Director Crowe. He knew he was due for a dressing-down. He shouldn't have gone in alone to Fort Detrick. It had been a bad call. He knew it.

But still riding the adrenaline surge from this morning's near disaster, Gray couldn't sit idle and simply wait. Director Crowe had gone off to a meeting over at DARPA headquarters in Arlington. There was no telling when he'd be back. In the meantime, Gray needed to move, to let off some steam.

He pulled on his small riding backpack.

'Have you heard who else has been summoned to the meeting with the director?' Monk asked.

'Who?'

'Kat Bryant.'

'Really?'

A nod.

Captain Kathryn Bryant had entered Sigma only ten months ago, but she had already completed a fast-track program in geology. There were rumors that she was also completing an engineering discipline. She would be only the second operative with a dual degree. Grayson was the first.

'Then it can't be a mission assignation,' Gray said. 'They wouldn't send someone so green out into the field.'

'None of us is *that* green.' Monk grabbed a towel and headed for the showers. 'She did come out of the intelligence branch of the Navy. Black ops, they say.'

'*They* say a lot of things,' Gray mumbled and crossed to the exit.

Despite the number of high IQs, Sigma was no less a rumor mill than any corporation. Even this morning's summons had followed a flurry of memos and a recall of operatives. Of course, some of this activity was the direct result of Gray's mission. The Guild had attacked one of their members. Speculation abounded. Was there a new leak, or had the ambush been planned based on old intel, prior to Sigma's move to Washington from DARPA's headquarters in Arlington and the purging of its operations there?

Either way, another rumor persisted in the halls of Sigma: a new mission was being planned, one commanded high up the chain, one of vital national interest. But nothing else was known.

Gray refused to play the rumor game. He would wait to hear from the commander himself. Besides, it's not like he would be going anywhere soon. He'd be warming the bench for some time.

So he might as well meet his other obligations.

Crossing out of the gym, Gray strode through the

labyrinth of hallways toward the elevator bay. The space still smelled of fresh paint and old cement.

The subterranean stronghold of Sigma central command was once an underground bunker and a fallout shelter. It had been a place to secure an important think tank during World War II, but it had long been abandoned and closed off. Few knew of its existence, buried beneath the mecca of Washington's scientific community: the campus of museums and laboratories that made up the Smithsonian Institution.

Now the underground warren had new tenants. To the world at large, it was just another think tank. Many of its members worked at laboratories throughout the Smithsonian, doing research and utilizing the resources at hand. The new site for Sigma had been chosen because of its proximity to all the research labs, covering a wide range of disciplines. It would have been too expensive to duplicate all the varied facilities. So Sigma had been buried at the heart of Washington's scientific community. The Smithsonian Institution became both a resource and a cover.

Gray pressed his hand on the elevator door's security pad. A blue line scanned his palm print. The doors whooshed open. He climbed inside and pressed the top button, marked LOBBY. The cage rose silently, climbing up from the fourth level.

He sensed more than felt the scan over his body, a proprietary search for hidden electronic data. It helped aid in the prevention of information being stolen out of the command center. It had its drawbacks. During the first week here, Monk had set off a system-wide alert after absentmindedly carrying in an unauthorized MP3 digital player after an afternoon run.

The doors opened into an ordinary-looking reception area, manned by two armed guards and a female receptionist. It could pass as a bank lobby. But the amount of surveillance and state-of-the-art countermeasures rivaled those at Fort Knox. A second entrance to the bunker, a large service access, equally guarded, lay hidden in a private garage complex, half a mile away. His motorcycle was over there, being repaired. So he was hoofing it to the Metro station where he had a mountain bike stored for emergencies.

'Good morning, Dr. Pierce,' the receptionist said.

'Hello, Melody.'

The young woman was unaware of what truly lay below, believing the fabricated story of the think tank, also named Sigma. Only the guards knew the truth. They nodded to Gray.

'Are you leaving for the day?' Melody asked.

'Only for an hour or so.' He slid his holographic ID card into the reader by the desk, then pressed his thumb on the screen, signing out of the command center. He had always thought the security countermeasures here were overkill. Not any longer.

The outer door's lock unhitched.

One of the guards opened the door, stepped out, and held it open for Gray. 'Good day, sir,' the guard said as Gray exited.

*Good* hardly described his day so far.

A long paneled corridor stretched ahead, followed by a single flight of stairs that led up into the public regions of the building. Entering a large hall, he passed a touring group of Japanese visitors led by a translator and guide. No one gave him a second glance.

Talk about hiding in plain sight.

As he crossed the tiled floor, he heard the tour leader's speech, spoken in rote, given a thousand times. 'The Smithsonian Castle was completed in 1855, with the cornerstone being laid by President James Polk. It is the largest and oldest of the Institution's structures and once housed the original science museum and research laboratories, but now it serves as the administrative office and Information Center for the Institution's fifteen museums, the National Zoo, and many research sites and galleries. If you'll follow me, next . . .'

Gray reached the outer doors, a side exit to the Smithsonian Castle, and pushed to freedom. He squinted at the bright sun, shielding his eyes. As he lifted his arm, he felt a twinge of protest from his ribs. The Tylenol with codeine must be wearing off.

Reaching the edge of the manicured gardens, he glanced back to the Castle. Nicknamed for its red-brick parapets, turrets, spires, and towers, it was considered one of the finest Gothic Revival structures in the United States and formed the heart of the Smithsonian Institution. The bunker had been tunneled out beneath it, built when the southwest tower had burned to the ground in 1866, requiring it to be rebuilt from the ground up. The secret labyrinth had been incorporated in the renovation, eventually becoming the subterranean fallout shelter, meant to protect the brightest minds of its generation . . . or at least those in Washington, D.C.

Now it hid Sigma's central command.

With a final glance at the U.S. flag flying over the highest tower, Gray headed across the Mall, aiming for the Metro station.

He had other responsibilities besides keeping America safe.

Something he had neglected for too long.


4:25 p.m.
ROME, ITALY

The two BMWs continued to pin the Mini Cooper. No matter how Rachel struggled, she could not pull free.

The guns in the back seats swung forward.

Before the assailants could open fire, Rachel shoved the

77

car into park and yanked her emergency brake. The car jolted with a scream of tearing metal. Her rearview mirror shattered. The effort threw off the gunmen's aim, but it was not enough to free her trapped car.

The BMWs continued to drag her car forward.

With her Mini Cooper now dead weight, Rachel dove for the car's floor well, gouging her left side on the gearshift knob. A spate of gunfire shattered through the driver's-side window, passing through where she had been sitting.

She wouldn't be so lucky a second time.

As their speed slowed, Rachel hit the controls to her convertible roof. The windows began to lower and the cloth roof folded back. Wind whistled inside.

She prayed the momentary distraction would buy her the time she needed. Bunching her legs under her, she leaped off the center console and used the lip of the passenger door to hurdle herself through the half-open roof. The white sedan was still crammed against the passenger side. She landed atop its roof and rolled into a half crouch.

By now, their speed had slowed to less than thirty kilometers per hour.

Bullets blasted from below.

She threw herself off the roof and flew toward a line of cars parked at the edge of the road. She struck the long roof of a Jaguar and slid belly-first off its edge and landed in a teeth-jarring tumble on the far side.

Dazed, she lay still. The bulk of parked cars shielded her from the open road. Half a block away, unable to brake fast enough, the BMWs suddenly roared and, with a squeal of tires, sped off.

In the distance, Rachel heard the *wha-wha* of police sirens.

Rolling onto her back, she searched her belt for her cell phone. The holster was empty. She had been making a call when the attackers swiped into her.

*Oh God . . .*

She struggled up. She had no fear that the assassins would return. Already multiple cars were stopping, blocked by her Mini Cooper stalled in the road.

Rachel had a larger concern. Unlike the first time, she had caught a glimpse of the black BMW's license plate.

SCV 03681.

She didn't need a registration search to know where the car had originated. The special plates were only issued by one agency.

SCV stood for *Stato della Città del Vaticano*.

Vatican City.

Rachel struggled up, head aching. She tasted blood from a split lip. It didn't matter. If she was attacked by someone with connections to the Vatican . . .

She gained her feet with her heart pounding. A driving fear fueled her strength. Another target was surely in danger.

'Uncle Vigor . . .'

11:03 a.m.
TAKOMA PARK, MARYLAND

'Gray! Is that you?'

Grayson Pierce hitched his bike over one shoulder and climbed the steps of the porch of his parents' home, a bungalow with a wooden porch and a wide overhanging gable.

He called through the open screen door. 'Yeah, Mom!'

He leaned the bike against the porch railing, earning a protest from his ribs. He had phoned the house from the Metro station, giving his mother fair warning of his arrival. He kept a Trek mountain bike locked up at the local station here for times like this.

'I have lunch almost ready.'

'What? You're cooking?' He swung open the screen

79

door with a pained cry of its spring hinges. It snapped closed behind him. 'Will wonders never cease?'

'Don't give me any of your lip, young man. I'm fully capable of making sandwiches. Ham and cheese.'

He crossed through the living room with its oak Craftsman furniture, a tasteful mix of modern and antique. He did not fail to note the fine coating of dust. His mother had never been much of a homemaker, spending most of her time teaching, first at a Jesuit high school back in Texas and now as an associate dean of biological sciences at George Washington University. His parents had moved out here three years ago, into the quiet historical district of Takoma Park, with its quaint Victorian homes and older shingle cottages. Gray had an apartment a couple of miles away, on Piney Branch Road. He had wanted to be close to his parents, to help out where he could.

Especially now.

'Where's Dad?' he asked as he entered the kitchen, seeing his father was not present.

His mother closed the refrigerator door, a gallon of milk in hand. 'Out in the garage. Working on another birdhouse.'

'Not another one?'

She frowned at him. 'He likes it. Keeps him out of trouble. His therapist says it's good for him to have a hobby.' She crossed with two plates of sandwiches.

His mother had come straight from her university office. She still wore her blue blazer over a white blouse, her blond-gray hair pulled back and bobby-pinned. Neat, professorial. But Gray noted the haggard edge to her eyes. She looked more drawn, thinner.

Gray took the plates. 'Dad's woodworking may help him, but does it always have to be birdhouses? There are only so many birds in Maryland.'

She smiled. 'Eat your sandwiches. Do you want any pickles?'

80

'No.' It was the way they always were. Small talk to avoid the larger matters. But some things couldn't be put off forever. 'Where did they find him?'

'Over by the 7-Eleven on Cedar. He got confused. Ended up heading the wrong way. He had enough presence of mind to call John and Suz.'

The neighbors must have then telephoned Gray's mother, and she in turn had called Gray, worried, half-panicked. But five minutes later, she had called again. His father was home and fine. Still, Gray knew he had better stop by for a short visit.

'Is he still taking his Aricept?' he asked.

'Of course. I make sure he does every morning.'

His father had been diagnosed with Alzheimer's, the very early stages, shortly after his parents had moved out here. It had started with small bouts of forgetfulness: where he had placed his keys, telephone numbers, the names of neighbors. The doctors said the move from Texas might have brought forth symptoms that had been latent. His mind had a difficult time cataloging all the new information after the cross-country move. But stubborn and determined, he had refused to go back. Eventually along with the forgetfulness came spats of frustrated anger. Not that such a line was ever hard for his father to cross.

'Why don't you take his plate out to him?' his mother asked. 'I have to call in to the office.'

Gray reached and took the sandwiches, letting his hand rest atop hers for a moment. 'Maybe we need to talk about that live-in nurse.'

She shook her head – not denying the need so much as simply refusing to discuss it. She pulled her hand from his. Gray had hit this wall before. His father would not allow it, and his mother felt it was her responsibility to care for him. But it was wearing on the household, on his mother, on their entire family.

'When was the last time Kenny came by?' he asked. His younger brother ran a computer start-up just across the border in Virginia, following in his father's footsteps as an engineer – electrical, though, not petroleum.

'You know Kenny . . .' his mother said. 'Let me get you a pickle for your father.'

Gray shook his head. Lately Kenny had been talking of moving to Cupertino, California. He had excuses for why the move was necessary, but beneath it all, Gray knew the truth. His brother merely wanted to escape, to get away. At least Gray understood that sentiment. He had done that himself, joining the Army. It must be a Pierce family trait.

His mother passed him the pickle jar to open. 'How is everything at the lab?'

'Going fine,' he said. He cracked the lid, fished out a dill, and placed it on the plate.

'I was reading about a bunch of budget cuts over at DARPA.'

'My job's not at risk,' he assured her. Neither of his folks knew of his role with Sigma. They thought he simply did low-level research for the military. They did not have the security clearance for the truth.

With the plate in hand, Gray headed for the back door.

His mother watched him. 'He'll be glad to see you.'

*If only I could say the same. . . .*

Gray headed for the garage out back. He heard the twangs of a country music station flowing from the open door. It brought back memories of line dancing at Mule-shoes. And other less pleasant recollections.

He stood at the entrance of the garage. His father crouched over a vise-gripped piece of wood, hand-planing an edge.

'Pop,' he said.

His dad straightened and turned. He was as tall as Grayson, but built stocky, wider shoulders, broader back. He had worked the oil fields while putting himself through college, earning a good practical degree in petroleum engineering. He had done well until an industrial accident at a well sheared away his left leg at the knee. The settlement and disability allowed him to retire at forty-seven.

That had been fifteen years ago.

Half of Grayson's life. The bad half.

His father turned toward him. 'Gray?' He wiped the sweat from his brow, smearing sawdust. A scowl formed. 'There was no need to come all the way out here.'

'How else would these sandwiches get to you?' He lifted the plate.

'Your mother made those?'

'You know Mom. She tried her best.'

'Then I'd better eat them. Can't discourage the habit.'

He pushed away from the workbench and hobbled stiff-legged on his prosthesis to a small fridge in the back. 'Beer?'

'I have to go back to work in a bit.'

'One beer won't kill you. I've some of that Sam Adams swill you like.'

His father was more of a Budweiser-and-Coors man. But the fact that he stocked his fridge with Sam Adams was about the equivalent of a pat on the back. Maybe even a hug.

He couldn't refuse.

Gray took the bottle and used the opener built into the edge of the worktable to pop it open. His father sidled over and leaned a hip on a stool. He lifted his own bottle, a Budweiser, in salute. 'It sucks to get old . . . but there's always beer.'

'So true.' Gray drank deeply. He wasn't sure he should be mixing codeine and alcohol – then again, it had been a long, long morning.

His father stared at him. The silence threatened to become quickly awkward.

'So,' Gray said, 'can't find your way home any longer.'

'Fuck you,' he responded with false anger, weakened by a grin and a shake of his head. His father appreciated honest talk. *Straight shooting,* as he used to say. 'At least I was no goddamn felon.'

'You can't let go of my stint in Leavenworth. *That* you keep remembering!'

His father tipped his beer bottle at Gray. 'I will as long as I damn can.'

Their eyes met. He saw something glint behind his father's banter, something he had seldom seen before. Fear.

The two had never had an easy relationship. His father had taken to heavy drinking after the accident, accompanied by severe bouts of depression. It was hard for a Texas oilman to suddenly become a housewife, raising two boys while his spouse went to work. To compensate, he had run the household like a boot camp. And Gray had always pushed the envelope, a born rebel.

Until at last, at eighteen, Gray had simply packed his bags and joined the Army, leaving in the middle of the night.

Afterward the two did not speak for a full two years.

Slowly his mother had brought them back together. Still, it had remained an uncomfortable détente. She had once said, 'You two are more alike than you are different.' Grayson had not heard scarier words.

'This goddamn sucks . . .' his father said softly, breaking the silence.

'Budweiser certainly does.' Grayson lifted his beer bottle. 'That's why I only drink Sam Adams.'

His father grinned. 'You're an asshole.'

'You raised me.'

'And I suppose it takes one to know one.'

'I never said that.'

His father rolled his eyes. 'Why do you even bother coming over?'

*Because I don't know how long you'll remember me,*
he thought, but dared not say it aloud. There remained a
tight spot behind his sternum, an old resentment that he
could not completely let go. There were words he wanted to say, wanted to hear . . . and a part of him knew he
was running out of time.

'Where did you get these sandwiches?' his father asked,
taking a bite and speaking around the mouthful. 'They're
pretty good.'

Gray kept his face passive. 'Mom made 'em.'

A flicker of confusion followed. 'Oh . . . yeah.'

Their eyes met again. Fear flared brighter in his father's
gaze . . . and shame. He had lost a part of his manhood
fifteen years ago and now he faced losing his humanity.

'Pop . . . I . . .'

'Drink your beer.' He heard an edge of familiar anger,
and Gray reflexively shied from it.

He drank his beer, sitting silently, neither able to speak.
Maybe his mother was right. They *were* too much alike.

His beeper finally went off at his waist. Gray grabbed
it too quickly. He saw the Sigma number.

'That's the office,' Gray mumbled. 'I . . . I have an
afternoon meeting.'

His father nodded. 'I should get back to this damn
birdhouse.'

They shook hands, two uneasy adversaries conceding
no contest.

Gray returned to the house, said his good-byes to his
mother, and collected up his bike. He mounted it and
quickly pedaled toward the Metro station. The phone number on his beeper had been followed by an alphanumeric
code.

Σ911.

An emergency.

Thank God.

The search for the truth behind the Three Magi had turned into a painstaking archaeological dig – but instead of hauling dirt and rock, Monsignor Vigor Verona and his crew of archivists were digging through crumbling books and parchments. The crew of *scrittori* had done the initial spadework in the main Vatican Library; now Vigor sifted for clues about the Magi in one of the most guarded areas of the Holy See: the Archivio Segretto Vaticano, the infamous Secret Archives of the Vatican.

Vigor strode down the long subterranean hall. Each lamp clicked on as he approached and switched off as he left it behind, maintaining a pool of illumination around him and his young student, Jacob. They crossed the length of the main Manuscript Depository, nicknamed the *carbonile,* or bunker. Built in 1980, the concrete hall rose two stories high, each level separated by a mesh metal floor, connected by steep stairs. On one side, miles of steel shelves contained various archival *regestra:* bound reams of parchments and papers. On the opposite wall stood the same metal shelves, only sealed and locked behind wire doors, protecting more-sensitive material.

There was a saying about the Holy See: the Vatican had too many secrets . . . and not enough. Vigor doubted the latter as he strode through the vast depository. It kept too many secrets, even from itself.

Jacob carried a laptop, maintaining a database on their subject. 'So there were not just *three* Magi?' he said as they headed toward the exit to the bunker.

They had come down here to digitize a photograph of a vase currently residing at the Kircher Museum. It had depicted not three kings, but *eight.* But even that number varied. A painting in the cemetery of Saint Peter showed *two,* and one at a crypt in Domitilla illustrated *four.*

'The Gospels were never specific on the number of Magi,' Vigor said, feeling the exhaustion of the long day setting in. He found it useful to talk through much of his thoughts, a firm believer in the Socratic method. 'Only the Gospel of Matthew directly refers to them, and even then only vaguely. The common assumption of *three* comes from the number of gifts borne by the Magi: gold, frankincense, and myrrh. In fact, they might not even have been kings. The word *magi* comes from the Greek word *magoi,* or "magician."'

'They were magicians?'

'Not as we might think. The connotation of *magoi* does not imply sorcery, but rather practitioners of hidden wisdom. Hence the "wise men" reference. Most biblical scholars now believe they were Zoroastrian astrologers out of Persia or Babylon. They interpreted the stars and foresaw the coming of a king to the west, portended by a single celestial rising.'

'The Star of Bethlehem.'

He nodded. 'Despite all the paintings, the star was not a particularly dramatic event. According to the Bible, no one in Jerusalem even noted it. Not until the Magi came to King Herod and brought it to his attention. The Magi had figured a newborn king, as heralded by the stars, must be born to royalty. But King Herod was shocked to hear of this news and asked them when they saw the star rise. He then used Hebrew holy books of prophecy to point out where this king might've been born. He directed the Magi to Bethlehem.'

'So Herod told them where to go.'

'He did, sending them as spies. Only on the way to Bethlehem, according to Matthew, the star reappeared and guided the Magi to the child. Afterward, warned by an angel, they left without telling Herod who or where the child was. Thence began the slaughter of the innocents.'

Jacob hurried to keep pace. 'But Mary, Joseph, and the newborn child had already fled to Egypt, warned by an angel as well. So what became of the Magi?'

'What indeed?' Vigor had spent most of the last hour chasing down Gnostic and Apocryphal texts with references to the Magi, from the Protevangelium of James to the Book of Seth. If the bones were stolen, was there motivation beyond pure profit? Knowledge could prove their best weapon in that case.

Vigor checked his watch. He was running out of time, but the Prefect of the Archives would continue the search, building the database with Jacob, who would forward their findings via e-mail.

'What about the historical names of the Magi?' Jacob said. 'Gaspar, Melchior, and Balthazar?'

'Supposition only. The names first appeared in *Excerpta Latina Barbari* in the sixth century. Further references follow that one, but I think they're more fairy tales than factual accounts; still, they may be worth following. I'll leave that for you and the Preffeto Alberto to research.'

'I'll do my best.'

Vigor frowned. It was a daunting task. Then again, did any of this really matter? Why steal the Magi bones?

The answer eluded him. And Vigor was unsure if the truth would be found among the thirty miles of shelves that made up the Secret Archives. But one consensus had begun to form from all the clues. Factual or not, the stories of the Magi hinted at some vast wealth of hidden knowledge, known only to a certain sect of magi.

But who were they really?

Magicians, astrologers, or priests?

Vigor passed the Parchment Room, catching a fresh whiff of insecticide and fungicide. The caretakers must have just sprayed. Vigor knew that some of the rare documents in the Parchment Room were turning purple, succumbing to a resistant violet fungus and leaving them in grave danger of being lost forever.

So much else here was also threatened . . . and not just from fire, fungus, or neglect, but from sheer volume. Only half of the material stored here had ever been indexed. And more was added each year, flooding in from Vatican ambassadors, metropolitan sees, and individual parishes.

It was impossible to keep up.

The Secret Archives themselves had spread like a malignant cancer, metastasizing out from its original rooms into old attics, underground crypts, and empty tower cells. Vigor had spent half a year researching the files of past Vatican spies, those who came before him, agents placed in government positions around the world, many written in code, reporting on political intrigue spanning a thousand years.

Vigor knew that the Vatican was as much a political entity as a spiritual one. And enemies of both sought to undermine the Holy See. Even today. It was priests like Vigor who stood between the Vatican and the world. Warriors in secret, holding the line. And while Vigor might not agree with everything done in the past or even the present, his faith remained solid . . . like the Vatican itself.

He was proud of his service to the papacy.

Empires might rise and fall. Philosophies might come and go. But in the end, the Vatican persisted, abided, remained stolid and steadfast. It was history, time, and faith all preserved in stone.

Even here, many of the greatest treasures of the world were protected in the Archive's locked vaults, safes, closets, and dark wooden cabinets called *armadi*. In one drawer was a letter from Mary Stuart on the day before she was beheaded; in another, the love letters between King Henry VIII and Anne Boleyn. There were documents pertaining to the Inquisition, to witch trials, to the Crusades, to letters from a khan of Persia and a Ming empress.

But what Vigor sought now was not so guarded.

It required only a long climb.

He had one more clue he wanted to investigate before he left for Germany with Rachel.

Vigor reached the small elevator to the upper rooms of the Archives, called the *piani nobli,* or the noble floors. He held the door for Jacob, closed it, and punched the button. With a shudder and bounce, the small cage rose.

'Where are we headed now?' Jacob asked.

'To the Torre dei Venti.'

'The Tower of the Winds? Why?'

'There is an ancient document kept up there. A copy of the *Description of the World* from the sixteenth century.'

'Marco Polo's book?'

He nodded as the elevator shuddered to a stop. They exited down a long corridor.

Jacob hurried to keep up. 'What do Marco Polo's adventures have to do with the Magi?'

'In that book, he relates myths out of ancient Persia, concerning the Magi and what became of them. It all centers on a gift given to them by the Christ child. A stone of great power. Upon that stone, the Magi supposedly founded a mystical fraternity of arcane wisdom. I'd like to trace that myth.'

The corridor ended at the Tower of the Winds. The empty rooms of this tower had become incorporated into the Secret Archives. Unfortunately, the room Vigor sought was at its very top. He cursed the lack of elevator and entered the dark stair.

He abandoned further lecturing, saving his breath for the long climb. The spiral stair wound round and round. They continued in silence until at last the stairs emptied into one of the Vatican's most unique and historic chambers.

The Meridian Room.

Jacob craned at the frescoes adorning the circular walls and ceilings, depicting scenes from the Bible with cherubs and clouds above. A single spear of light, admitted through a quarter-sized hole in the wall, pierced the dusty air and spiked down atop the room's marble slab floor, which was carved with the signs of the zodiac. A line marking the meridian cut across the floor. The room was the sixteenth-century solar observatory used to establish the Gregorian calendar and where Galileo had attempted to prove his case that the Earth revolved around the sun.

Unfortunately he had failed – certainly a low point between the Catholic Church and the scientific community. Ever since, the Church had been trying to make up for its shortsightedness.

Vigor took a moment to slow his breathing after the long climb. He wiped sweat from his brow and directed Jacob to a neighboring chamber off the Meridian Room. A massive bookshelf covered its back wall, crammed with books and bound *regestra*.

'According to the master index, the book we seek should be on the third shelf.'

Jacob stepped through, tripping the wire that ran across the threshold.

Vigor heard the twang. No time for warning.

The incendiary device exploded, blowing Jacob's body out the doorway and into Vigor.

They fell backward as a wall of flames roared outward, rolling over them, like the brimstone breath of a dragon.

# 4

## DUST TO DUST

The mission had been assigned crimson priority, black assignation, and silver security protocols. Director Painter Crowe shook his head at the color-coding. Some bureaucrat had visited a Sherwin-Williams store one too many times.

All the designations boiled down to one bottom line: Do not fail. When matters of national security were involved, there was no second place, no silver medal, no runner-up.

Painter sat at his desk and reviewed his ops manager's report. All seemed in order. Credentials established, safehouse codes updated, equipment checks completed, satellite schedules coordinated, and a thousand other details arranged. Painter ran a finger down the projected cost analysis. He had a budget meeting next week with the Joint Chiefs.

He rubbed his eyes. This had become his life: paperwork, spreadsheets, and stress. It had been a grueling day. First the Guild ambush, now an international operation to launch. Still, a part of him thrilled at the new challenges and responsibilities. He had inherited Sigma from its founder, Sean McKnight, now director of all of DARPA. Painter refused to disappoint his mentor. All morning, the two had discussed the ambush at Fort Detrick and the upcoming mission, strategizing like old

92

times. Sean had been surprised by Painter's choice of team leader, but it was ultimately his decision.

So the mission was a go.

All that was left was to brief the operatives. Flight time was set for 0200. There was not much time. A private jet was already being fueled and loaded at Dulles, courtesy of Kensington Oil, a perfect cover. Painter had arranged this last himself, calling on a favor from Lady Kara Kensington. She had been amused to be helping Sigma again. 'Can't you Americans do anything by yourselves?' she had chided him.

The intercom buzzed on his desk.

He hit the button. 'Go ahead.'

'Director Crowe, I have Drs. Kokkalis and Bryant here.'

'Send them in.'

A chime sounded at the door as the lock released. Monk Kokkalis pushed in first, but he held the door for Kathryn Bryant. The woman stood a head taller than the stocky former Green Beret. She moved with a leonine grace of constrained power. Her auburn hair, straight to the shoulder, was braided and as conservative as her attire: navy blue suit, white blouse, leather pumps. Her only flash of color was a jeweled pin on her lapel, a tiny frog. Gold enameled in emerald. A match to the flash of her green eyes.

Painter knew why she wore the golden pin. The frog had been a gift from an amphibious team she had once joined during a marine recon operation for naval intelligence. She had saved two men, proving her prowess with a dagger. But one teammate never came back. She wore the pin in his memory. Painter believed there was more to the story, but her files did not elaborate further.

'Please take a seat,' Painter said, acknowledging them both with a nod. 'Where's Commander Pierce?'

Monk shifted in his seat. 'Gray . . . Commander Pierce

had a family emergency. He just arrived back. He'll be up in a moment.'

*Covering for him,* Painter thought. Good. It was one of the reasons he had chosen Monk Kokkalis for this mission, pairing him up with Grayson Pierce. They complemented each other's skills – but more importantly, they suited each other's personalities. Monk could be a tad staid, by-the-book, while Grayson was more reactionary. Still, Grayson listened to Monk, more so than any other member of Sigma. He tempered the steel in Gray. Monk had a way of joking and humoring that proved as convincing as any well-debated argument. They made a good pair.

On the other hand . . .

Painter noted how stiffly Kat Bryant sat, still at attention. She was not nervous, more wary with an edge of excitement. She exuded confidence. Maybe too much. He had decided to include her on this mission due to her intelligence background, more than her current study of engineering. She was experienced with protocols in the EU, especially around the Mediterranean. She knew microelectronic surveillance and counterintelligence. But more importantly, she had dealings with one of the Vatican operatives who would be jointly overseeing this investigation, Monsignor Verona. The two had worked together on an international art theft ring.

'We might as well get the paperwork out of the way while we await Commander Pierce.' Painter passed out two thick dossiers in black file jackets, one each to Bryant and Kokkalis. A third waited for Pierce.

Monk glanced at the silver $\Sigma$ emblazoned on the folder.

'That'll fill in all the finer details for this op.' Painter tapped the touch screen built into his desktop. The three Sony flat-panel screens – one behind his shoulder, one to the left, and one to the right – changed from panoramic views of mountain landscapes rendered in high definition to the same silver Σ. 'I'll be doing the mission briefing myself, rather than the usual ops manager.'

'Compartmentalizing the intel,' Kat said softly, her Southern accent softening the edges of her consonants. Painter knew she could make all trace of her accent disappear when she needed too. 'Due to the ambush.'

Painter nodded. 'Information is being restricted in advance of a system-wide check of our security protocols.'

'Yet we're still going ahead with a new mission?' Monk asked.

'We have no choice. Word from –'

The buzz of the intercom interrupted. Painter hit the button.

'Director Crowe,' his secretary announced, 'Dr. Pierce has arrived.'

'Send him in.'

The door chimed open, and Grayson Pierce strode inside. He wore black Levi's dressed up with black leather shoes and a starched white shirt. His hair was slicked down, still wet from a shower.

'Sorry,' Grayson said, stopping between the two other agents. A certain hardness in his eyes belied any real sorrow. He kept a stiff posture, ready for reprimand.

And he deserved it. After the security breach, now was not the time to be thumbing his nose at command. However, a certain modicum of insubordination had always been tolerated at Sigma command. These men and women were the best of the best. You couldn't ask them to act independently out in the field, then expect them to bend to totalitarian authority here. It required a deft hand to balance the two.

Painter stared at Grayson. With the increased security, Painter was well aware the man had received an urgent call from his mother and had checked out of the command center. Behind the stolid stare of the other, Painter noted a glassy-eyed fatigue. Was it from the ambush or his home situation? Was he even fit for this new assignment?

Grayson did not break eye contact. He simply waited.

The meeting had a purpose beyond just a briefing. It was also a test.

Painter waved to a seat. 'Family is important,' he said, releasing the man. 'Just don't let your tardiness become a habit.'

'No, sir.' Grayson crossed and sat, but his eyes flicked from the emblazoned flat-screen monitors to the dossiers on his fellow agents' laps. A crease formed between his brows. The lack of reprimand had unsettled him. Good.

Painter slid the third folder toward Grayson. 'We were just starting the mission briefing.'

He took the folder. A look of wary bewilderment narrowed his eyes, but he kept silent.

Painter leaned back and tapped the screen on his desk. A Gothic cathedral appeared on the left screen, an exterior shot. An interior view appeared on the right. Bodies lay sprawled everywhere. Behind his shoulder, he knew a picture of a chalked outline marked off an altar, still bloodstained, outlining the sprawl of a murdered priest. Father Georg Breitman.

Painter watched the agents' gazes travel over the images.

'The massacre in Cologne,' Kat Bryant said.

Painter nodded. 'It occurred near the end of a midnight mass celebrating the feast day of the biblical Wise Men. Eighty-five people were killed. The motive appears to be simple robbery. The cathedral's priceless reliquary was broken into.' Painter flicked through additional images of the golden sarcophagus and the shattered remains of its security cage. 'The only items stolen were the shrine's contents. The supposed bones of the biblical Magi.'

'Bones?' Monk asked. 'They leave behind a crate of solid gold and take a bunch of bones? Who would do that?'

'That remains unknown. There was only one survivor of the massacre.' Painter brought up an image of a young man being carried out in a stretcher, another of the same man in a hospital bed, eyes open but glazed with shock. 'Jason Pendleton. American. Age twenty-one. He was found hiding in a confessional booth. He was barely coherent when first discovered, but after a regimen of sedatives, he was able to give a tentative report. The party involved were robed and cloaked as monks. No faces were ID'd. They stormed the cathedral. Armed with rifles. Several people were shot, including the priest and archbishop.'

More pictures flashed across the screens: bullet wounds, more chalked outlines, a web of red yarns marking the trajectory of shots. It looked like a typical crime scene, just with an unusual backdrop.

'And how does this involve Sigma?' Kat asked.

'There were other deaths. Inexplicable deaths. To break into the security vault, the assailants employed some device that not only shattered the metal and bullet-proof cage, but also, at least according to the survivor, triggered a wave of death across the cathedral.'

Painter reached out and hit a key. Across all three screens, views of various corpses appeared. The agents' expressions remained passive. They had all seen their share of death. The bodies were contorted, heads thrown back. One image was a close-up of one of the faces. Eyes were open, corneas gone opaque, while black trails of bloody tears leached from the corners. Lips were stretched back, frozen in a rictus of agony, teeth bared, gums bleeding. The tongue was swollen, cracked, black-ened at the edges.

Monk, with his medical and forensic training, shifted straighter, eyes pinched. He might play the absentminded clown, but he was a keen observer, his strongest suit.

'Full autopsy reports are in your folders,' Painter said.

'The initial conclusion from the coroners is that the deaths were due to some manifestation of an epileptiform seizure. An extreme convulsive event coupled with severe hyperthermia, spiking core temperature and resulting in the complete liquefaction of the outer surfaces of the brain. All died with their hearts in a contracted state, so intensely squeezed that no blood could be found in the chambers. One man's pacemaker had exploded in his chest. A woman with a metal pin in a femur was found with her leg still on fire, hours later, smoldering from the inside out.'

The agents kept their faces stoic, but Monk narrowed one eye and Kat's complexion seemed to have blanched to a pale white. Even Grayson stared a bit too fixedly at the images, unblinking.

But Gray was the first to speak. 'And we're sure the deaths are connected to the device employed by the thieves.'

'As sure as we can be. The survivor reported feeling an intense pressure in his head as the device was turned on. He described it like descending in an airplane. Felt in the ears. The deaths occurred at this time.'

'But Jason lived,' Kat said, taking a deep breath.

'Some others did, too. But the unaffected were subsequently shot by the perpetrators. Slaughtered in cold blood.'

Monk stirred. 'So some people succumbed, others did not. Why? Was there any commonality between the victims of the seizures?'

'Only one. A fact even noted by Jason Pendleton. The only ones to suffer the seizures appear to be those who had partaken of the Communion service.'

Monk blinked.

'It is for this reason that the Vatican made contact with U.S. authorities. And the chain of command dropped this into our laps.'

'The Vatican,' Kat said.

Painter read the understanding in her eyes. She now understood why she had been handpicked for this mission, interrupting her doctoral program in engineering.

Painter continued, 'The Vatican fears repercussions if it becomes widely known that some group may be targeting the Communion service. Possibly poisoning its wafers. They want answers as soon as possible, even if it means bending international law. Your team will be working with two intelligence agents in association with the Holy See. They'll be targeting why all this death seemed aimed to cover the theft of the bones of the Magi. Was it purely a symbolic gesture? Or was there more to the theft?'

'And our end goal?' Kat asked.

'To find out who perpetrated the crime and what device they employed. If it could kill in such a specific and targeted manner, we need to know what we're dealing with and who controls it.'

Grayson had remained quiet, staring at the gruesome images with more of a clinical stare. 'Binary poison,' he finally mumbled.

Painter glanced to the man. Their eyes matched, mirroring each other, both a stormy blue.

'What was that?' Monk asked.

'The deaths,' Grayson said, turning to him. 'They were not triggered by a single event. The cause had to be twofold, requiring an intrinsic and extrinsic factor. The device – the extrinsic factor – triggered the mass seizure. But only those who had participated in the Communion service responded. So there must be an intrinsic factor as yet unknown.'

Grayson turned back to Painter. 'Was any wine passed out during the service?'

'Only to a handful of the parishioners. But they also consumed the Communion bread.' Painter waited, watching the strange gears shift in the man's head, seeing him come to a conclusion that had taken experts even longer to reach. There was a reason beyond brawn and reflex for why Grayson had caught Painter's eye.

'The Communion bread *must* have been poisoned,' Grayson said. 'There is no other explanation. Something was intrinsically seeded into the victims through the consumption of the hosts. Once contaminated, they were susceptible to whatever force was generated by the device.' Grayson's eyes met Painter's again. 'Were the host wafers examined for any contamination?'

'There was not enough left in the victims' stomach contents to analyze properly, but there were wafers left over from the service. They were sent to labs throughout the EU.'

'And?'

By now, the glassy fatigue had vanished from the man's eyes, replaced by a laser-focused attention. He was plainly still competent for duty. But the test was not over.

'Nothing was found,' Painter continued. 'All analyses showed nothing but wheat flour, water, and the usual bakery ingredients for making unleavened bread wafers.'

The crease deepened between Grayson's brows. 'That's impossible.'

Painter heard the stubborn edge to his voice, almost belligerent. The man remained firmly confident in his assessment.

'There *must* be something,' Grayson pressed.

'Labs at DARPA were also consulted. Their results were the same.'

'They were wrong.'

Monk reached out a restraining arm.

Kat crossed her arms, settled on the matter. 'Then there must be another explanation for –'

'Bullshit,' Grayson said, cutting her off. 'The labs were all wrong.'

Painter restrained a smile. Here was the *leader* waiting

to come out in the man: sharp of mind, doggedly confident, willing to listen but not easily swayed once his mind was set.

'You're right,' Painter finally said.

While Monk's and Kat's eyes widened in surprise, Grayson merely leaned back in his seat.

'Our labs here did find something.'

'What?'

'They carbonized the sample down to its component parts and separated out all the organic components. They then removed each trace element as the mass spectrometer measured it. But after everything was stripped away, they still had a quarter of the dry weight of the host remaining on their scales. A dry whitish powder.'

'I don't understand,' Monk said.

Grayson explained. 'The remaining powder couldn't be detected by the analyzing equipment.'

'It was sitting on the scales, but the machines were telling the technicians nothing was there.'

'That's impossible,' Monk said. 'We have the best equipment in the world here.'

'But still they couldn't *detect* it.'

'The powdery substance must be totally inert,' Grayson said.

Painter nodded. 'So the lab boys here tested it further. They heated it to its melting point, 1,160 degrees. It melted and formed a clear liquid that, when the temperature dropped, hardened to form a clear amber glass. If you ground the glass in a mortar and pestle, it again formed the white powder. But in every stage it remained inert, undetectable by modern equipment.'

'What can do that?' Kat asked.

'Something we all know, but in a state that was only discovered in the last couple decades.' Painter flicked to the next picture. It showed a carbon electrode in an inert gas chamber. 'One of the technicians worked at Cornell

101

University, where this test was developed. They performed a fractional vaporization of the powder coupled with emission spectroscopy. Using an electroplating technique, they were able to get the powder to anneal back to its more common state.'

He tapped up the last picture. It was a close-up of the black electrode, only it was no longer *black*. 'They were able to get the converted substance to adhere to the carbon rod.'

The black electrode, plated now, shone under the lamp, brilliant and unmistakable.

Grayson leaned forward in his seat. 'Gold.'

6:24 p.m.
ROME, ITALY

The car's siren wailed in Rachel's ears. She sat in the passenger seat of the Carabinieri patrol, bruised, aching, head throbbing. But all she could feel was an icy certainty that Uncle Vigor was dead. Fear threatened to strangle her, shortening her breath and narrowing her vision.

Rachel half-heard the patrolman speaking into his radio. His vehicle had been the first on the scene of her ambush on the streets. She had refused medical care and used her authority as a lieutenant to order the man to take her to the Vatican.

The car reached the bridge spanning the Tiber River. Rachel continued to stare toward her destination. Across the channel, the shining dome of St. Peter's appeared, rising above all else. The setting sun cast it in hues of silver and gold. But what she saw rising behind the basilica lifted her from her seat. Her hands grabbed the edge of the dashboard.

A sooty column of black smoke coiled into the indigo sky.

'Uncle Vigor . . .'

102

Rachel heard the sounds of additional sirens echoing up the river. Fire engines and other emergency vehicles.

She grabbed the patrolman's arm. She itched to shove the man out of the way and drive herself. But she was still shaken up. 'Can you go any faster?'

Carabiniere Norre nodded. He was young, new to the force. He wore the black uniform with the red stripe down the legs and silver sash across his chest. He twisted the wheel and rode up onto a sidewalk to clear past a knot of traffic. The closer they got to the Vatican, the worse the congestion became. The convergence of emergency vehicles had snarled all traffic in the area.

'Aim for St. Anne's Gate,' she ordered.

He wheeled around and managed to cut down an alley to get them within three blocks of Porta Sant'Anna. Directly ahead, the source of the fire became clear. Beyond the walls of Vatican City, the Tower of the Winds was the second-highest point of all of Vatican City. Its top floors blazed with flames, becoming a stone torch.

*Oh no . . .*

The tower housed a part of the Vatican Archives. She knew her uncle had been searching the libraries of the Holy See. After her attack, the fire couldn't be a mere accident.

The car suddenly braked sharply, throwing Rachel forward in her seat restraints. Her eyes were torn away from the blazing tower.

All traffic forward was blocked.

Rachel could not wait any longer. She yanked on the door handle and began to roll out.

Fingers gripped her shoulder, restraining her. 'Tenente Verona,' Carabiniere Norre said. 'Here. You may need this.'

Rachel stared down at the black pistol, a Beretta 92, the man's service weapon. She took it with a nod of thanks. 'Alert the station. Let General Rende of the TPC know that I've returned to the Vatican. He can reach me through the Secretariat's Office.'

He nodded. 'Be careful, Tenente.'

With sirens wailing from every direction, Rachel set off on foot. She shoved the pistol into the waistband of her belt and tugged her blouse free so it hung over and hid the Beretta. Out of uniform, it would not be good to be seen running toward an emergency situation with an exposed weapon.

Crowds filled the sidewalks. Rachel took to shimmying between the cars stalled in the streets, and even slid across the hood of one to continue forward. Ahead she spotted a red municipal fire engine edging through St. Anne's Gate. It was a narrow fit. A contingent of Swiss Guards formed a barricade to either side, on high alert. No ceremonial halberds here. Each man had an assault rifle in hand.

Rachel pushed toward the guard line.

'Lieutenant Verona with the Carabinieri Corps!' she yelled, arms up, ID in hand. 'I must reach Cardinal Spera!'

Expressions remained hard, unbending. Clearly they had been ordered to block all entrance to the Holy See, closing it off to all but emergency personnel. A Carabinieri lieutenant had no authority over the Swiss Guards.

But from the back of the line, a single guard pushed forward, dressed in midnight blue. Rachel recognized him as the same guard to whom she had spoken earlier. He shoved through the line and met her.

'Lieutenant Verona,' he said. 'I've been ordered to escort you inside. Come with me.'

He turned on a heel and led her away.

She hurried to keep up as they crossed through the gate. 'My uncle . . . Monsignor Verona . . .'

'I know nothing except to escort you to the *eliport*.' He

directed her to an electric groundskeeper's cart parked just past the gate. 'Orders from Cardinal Spera.'

Rachel climbed inside. The lumbering fire engine rolled ahead of them and entered the wide yard that fronted the Vatican Museums. It joined the other emergency vehicles, including a pair of military vehicles mounted with submachine guns.

With clearance now, the guardsman turned their cart to the right, skirting the emergency traffic jam in front of the museums. Overhead, the tower continued to blaze. From somewhere on the far side, a jet of water exploded upward, trying to reach the fiery top levels. Flames lapped from windows of the top three floors. Clouds of black smoke billowed and churned. The tower was a tinderbox, stoked with masses of books, parchments, and scrolls.

It was a disaster of vast scale. What fire didn't destroy, water and smoke would ruin. Centuries of archives, mapping Western history, gone.

Still, Rachel found all her fears centered on one concern.

Uncle Vigor.

The cart zipped past the city's garage and continued down a paved road. It paralleled the Leonine Wall, the stone-and-mortar cliff that enclosed Vatican City. They circled the museum complex and reached the vast gardens covering the back half of the city-state. Fountains danced in the distance. The world was painted in shades of green. It seemed too pastoral for the hellish landscape behind them of smoke, fire, and siren wails.

They continued in silence to the very back of the grounds.

Their destination appeared ahead. Tucked into a walled alcove was the Vatican heliport. Converted from old tennis courts, the airfield was little more than a vast acre of concrete and some outbuildings.

105

On the tarmac, a single helicopter rested on its skids, isolated from the tumult. Its blades were slowly beginning to spin, gaining speed. The engine whined. Rachel knew the solid white aircraft. It was the pope's private helicopter, nicknamed the 'Holycopter.'

She also recognized the black robe and red sash of Cardinal Spera. He stood at the open door to the passenger compartment, ducked slightly from the spinning blades. One hand held his scarlet skullcap in place.

He turned, drawn by the motion of the cart, and lifted an arm in greeting. The motor cart braked a short distance away. Rachel hardly waited for it to stop and leapt out. She hurried toward the cardinal.

If anyone knew the fate of her uncle, it would be the cardinal.

Or one other . . .

From the back of the helicopter, a figure stepped out and hurried toward her. She rushed to meet him and hugged him tight under the whirling blades of the helicopter.

'Uncle Vigor . . .' Tears ran down her face, hot, melting through the ice around her heart.

He pulled back. 'You're late, child.'

'I was distracted,' she answered.

'So I heard. General Rende passed on word of your attack.'

Rachel glanced back to the flaming tower. She smelled the smoke in his hair. His eyebrows were singed. 'It seems I wasn't the only one attacked. Thank God you're okay.'

Her uncle's face darkened, his voice tightened. 'Unfortunately, not all were so blessed.'

She met his eyes.

'Jacob was killed in the blast. His body shielded mine, saved me.' She heard the anguish in his words, even over the roar of the helicopter. 'Come, we must get away.'

He directed her to the helicopter.

Cardinal Spera nodded to her uncle. 'They must be stopped,' he said cryptically.

Rachel followed her uncle into the helicopter. They strapped themselves in as the door was shoved closed. The thick insulation muffled a good portion of the engine noise, but Rachel heard the helicopter rev up. It immediately lifted from its skids and rose smoothly into the air.

Uncle Vigor settled against his seatback, head bowed, eyes closed. His lips trembled, speaking a silent prayer. For Jacob . . . perhaps for themselves.

Rachel waited until he opened his eyes. By then, they were winging away from the Vatican and out over the Tiber. 'The attackers,' Rachel began, '. . . they were driving vehicles with Vatican license plates.'

Her uncle nodded, unsurprised. 'It seems that the Vatican not only has spies abroad, but is also spied against within its own midst.'

'Who – ?'

With a groan, Uncle Vigor cut her off. He sat straighter, reached into his jacket, and removed a folded slip of paper. He passed it to her. 'The survivor of the Cologne massacre described this for a sketch artist. He saw it embroidered on the chest of one of the attackers.'

Rachel unfolded the slip of paper. Drawn in surprising detail was the coiled figure of a red dragon, wings blazed out, tail twisted and serpentine, wrapped around its own neck.

She lowered the drawing and glanced to her uncle.

'An ancient symbol,' her uncle said. 'Dating back to the fourteenth century.'

'Symbol of what?'

'The Dragon Court.'

Rachel shook her head, not recognizing the name.

'They are a medieval alchemical cult created by a schism in the early Church, the same schism that saw the rise of popes and antipopes.'

Rachel was familiar with the reign of Vatican anti-popes, men who sat as head of the Catholic Church but whose election was later declared uncanonical. They arose for a variety of reasons, the most common being the usurpation and exile of the legitimately elected pope, usually by a militant faction backed by a king or emperor. From the third to fifteenth century, forty antipopes had risen to sit on the papal throne. The most tumultuous era, though, was during the fourteenth century, when the legitimate papacy was driven out of Rome and into France. For seventy years, popes reigned in exile, while Rome was governed by a series of corrupt antipopes.

'What does such an ancient cult have to do with the situation now?' she asked.

'The Dragon Court is still active today. Its sovereignty is even recognized by the EU, similar to the Knights of Malta, who hold observer status at the United Nations. The shadowy Dragon Court has been linked to the European Council of Princes, the Knights Templar, and the Rosicrucians. The Dragon Court also openly admits to having members within the Catholic Church. Even here in the Vatican.'

'Here?' Rachel could not keep the shock from her voice. She and her uncle had been targeted. By someone inside the Vatican.

'A few years back, there was quite a scandal,' Uncle Vigor continued. 'A former Jesuit priest, Father Malachi Martin, wrote of a "secret church" within the Church. He was a scholar who spoke seventeen languages, authored many scholarly texts, and was a close associate of Pope John XXIII. He worked here in the Vatican for twenty years. His last book, written just before he died, spoke of an alchemical cult within the Vatican itself, performing rites in secret.'

Rachel felt a sickening lurch in her stomach that had nothing to do with the helicopter banking in the direction of the international airport in nearby Fiumicino. 'A secret church within the Church. This is who may have been involved in the Cologne massacre? Why? What's their purpose?'

'For stealing the bones of the Magi? I have no clue.'

Rachel allowed this revelation to filter through her mind. To catch a criminal required first knowing them. Ascertaining motive often proved more informative than physical evidence.

'What else do you know about the Court?' she asked.

'Despite their long history, not much. Back in the eighth century, Emperor Charlemagne conquered ancient Europe in the name of the Holy Church, smashing pagan nature-cult religions and replacing their beliefs with Catholicism.'

Rachel nodded, well acquainted with the brutal tactics of Charlemagne.

'But tides turn,' Uncle Vigor continued. 'What was once unfashionable becomes fashionable again. By the twelfth century, a resurgence in Gnostic or mystical belief began to arise, taken up in secret by the same emperors who had once beaten it down. A schism slowly formed as the Church moved toward the Catholicism we know today, while the emperors continued their Gnostic practices. The schism came to a head during the end of the fourteenth century. The exiled papacy in France had just returned. To make peace, Holy Roman Emperor Sigismund of Luxembourg backed the Vatican politically, even outwardly abolishing Gnostic practices among the lower classes.'

'Only the lower classes?'

'The aristocracy was spared. While the emperor beat down mystical beliefs among commoners, he created a secret society among the royal families of Europe, one dedicated to alchemical and mystical pursuits. The Ordinis Draconis. The Imperial Royal Dragon Court. It continues to this day. But there are many sects in different countries; some are benign, merely ceremonial or fraternal, but others have sprouted up that are led by vitriolic leaders. I would wager if the Dragon Court is involved, it is one of these rabid subsects.'

Rachel slipped instinctually into interrogation mode. *Know your enemy.* 'And what's the goal of these nastier sects?'

'As a cult of aristocracy, these extreme leaders believe they and their members are the rightful and chosen rulers of mankind. That they were born to rule by the purity of their blood.'

'Hitler's master-race syndrome.'

A nod. 'But they seek more. Not just kingship. They seek all forms of ancient knowledge to further their cause of domination and apocalypse.'

'To tread where even Hitler feared to go,' Rachel mumbled.

'Mostly they've maintained an austere air of superiority while manipulating politics behind a screen of secrecy and ritual, working with such elite groups as Skull and Bones in America and the Bilderburg think tank in Europe. But now someone is showing their hand, brazenly, bloodily.'

'What does it mean?'

Uncle Vigor shook his head. 'I fear this sect has discovered something of major importance, something that draws them out of hiding and into the open.'

'And the deaths?'

'A warning to the Church. Like the attacks upon ourselves. The simultaneous murder attempts today couldn't be coincidence. They had to have been ordered by the Dragon Court, to slow us, to scare us. It couldn't be coincidence. This particular Court is flexing its muscles, growling for the Church to back off, shedding the skin it's worn for centuries.'

110

'But to what end?'

Uncle Vigor leaned back with a sigh. 'To achieve the goal of all madmen.'

Rachel continued to stare at him.

He answered with one word. 'Armageddon.'

Gray shook his tumbler, clinking the ice.

Kat Bryant glanced from her seat across the plush cabin of the private jet. She didn't say anything, but her furrowed brow spoke volumes. She had been concentrating on the mission dossier – for the second time. Gray had already read it from cover to cover. He saw no need to peruse it again. Instead, he had been studying the gray-blue slate of the Atlantic Ocean, trying to figure out why he had been pegged as mission leader. At forty-five thousand feet, he still had no answer.

Swiveling his chair, he stood and crossed to the antique mahogany bar at the back of the cabin. He shook his head again at the opulence here: Waterford crystal, burled walnut, leather seating. It looked like an upscale English pub.

But at least he knew the bartender.

'Another Coke?' Monk asked.

Gray placed his glass on the bar. 'I think I've reached my limit.'

'Lightweight,' his friend mumbled.

Gray turned and faced the cabin. His father had once told him that acting the part was halfway to becoming that part. Of course, he had been referring to Gray's stint as a rig hand at an oil field, one overseen by his engineer father. He had been only sixteen, spending a summer in the hot sun of East Texas. It had been brutal work, when other of his high school friends had been summering on

111

the beaches of South Padre Island. His father's admonishment still rang in his head. *To be a man, you first have to act like one.*

Perhaps the same could be said for being a leader.

'Okay, enough with hitting the books,' he said, drawing Kat's eyes. He glanced to Monk. 'And I think you've explored the depth of this flying liquor cabinet long enough.'

Monk shrugged and came around into the main cabin area.

'We have less than four hours of flight time,' Gray said. With their jet, a custom Citation X, traveling just under sonic speeds, they would be landing at two A.M. German time, the dead of night. 'I suggest we all try to get some sleep. We'll be hitting the ground running once we're there.'

Monk yawned. 'You don't have to tell me twice, Commander.'

'But first let's compare notes. We've had a lot thrown at us.'

Gray pointed to the seats. Monk dropped into one. Gray joined them, facing Kat across a table.

While Gray had known Monk since joining Sigma, Captain Kathryn Bryant remained a relative unknown. She was so steeped in study that few at Sigma knew her well. She was mostly defined by her reputation since being recruited. One operative described her as a walking computer. But her reputation was also clouded by her former role as an intelligence operative. Overseeing black ops, it was rumored. But no one knew for sure. Her past was beyond the classification of even her fellow Sigma members. Such secrecy only isolated her further from men and women who had risen through the ranks in units, teams, and platoons.

Gray had his own problems with her past. He had personal reasons for disliking those in the intelligence field. They operated aloof, far from the battlefield, farther than even bomber pilots, but more deadly. Gray bore blood on his hands because of poor intel. Innocent blood. He could not shake a certain level of distrust.

He stared at Kat. Her green eyes were hard. Her whole body seemed starched. He pushed aside her past. She was his teammate now.

He took a deep breath. He was her leader.

*Act the part . . .*

He cleared his throat. Time to get to business. He lifted one finger. 'Okay, first, what do we know?'

Monk answered, his face dead serious. 'Not much.'

Kat maintained a fixed expression. 'We know the perpetrators are somehow involved with the cult society known as the Royal Dragon Court.'

'That's as good as saying they're involved with Hari Krishnas,' Monk countered. 'The group is as shadowy and weedy as crabgrass. We don't have a clue who is truly behind all this.'

Gray nodded. They had been faxed this information while en route. But more disturbingly, news had reached them of an attack upon their counterparts in the Vatican. It had to be the work of the Dragon Court again. But why? What sort of clandestine war zone were they flying into? He needed answers.

'Let's break this down then,' Gray said, realizing he sounded like Director Crowe. The other two looked at him expectantly. He cleared his throat. 'Back to the basics. Means, motive, and opportunity.'

'They had plenty of opportunity,' Monk said. 'Striking after midnight. When the streets were mostly empty. But why not wait until the cathedral was empty, too?'

'To send a message,' Kat answered. 'A blow against the Catholic Church.'

'We can't make that assumption,' Monk said. 'Look at it more broadly. Maybe it was all sleight of hand. Meant to misdirect. To commit a crime so bloody that all attention would be pulled from the rather insignificant theft of some dusty bones.'

Kat didn't look convinced, but she was difficult to read, playing her cards close to the chest. Like she had been trained.

Gray settled the matter. 'Either way, for now, exploring *opportunity* offers no inroads into who perpetrated the massacre. Let's move on to motive.'

'Why steal bones?' Monk said with a shake of his head and sat back. 'Maybe they mean to ransom them back to the Catholic Church.'

Kat shook her head. 'If it was only money, they would've stolen the golden reliquary. So it must be something else about the bones. Something we have no clue about. So maybe it's best we leave that thread to our Vatican contacts.'

Gray frowned. He was still uncomfortable working jointly with an organization like the Vatican, an establishment built on secrets and religious dogma. He had been raised Roman Catholic, and while he still felt strong stirrings of faith, he had also studied other religions and philosophies: Buddhism, Taoism, Judaism. He had learned much, but he never could answer one question from his studies: What was he seeking?

Gray shook his head. 'For now, we'll mark the motivation for this crime with another big question mark. We'll pursue that in more depth when we meet with the others. That leaves only *means* to discuss.'

'Which goes back to the whole financial discussion,' Monk said. 'This operation was well planned and swiftly executed. From the manpower alone, this was an expensive operation. Money backed this theft.'

'Money and a level of technology that we don't understand,' Kat said.

Monk nodded. 'But what about that weird gold in the Communion bread?'

'Monatomic gold,' Kat mumbled, creasing lines around her lips.

Gray pictured the gold-plated electrode. They had been given reams of data in their dossier on this strange gold, culled from labs around the world: British Aerospace, Argonne National Laboratories, Boeing Labs in Seattle, the Niels Bohr Institute in Copenhagen.

The powder had not been ordinary gold dust, the flaky form of metallic gold. It had been an entirely new elemental state of gold, classified as *m-state*. Rather than its usual metallic matrix, the white powder was gold broken down into individual atoms. Monatomic, or m-state. Until recently, scientists had no idea that gold could transmute, both naturally and artificially, into an inert white powder form.

But what did it all mean?

'Okay,' Gray said, 'we've all read the files. Let's round-robin that topic. See if it leads anywhere.'

Monk spoke up. 'First, it's not just gold that does this. We should keep that in mind. It seems any of the transitional metals on the periodic table – platinum, rhodium, iridium, and others – can also dissolve into a powder.'

'Not dissolve,' Kat said. She glanced down to the dossier with its photocopied articles from *Platinum Metals Review, Scientific American,* even *Jane's Defense Weekly,* the journal of the UK's Ministry of Defense. It appeared as if she itched to open the folder.

'The term is *disaggregate*,' she continued. 'These m-state metals break down into both individual atoms and microclusters. From a physics standpoint, this state arises when time-forward and time-reverse electrons fuse around the nucleus of the atom, causing each atom to lose its chemical reactivity to its neighbor.'

'You mean they stop *sticking* to each other.' Monk's eyes danced a bit with amusement.

'To put it crudely,' Kat said with a sigh. 'It's this lack of chemical reactivity that makes the metal lose its *metallic* appearance and disaggregate into a powder. A powder undetectable to ordinary lab equipment.'

'Ah . . .' Monk muttered.

Gray frowned at Monk. He shrugged. Gray knew his friend was playing dumb.

'I think,' Kat went on, oblivious of the exchange, 'that the perpetrators knew about this lack of chemical reactivity and trusted the gold powder would never be discovered. It was their second mistake.'

'Their second?' Monk asked.

'They left alive a witness. The young man. Jason Pendleton.' Kat opened her dossier folder. It seemed she couldn't resist the temptation after all. 'Back to the matter of the gold. What about this one paper on superconductivity?'

Gray nodded. He had to give Kat credit. She had zeroed in on the most intriguing aspect of these m-state metals. Even Monk sat straighter now.

Kat continued, 'While the powder appears inert to analyzing equipment, the atomic state is far from low-energy. It was as if each atom took all the energy it used to react to its neighbor and turned it *inward* on itself. The energy deformed the atom's nucleus, stretching it out to an elongated shape, known as . . .' She searched the article at her fingertips. Gray noted it had been marked up with a yellow highlighter.

'An asymmetrical high-spin state,' she said. 'Physicists have known that such high-spin atoms can pass energy from one atom to the next with no net energy loss.'

'Superconductivity,' Monk said with no dissembling.

'Energy passed into a superconductor would continue to flow through the material with no loss of power. A perfect superconductor would allow this energy to flow infinitely, until the end of time itself.'

Silence settled over them as they all pondered the many perplexities here.

Monk finally stretched. 'Great. We've ground the mystery down to the level of the atomic nucleus. Let's pull back. What does any of this have to do with the murders at the cathedral? Why poison the wafers with this weird gold powder? How did the powder kill?'

They were all good questions. Kat closed her dossier, conceding that no answers would be found there.

Gray was beginning to understand why the director had given him these two partners. It went beyond their backgrounds as an intelligence specialist and a forensics expert. Kat had a focused ability to concentrate on minutiae, to pick out details others might miss. But Monk, no less sharp, was better at looking at the bigger picture, spotting trends across a broader landscape.

But where did that leave him?

'It seems we still have much to investigate,' he finished lamely.

Monk lifted one eyebrow. 'As I said from the start, we don't have a lot to go on.'

'That's why we've been called in. To solve the impossible.' Gray checked his watch, stifling a yawn. 'And to do that, we should grab as much downtime as we can until we land in Germany.'

The other two nodded. Gray stood and crossed to a seat a short distance away. Monk grabbed pillows and blankets. Kat closed the shades on the windows, dimming the cabin. Gray watched them.

His team. His responsibility.

*To be a man, you first have to act like one.*

Gray accepted his own pillow and sat down. He did not recline his seat. Despite his exhaustion, he did not expect to get much sleep. Monk toggled down the overhead lights. Darkness descended.

'Good night, Commander,' Kat said from across the cabin.

As the others settled, Gray sat in the darkness, wondering how he got here. Time stretched. The engines rumbled white noise. Still, any semblance of sleep escaped him.

In the privacy of the moment, Gray reached into the pocket of his jeans. He slipped out a rosary, gripping the crucifix at the end, hard enough to hurt his palm. It was a graduation gift from his grandfather, who had died only two months after that. Gray had been in boot camp. He hadn't been able to attend the funeral. He leaned back. After today's briefing, he had called his folks, lying about a last-minute business trip to cover his absence.

*Running again* . . .

Fingers traveled down the hard beads of his rosary.

He said no prayers.


10:24 p.m.
LAUSANNE, SWITZERLAND

Château sauvage crouched in the mountain pass of the Savoy Alps like a stone giant. Its battlements were ten feet thick. Its single four-square tower crested its walls. The only access to its gates was over a stone bridge spanning the pass. While it was not the largest castle of the Swiss canton, it was certainly one of the oldest, constructed during the twelfth century. Its roots were even older. Its battlements were built on the ruins of a Roman *castra,* an ancient military fortification from the first century.

It was also one of the oldest privately owned castles, belonging to the Sauvage family since the fifteenth century, when the Bernese army wrested control of Lausanne from the decadent bishops during the Reformation. Its parapets overlooked Lake Geneva far below and the handsome cliff-side city of Lausanne, once a fishing village, now a cosmopolitan town of lakeside parks, museums, resorts, clubs, and cafés.

The castle's current master, Baron Raoul de Sauvage, ignored the lamp-lit view of the dark city and descended the stairs that led below the castle. He had been summoned. Behind him, a huge wooly dog, weighing a massive seventy kilos, followed his steps. The Bernese mountain dog's black-and-brown shaggy coat brushed the ancient stone steps.

Raoul also had a kennel of pit-fighting dogs, massive hundred-kilo brutes from Gran Canaria, short-haired, thick-necked, tortured to a savage edge. He bred champions of the blood sport.

But right now, Raoul had matters even bloodier to settle.

He passed the dungeon level of the castle with its stone caves. The cells now housed his extensive wine collection, a perfect cellar, but one section harkened back to the old days. Four stone cells had been updated with stainless steel gates, electronic locks, and video surveillance. Near the cells, one large room still housed ancient torture devices . . . and a few modern ones. His family had helped several Nazi leaders escape out of Austria after World War II, families with ties to the Hapsburgs. They had been hidden down here. As payment, Raoul's grandfather had taken his share, his 'toll' as he called it, which had helped keep the castle within the family.

But now, at the age of thirty-three, Raoul would surpass his grandfather. Raoul, born a bastard to his father, had been given title to both estate and heritage at the age of sixteen, when his father died. He was the only living male offspring. And among the Sauvage family, genetic ties were given precedence over those of marriage. Even his birth had been conceived by arrangement.

Another of Grandfather's tolls.

The Baron of Sauvage climbed down even deeper into the mountainside, hunching away from the roof, followed by his dog. A string of bare electrical lights illuminated his way.

The stone steps became natural hewn rock. Here

Roman legionnaires had tread in ancient times, often leading a sacrificial bull or goat down to the cave below. The chamber had been converted into a *mithraeum* by the Romans, a temple to the god Mithra, a sun god imported from Iran and taken to heart by the empire's soldiers. Mithraism predated Christianity yet bore uncanny similarities. Mithra's birthday was celebrated on December 25. The god's worship involved baptism and the consumption of a sacred meal of bread and wine. Mithra also had twelve disciples, held Sunday sacred, and described a heaven and a hell. Upon his death, Mithra was also buried in a tomb, only to rise again in three days.

From this, some scholars claimed Christianity had incorporated Mithraic mythology into its own ritual. It was not unlike the castle here, the new standing on the shoulders of the old, the strong surpassing the weak. Raoul saw nothing wrong with this, even respected it.

It was the natural order.

Raoul descended the last steps and entered the wide subterranean grotto. The roof of the cave was a natural stone dome, crudely carved with stars and a stylized sun. An old Mithraic altar, where young bulls had been sacrificed, stood on the far side. Beyond it ran a deep cold spring, a small river. Raoul imagined the sacrificed bodies had been dumped into it to be carried away. He had disposed of a few of his own that way, too . . . those not fed to his dogs.

At the entrance, Raoul shed his leather duster. Beneath the coat, he wore an old rough-spun shirt embroidered with the coiled dragon, the symbol of the Ordinis Draconis, his birthright going back generations.

'Stay, Drakko,' he ordered the dog.

The Bernese mountain dog dropped to its haunches. It knew better than to disobey.

As did the dog's owner . . .

Raoul acknowledged the cave's occupant with a half bow, then proceeded forward.

The Sovereign Grand Imperator of the Court waited for him before the altar, dressed in the black leathers of a motorcycle outfit. Though he was two decades older than Raoul, the man matched his height and breadth of shoulder. He showed no withering of age, but remained stolid and firm of muscle. He kept his helmet in place, visor down.

The leader had entered through the secret back entrance to the Grotto . . . along with a stranger.

It was forbidden for anyone outside the Court to view the Imperator's face. The stranger had been blindfolded as an extra precaution.

Raoul also noted the five bodyguards at the back of the cavern, all armed with automatic weapons, the elite guard of the Imperator.

Raoul strode forward, right arm across his chest. He dropped to a knee before the Imperator. Raoul was head of the Court's infamous *adepti exempti*, the military order, an honor going back to Vlad the Impaler, an ancient ancestor of the Sauvage family. But all bowed to the Imperator. A mantle Raoul hoped to one day assume for himself.

'Stand,' he was ordered.

Raoul gained his feet.

'The Americans are already under way,' the Imperator said. His voice, muffled by the helmet, was still heavy with command. 'Are your men ready?'

'Yes, sir. I handpicked a dozen men. We only await your order.'

'Very good. Our allies have lent us someone to assist on this operation. Someone who knows these American agents.'

Raoul grimaced. He did not need help.

'Do you have a problem with this?'

'No, sir.'

'A plane awaits you and your men at the Yverdon airfield. Failure will not be tolerated a second time.'

Raoul cringed inwardly. He had led the mission to steal the bones in Cologne, but he had failed to purge the sanctuary. There had been one survivor. One who had pointed in their direction. Raoul had been disgraced.

'I will not fail,' he assured his leader.

The Imperator stared at him, an unnerving gaze felt through the lowered visor. 'You know your duty.'

A final nod.

The Imperator strode forward, passing Raoul, accompanied by his bodyguards. He was headed for the castle, taking over the chateau here until the end game was completed. But first Raoul had to finish clearing the mess he had left behind.

It meant another trip to Germany.

He waited for the Imperator to leave. Drakko trotted after the men, as if the dog scented the true power here. Then again, the leader had visited the castle often during the last ten years, when the keys to damnation and salvation had fallen into their laps.

All due to a fortuitous discovery at the Cairo Museum . . .

Now they were so close.

With his leader gone, Raoul finally faced the stranger. What he saw, he found lacking, and he let his scowl show it. But at least the stranger's garb, all black, was fitting.

As was the bit of silver decoration.

From the woman's pendant, a silver dragon dangled.

# DAY
# TWO

DAY
TWO

# 5

## FRANTIC

For Gray, churches at night always held a certain haunted edge. But none more so than this house of worship. With the recent murders, the Gothic structure exuded a palpable dread.

As his team crossed the square, Gray studied the Cologne cathedral, or the Dom, as it was called by the locals. It was lit up by exterior spotlights, casting the edifice into silver and shadow. Most of the western façade was just two massive towers. The twin spires rose close together, jutting up from either side of the main door, only meters apart for most of their lengths until the towers tapered to points with tiny crosses at the tips. Each tier of the five-hundred-foot structures had been decorated with intricate reliefs. Arched windows climbed the towers, all aiming toward the night sky and the moon far above.

'Looks like they left the light on for us,' Monk said, gaping at the spotlighted cathedral. He hitched his backpack higher on his shoulder.

They were all dressed in dark civilian clothes, meant not to stand out. But beneath, each team member wore a clinging undergarment of liquid body armor. Their rucksacks, black Arcteryx backpacks, were stuffed with tools of the trade, including weapons from a CIA contact who had met them at the airport: Glock M-27 compact pistols, chambered in .40-caliber hollowpoints, fitted with tritium night sights.

Monk also had a Scattergun-built shotgun, strapped to his left thigh, hidden under a long jacket. The weapon had been custom-designed for such service, snub-nosed and compact, like Monk himself, with a Ghost Ring sight system for riflelike accuracy in low light. Kat went more low-tech. She managed to hide eight daggers on her body. A blade lay only a fingertip away, no matter her position.

Gray checked his Breitling dive watch. The hands glowed a quarter after two o'clock. They had made excellent time.

They crossed the square. Gray searched the dark corners for anything suspicious. All seemed quiet. At this hour on a weekday, the place was nearly deserted. Only a few stragglers. And most of those weaved a bit as they walked, the pubs having let out. But there were signs of earlier crowds. Piles of flowers from mourners littered the square's edges, along with the discarded beer bottles of gawkers. Mounds of melted wax candles marked memorial shrines, some with photos of relatives who had died. A few tapers still burned, tiny flickers in the night, lonely and forlorn.

A full candlelit vigil was under way at a neighboring church, an all-night memorial service, with a live feed from the pope. It had been coordinated to empty the square this night.

Still, Gray noted that his teammates kept a wary watch on their surroundings. They were not taking any chances.

Parked in front of the cathedral was a panel truck with the municipal *Polizei* logo on its side. It had served as the main base of operation for the forensic teams. Upon landing, Gray had been informed by the ops manager of this mission, Logan Gregory, Sigma's second-in-command, that all local investigative teams had been pulled out by midnight but would be returning in the morning. Zero-

126

six-hundred. Until then, they had the church to themselves.

Well, not entirely to themselves.

One of the flanking side doors to the cathedral opened as they neared. A tall, thin figure stood limned against the light inside. An arm lifted.

'Monsignor Verona,' Kat whispered under her breath, confirming the identity.

The priest crossed to the police cordon that had been placed around the cathedral. He spoke to one of the two guards on duty, posted to keep the curious away from the crime scene, then motioned the trio through the barricade.

They followed him to the open doorway.

'Captain Bryant,' the monsignor said, smiling warmly. 'Despite the tragic circumstances, it's wonderful to see you again.'

'Thank you, Professor,' Kat said, returning an affectionate grin. Her features softened with genuine friendship.

'Please call me Vigor.'

They entered the cathedral's front vestibule. The monsignor pulled the door closed and locked it. He scrutinized Kat's two companions.

Gray felt the weight of his study. The man was nearly his height, but more wiry of build. His salt-and-pepper hair had been combed straight back, curling in waves. He wore a neatly trimmed goatee and was dressed casually in midnight-blue jeans and a black V-neck sweater, revealing the Roman collar of his station.

But it was the steady fix of his gaze that most struck Gray. Despite his welcoming manner, there was a steely edge to the man. Even Monk straightened his shoulders under the priest's attention.

'Come inside,' Vigor said. 'We should get started as soon as possible.'

The monsignor led the way to the closed doors of the nave, opened them, and waved the group inside.

As he entered the heart of the church, Gray was immediately struck by two things. First by the smell. The air, while still redolent with incense, also wafted an underlying stench of something burnt.

Still, that was not all that caught Gray's attention. A woman rose from a pew to greet them. She looked like a young Audrey Hepburn: snowy skin, short ebony hair parted and swept behind her ears, caramel-colored eyes. She offered no smile. Her gaze swept over the newcomers, settling a moment longer on Gray.

He recognized the familial resemblance between her and the monsignor, more from the intensity of her scrutiny than any physical features.

'My niece,' Vigor introduced. 'Lieutenant Rachel Verona.'

They finished their introductions quickly. And though there was no outward animosity, their two camps still remained separate. Rachel kept a wary distance, as if ready to go for her gun if necessary. Gray had noted a holstered pistol under her open vest. A 9mm Beretta.

'We should get started,' Vigor said. 'The Vatican was able to gain us some privacy, demanding time to sanctify and bless the nave after the last body was removed.'

The monsignor led the way down the central aisle.

Gray noted sections of the pews had been marked off with masking tape. Place cards had been affixed to each with the names of the deceased. He stepped around the chalked outlines on the floor. Blood had been wiped up, but the stain had seeped into the mortar of the stone floor. Yellow plastic markers fixed the positions of shell casings, long gone to forensics.

He glanced across the nave, picturing how it must have looked upon first entering. Bodies sprawled everywhere; the smell of burnt blood, richer. He could almost sense an echo of the pain, trapped in the stone as much as the reek. It shivered over his skin. He was still enough of a Roman Catholic to find such murder disturbing beyond mere violence. It was an affront against God. Satanic.

Had that been part of the motivation?

To turn a feast into a Black Mass.

The monsignor spoke, drawing his attention back. 'Over there was where the boy was found hiding.' He pointed to a confessional booth against the north wall, halfway up the long nave.

Jason Pendleton. The lone survivor.

Gray took some degree of grim satisfaction that not all had died that bloody night. The attackers had made a mistake. They were fallible. Human. He centered himself with this thought. Though the act was demonic, the hand that committed it was as human as any other. Not that there weren't demons in human form.

But humans could be caught and punished.

They reached the raised sanctuary with the slab-marble altar and the tall-backed *cathedra,* the bishop's seat. Vigor and his niece made the sign of the cross. Vigor dropped to one knee, then got up. He led them through a gate in the chancel railing. Beyond the railing, the altar was also marked in chalk, the travertine marble stained. Police tape cordoned off a section to the right.

Crashed onto the floor, cracking the stone tile, a golden sarcophagus lay on its side. Its top rested two steps down. Gray shrugged off his backpack and lowered to one knee.

The golden reliquary, when whole, plainly formed a miniature church, carved with arched windows and etched scenes done in gold, rubies, and emeralds, depicting Christ's life, from his adoration by the Magi to his scourging and eventual crucifixion.

Gray donned a pair of latex gloves. 'This is where the bones were enshrined?'

Vigor nodded. 'Since the thirteenth century.'

129

Kat joined Gray. 'I see they've already dusted it for prints.' She pointed to the fine white powder clinging to cracks and crevices in the reliefs.

'No prints were found,' Rachel said.

Monk glanced across the cathedral. 'And nothing else was taken?'

'A full inventory was conducted,' Rachel continued. 'We've already had a chance to interview the entire staff, including the priests.'

'I may want to speak to them myself,' Gray mumbled, still studying the box.

'Their apartments are across a cloistered yard,' Rachel responded, voice hardening. 'No one heard or saw anything. But if you want to waste your time, feel free.'

Gray glanced up at her. 'I only said I *may* want to speak to them.'

She met his gaze without shrinking. 'And I was under the impression that this investigation was a *joint* effort. If we're going to recheck each other's work at every step, we'll get nowhere.'

Gray took a steadying breath. Only minutes into the investigation, and already he had stepped on jurisdictional toes. He should have interpreted her earlier wariness and trodden more lightly.

Vigor placed a hand on his niece's shoulder. 'I assure you the interrogation was thorough. Among my colleagues, where prudence of tongue often surpasses good sense, I doubt you'd gain any further details, especially when being interviewed by someone not wearing a clerical collar.'

Monk spoke up. 'That's all well and good. But can we get back to me?' All eyes turned to him. He wore a crooked grin. 'I believe I was asking if anything else was taken.'

Gray felt the attention shift from him. As usual, Monk had his back. A diplomat in body armor.

Rachel fixed Monk with her uncompromising gaze. 'As I said, nothing was –'

'Yes, thank you, Lieutenant. But I was curious if any other relics are kept here at the cathedral. Any relics that the thieves *didn't* take.'

Rachel frowned in confusion.

'I figured,' Monk explained, 'that what the thieves didn't take may be as informative as what they did.' He shrugged.

The woman's face relaxed a touch, contemplating this angle. The anger bled away.

Gray inwardly shook his head. How did Monk do that?

The monsignor answered Monk. 'There's a treasure chamber off the nave. It holds the reliquaries from the original Romanesque church that once stood here: the staff and chain of Saint Peter, along with a couple of pieces of the Christ's cross. Also a Gothic bishop's staff from the fourteenth century and a jewel-encrusted elector's sword from the fifteenth.'

'And nothing was stolen from the treasure chamber.'

'It was all inventoried,' Rachel answered. Her eyes remained pinched in concentration. 'Nothing else was stolen.'

Kat crouched down with Gray, but her eyes were on those still standing. 'So only the bones were taken. Why?'

Gray turned his attention to the open sarcophagus. He slipped a penlight from his nearby backpack and examined the interior. It was unlined. Just flat gold surfaces. He noted a bit of white powder sifted over the bottom surface. More latent powder? Bone ash?

There was only one way to find out.

He turned back to his pack and pulled out a collection kit. He used a small battery-powered vacuum to sniff up some of the powder into a sterile test tube.

'What are you doing?' Rachel asked.

'If this is bone dust, it may answer a few questions.'

'Like what?'

He sat back and examined the test tube. There was no more than a couple grams of gray powder. 'We might be able to test the dust for age. Find out if the stolen bones were from someone who lived during Christ's time. Or not. Maybe the crime was to recover the family bones of someone in the Dragon Court. Some old lord or prince.'

Gray sealed the test tube and packed the sample away. 'I'd also like to get samples of the broken glass from the security vault. It might give us some answers as to how the device shattered bulletproof glass. Our labs can examine the crystalline microstructure for fracture patterns.'

'I'll get on that,' Monk said, slinging off his pack.

'What about the stonework?' Rachel asked. 'Or other materials inside the cathedral?'

'What do you mean?' Gray asked.

'Whatever triggered the deaths among the parishioners might have affected the stone, marble, wood, plastic. Something that could not be seen with the naked eye.'

Gray had not considered that. He should have. Monk met his eyes and shrugged his brows. The carabiniere lieutenant was proving herself to be more than a pretty package.

Gray turned to Kat to organize a collection methodology. But she seemed preoccupied. From the corner of his eye, he had noted her interest in the reliquary, all but ducking her head inside to investigate. She now crouched on the marble floor, bent over something she was working on.

'Kat – ?'

She held up a tiny mink-haired brush. 'One moment.' In her other hand, she held a small butane pistol-lighter. She squeezed the trigger and a tiny blue flame hissed from the end. She applied the flame to a pile of powder, plainly whisked from the reliquary with the brush.

After a couple seconds, the gray powder melted, bubbling and frothing into a translucent amber liquid. It dribbled over the cold marble and hardened into glass. The sheen against the white marble was unmistakable.

'Gold,' Monk said. All eyes had been drawn to the experiment.

Kat sat back, extinguishing her torch. 'The residual powder in the reliquary . . . it's the same as in the tainted wafers. Monatomic, or m-state, gold.'

Gray remembered Director Crowe's description of the lab tests, how the powder could be melted down to a slag glass. A glass made of solid gold.

'That's gold?' Rachel asked. 'As in the precious metal?'

Sigma had provided the Vatican with cursory information on the tainted wafers, so their bakeries and supplies could be examined for further tampering. Its two spies had also been informed, but plainly they had their doubts.

'Are you sure?' Rachel asked.

Kat was already busy proving her assertion. She had an eyedropper in hand and dribbled its contents onto the glass. Gray knew what filled the eyedropper. They had all been supplied it by the labs back at Sigma for just this purpose. A cyanide compound. For years, miners had been using a process called heap leach cyanide recovery to dissolve gold out of old tailings.

Where the drop touched, the glass etched as if burned by acid. But rather than frosting the glass, the cyanide carved a trail of pure gold, a vein of metal in glass. There was no doubt.

Monsignor Verona stared, unblinking, one hand fingering his clerical collar. He mumbled, 'And the streets of New Jerusalem will be paved with gold so pure as to be transparent glass.'

Gray glanced quizzically at the priest.

Vigor shook his head. 'From the Book of Revelations . . . don't mind me.'

133

But Gray saw the way the man drew inward, turning half away, lost in deeper thoughts. Did he know more? Gray sensed the priest was not so much holding back as needing time to dwell on something.

Kat interrupted. She had been leaning over her sample with a magnifying lens and an ultraviolet lamp. 'I think there might be more than gold here. I can spot tiny pools of silver in the gold.'

Gray shifted closer. Kat allowed him to peer through her lens, shadowing the glass with her hand so the blue sheen of the ultraviolet light better illuminated the sample. The veins of metallic gold did indeed seem pocked with silvery impurities.

'It might be platinum,' Kat said. 'Remember that the monatomic state occurs not just in gold but *any* of the transitional metals on the periodic table. Including platinum.'

Gray nodded. 'The powder might not be pure gold, but a mix of several of the platinum series. An amalgam of various m-state metals.'

Rachel continued to stare at the etched glass. 'Could the powder just be from the wearing down of the old sarcophagus? The gold crumbling with age or something?'

Gray shook his head. 'The process to turn metallic gold into its m-state is complicated. Age alone won't do this.'

'But the lieutenant might be onto something,' Kat said. 'Maybe the device affected the gold in the reliquary and caused some of the gold to transmute. We still have no idea by what mechanism the device –'

'I may have one clue,' Monk said, cutting her off.

He stood by the shattered security case, where he had been collecting shards. He stepped to a bulky iron cross resting in a stanchion not far from the case.

'It looks like one of our forensic experts missed a shell,' Monk said. He reached out and plucked a hollow casing from beneath the feet of the crucified Christ figure. He took a step back again, held the casing out toward the cross, and let it go. It flew through six inches of air, and with a *ping*, stuck again to the cross.

'It's magnetized,' Monk said.

Another *ping* sounded. Louder. Sharper. The cross spun half a turn in its stanchion.

For half a second, Gray did not comprehend what had happened.

Monk dove for the altar. 'Down!' he screamed.

Other shots rang out.

Gray felt a kick to his shoulder, throwing him off kilter, but his body armor saved him from real injury. Rachel grabbed his arm and yanked him into a row of pews. Bullets chewed wood, sparked off marble and stone.

Kat ducked with the monsignor, shielding him with her body. She took a glancing shot to the thigh, half collapsing, but they fell together behind the altar with Monk.

Gray had only managed a quick glimpse of their attackers.

Men in hooded robes.

A sharp pop sounded. Gray glanced up to see a fist-sized black object arc across the breadth of the church.

'Grenade!' he screamed.

He scooped up his pack and shoved Rachel down the pew. They scrambled low and ran for the south wall.

3:20 a.m.

Monk barely had time to react when Gray yelled. He grabbed Kat and the monsignor and flattened himself against them behind the stone altar.

The grenade hit the far side and exploded, sounding like a mortar blast. A cascade of marble shattered upward and outward, pelting the wooden pews. Smoke rolled and billowed up.

135

Half deafened by the blast, Monk simply hauled Kat and Vigor to their feet. 'Follow me!'

It was death to stay out here in the open. Toss one grenade behind the altar, and they were all hamburger. They needed a more defensible position.

Monk dashed toward the north wall. Behind him, gunfire remained fierce. Gray was striking for the opposite wall. Just as well. Once in position, they could set up a crossfire across the center of the church.

Clear of the altar, Monk pounded across the sanctuary. He aimed for the nearest shelter, spotting a wide wooden door. The gunmen finally noted their escape. Shots spattered against the marble floor, ricocheted off a column, and tore into pews. The shots came from all directions now. More of the assailants had taken up positions deeper in the church, coming in other doors, cutting off escape, surrounding them.

They needed cover.

Monk yanked his own weapon from its straps. The snub-nosed shotgun. On the fly, he lifted the barrel in the crook of his left elbow and pulled the trigger. Along with the blast, he heard a sharp grunt from several pews away. Accuracy was not necessary with a Scattergun.

Shoving the barrel forward, he took crude aim at the door handle. It was too much to hope it was an exit to the outside, but it would at least get them clear of the central nave. From a few steps away, he pulled the trigger as he heard a faint protest from Monsignor Verona.

But there was no time for debate.

The blast punched a fist-sized hole through the door, taking the entire handle and lock with it. Still running, Monk hit the door. It banged open under his shoulder. He fell inside, followed by Kat and the monsignor. Kat turned, limping, and shoved the door closed.

'No,' the priest said.

Monk now understood the reason for his protest.

136

The vaulted room was the size of a single-car garage. He stared at the glass cases crowded with old robes and insignia, bits of sculpture. Gold shone from some of the cases.

It was the cathedral's Treasure Chamber.

There was no exit.

Trapped.

Kat took up position, Glock in hand, and peered out the blasted hole. 'Here they come.'


3:22 a.m.

Rachel reached the end of the pew, out of breath, heart thundering in her ears. Shots continued to pound their position, coming from all sides, gouging out chunks of wood from the flanking pews.

The grenade blast still echoed in her head, but her hearing was returning. Surely the priests and staff in the rectory had heard the explosion and had called the police.

The gunfire relented momentarily as the robed assailants repositioned themselves, closing up the center aisle.

'Make for that wall,' Gray urged. 'Behind the pillars. I'll cover you.'

Rachel spotted the nest of pylons that supported the vaulted roof. It offered better shelter than being pinned between a row of seats. She glanced back to the American.

'On my signal,' he said, crouching down. Their eyes met. She saw a thread of healthy fear, but also a determined concentration. He nodded to her, shifted around, readied himself, then shouted, 'Go!'

Rachel dove out the end of the pew as gunfire erupted behind her, louder than their assailants'. The commander's guns had no silencers.

She hit the marble floor and rolled behind the trio of pillars. She gained her feet immediately, back to the giant

137

pillar. Carefully peeking around the curve, she spotted Commander Pierce backpedaling toward her, both pistols blazing.

A robed man down the end of the same pew fell backward, punched by the impacts. Another down the center aisle cried out and grabbed his neck as a spat of red arced out. The others had ducked from the American's attack. Across the church, Rachel spotted five or six men converging on the door to the cathedral's Treasure Chamber, firing almost nonstop.

As Commander Pierce reached her position, panting, Rachel swung to check the other side of her pillar, peering along the wall. So far no one had circled this way yet. But she had to assume they would soon.

'What now?' she asked, removing her pistol from a shoulder holster, the Beretta given to her by the Carabinieri driver back in Rome.

'This line of columns parallels the wall. We stick to cover. Shoot anything that moves.'

'And our goal?'

'To get the hell out of this death trap.'

Rachel frowned. What about the others?

The American must have noted her worry. 'We'll head for the streets. Draw off as many of the bastards as we can.'

She nodded. They would play decoy. 'Let's go.'

The pillars along the south wall were spaced only two meters apart. They proceeded briskly, staying low, using the rows of neighboring pews out in the nave as additional cover. Commander Pierce fired high, while Rachel discouraged any assailants from entering the alleyway between the wall and the pillars, picking off any shadows that moved.

The ploy worked. More gunfire concentrated on their position. But it also slowed them down, putting them at risk of a second grenade attack. They had only made it halfway down the nave, and it became impossible to leap from pillar to pillar.

The American took a blow to the back, splaying him out on the ground. Rachel gasped. But he pushed back up.

Rachel shifted down the alley, sticking close to the wall, pointing her gun back and forth. With her concentration fixed outward, she made the same mistake as the assailants had the prior night.

The door to the confessional swung open behind her. Before she could move, an arm lashed out and wrapped around her neck. Her weapon was knocked from her fingers. The cold steel of a gun barrel pressed against her neck.

'Don't move,' a deep bass voice ordered as the commander swung around. The attacker's arm felt like a tree trunk, strangling her breathing. He was tall, a giant of a man, practically hauling her to her toes. 'Drop your weapons.'

The gunfire died out. It was clear now why a second grenade hadn't been lobbed toward them. While the two of them thought they were escaping, the gunmen had been merely driving them into this trap.

'I'd do as he says,' a new voice said silkily, coming from the penitent's booth neighboring the priest's confessional. The door opened and a second figure stepped out, dressed in black leather.

It was no monk, but a woman. Slender, Eurasian.

She lifted her pistol, a black Sig Sauer. She pointed it at Gray's face. '*Déjà vu*, Commander Pierce?'


3:26 a.m.

The door was a problem. With the lock blown off, every strike of a bullet threatened to pop the door open. And they dared not keep it shouldered closed. Most of the

139

rounds were stopped by the wood planks, but a few still found weak spots and cracked through, making Swiss cheese out of the door.

Monk kept one boot against the frame, anchoring the door with his heel, while keeping his body off to the side. Bullets pounded against the door, the impacts rattling up to his knee.

'Hurry it up back there,' he urged.

He pointed his shotgun out the hole in the door and fired blindly. The smoking shell casing ejected out of the weapon's chamber, hit one of the long glass treasure cases, and bounced off of it. Beyond the door, the spray of the Scattergun kept the assailants wary, firing from a distance. It seemed the attackers knew their prey was trapped.

So what were they waiting for?

Monk expected a grenade to be lobbed against the door at any moment. He prayed the insulation of the stone wall would keep him alive. But what then? With the door blown away, they had no chance at all in here.

And rescue was unlikely. Monk had heard the chatter of Gray's weapon echo across the church. It sounded like he was retreating toward the main doors. Monk knew that the commander was helping to draw the fire off their location. It was the only reason they were still alive.

But now Gray's weapon had gone silent.

They were on their own.

A fresh barrage struck the door, rattling the frame, jarring his anchored leg. His thigh burned from the effort and had begun to tremble. 'Guys, now or never!'

A rattle of keys drew his eye. Monsignor Verona had been struggling with a key ring, given to him by the cathedral's caretaker. He fought to get the third bulletproof case open. Finally, with a cry of relief, he found the right key, and the front of the case swung open like a gate.

Kat reached over his shoulder and grabbed a long

140

sword from the case. A fifteenth-century decorative weapon with a gold and jeweled hilt. But the blade, three feet long, was polished steel. She yanked it free and hauled it across the chamber. She kept out of the direct line of fire and stabbed the sword between the door and its frame, jamming and securing the door.

Monk pulled back his leg, rubbing his sore knee. ''Bout time.' He again shoved his shotgun through the hole in the door and fired – more in irritation than any hope of hitting anyone.

With the scatter of shot driving the attackers back a step, Monk risked a fast glance out. One of the assailants lay sprawled on his back, head half gone, blood pooled. One of his blind shots had found a target.

But now his attackers were finished taking potshots.

A black smooth pineapple bounced down the pew, aimed right at their door. Monk flung himself flat against the stone.

'Fire in the hole!'

3:28 a.m.

The explosion across the church drew all eyes – except Gray's. There was nothing he could do for the others.

A grim smile creased the tall man's face. 'It seems your friends –'

Rachel moved. With the momentary distraction, her captor must have loosened his grip, perhaps underestimating the slim woman. Rachel dropped her head and snapped it back briskly, smacking the man's lower jaw hard enough to hear his teeth crack together.

Moving with surprising speed, she struck the encircling arm with the heel of her hand and dropped at the same time. She elbowed her assailant a sharp blow to the midriff, then twisted and punched a fist into the man's crotch.

Gray swung his pistol toward the Dragon Lady. But the woman was quicker, stepping forward and placing her gun between his eyes, an inch away.

To the side, the tall man crumpled around his waist, falling to a knee. Rachel kicked his gun aside.

'Run!' Gray hissed at her, but he kept his eyes on the Dragon Lady.

The Guild operative met his gaze – then did the oddest thing. She flicked the muzzle of her gun in the direction of the exit and motioned with her head.

She was letting him go.

Gray stepped back. She didn't fire, but she kept her gun focused on him, ready if he tried to make a move against her.

Rather then ponder the impossibility, Gray swung around and fired at the nearest monks, dropping the two closest. They had been distracted by the grenade blast and missed the lightning-fast change in power here.

Gray grabbed Rachel by the arm and hauled ass toward the exit doors.

A pistol shot sounded directly behind him. He was struck in the upper arm and spun slightly, skipping steps. The Dragon Lady's pistol smoked. She had shot Gray as she helped the tall man up. Blood dribbled down her face. A self-inflicted wound, covering her subterfuge. She had purposefully missed her shot.

Rachel steadied him and ducked behind the last pillar. The door to the outer vestibule lay directly ahead. No one stood in their way.

Gray risked a glance toward the gunfire at the back of the cathedral. Smoke billowed from the blasted doorway. The handful of gunmen fired a continual barrage through the opening, making sure no one escaped this time. Then one of the men tossed a second grenade – right through the blasted doorway.

The other gunmen ducked as it blew.

Smoke and debris shattered outward.

Gray turned away. Rachel had also witnessed the attack. Tears welled in her eyes. He felt her sag against him, legs weakening. Something deep inside him ached at her grief. He had lost teammates in the past. He was trained to mourn later.

But she had lost family.

'Keep moving,' he said gruffly. It was all he could do. He had to get her to safety.

She glanced to him and seemed to gain strength from his hard countenance. It was what she needed. Not sympathy. Strength. He had seen it in the field before, men under fire. She stood straighter.

He squeezed her arm.

She nodded. Ready.

Together they ran and slammed through the outer doors.

A pair of assassins manned the foyer, posted over the dead bodies of two men in German police uniforms. The guards at the cordon. The pair of monks was not caught by surprise. One of the men fired immediately, driving Rachel and Gray to the side. They would not make it to the outer doors, but another doorway lay to their immediate left.

With no choice, they dodged through it. The second man raised his weapon. A wall of fire cascaded toward them. He had a goddamn flamethrower. Gray slammed the door, but flames licked under the jamb. Gray danced back. There was no lock on the door.

He glanced behind him.

Steps spiraled up.

'The tower stair,' Rachel said.

Gunshots struck the door.

'Go,' he said.

He pushed Rachel ahead of him, and they fled up the stairs, winding around and around. Behind and below,

143

the door crashed open. He heard a familiar voice, yelling in German. 'Get the bastards! Burn them alive!'

It was the tall man, the leader of the monks.

Footsteps pounded on the stone steps.

With the twist of the staircase, neither party had a clear shot at the other, but that still put the advantage with their pursuers. As Gray and Rachel ran, a fountain of flames chased them, sputtering up after them, whisking around the bend in the tower stairs.

Around and around they ran. The steps grew more narrow as they climbed the constricting throat of the steepled tower. Tall stained-glass windows dotted the way, but they were too thin to climb through, no more than arrow slits.

At last the steps reached the belfry of the tower. A massive free-swinging bell hung over the tower's steel-grated well. A deck lay around the bell.

Here at least the windows were wide enough to climb through and held no glass to muffle the mighty bell's peals – but the way through them was sealed by bars.

'A public observation deck,' Rachel said. She kept a gun, one borrowed from Gray, fixed on the opening to the stairs.

Gray hurried around. There was no other way out. The city views opened around him: the Rhine River sparkled, spanned by the arched Hohenzollern Bridge; the Ludwig Museum was lit up brilliantly, as were the blue sails of the Cologne Musical Dome. But there was no escape to the streets below.

Distantly he heard police sirens, a forlorn and eerily foreign wail.

Gray raised his eyes, calculating.

A shout rose from Rachel. Gray turned as a jet of flames erupted from the stairwell. Rachel fled back, joining him.

They had run out of time.

Below, in the cathedral, Yaeger Grell entered the blasted chamber, gun in hand. He had waited until the smoke from the second grenade had cleared out. His two partners had gone to join the others in setting up the final incendiary bombs near the entrance to the church.

He would join them – but first he wanted to see the damage done to those who had killed Renard, his brother-in-arms. He stepped through, readying himself for the stench of bloody flesh and burst bowel.

The remains of the door made the footing treacherous. He led with his gun. As he took a second step, something struck his arm. He backed a step, stunned, not comprehending. He stared down at the severed stump of his wrist as blood spurted. There was no pain.

He glanced up in time to see a sword – a sword! – swinging through the air. It reached his neck before the surprise faded from his features. He felt nothing as his body pitched forward, his head impossibly thrown back.

Then he kept falling, falling, falling . . . as the world went black.

Kat stepped back and lowered the jeweled sword. She bent, grabbed an arm, and dragged the body out of direct view of the doorway. Her head still rang from the grenade blast.

She whispered to Monk – at least she hoped she whispered. She couldn't even hear her own words. 'Help the monsignor.'

Monk stared from the decapitated body back to the bloody sword in her hand, his eyes wide with a shock, but also grudging respect. He stepped over to one of the treasure cases and manhandled the monsignor free of one

145

of the displays. All three of them had hidden inside a bulletproof case after the first grenade blast, knowing a second grenade would follow.

It had.

But the security cases had done their job, protecting the most valuable treasure of all: their lives. The shrapnel had cut through the room, but shielded behind the bulletproof glass, they had survived.

It had been her idea.

Afterward, with the concussion still echoing in her head, Kat had rolled out of her case and found the jeweled sword on the floor. It proved a more circumspect weapon than her pistol. She had not wanted a blast to alert the other gunmen.

Still, her hand shook. Her body remembered the last knife fight she had been in . . . and the aftermath. She tightened her grip on the sword's hilt, drawing strength from the hard steel.

Behind her, Monsignor Verona stumbled to his feet. He glanced to his limbs as if surprised to find them still attached.

Kat returned to the door. Except for their dead comrade, none of the other gunmen seemed to be paying attention. They were massed by the entrance.

'We should move.' Kat motioned them out. Sticking to the wall, she led them away from the front exits, away from the guards. She reached the corner where the nave crossed with the transept. Kat waved them around the corner of the intersection.

Once out of the direct view of the gunmen, the monsignor pointed down the length of the transept. 'That way,' he whispered.

There was another set of doors back there. Another exit. Unguarded.

With the fifteenth-century sword clutched in her fist, Kat hurried them forward. They had survived.

But what about the others?

Rachel fired her gun down the throat of the spiral stair-case, counting down the rounds in the second clip. Nine bullets. They had more ammunition, but no time to load another magazine. Commander Pierce was too busy.

With no other recourse, she shot blindly, sporadically, keeping the attackers at bay. Spouts of flame continued to harass her, licking forth like the tongue of a dragon.

The stalemate could not last much longer.

'Gray!' she yelled, skipping the formalities of rank.

'Another second,' he answered from around the far side of the bell.

As the flames faltered from the stairwell, Rachel aimed and squeezed the trigger. She had to hold them off. The bullet struck the stone wall and ricocheted down the staircase.

Then her pistol's slide locked open.

Out of bullets.

She backed away and circled the bell to the far side.

Gray had his pack off and had tied a rope around one of the window bars. He had the other end wrapped around his waist and the slack over one arm. He had used a hand jack in a tool kit to pry apart two of the window's bars, just wide enough to climb through.

'Hold the slack,' he said.

She took the nylon rope, about five meters in length. Behind her, a fresh billow of flame jettisoned from the stairwell. The others were testing again, moving forward.

Gray grabbed his pack and squeezed between the bars. Once out on the stone parapet, he donned the backpack and turned back to her. 'The rope.'

She passed it to him. 'Be careful.'

'A little late for that.'

He stared down between his toes. Not a wise thing to do, Rachel thought. The hundred-meter drop would weaken anyone's knees . . . and strength of leg was most important now.

Gray faced forward from the ledge of the cathedral's south spire.

Four meters away, over a fatal drop, stood the north spire, a twin to this one. Off limits to the public, there were no bars across the far window. But there was also no hope of jumping from window to window, not from a standing position. Instead, Gray planned to dive straight out and grab whatever handhold he could on the decorated façade of the opposite tower.

The risk was great, but they had no other recourse.

They had to jump ship.

Gray bent his knees. Rachel held her breath, one hand fisted at the hollow of her neck.

Without a second's hesitation, Gray simply leaned out and leapt, arching the length of his body, flinging away the coil of slack rope. He flew across the gap and struck just below the window ledge. He lunged out with both arms and grabbed ahold of the sill, miraculously catching it. But the impact bounced him back. His arms could not hold him. He began to fall.

'Your left foot!' she yelled to him.

He heard her. His left toe scrambled against the stone surface and found the demon-faced gargoyle on the lower tier. He planted his foot atop its head.

With his plummet stopped, he regained a handful of ledge above and found another toehold for his right leg, clinging like a fly to a wall. He took a deep breath, steadying himself, then climbed and manhandled himself through the window.

Rachel risked a glance behind her, ducking to peer under the bell. The flames had stopped. She knew the others understood the significance of her sudden ceasefire.

Rachel could wait no longer. She shimmied through the

bars. The ledge was slick with pigeon guano, the winds gusting and treacherous.

Across the gap, Gray had secured his end of the rope, forming a bridge. 'Hurry! I have you.'

She met his eyes across the gap and found firm assurance.

'I have you,' he repeated.

Swallowing, she reached out. Don't look down, she thought, and grabbed the rope. Hand over hand. That's all she needed to do.

She leaned out, both fists white-knuckled to the rope, toes still on the ledge. She heard the bell ring behind her. Startled, she glanced over a shoulder and watched a dumbbell-shaped silver cylinder bounce across the stone deck.

She didn't know what it was – but it certainly wasn't good.

Needing no other encouragement, Rachel swung out on the rope and quickly scrambled across the bridge, legs kicking, hand over hand. Gray caught her around the midriff.

'Bomb,' she gasped out, tossing her head back to indicate the far tower.

'What – ?'

The blast cut off any further words. Buffeted from behind, Rachel was shoved through the casement and into Gray's chest. They both fell in a tangle to the floor of the bell tower. A wall of blue flame rolled over them through the window, blast-furnace hot.

Gray held her tight, shielding her with his own body.

But the flames quickly dissipated in the gusty winds.

Gray rolled aside as Rachel elbowed up. She stared back toward the south tower. The spire was aflame. Spats of fire licked and roiled from the four windows. The bell clanged within the conflagration.

Gray joined her. He hauled in the rope. The knot on

the far side had burned away, severing the bridge. Across the gap, the window bars glowed a fiery red.

'Incendiary device,' he said.

The flames rippled in the strong winds, like a candle in the night. A final memorial to those killed, both last night and tonight. Rachel pictured the rakish smile of her uncle. Dead. Grief welled through her . . . along with something hotter and sharper. She stumbled back, but Gray caught her.

Police sirens wailed across the city, echoing up to them.

'We must go,' he said.

She nodded.

'They'll think us dead. Let's keep it that way.'

She allowed herself to be led to the stairwell. They hurried down, winding around and around. Sirens grew even louder – but closer, an engine coughed to life, revving gutturally, followed by a second.

Gray checked the window. 'They're fleeing.'

Rachel stared out. Three stories below, a pair of black vans pulled away, racing across the pedestrian square.

'C'mon,' Gray said. 'I have a bad feeling about this.'

He hurried down, skipping steps. Rachel rushed after him, trusting his instinct.

They hit the foyer at a dead run. One of the doors to the nave had been left ajar. Rachel glanced into the church – toward where her uncle had been killed. But something drew her eye, closer, on the floor, draped down the center aisle.

Silver barbells.

A dozen or more. Daisy-chained with red wires.

'Run!' she yelled, turning on a heel.

Together they hit the main doors and flew into the square.

Without a word, they fled toward the only shelter. The panel truck of the German Polizei sat on the square. They dove behind it just as the devices exploded.

It sounded like fireworks going off, one after the other, in succession.

A shatter of glass accompanied, loud enough to be heard above the popping explosions. Rachel glanced up. The giant Bavarian stained-glass window above the main door, dating from the Middle Ages, blew out in a brilliant cascade of fire and jeweled glass.

She tucked tight to the truck as the shower of glass pelted the square all around them in a rain of death.

Something hit the far side of the truck with a resounding crash. Rachel bent and stared past the wheels. On the far side, one of the massive wooden doors of the cathedral lay on the street, aflame.

Then a new noise intruded. Surprised voices. Muffled. Coming from *inside* the truck. Rachel glanced to Gray. He suddenly had a knife in hand, making it appear as if by magic.

They circled around the back of the van.

Before they could touch the handle, the door popped open.

Rachel stared in disbelief as Gray's stocky team member stumbled out. He was followed by his female partner, bearing a longsword in hand. And lastly by a familiar, welcome figure.

'Uncle Vigor!' Rachel clasped him in a bear hug.

He returned her embrace. 'Why is it,' he asked, 'that everyone seems determined to blow me up?'


4:45 a.m.

An hour later, Gray paced the hotel room, still edgy, nerves stretched thin. They had taken up the room here using false identification, determining it was best to get off the streets as soon as possible. Hotel Cristall on Ursulaplatz was located less than half a mile from the cathedral, a small boutique establishment with an oddly

151

Scandinavian décor of primary colors.

They had gone to ground here to regroup, establish a plan of action.

But first they needed more intel.

A key scuffled in the door lock. Gray placed a palm on his pistol. He wasn't taking any chances. But it was only Monsignor Verona returning from a scouting expedition.

Vigor pushed into the room. His expression had gone very grim.

'What?'

'The boy's dead,' the monsignor said.

The others gathered closer.

Vigor explained, 'Jason Pendleton. The boy who survived from the massacre. It's just been reported on the BBC. He was killed in his hospital room. Cause of death is still unknown, but foul play is highly suspected. Especially coinciding with the firebombing of the cathedral.'

Rachel shook her head sadly.

Earlier, Gray had been relieved to find everyone alive, only bruised and shaken. He had failed to consider the survivor of the first massacre. But it made a certain horrible sense. The cathedral attack had obviously been a whitewash operation, to erase any residual trail. And of course, that would include silencing the only witness.

'Did you learn anything else?' Gray asked.

He had sent the monsignor down to the lounge after they had checked into the hotel, to investigate the state of affairs at the cathedral. The monsignor was best suited. He spoke the language fluently, and his clerical collar would place him above suspicion.

Even now, Klaxons and sirens wailed across the city. Out the window, they had a view of Cathedral Hill. A bevy of fire engines and other emergency vehicles gathered there, flashing their blues and reds. Smoke clouded the night sky. The streets were crowded with spectators and news vans.

'I learned nothing more than we already know,' Vigor said. 'The fire is still raging inside the church. It hasn't spread. I saw an interview with one of the priests from the rectory. No one was harmed. But they're reporting concern about the whereabouts of myself and my niece.'

'Good,' Gray said, earning a glance from Rachel. 'As I said before, they think we were eliminated for the moment. We should maintain that ruse for as long as possible. As long as they don't know we're alive, they'll be less likely to be looking over their shoulders.'

'And less likely to be gunning for us,' Monk said. 'I especially like that part.'

Kat was working on a laptop wired to a digital camera. 'The photos are uploading now,' she said.

Gray stood and stepped to the desk. Monk and the others had sought not only a hiding place in the van after their escape, but also a vantage to get some photographs of the assailants. Gray was impressed with their resourcefulness.

Black-and-white thumbnail images filled the screen.

'There,' Rachel said, pointing to one. 'That's the guy who grabbed me.'

'The leader of the group,' Gray said.

Kat double-clicked the image and brought up a full-scale photo. He was frozen in mid-stride as he exited the cathedral. He had dark hair, cut long, almost to the shoulder. No facial hair. Aquiline features. Rocky and expressionless. Even in the photo, he gave off an air of superiority.

'Look at that smug bastard,' Monk said. 'The cat who ate the canary.'

'Does anyone recognize him?' Gray asked.

Heads shook.

'I can uplink it to Sigma's facial-recognition software,' Kat said.

'Not yet,' Gray said. He answered her frown. 'We need to stay incommunicado.'

153

He glanced around the room. While normally he preferred to operate on his own, free from Big Brother watching over his shoulder, he could no longer play lone wolf. He had a team now, a responsibility beyond his own skin. His eyes found Vigor and Rachel. And it wasn't even just his own team any longer. They were all looking to him. He suddenly felt overwhelmed. He desired nothing more than to check in with Sigma, consult with Director Crowe, pawn off his responsibility.

But he couldn't . . . at least not yet.

Gray gathered his thoughts and his resolve. He cleared his throat. 'Someone knew we were alone in the cathedral. Either they were already spying on the church or they had prior intel.'

'A leak,' Vigor said, rubbing the beard under his lower lip.

'Possibly. But I can't say for sure where it might have originated.' Gray glanced to Vigor. 'From our end or yours.'

Vigor sighed and nodded. 'I fear we may be to blame. The Dragon Court has always claimed members inside the Vatican. And with the ambush here following on the heels of the attacks against Rachel and myself, I can't help but think the problem may lie at the Holy See itself.'

'Not necessarily,' Gray answered. He turned back to the laptop and pointed to another thumbnail picture. 'Bring that one up.'

Kat double-clicked. An image of a slender woman climbing into the back of one of the two vans swelled across the monitor. Her face was only in silhouette.

Gray glanced to the others. 'Anyone know her?'

More shakes.

Monk leaned closer. 'But I wouldn't mind knowing her.'

'This is the woman who attacked me at Fort Detrick.'

Monk backed away, suddenly finding the woman less appealing. 'The Guild operative?'

Vigor and Rachel wore confused expressions. Gray didn't have time to go into the full history of the Guild, but he gave a brief overview of the organization: its terrorist-cell structure, its ties to Russian *mafiya*, and its interest in new technologies.

Once he was finished, Kat asked, 'So you think the problem might be at our end?'

'After Fort Detrick . . . ?' Gray frowned. 'Who can tell where the security leak lies? But the fact that the Guild is here, operating alongside the Dragon Court, I can't help but think that they've been drawn in because of our involvement. But I think they're as late to the game as we are.'

'Why do you say that?' Rachel asked.

Gray pointed at the screen. 'The Dragon Lady let me escape.'

Stunned silence followed.

'Are you sure?' Monk asked.

'Damn sure.' Gray rubbed his bruised upper arm where she had shot him as he fled.

'Why would she do that?' Rachel asked.

'Because she's playing the Dragon Court. Like I said, I think the only reason the Guild has been called into this venture is because Sigma became involved. The Court wanted the Guild's assistance to capture or eliminate us.'

Kat nodded. 'And if we were dead, then the Guild would no longer be needed. The partnership would end, and the Guild would never find out what the Dragon Court knows.'

'But now the Court thinks we were killed,' Rachel said.

'Exactly. And that's another reason to keep that ruse going for as long as possible. If we're dead, the Court will sever its ties with the Guild.'

'One less opponent,' Monk said.

Gray nodded.

'What do we do next?' Kat asked.

That was a mystery. They had no leads . . . except one. Gray glanced over to his pack. 'The powder we recovered from the reliquary. It must hold a key to all this. But I don't know what lock it fits. And if we can't send it to Sigma to test . . .'

Vigor spoke up. 'I think you're right. The answer lies in the powder. But a better question than "What is it –"'

The monsignor suddenly halted, his eyes narrowed. He placed a hand on his forehead. 'What is it . . .' he mumbled under his breath.

'Uncle?' Rachel asked with concern.

'Something . . . it's right at the corner of my brain.'

Gray remembered a similar expression of intense internal concentration when the monsignor had quoted a verse from the Book of Revelations.

The priest balled a fist. 'I can't put it together. Like trying to catch a soap bubble in your palm.' He shook his head. 'Maybe I'm too tired.'

Gray sensed the man was being truthful . . . for the most part. But he was holding something back, something triggered by the words *what is it*. For a flicker, Gray saw fear shine behind the confusion.

'So, what's the better question?' Monk asked, returning to the original train of thought. 'You started to say something about a better question than what the powder might be.'

Vigor nodded, focusing back. 'Right. Maybe we should be asking *how* the powder got there. Once every few years, the bones are carefully taken from the reliquary and the sarcophagus is cleaned. I'm sure they dusted and wiped out the interior.'

Kat sat straighter. 'Before the attack, we were wondering if the device somehow altered the gold of the sarcophagus, transmuted the lining into the white powder.'

'That's how it got there?' Rachel asked.

'Could be,' Monk said. 'Remember the magnetized cross back at the church. Something weird happened in there, and it affected metals. So why not gold, too?'

Gray wished he had had more time to collect samples, to perform more tests. But with the cathedral firebombed –

'No,' Kat said, sighing in exasperation. 'Remember. The powder was not just gold. We also spotted other elements. Maybe platinum or something else in that transitional group of metals that can also disaggregate into m-state powdery form.'

Gray slowly nodded, remembering the silvery inclusions in the molten gold.

'I don't think the powder came from the sarcophagus case,' Kat said.

Monk frowned. 'But if it's not coming from the gold in the case and if the box is Windexed every couple of years . . . then where else could it be coming from?'

Gray's eyes widened with understanding. He understood Kat's consternation. 'It came from the *bones*.'

'There is no other explanation,' Kat agreed.

Monk balked, shaking his head. 'That's easy to say. We have no bones to test your hypothesis. They have them all.'

Rachel and Vigor exchanged a sudden glance.

'What?' Gray asked.

Rachel met his gaze. He read the excitement in her expression. 'They don't have all the bones.'

Gray's brow furrowed. 'Where – ?'

Vigor answered. 'In Milan.'

157

# 6

## DOUBTING THOMAS

Gray and the others fell out of the rented Mercedes E55 sedan and stumbled onto the pedestrian plaza of the lakeside town of Como. Morning strollers and window-shoppers dotted the cobblestone square that led down to a promenade bordering the still blue waters.

Kat yawned and stretched, a cat slowly waking. She checked her watch. 'Three countries in four hours.'

They had driven all night. Across Germany to Switzerland, then over the Alps into Italy. They had traveled by car, rather than by train or plane, to maintain their anonymity, passing borders with false identification. They did not want to alert anyone that their group had survived the attack in Cologne.

Gray planned on contacting Sigma command after they had secured the bones from the basilica in Milan and had reached the Vatican. Once ensconced in Rome, they would regroup and strategize with their respective superiors. Despite the risk of a leak, Gray needed to debrief Washington on the events in Cologne, to reevaluate the mission's parameters.

In the meantime, the plan was to rotate drivers while en route from Cologne to Milan, to let everyone get a bit of shut-eye. It hadn't worked out that way.

Out of the car, Monk stood at the edge of the plaza, bent over, hands on his knees, slightly green in the face.

'It's her driving,' Vigor said, patting Monk on the back. 'She goes a bit fast.'

'I've been on fighter planes, doing goddamn loopty-loops,' he grumbled. 'This . . . this was worse.'

Rachel climbed out of the driver's seat and closed the door to the rental car. She had driven the entire way at breakneck speed, flying down the German Autobahn and taking the hairpin turns of the Alpine roads at physics-defying velocities.

She pushed her blue-tinted sunglasses to her forehead. 'You just need some breakfast,' she assured Monk. 'I know a nice bistro along the Piazza Cavour.'

Despite some reservations, Gray had agreed to stop for food. They needed gas, and the place was remote. And with the attack only six hours old, confusion still reigned back in Cologne. By the time it was known that their bodies were not among the dead at the cathedral, they would be in Rome. In a few more hours, the necessity for maintaining the ruse of their deaths would be over.

In the meantime, they were all road-weary and famished.

Rachel led the way across the plaza toward the banks of the lake. Gray followed her with his eyes. Despite the overnight drive, she moved with no sign of fatigue. If anything, she seemed enlivened by her Alpine racing, like it was her form of yoga. The haunted look in her eye from the night of terror had faded with each passing mile.

He found himself both relieved at her resilience and somewhat disappointed. He remembered her hand squeezing his as they ran. The worry in her eyes as she straddled the ledge of the cathedral's tower. The way her eyes fixed on him at that moment, trusting him, needing him.

That woman was gone.

Ahead, the view opened up, drawing his eye. The lake was a blue jewel set within the rugged green peaks of the lower Alps. A few of the mountains were still tipped with snow, reflected in the placid waters.

'Lago di Como,' Vigor said, striding beside Gray. 'Virgil once described this as the world's greatest lake.'

They reached a gardened promenade. The path was fringed with sprawls of camellias, azaleas, rhododendrons, and magnolias. The cobbled walkway continued along the edge of the lake, lined by chestnut trees, Italian cypresses, and white-barked laurels. Out in the waters, tiny sailboats skimmed along with the mild morning breezes. Up in the green hills, clusters of homes perched precariously atop cliff faces, shaded in hues of cream, gold, and terra-cotta red.

Gray noted the beauty and fresh air seemed to be reviving Monk, or at least the solid footing was. Kat's eyes also took in the sights.

'Ristorante Imbarcadero,' Rachel said, pointing across the piazza.

'A drive-through restaurant would've been fine,' Gray said, checking his watch.

'Maybe for you,' Monk said dourly.

Vigor stepped next to him. 'We made good time. We'll reach Milan in another hour.'

'But the bones –'

Vigor silenced him with a frown. 'Commander, the Vatican is well aware of the risk to the relics in the Basilica of Sant'Eustorgio. I was already under orders to stop in Milan to collect them on my way back to Rome. In the meantime, the Vatican has secured the bones in the basilica's safe, the church has been locked down, and the local police have been alerted.'

'That won't necessarily stop the Dragon Court,' Gray said, picturing the devastation in Cologne.

'I doubt they'd strike in full daylight. The group skulks in shadows and darkness. And we'll be in Milan before noon.'

Kat added, 'It won't delay us much to place a take-out order and be back on the road.'

160

Though far from satisfied, Gray conceded the point. The group needed to refuel as much as their automobile.

Reaching the restaurant, Rachel opened a gate to a bougainvillea-adorned terrace overlooking the lake. 'The Imbarcadero serves the best local dishes. You should try the *risotto con pesce persico*.'

'Golden perch with risotto,' Vigor translated. 'It is wonderful here. The fillets are rolled in flour and sage, shallow fried, and served crisp on a thick bed of risotto, soaking in butter.'

Rachel guided them to a table.

Somewhat mollified, Gray allowed himself to appreciate Rachel's enthusiasm. She spoke rapidly in Italian to an older man in an apron who came out to greet them. She smiled easily, making small talk. They hugged afterward.

Rachel turned back and waved to the seats. 'If you want something lighter, try the courgette flowers stuffed with bread and boraggine. But definitely have a small plate of agnolotti.'

Vigor nodded. 'A ravioli with aubergine and bufala mozzarella.' He kissed his fingertips in appreciation.

'So I take it you've eaten here a few times,' Monk said, dropping heavily into a seat. He eyed Gray.

So much for anonymity.

Vigor patted Monk's shoulder. 'The owners are friends of our family, going back three generations. Rest assured, they know how to be discreet.' He waved to a rotund server. '*Ciao, Mario! Bianco Secco di Montecchia, per favore!*'

'Right away, *Padre*! I also have a nice *Chiaretto* from Bellagio. Came by ferry last night.'

'*Perfetto!* A bottle of each then while we wait!'

'Antipasti?'

'Of course, Mario. We are not barbarians.'

Their order was placed with much bravado and laughter: salmon salad with apple vinegar, barley stew, breaded veal, tagliatelle pasta with whitefish, something called pappardelle.

Mario brought out a platter as large as the table, piled with olives and an assortment of antipasti . . . along with two bottles of wine, one red, one white.

'*Buon appetito!*' he said loudly.

It seemed Italians made a feast out of every meal – even take-out orders. Wine flowed. Glasses lifted. Bits of salami and cheese were passed around.

'*Salute,* Mario!' Rachel cheered as they finished the platter.

Monk leaned back, attempted to stifle a belch and failed. 'That alone overfilled the tank.'

Kat had eaten just as much, but she was now studying the dessert menu with the same intensity with which she had read the mission dossier.

'*Signorina?*' Mario asked, noting her interest.

She pointed to the menu. '*Macedonia con panna.*'

Monk groaned.

'It's only fruit salad with cream.' She glanced at the others, eyes wide. 'It's light.'

Gray sat back. He didn't suppress the bravado. He sensed they all needed this momentary respite. Once under way, the day would be a blur. They'd blow into Milan, grab the relic bones, and then take one of the hourly high-speed trains into Rome, getting there before nightfall.

Gray had also used the time to study Vigor Verona. Despite the festivities, the monsignor seemed lost to his own thoughts again. Gray could see the gears churning in the man's head.

Vigor suddenly focused on him, matched his gaze. He pushed back from the table. 'Commander Pierce, while we're waiting on the kitchen, I wonder if I might have a private word. Perhaps we could stretch our legs on the promenade.'

Gray settled his glass and stood. The others glanced to them curiously, but Gray nodded for them to remain there.

Vigor led the way off the terrace and onto the main promenade that bordered the lake. 'There's something I'd like to discuss with you and perhaps get your opinion.'

'Certainly.'

They walked down a block, and Vigor stepped to a stone railing that abutted an empty dock. They had privacy here.

Vigor kept his view on the lake, tapping one fist on the railing. 'I understand that the Vatican's role in all of this is centered on the theft of the relics. And once we return to Rome, I suspect you plan on cutting ties and pursuing the Dragon Court on your own.'

Gray considered vacillating, but the man deserved an honest answer. He could not risk further endangering this man and his niece. 'I think it's best,' he said. 'And I'm sure both our superiors will agree.'

'But I don't.' A bit of heat entered his words.

Gray frowned.

'If you're right about the bones being the source for the strange amalgam powder, then I believe our roles here are more deeply entwined than either organization suspected.'

'I don't see how.'

Vigor glanced to him again with that focused intensity that seemed to be a Verona family trait. 'Then let me convince you. First, we know the Dragon Court is an aristocratic society involved in the search for secret or lost knowledge. They've concentrated on ancient Gnostic texts and other arcana.'

'Mystical mumbo jumbo.'

Vigor turned to him, cocking his head. 'Commander Pierce, I believe you yourself have undergone a study of alternate faiths and philosophies. From Taoism to some of the Hindi cults.'

Gray flushed. It was easy to forget that the monsignor was an experienced field operative for the Vatican *intelligenza*. Clearly a dossier had been gathered on him.

'To seek spiritual truth is never wrong,' the monsignor continued. 'No matter the path. In fact, the definition of *gnosis* is 'to seek truth, to find God.' I can't even fault the Dragon Court in this pursuit. Gnosticism has been a part of the Catholic Church since its inception. Even predates it.'

'Fine,' Gray said, unable to keep a trace of irritation out of his voice. 'What does any of this have to do with the massacre at Cologne?'

The monsignor sighed. 'In some ways, the attack today could be traced back to a conflict between two apostles. Thomas and John.'

Gray shook his head. 'What are you talking about?'

'In the beginning, Christianity was an outlaw religion. An upstart faith like none other in its time. Unlike other religions that collected dues as a required part of their faith, the young Christian family contributed money voluntarily. The funds went to feed and house orphans, bought food and medicine for the sick, paid for coffins for the poor. Such support of the downtrodden attracted large numbers of people, despite the risks of belonging to an outlawed faith.'

'Yes, I know. Christian good works and all that. Still, what does – '

Gray was cut off by a raised palm. 'If you'll let me continue, you might learn something.'

Gray bridled but kept silent. Besides being a Vatican spy, Vigor was also a university professor. He plainly didn't like his lectures being interrupted.

'In the early years of the church, secrecy remained paramount, requiring surreptitious meetings in caves and crypts. This led to different groups being cut off from one another. First by distance, with major sects in Alexandria,

164

Antioch, Carthage, and Rome. Then, with such isolation, individual practices began to diverge, along with differing philosophies. Gospels were popping up everywhere. The ones collected in the Bible: Matthew, Mark, Luke, and John. But also others. The Secret Gospel of James, of Mary Magdalene, of Philip. The Gospel of Truth. The Apocalypse of Peter. And many others. With all these gospels, different sects began to develop around them. The young church began to splinter.'

Gray nodded. He had attended the Jesuit high school where his mother had taught. He knew some of this history.

'But in the second century,' Vigor continued, 'the bishop of Lyons, Saint Irenaeus, wrote five volumes under the title *Adversus Haereses. Against Heresies.* Its full title was *The Destruction and Overthrow of Falsely So-called Knowledge.* It was the moment where all early Gnostic beliefs were sifted out of the Christian religion, creating the fourfold Gospel canon, limiting the Gospels to Matthew, Mark, Luke, and John. All others were deemed heretical. To paraphrase Irenaeus, just as there are four regions of the universe, and four principal winds, the church needed only four pillars.'

'But why pick those four gospels out of all the others?'

'Why indeed? Therein lies my concern.'

Gray found his attention focused more fully. Despite his irritation at being lectured, he was curious where all this was leading.

Vigor stared out across the lake. 'Three of the Gospels – Matthew, Mark, and Luke – all tell the same story. But the Gospel of John relates a very different history, even events in Christ's life don't match the chronology in the others. But there was a more fundamental reason why John was included in the standardized Bible.'

'Why?'

'Because of his fellow apostle, Thomas.'

'As in *Doubting* Thomas?' Gray was well versed on the story of the one apostle who refused to believe Christ had resurrected, not until he could see it with his own eyes.

Vigor nodded. 'But did you know that *only* the Gospel of John tells the story of Doubting Thomas? Only John portrays Thomas as this dull-witted and faithless disciple. The other Gospels revere Thomas. Do you know why John tells this disparaging account?'

Gray shook his head. In all his years as a Roman Catholic, he had never noticed this imbalance in viewpoint.

'John sought to discredit Thomas, or more specifically, the followers of Thomas, who were numerous at that time. Even today you can still find a strong following of Thomas Christians in India. But in the early church, there was a fundamental schism between the gospels of Thomas and John. They were *so* different that only one gospel could survive.'

'What do you mean? How different could they be?'

'It goes back to the very beginning of the Bible, to Genesis, to the opening line. 'Let there be light.' Both John and Thomas identify Jesus with this primordial light, the light of creation. But from there, their interpretations widely diverge. According to Thomas, the light not only brought the universe into being but still exists within all things, especially within mankind, who was made in the image of God, and that the light is hidden within each person, only waiting to be found.'

'And what about John?'

'Now, John took a totally different view of matters. Like Thomas, he believed the primordial light was embodied by Christ, but John declared that *only* Christ held this light. The rest of the world remained forever in darkness, including mankind. And that the path back to this light, back to salvation and God, could only be found through the worship of the divine Christ.'

'A much narrower view.'

'And more pragmatic for the young church. John offered a more orthodox method for salvation, of coming into the light. Only through the worship of Christ. It was this simplicity and directness that appealed to the church leaders during this chaotic time. Contrarily Thomas suggested everyone had an innate ability to find God, by looking within, requiring no worship.'

'And that had to be squashed out.'

A shrug.

'But which is right?'

Vigor grinned. 'Who knows? I don't have all the answers. As Jesus said, "Seek and you shall find."'

Gray pinched his brows. That line sounded pretty Gnostic to him. He glanced out to the lake, watching the sailboats scud past. Light shone brilliantly off the waters. *Seek and you shall find.* Had that been the path he had been on himself by studying so many philosophies? If so, he had come to no satisfactory answers.

And speaking of unsatisfactory answers . . .

Gray turned back to Vigor, realizing how far off track they had gotten. 'What does all this have to do with the massacre in Cologne?'

'Let me tell you.' He held up one finger. 'First, I think this attack harkens back to the age-old conflict between John's orthodox faith and Thomas's ancient Gnostic tradition.'

'With the Catholic Church on one side and the Dragon Court on the other?'

'No, that's just it. I've been pondering this all night. The Dragon Court, while it seeks knowledge through Gnostic mysteries, does not ultimately seek God, only *power.* They want a new world order, a return to feudalism, with themselves at the helm, confident that they are genetically superior to lead mankind. So no, I don't think the Dragon Court represents the Gnostic side of this ancient conflict. I think they are perverters of it, power-hungry scavengers. But they definitely have roots back to that tradition.'

Gray grudgingly conceded the point, but he was far from swayed.

Vigor must have sensed this. He lifted a second finger. 'Point two. In the Gospel of Thomas, there's a story that tells of how Jesus pulled Thomas aside one day and told him three things in secret. When the other apostles asked him what was told to him, he answered, "If I tell you even one of the things, you will pick up stones and throw them at me; and a fire will come out of the stones and burn you up."'

Vigor stared at Gray, waiting, as if it were a test.

Gray was up for it. 'A fire from stones that burns. Like what happened to the parishioners at the church.'

He nodded. 'I've thought of that quote since I first heard of the murders.'

'That's a pretty thin connection,' Gray said, unconvinced.

'It might be if I didn't have a third historical point to make.' Vigor lifted a third finger.

Gray felt like a lamb being led to the slaughter.

'According to historical texts,' Vigor explained, 'Thomas went on to evangelize in the East, all the way to India. He baptized thousands of people, built churches, spread the faith, and eventually died in India. But in that region, he was most famous for one act, one act of baptism.'

Gray waited.

Vigor concluded with great emphasis. 'Thomas baptized the Three Magi.'

Gray's eyes widened. His mind whirled with the threads here: Saint Thomas and his Gnostic tradition, secrets whispered by Christ, deadly fire cast from stones, and all of it tied back to the Magi again. Did the connection extend further? He pictured the photographs of the dead in Germany. The wracked bodies. And the coroner's report of the liquefaction of the outer layers of the victims' brains. He also remembered the smell of seared flesh in the cathedral.

Somehow the bones were tied to those deaths.

But how?

If there was a historical trail leading to any clues, it was beyond his scope of experience and knowledge to follow. He recognized this and faced the monsignor.

Vigor spoke, confident of his argument. 'As I said from the start, I think there is more to the deaths at the cathedral than technology. I think whatever happened is entwined intimately with the Catholic Church, its early history, and possibly even before its founding. And I am certain I can be a continuing asset to this investigation.'

Gray bowed his head in thought, slowly won over.

'But not my niece,' Vigor finished, revealing at last why he had pulled Gray aside. He held out his hand. 'Once we return to Rome, I will send her back to the Carabinieri. I will not risk her again.'

Gray reached out and shook the monsignor's hand.

Finally something the two of them could agree on.


10:45 a.m.

Rachel heard a step behind her, expecting it to be Mario returning with their order. Glancing up, she almost fell out of her seat as she gazed at the elderly woman who stood there, leaning on a cane, dressed in navy slacks and a blue summer frock with a daffodil pattern. Her white hair was curled, her eyes flashing in amusement.

Mario stood behind the visitor, a broad smile on his face. 'Surprise, no?'

Rachel gained her feet as Gray's two partners looked on. '*Nonna?* What are you doing here?'

Her grandmother patted Rachel on a cheek, speaking in Italian. 'Your crazy mother!' She fluttered her fingers in the air. 'She goes off to see you in Rome. Leaves me alone with that Signore Barbari to watch over me. Like I need such care. Besides, he always smells of cheese.'

'Nonna . . .'

A wave of a hand held her off. 'So I come to our villa. I took the train. And then Mario calls me to tell me that you and Viggie are here. I tell him not to tell you.'

'It's a good surprise, no?' Mario repeated, glowing proudly. He must have been biting his thumb the entire time not to say anything.

'Who are your friends?' her *nonna* asked.

Rachel introduced them. 'This is my grandmother.'

She shook each of their hands and switched to English. 'Call me Camilla.' She eyed Monk up and down. 'Why do you cut off all your hair? A shame. But you have nice eyes. Are you *italiano*?'

'No, Greek.'

She nodded sagely. 'That's not too bad.' She turned to Kat. 'Is Signor Monk your boyfriend?'

Kat crinkled her brow in surprise. 'No,' she said a tad too tartly. 'Certainly not.'

'Hey,' Monk interjected.

'You make a nice couple,' *Nonna* Camilla declared, stating it as if it were set in stone. She turned to Mario. 'A glass of that wonderful *Chiaretto, per favore,* Mario.'

He whisked off, still beaming.

Rachel settled to her seat and spotted Gray and her uncle returning from their private meeting. As they crossed toward her, she noted that Gray would not meet her eye. She knew why her uncle had walked off with Commander Pierce. And from the man's avoidance, she could guess the outcome.

Rachel suddenly had no interest in her wine.

Uncle Vigor noticed the additional guest at their table. Shock shattered his grim expression.

The surprise was again explained, along with further introductions.

170

As Gray Pierce was introduced, her grandmother glanced askance at Rachel, one eyebrow raised, before fixing her gaze on the American. She clearly liked what she saw: stubbled dark chin, storm-blue eyes, lanky black hair. Rachel knew her grandmother had a strong match-making streak, a genetic trait in all Italian matrons.

Her grandmother leaned toward Rachel. 'I see beautiful babies,' she whispered, her eyes still on Gray. '*Bellissimo bambini.*'

'*Nonna,*' she warned.

Her grandmother shrugged and raised her voice. 'Signore Pierce, are you *italiano?*'

'No, I'm afraid not.'

'Would you like to be? My granddaughter – '

Rachel cut her off. '*Nonna,* we don't have much time.' She made a show of checking her wristwatch 'We have business in Milan.'

The grandmother brightened. 'Carabinieri work. Tracking stolen art?' She eyed Uncle Vigor. 'Something taken from a church?'

'Something like that, *Nonna*. But we can't talk about an open investigation.'

Her grandmother crossed herself. 'Horrible . . . stealing from a church. I read about the murders up in Germania. Terrible, just terrible.' She glanced around the table, taking in the strangers. Her eyes narrowed ever so slightly, settling on Rachel.

Rachel noted the sharp-eyed realization in her grandmother's gaze. Despite her outward appearance, nothing slipped past her *nonna*. The theft of the Magi bones was all over the newspapers. And here they were traveling with a group of Americans, near the border of Switzerland, heading back *into* Italy. Had her *nonna* guessed their real purpose?

'Terrible,' her grandmother repeated.

A server arrived laden with two heavy bags of food. A

loaf of bread poked from each like a pair of baguette masts. Monk rose to accept the burden with a broad smile.

Uncle Vigor spoke, leaning forward to kiss both her cheeks. 'Momma, we'll see you back home in Gandolfo in a couple of days. Once this business is finished.'

As Gray stepped past, *Nonna* Camilla took his hand and pulled him down closer. 'You watch after my granddaughter.'

Gray looked up to Rachel. 'I will, but she takes pretty good care of herself.'

Rachel felt a sudden flush of heat as his eyes met hers. Feeling ridiculous, she glanced aside. She wasn't a schoolgirl. Far from it.

Her *nonna* gave Gray a peck on the cheek. 'We Verona women always take care of ourselves. You remember that.'

Gray smiled. 'I will.'

She patted him on his backside as he stepped away. '*Ragazzo buono.*'

As the others headed out, her grandmother motioned Rachel to stay. She then reached out, turned back the corner of Rachel's open vest, and exposed the empty holster. 'You lost something, no?'

Rachel had forgotten she was still wearing the empty shoulder belt. She had left her borrowed Beretta back at the cathedral. But her *nonna* had noticed.

'A woman should never leave the house naked.' Her grandmother reached down and collected her purse. She opened it and pulled out the matte-black handle of her prized Nazi P-08 Luger. 'You take mine.'

'*Nonna!* You shouldn't be carrying that around.'

Her grandmother dismissed her concern with a wave. 'The trains are not that safe for a woman alone. Too many Gypsies. But I think you maybe need this more than me.'

172

Her grandmother's gaze weighed heavily on her, making it plain she understood the danger of Rachel's mission.

Rachel reached out and closed her purse with a snap. '*Grazie, Nonna.* But I'll be fine.'

Her grandmother shrugged. 'Terrible business up in Germania,' she said with a significant roll of her eyes. 'Best to be careful.'

'I will, *Nonna.*' Rachel began to turn away, but her wrist was grabbed.

'He likes you,' her grandmother said. 'Signore Pierce.'

'*Nonna.*'

'You would make *bellissimo bambini.*'

Rachel sighed. Even with danger threatening, her grandmother knew how to stay focused. Babies. The true treasures of *nonne* everywhere.

She was saved by Mario arriving with the bill. She stepped aside and paid it in cash, leaving enough to cover her *nonna*'s lunch. She then gathered up her things, kissed her grandmother, and headed out to the piazza to join the others.

But she carried her grandmother's spirit with her. Verona women certainly did know how to take care of themselves. She met her uncle and the others at the car. She fixed Gray with her best poisonous stare. 'If you think you're going to kick me off this investigation, you can walk to Rome.'

Keys in hand, she rounded the Mercedes, satisfied by the surprised look on the man's face as he glanced back to Uncle Vigor.

She had been ambushed, shot at, and firebombed. She wasn't about to be left at the side of the road.

She pulled her door open, but she kept the other doors locked. 'And that goes for you, too, Uncle Vigor.'

'Rachel . . .' he tried to argue.

She slid into the driver's seat, slammed her door, and keyed the ignition.

'Rachel!' Her uncle knocked on the window.

She shifted into gear.

'*Va bene!*' her uncle yelled to her over the supercharged engine, agreeing. 'We stay together.'

'Swear it,' she called back, keeping her palm on the gear knob.

'*Dio mio* . . .' He rolled his eyes heavenward. 'And you wonder why I became a priest. . . .'

She revved her engine.

Uncle Vigor placed a palm on the window. 'I submit. I swear. I should never have tried to go against a Verona woman.'

Rachel twisted and locked eyes on Gray. He had remained silent, his face hard. He looked ready to hotwire a car and take off on his own. Had she overplayed her hand? But she sensed she needed to make a strong stand now.

Slowly Gray's blue eyes shifted with a glacial coolness to her uncle, then back to Rachel. As they faced each other, at that moment, Rachel felt how deeply she wanted to remain, down to the marrow of her bones. Maybe he understood. Gray ever so slowly nodded, a barely perceptible movement.

It was enough of a concession.

She unlocked the doors. The others climbed in.

Monk was last. 'I was fine with walking.'

11:05 a.m.

From the backseat, Gray watched Rachel.

She had donned her blue-tinted sunglasses, which made her expression all but unreadable. Her lips, though, were pressed tightly. The muscles of her long neck remained taut as bowstrings as she glanced around for traffic. Despite the fact they had relented, she was still angry.

174

How had Rachel even known what had been decided between her uncle and himself? Her intuitive capacity was impressive, along with her no-nonsense approach to conflict. But he also remembered her vulnerability in the tower, her eyes meeting his across the gap between the two spires. Yet, even then, among the bullets and flames, she had not crumbled.

For a moment, he caught a glance from Rachel in the rearview mirror, her eyes shaded by her glasses. Still, he knew she was studying him. Too conscious of the scrutiny, he glanced away.

He balled a fist on a knee at his reaction.

Gray had never met a woman who so confounded him. He'd had girlfriends before but nothing that lasted more than six months, and even that relationship had been in high school. He'd been too hotheaded in his youth, then too devoted to his career in the military, first in the Army, then in the Rangers. He never called one place home for longer than six months, so romance was usually no more than a long weekend leave. But in all his dalliances, he had never met a woman who was as frustrating as she was intriguing: a woman who laughed easily over lunch, but who could turn hard as a polished diamond.

He leaned back as the countryside flashed past. They left behind the lake country of Northern Italy and descended the foothills of the Alps. The journey was a short one. Milan lay only a forty-minute drive away.

Gray knew enough about himself to understand part of his attraction to Rachel. He was never fascinated by the middle of the road, the mundane, the undecided. But neither was he a fan of extremes: the brash, the strident, the discordant. He had preferred harmony, a merging of extremes where balance was achieved but uniqueness was not lost.

Basically the Taoist yin-and-yang view of the cosmos. Even his own career reflected this – the scientist and the soldier. His field of disciplines sought to incorporate biology and physics. He had once described this choice to Painter Crowe. 'All chemistry, biology, mathematics boil down to the positive and the negative, the zero and the one, the light and the dark.'

Gray found his attention drifting back to Rachel. Here was this same philosophy in shapely flesh.

He watched Rachel lift a hand and knead a kink from her neck. Her lips were slightly parted as she found the sweet spot and rubbed. He wondered what those lips would taste like.

Before he let this thought drift further, she whipped the Mercedes around a tight curve, throwing Gray against the door frame. She dropped her hand, downshifted, gassed the engine, and took the turn even faster.

Gray hung on. Monk groaned.

Rachel merely wore a ghost of a smile.

Who wouldn't be fascinated by this woman?

6:07 a.m.
WASHINGTON, D.C.

Eight hours and no word.

Painter paced the length of his office. He had been here since ten o'clock the prior night – as soon as the news reached him about the explosion at the Cologne Cathedral. Since then, information had been filtering in slowly.

Too slowly.

The source of the incineration: bombs filled with black powder, white phosphorus, and the incendiary oil LA-60. It had taken three hours until the fire was contained enough to attempt entry. But the interior was a smoky, toxic shell, burned down to the stone walls and floors. Charred skeletal remains were discovered.

Was it his team?

Another two hours passed until a report came in that the slag remains of weapons had been found with two of the bodies. Unidentified assault rifles. No such weapons had been deployed with his team. So at least some of the bodies had been unknown assailants.

But what about the others?

Satellite surveillance out of NRO proved useless. No eyes in the skies had been sampling the area at that hour. On the ground, business and municipal cameras in the vicinity were still being canvassed. Eyewitnesses were few. One homeless man, sleeping near Cathedral Hill, reported seeing a handful of people fleeing the burning cathedral. But his blood alcohol level was over .15. Stumbling drunk.

All else was quiet. The safe house in Cologne hadn't been breeched. And so far, not a word from the field.

Nothing.

Painter could not help but fear the worst.

A knock at his half-open door interrupted him.

He turned and waved Logan Gregory into the office. His second-in-command had reams of paper tucked under his arm and dark circles under his eyes. Logan had refused to go home, sticking at his side all night long.

Painter looked on expectantly, hoping for a good word.

Logan shook his head. 'Still no hits on their aliases.' They had been checking hourly at airports, train stations, and bus lines.

'Border crossings?'

'Nothing. But the EU is pretty much an open sieve. They could have crossed out of Germany any number of ways.'

'And the Vatican still hasn't heard anything?'

Another shake of his head. 'I spoke to Cardinal Spera just ten minutes ago.'

A chime sounded from his computer. He strode around

his desk and tabbed the key to initiate the video-conferencing feature. He faced the plasma screen hanging on the left wall. A pixilating image appeared of his boss, the head of DARPA.

Dr. Sean McKnight was at his office in Arlington. He had abandoned his usual suit jacket and had the cuffs on his shirt rolled up. No tie. He ran a hand through his graying red hair, a familiar tired gesture.

'I got your request,' his boss started.

Painter straightened from where he had been leaning on his desk. Logan had retreated to the door, staying out of camera view. He made a move to step out, to offer privacy, but Painter motioned him to stay. His request wasn't a matter of security.

Sean shook his head. 'I can't grant it.'

Painter frowned. He had asked for an emergency pass to go to the site himself. To be on hand in Germany during the investigation. There might be clues others missed. His fingers curled into a fist in frustration.

'Logan can oversee things here,' Painter argued. 'I can be in constant communication with command.'

Sean's demeanor hardened. 'Painter, you *are* command now.'

'But –'

'You're no longer a field operative.'

The pain must have been evident in his expression.

Sean sighed. 'Do you know how many times I've sat in my office waiting to hear from you? How about your last operation in Oman? I thought you were dead.'

Painter glanced down to his desk. Binders and papers were piled everywhere. There was no relief to be found among them. He had never suspected how agonizing this job had been for his boss. Painter shook his head.

'There is only one way of handling matters like this,' his boss said. 'And believe me, they'll happen on a regular basis.'

Painter faced the screen. An ache had settled behind his breastbone, throbbing and hot.

'You have to trust your agents. You put them into the field, but once they're let loose, you have to have confidence. You picked the team leader for this op and his support. Do you trust they are capable of handling a hostile situation?'

Painter pictured Grayson Pierce, Monk Kokkalis, and Kat Bryant. They were some of the best and brightest in the force. If anyone could survive . . .

Painter slowly nodded. He did trust them.

'Then let them run their game. Like I did you. A horse runs best with only the lightest touch of the reins.' Sean leaned forward. 'All you can do now is wait for them to contact you. That is your responsibility to them. To be ready to respond. Not to run off to Germany.'

'I understand,' he said, but it didn't offer much solace. The ache continued inside his rib cage.

'Did you get that package I sent you last week?'

Painter glanced up, a half-smile forming. He had gotten a care package from his director. A crate of Tums antacids. He had thought it was a gag gift, but now he wasn't so sure.

Sean settled back into his chair. 'That's all the relief you'll ever get in this business.'

Painter recognized the truth in his mentor's words. Here was the true burden of leadership.

'It was easier in the field,' he finally mumbled.

'Not always,' Sean reminded him. 'Not always by a long shot.'


12:10 p.m.
MILAN, ITALY

Locked up tight,' Monk said. 'Just like the monsignor said.'

179

Gray could not argue. It all looked good. He itched to get inside, grab the bones, and head out of here.

They stood on a shaded sidewalk bordering the unassuming façade of the Basilica of Saint Eustorgio, near one of the side doors. The front was humble adorned red brick; behind it rose a single clock-tower steeple, surmounted by a cross. The tiny sun-baked square was empty for the moment.

A few minutes ago, a municipal patrol car had looped past, going slow, keeping watch. All seemed quiet.

Following Kat's recommendation, they had searched the entire church's periphery from a circumspect distance. Gray had also used a set of telescoping lenses to peer discreetly through several windows. The five side chapels and central nave appeared deserted.

Sunlight blazed off the pavement. The day had grown hot.

But Gray still felt cold, unsure.

Would he be less cautious if it were only himself?

'Let's do this,' he said.

Vigor stepped to the side door and reached for the large iron knocker, a ring containing a simple cross.

Gray stayed his hand. 'No. We've kept our approach quiet. Let's keep it that way.' He turned to Kat and pointed to the lock. 'Can you get it open?'

Kat dropped to a knee. Monk and Gray shielded her work with their bodies. While Kat studied the lock, her fingers fished through a lock-picking kit. With the meticulous skill of a surgeon, she set to work on the door's lock.

'Commander,' Vigor said. 'To violate a church . . .'

'If you were already invited entry by the Vatican, it's no violation.'

A snick of a latch ended the matter. The door opened an inch.

Kat gained her feet and shouldered her pack.

Gray waved the others back. 'Monk and I will go in alone. Scout the terrain.' He reached to his collar and secured an earpiece in place. 'Radio up while we have a chance. Kat, stay here with Rachel and Vigor.'

Gray taped on a throat mike for subvocalization.

Vigor stepped forward. 'Like I said before, priests are more likely to speak to someone wearing a collar. I'll go with you.'

Gray hesitated – but the monsignor made sense. 'Stay behind us at all times.'

Kat did not protest being left holding the door, but Rachel's eyes sparked fire.

'We need someone to cover our backs if things go south,' he explained, speaking directly to Rachel.

Her lips tightened, but she nodded.

Satisfied, he turned and opened the door enough to slip through. The dark foyer was cool. The doors to the nave were closed. He saw nothing amiss. The quiet of the sanctuary felt heavy, like being underwater.

Monk closed the outer door and flipped his long coat aside to rest a hand on his shotgun. Vigor obeyed his instructions and shadowed Monk.

Gray moved to the central door of the inner nave. He pushed it open with the palm of his hand. He had his Glock in the other.

The nave was brighter than the foyer, full of natural light from the basilica's windows. Its polished marble floor reflected the illumination, appearing almost wet. The basilica was much smaller than the cathedral in Cologne. Rather than cross-shaped, it was just a single long hall, a straight nave that ended at the altar.

Gray froze and watched for movement. Despite the ample light, there were plenty of places for people to hide. A line of pillars supported the arched roof. Five tiny chapels jetted out from the right wall, sheltering the tombs of martyrs and saints.

181

Nothing moved. The only noise was the distant rumble of traffic, sounding as if coming from another world.

Gray entered and moved down the center of the nave, pistol ready.

Monk stepped wide, positioning himself to keep the entire nave covered. They crossed the hall in silence. There was no sign of the church's staff.

'Perhaps they all went out for a late lunch,' Monk sub-vocalized into his radio.

'Kat, can you hear me?' Gray asked.

'Loud and clear, Commander.'

They reached the end of the nave.

Vigor pointed to the right, to the chapel closest to the altar.

Tucked into the chapel's corner, a gigantic sarcophagus lay half in shadow. Like the reliquary in Cologne, the Shrine of the Magi here was shaped like a church, but rather than gold and jewels, the sarcophagus had been carved out of a single block of Proconnesio marble.

Gray led the way toward it.

The shrine stood over twelve feet tall from its base to pitched roof and stretched seven feet wide by twelve long. The only access to the interior was through a small barred window low in the front face.

'*Finestra confessionis,*' Vigor whispered, pointing to the window. 'So one can observe the relics while kneeling.'

Gray approached. Monk stood guard. He still didn't like this situation. He bent and peered through the small window. Behind glass, a white silk-lined chamber opened.

The bones had been removed, just as the monsignor had described. The Vatican was taking no chances. And neither would he.

'The rectory is located off the church's left side,' Vigor said, a bit too loudly. 'That's where the offices and apartments are. It's connected through the sacristy.' He point-ed across the church.

182

As if responding to his signal, a door smacked open across the nave. Gray dropped to a knee. Monk yanked the monsignor behind a pillar, swinging up his shotgun.

A single figure strode out, oblivious of the intruders.

It was a young man dressed in black with a clerical collar.

A priest.

He was alone. He crossed and began lighting a set of candles on the far side of the altar.

Gray waited until the man was only two yards away. Still, no others appeared. Slowly he gained his feet, coming into view.

The priest froze when he spotted Gray, his arm half-raised in lighting another candle. His expression turned to shock when he spotted the pistol in Gray's hand. *'Chi sei?'*

Still, Gray hesitated.

Vigor stepped out of hiding. *'Padre . . .'*

The priest jumped, and his eyes flicked to the monsignor. He immediately noted the matching collar; confusion surpassed fear.

'I am Monsignor Verona,' Vigor introduced, stepping forward. 'Do not be afraid.'

'Monsignor Verona?' Worry etched the man's features. He backed a step.

'What's wrong?' Gray asked in Italian.

The priest shook his head. 'You can't be Monsignor Verona.'

Vigor stepped forward and showed him his Vatican ID.

The man glanced from it back to Vigor.

'But a . . . a man came here early this morning, just after dawn. A tall man. Very tall. With identification as Monsignor Verona. He bore papers with proper seals from the Vatican. To take the bones.'

Gray exchanged a look with the monsignor. They had already been outmaneuvered. Instead of brute force, the

Dragon Court had slipped in more slyly this time. By necessity. Because of the increased security. With the real Monsignor Verona believed dead, the Court had assumed his role. Like everything else, they must have known about Vigor's side mission here to collect the relics. They had used the intelligence to slip the last bones through the intensified security here.

Gray shook his head. They continued to be a step behind.

'Damn it,' Monk said.

The priest frowned at him. Clearly he understood enough English to find affront at the man's language in a house of God.

'*Scusi,*' Monk responded.

Gray understood Monk's frustration, doubly so as mission leader. He bit back his own curse. They had moved too slowly, played too cautiously.

His radio buzzed.

Kat came on the line. She must have overheard enough of the conversation. 'Is it all clear, Commander?'

'Clear . . . and too late,' he answered back sourly.

Kat and Rachel joined them. Vigor introduced the others.

'So the bones are gone,' Rachel said.

The priest nodded. 'Monsignor Verona, if you'd like to see the paperwork, we have it in the safe in the sacristy. Maybe that would help.'

'We could check it for fingerprints,' Rachel said tiredly, the exhaustion finally hitting her. 'They may have been careless. Not expecting we'd be on their heels. It might flush out whoever betrayed us in the Vatican. It could be our only new lead.'

Gray nodded. 'Bag it up. We'll see what we can find here.'

Rachel and Monsignor Verona headed across the nave.

Gray turned away and strode over to the sarcophagus.

'Any ideas?' Monk asked.

'We still have the gray powder we collected from the golden reliquary,' he said. 'We'll regroup in the Vatican, alert everyone of what's happened, and test the powder more thoroughly.'

As the sacristy door closed, Gray knelt down by the tiny window again, wondering if praying would help. 'We should vacuum out the interior,' he said, struggling to remain clinical. 'See if we can confirm the presence of the amalgam powder here, too.'

He leaned closely, cocking his head, not sure what he was looking for. But he found it anyway. A mark on the silk-lined roof of the reliquary chamber. A red seal pressed into the white silk. A tiny curled dragon. The ink looked fresh . . . too fresh.

But it was not ink. . . .

Blood.

A warning left behind by the Dragon Lady.

Gray straightened, suddenly knowing the truth.

# 7

# ROLLING THE BONES

Once inside, the priest closed the door to the sacristy. It was the chamber where the clergy and altar boys robed themselves prior to Mass.

Rachel heard the lock click behind her.

She half turned and found a pistol leveled at her chest. Held in the hand of the priest. His eyes had gone as cold and hard as polished marble.

'Don't move,' he said firmly.

Rachel backed a step. Vigor slowly raised his hands.

To either side were closets hung with clerical garments and vestments, used daily by the priests to say Mass. A table held a row of silver chalices, haphazardly arranged for the same. A large gilded silver crucifix, mounted on a wrought-iron pole, leaned against one corner, meant to lead a processional.

The door on the opposite end of the sacristy opened.

A familiar bull of a man entered, filling the doorway. It was the man who attacked her in Cologne. He carried a long knife in one hand, the blade wet and bloody. He stepped into the room and used a blessed stole hanging in a closet to wipe it clean.

Rachel felt Vigor wince next to her.

The blood. The missing priests. Oh God . . .

The tall man no longer wore a monk's garb, but ordinary street clothes, charcoal khakis and a black T-shirt, over which he wore a dark suit jacket. He carried a pistol in a shoulder holster beneath it and wore a radio headset over one ear, the mike at his throat.

'So you both survived Cologne,' he said, his eyes traveling up and down Rachel's form, as if sizing up a prized calf at a country fair. 'How very fortunate. Now we can become better acquainted.'

He tipped his throat mike up and spoke into it. 'Clear the church.'

Behind her, Rachel heard doors slam open in the nave. Gray and the others would be caught off guard. She waited for a spate of gunfire or the blast of a grenade. But all she heard was the patter of boots on marble. The church remained silent.

The same must have been noted by their captor.

'Report,' he ordered into his mike.

Rachel did not hear the reply, but she knew from the darkening of his face that the news was not good.

He shoved forward, passing between Vigor and Rachel.

'Watch them,' he growled to the fake priest. A second gunman had taken up post by the back exit to the sacristy.

Their captor yanked open the door to the nave. An armed figure strode over to him, accompanied by the Eurasian woman, holding her Sig Sauer pistol at her side.

'No one's here,' the man reported.

Rachel spotted other gunmen searching the main nave and side chapels.

'All exits have been guarded.'

'Yes, sir.'

'At all times.'

'Yes, sir.'

The giant's eyes settled on the Asian woman.

She shrugged. 'They might have found an open window.'

With a grumble, he cast a final search around the basilica, then swung around with a sweep of his suit jacket. 'Keep searching. Send three men to canvass the outside.

187

They can't have gotten far.'

As the giant turned, Rachel made her move.

Reaching behind her, she snatched the ceremonial pole with the silver crucifix and rammed its butt end square into the man's solar plexus. He grunted and fell back into the priest. She yanked the pole back, under her elbow, and slammed the cross end into the gunman's face behind her.

His pistol blasted, but the shot went wild as he fell back out the door.

Rachel followed him, tumbling out the back exit into a narrow hallway, her uncle on her heels. She slammed the door and propped the pole against it, jamming it against the hallway's far wall.

Beside her, Uncle Vigor smashed a heel on the fallen gunman's hand. Bones cracked. He then kicked the man square in the face. His head bounced against the stone floor with a thud, then his form went slack.

Rachel bent down and grabbed his pistol.

Crouched, she searched both ways down the windowless hall. No other men were about. The additional forces must have been placed to ambush Gray and his team. A large crash rattled the door in its frame. The Bull was trying to break through.

She dropped flat to the floor and searched beneath the jam. She watched the play of light and shadow. She aimed for darkness and fired.

The bullet sparked off the marble floor, but she heard a satisfying bellow of surprise. A little hotfoot should slow the Bull.

She rolled to her feet. Uncle Vigor had crossed down the hall a few steps.

'I hear someone groaning,' he whispered. 'Back here.'

'We don't have time.'

Ignoring her, Uncle Vigor continued deeper. Rachel followed. Without a frame of reference, one way was no worse than the other. They reached a door cracked open. Rachel heard a moan from inside.

She shouldered in, gun ready.

The room had once been a small dining hall. But now it was a slaughterhouse. One priest lay facedown in a pool of blood on the floor, the back of his head a pulp of brain, bone, and hair. Another black-robed figure lay sprawled on one of the tables, spread-eagled, tied to the bench legs. An older priest. His robes had been stripped to the waist. His chest was a pool of blood. His head was missing both ears. There was also the smell of burned flesh.

Tortured.

To death.

A sobbing moan sounded to the left. On the floor, tied hand and foot, was a young man, stripped to boxer shorts, gagged. He had a black eye and blood dribbled from both nostrils. From his half-naked form, it was plain where the clerical garb for the fake priest had come from.

Vigor came around the table. When the man spotted him, he struggled, eyes wild, frothing around his gag.

Rachel held back.

'It's all right,' Vigor soothed.

The man's eyes fixed on Vigor's collar. He stopped struggling, but he was still wracked with sobs. Vigor reached out to free the gag. The man shook and spat it out. Tears flowed down his cheeks.

'*Molti . . . grazie,*' he said, his voice weak with shock.

Vigor cut the plastic ties with a knife.

As he worked, Rachel locked the door to the dining room and jammed a chair under the knob for good measure. There were no windows, only a door leading deeper into the rectory. She kept her gun pointed that way and crossed to a phone on the wall. No dial tone. The phone lines had been cut.

She fished out Gray's cell phone and dialed 112, the

universal EU emergency number. Once connected, she identified herself as a Carabinieri lieutenant, though she didn't give her name, and called for an immediate medical, police, and military response.

With the alarm raised, she pocketed her phone.

Outgunned, it was all she could do.

For herself . . . and for the others.


12:45 p.m.

Footsteps approached Gray's hiding place. He held perfectly still, not breathing. The steps stopped nearby. He strained to listen.

A man spoke. A familiar voice, angry. It was the leader of the monks. 'The Milan authorities have been alerted.'

There was no reply, but Gray was certain two people had approached.

'Seichan?' the man asked. 'Did you hear me?'

A bored voice answered. It was equally recognizable. The Dragon Lady. But now she had a name. *Seichan.*

'They must have gone out a window, Raoul,' she said, returning the favor and naming the leader. 'Sigma is slippery. I warned you as much. We've secured the remaining bones. We should be gone before Sigma returns with reinforcements. The police may already be on the way.'

'But that bitch . . .'

'You can settle matters with her later.'

The footsteps departed. It sounded like the heavier of the two was limping. Still, the Dragon Lady's words remained with Gray.

*You can settle matters with her later.*

Did that mean Rachel had escaped?

Gray was surprised at the depth of his relief.

A door slammed on the far side of the church. As the sound echoed away, Gray strained his ears. He heard no more footsteps, no tread of boots, no voices.

To be cautious, he waited a full minute longer.

With the church silent, he nudged Monk, who lay spooned next to him. Kat lay scrunched on Monk's other side. They rolled with a sickening crunch of desiccated bone and reached overhead. Together they shifted the stone lid to the sepulcher.

Light spilled into the tomb, their makeshift bunker.

After spotting the Dragon Lady's warning in blood, Gray had known they'd been ensnared. All exit doors would be guarded. And with Rachel and her uncle vanished into the sacristy, there was nothing he could do to help.

So Gray had led the others into the neighboring chapel, to where a massive marble sepulcher rested on twisted Gothic columns. They had shifted its lid enough to climb inside, then pulled the lid back over them just as doors crashed open all across the church.

With the search ended, Monk climbed out, shotgun in hand, and shook his body with a disgusted grumble. Bone dust shivered from his clothes. 'Let's not do that again.'

Gray kept his pistol ready.

He saw an object on the marble floor, a few steps away from where they had been hidden. A copper coin. Easy to miss. He picked it up. It was a Chinese *fen*, or penny.

'What is it?' Monk asked.

He closed his fingers over it and stood, pocketing it. 'Nothing. Let's go.'

He headed across the nave toward the sacristy, but he glanced back to the crypt. Seichan had known.

12:48 p.m.

Rachel kept guard as Vigor helped the priest stand.

'They . . . they killed everyone,' the young man said. He needed Vigor's arm to keep his feet. The man's eyes avoided the bloody figure on the table. He covered his

191

face with one hand and groaned. 'Father Belcarro . . .'

'What happened?' Vigor asked.

'They came an hour ago. They had papal seals and papers, identification. But Father Belcarro had a faxed picture.' The priest's eyes widened. 'Of you. From the Vatican. Father Belcarro knew the lie immediately. But by that time, the monsters were already here. The phone lines were severed. We were locked inside, cut off. They wanted the combination to Father Belcarro's safe.'

The man turned from the bloody form, guiltily. 'They tortured him. He would not speak. But they did worse things then . . . so much worse. They made me watch.'

The young priest grabbed her uncle's elbow. 'I couldn't let it continue. I . . . I told them.'

'And they took the bones from the safe?'

The priest nodded.

'Then all is lost,' Vigor said.

'Still, they wanted to be sure,' the priest continued, seemingly deaf, babbling on. He glanced to the tortured figure, knowing he had been destined to share the same fate. 'Then you arrived. They stripped me, gagged me.'

Rachel pictured the fake priest who had worn the man's cassock. The subterfuge must have been devised to lure Rachel and Kat off the street and into the church.

The priest stumbled to the body of Father Belcarro. He folded back the older man's robe, covering the mutilated face as if hiding his own shame. Then the priest reached into a pocket of the bloody robe. He pulled out a pack of cigarettes. It seemed the elderly father had not shed all his vices . . . nor had the young priest.

Fingers shaking, the man peeled back the top and shook out the contents. Six cigarettes – and a broken stub of chalk. The man dropped the cigarettes and held out the ochre bit.

Vigor took it.

Not chalk. Bone.

'Father Belcarro feared sending away all the holy relics,' the young priest explained. 'In case something happened. So he kept a bit aside. For the church.'

Rachel wondered how much of this subterfuge was motivated by a selfless desire to preserve the relics and how much was due to pride, and the memory of the last time the bones had been stolen from Milan. Carted off to Cologne. Much of the basilica's fame was centered on those few bones. But either way, Father Belcarro had died a martyr. Tortured while hiding the holy relic on his own body.

A loud blast made them all jump.

The priest fell back to the floor.

But Rachel recognized the gauge of the weapon.

'Monk's shotgun . . .' she said, eyes widening with hope.


2:04 p.m.

Gray reached through the smoking hole in the sacristy door.

Monk shouldered the shotgun. 'I'm really going to owe the Catholic Church a month's salary for carpentry repair.'

Gray shoved aside the pole blocking the way and opened the door. After the shotgun blast, there was no further need for subterfuge. 'Rachel! Vigor!' he called as he entered the rectory hall.

A scuffle sounded from down the hall. A door opened. Rachel stepped out, pistol in hand. 'Over here!' she urged.

Uncle Vigor led a half-naked man out into the hallway. The man looked pale and haunted, but he seemed to gain strength from their presence.

Or maybe it was the sound of the approaching sirens.

'Father Justin Mennelli,' Vigor said in introduction.

They quickly compared notes.

'So we have one of the bones,' Gray said, surprised.

'I suggest we get the relic back to Rome as soon as possible,' Vigor said. 'They don't know we have it, and I want to be behind the Leonine Walls of the Vatican before they do.'

Rachel nodded. 'Father Mennelli will let the authorities know what happened here. He'll leave out the details of our presence – and of course, about the relic we have.'

'There's an ETR train leaving for Rome in ten minutes.' Vigor checked his watch. 'We can be in Rome by six o'clock.'

Gray nodded. The more under-the-radar they operated, the better. 'Let's go.'

They headed out. Father Mennelli led them to a side exit not far from where they had parked. Rachel climbed into the driver's seat as usual. They sped off as sirens converged.

As Gray settled back, he fingered the Chinese coin in his pocket. He sensed he had missed something.

Something important.

But what?


3:39 p.m.

An hour later, Rachel crossed from the bathroom to the first-class compartment in the ETR 500 train. Kat accompanied her. It was decided no one would leave the group by themselves. Rachel had wet her face, combed her hair, and brushed her teeth while Kat waited outside the door.

After the horrors in Milan, she had needed a personal moment in the cubicle. For a full minute, she had simply stared at herself in the mirror, teetering between fury and a need to cry. Neither won out, so she had washed her face.

It was all she could do.

But it did make her feel better, a private absolution.

As she strode down the hall, she barely felt the tremble

194

of the tracks under her heels. The Elettro Treno Rapido was Italy's newest and fastest train, connecting a corridor from Milan to Naples. It traveled at a blistering three hundred kilometers per hour.

'So, what's the story on your commander?' Rachel asked Kat, taking advantage of the time alone with the woman. Also, it felt good to talk about a subject outside of murder and bones.

'What do you mean?' Kat did not even look over.

'Is he involved with anyone back home? A girlfriend maybe?'

This question earned a glance. 'I don't see how his personal life –'

'What about you and Monk?' Rachel said, cutting her off, realizing how her original question sounded. 'With *all* your professions, do you have time for personal lives? What about the risks?'

Rachel was curious how these people balanced their regular lives with all the cloak-and-dagger. She had a hard enough time finding a man who could handle her position as a lieutenant in the Carabinieri Force.

Kat sighed. 'It's best not to get too involved,' she said. Her fingers had wandered to a tiny enameled frog pinned to her collar. Her voice grew stiffer, but it sounded more like bolstering than true strength. 'You form friendships where you can, but you shouldn't let it go any further. It's easier that way.'

Easier for whom? Rachel wondered.

She let the matter drop as they reached their compartments. The team had booked two cabins. One was a sleeping compartment to allow them to take short cat-naps in shifts. But no one was sleeping yet. Everyone had gathered in the other cabin, seated on either side of a table. The shades had been drawn across the windows.

Rachel slid in next to her uncle, Kat next to her team-mates.

195

Gray had unboxed an assortment of compact analyzing equipment from his backpack and wired it to a laptop. Other tools were neatly aligned in front of him. In the center of the table, resting on a stainless steel sample tray, was the relic from one of the Magi.

'It was lucky that this bit of finger bone escaped their net,' Monk said.

'Luck had nothing to do with it,' Rachel bristled. 'It cost good men their lives. If we hadn't come when we did, I suspect we would've lost this bit of bone, too.'

'Luck or not,' Gray grumbled, 'we have the artifact. Let's see if it can solve any mysteries for us.'

He slipped on a pair of glasses outfitted with a jeweler's magnifying loupe and donned a pair of latex gloves. With a tiny trepanning drill, he cored a thin sliver through the center of the bone, then used a mortar and pestle to grind the sample to a powder.

Rachel watched his meticulous work. Here was the scientist in the soldier. She studied the movements of his fingers, efficient, no wasted effort. His eyes focused fully on the task at hand. Two perfectly parallel lines furrowed his brow, never relaxing. He breathed through his nose.

She had never imagined this side of him, the man who leapt between fiery towers. Rachel had a sudden urge to tip his chin up, to have him look at her with that same intensity and focus. What would that be like? She pictured the depth of his blue-gray eyes. She remembered his touch, his hand in hers, both strength and tenderness, somehow at the same time.

Warmth swelled through her. She felt her cheeks flush and had to glance away.

Kat stared up at her, expressionless but still somehow making her feel guilty, her words too fresh. *It's best not to get too involved. It's easier that way.*

Maybe the woman was right. . . .

'With this mass spectrometer,' Gray finally mumbled,

drawing back her attention, 'we can determine if any of the m-state metal is in the bones. Attempt to rule out, or in, the possibility that the Magi bones were the source of the powder found in the gold reliquary.'

Gray mixed the powder with distilled water, then sucked the silty liquid into a pipette and transferred it to a test tube. He inserted the sample tube into the compact spectrometer. He prepared a second test tube of pure distilled water and held it up.

'This is a standard to calibrate,' he explained, and placed the tube into another slot. He pressed a green button and turned the laptop screen toward the group so all could see. A graph appeared on the screen with a flat line across it. A few tiny barbs jittered the straight line. 'This is water. The intermittent spikes are a few trace impurities. Even distilled water is not a hundred percent pure.'

Next, he switched a dial so it pointed to the slot with the silty sample. He pressed the green button. 'Here is the breakdown of the pulverized bone.'

The graph on the screen cleared and refreshed with the new data.

It looked identical.

'It hasn't changed,' Rachel said.

With his brow pinched, Gray repeated the test, even taking out the tube and shaking it up. The result was the same each time. A flat line.

'It's still reading like distilled water,' Kat said.

'It shouldn't,' Monk said. 'Even if the old magi had osteoporosis, the calcium in the bone should be spiking through the roof. Not to mention carbon and a handful of other elements.'

Gray nodded, conceding. 'Kat, do you have some of that cyanide solution?'

She swung to her pack, fished through it, and came up with a tiny vial.

Gray soaked a cotton-tipped swab, then pinched the

bone between his gloved fingers. He rubbed the wet swab across the bone, pressing firmly, rubbing as if he were polishing silver.

But it was not silver.

Where he rubbed, the brownish-yellow bone turned a rich gold.

Gray glanced up at the group. 'This isn't bone.'

Rachel could not keep the awe and shock from her voice. 'It's solid gold.'


5:12 p.m.

Gray spent half the train trip disproving Rachel's statement. There was more than just gold in these bones. Also it wasn't heavy *metallic* gold, but that strange gold glass again. He attempted to backward engineer the exact composition.

While he worked, he also grappled another problem. Milan. He went over and over again the events at the basilica. He had walked his team into a trap. He could forgive last night's ambush up in Germany. They had been caught with their pants down. No one could have anticipated such a savage attack at the cathedral in Cologne.

But the close call in Milan could not be so easily dismissed. They had gone into the basilica prepared – but still came close to losing everything, including their lives.

So where did the fault lie?

Gray knew the answer. He had fucked up. He should never have stopped at Lake Como. He should not have listened to Kat's words of caution and wasted so much time canvassing the basilica, exposing themselves, giving the Court time to spot them and prepare a trap.

Kat was not to blame. Caution was part and parcel of intelligence work. But fieldwork also required swift and certain action, not hesitation.

198

Especially in its leader.

Up until now, Gray had been going by the book, staying overly cautious, being the leader that was expected of him. But maybe that was the mistake. Hesitation and second-guessing were not Pierce family traits. Not in the father, not in the son. But where was the line between caution and foolhardiness? Could he ever achieve *that* balance?

Success on this mission – and possibly their lives – would depend on it.

Finished with his analysis, Gray leaned back. He had blistered his thumb, and the cabin reeked of methyl alcohol. 'It's not pure gold,' he concluded.

The others glanced to him. Two were working, two drowsing.

'The fake bone is a mixture of elements across the platinum group,' Gray explained. 'Whoever crafted this, they mixed a powdery amalgam of various transitional metals and melted it down to glass. As it cooled, they molded the glass and roughed up the surfaces to a chalky complexion, making it *appear* like bone.'

Gray began putting away his tools. 'It's predominantly composed of gold, but there's also a large percentage of platinum and smaller amounts of iridium and rhodium, even osmium and palladium.'

'A regular potpourri,' Monk said with a yawn.

'But a potpourri whose exact recipe may be forever unknown,' Gray said, frowning at the abused piece of bone. He had preserved three-quarters of the artifact untouched and put the remaining quarter through the battery of tests. 'With the m-state powder's stubborn lack of reactivity, I don't think any analyzing equipment could tell you the exact ratio of metals. Even testing alters the ratio in the sample.'

'Like the Heisenberg Uncertainty Principle,' Kat said, feet up on the opposite bench, her laptop on her thighs.

She tapped as she spoke. 'Even the act of looking changes the reality of what's being observed.'

'So if it can't be completely tested –' Monk's words were cut off by another jaw-popping yawn.

Gray patted Monk on the shoulder. 'We'll be in Rome in another hour. Why don't you catch some sleep in the next room?'

'I'm fine,' he said, stifling another yawn.

'That's an order.'

Monk stood with a long stretch. 'Well, if it's an order . . .' He rubbed his eyes and headed out the door.

But he paused in the doorway. 'You know,' he said bleary-eyed, 'maybe they had it all wrong. Maybe history misinterpreted the words *the Magi's bones*. Rather than referring to the skeleton of those guys, maybe it meant the bones were *made* by the Magi. Like it was their property. The Magi's bones.'

Everyone stared at him.

Under the combined scrutiny, Monk shrugged and half fell out the door. 'Hell, what do I know? I can hardly think straight.' The door closed.

'Your teammate might not be so far off base,' Vigor said as silence settled around the cabin.

Rachel stirred. Gray glanced up. Until the recent exchange, Rachel had been leaning against her uncle and had napped for a short while. Gray had watched her breathing from the corner of his eye. In slumber, all hard edges softened in the woman. She seemed much younger.

She stretched one arm in the air. 'What do you mean?'

Vigor worked on Monk's laptop. Like Kat, he was connected to the DSL line built into the new train's first-class cabins. They were searching for more information. Kat concentrated on the science behind the white gold, while Vigor searched for more history connecting the Magi to this amalgam.

The monsignor's eyes remained on his screen. 'Some-body forged those fake bones. Somebody with a skill barely reproducible today. But who did it? And why hide them in the heart of a Catholic cathedral?'

'Could it be someone connected to the Dragon Court?' Rachel asked. 'Their group traces back to the Middle Ages.'

'Or someone within the Church itself?' Kat said.

'No,' Vigor said firmly. 'I think there is a third group involved here. A brotherhood that's existed before either group.'

'How can you be certain?' Gray asked.

'In 1982, some of the Magi burial cloths were tested. They dated to the second century. Well before the Dragon Court was founded. Before even Queen Helena, mother of Constantine, discovered the bones somewhere in the East.'

'And no one tested the bones?'

Vigor glanced to Gray. 'The Church forbade it.'

'Why?'

'It takes a special papal dispensation to allow bones to be tested, especially relics. And the relics of the Magi would require extraordinary dispensation.'

Rachel explained, 'The Church doesn't want its most precious treasures to be ruled fake.'

Vigor frowned at Rachel. 'The Church places much weight on faith. The world certainly could use more of it.'

She shrugged, closed her eyes, and settled back down.

'So if not the Church or the Court, who forged the bones?' Gray asked.

'I think your friend Monk was correct. I think an ancient fraternity of mages fabricated them. A group that may predate Christianity, possibly going back to Egyptian times.'

'Egyptians?'

Vigor clicked the mouse on his laptop, bringing up a

file. 'Listen to this. In 1450 B.C., Pharaoh Tuthmosis III united his best master craftsmen into a thirty-nine-member group called the Great White Brotherhood – named from their study of a mysterious *white* powder. The powder was described as forged from gold, but shaped into pyramidal cakes, called "white bread." The cakes are depicted at the temple of Karnak as tiny pyramids, sometimes with rays of light radiating out.'

'What did they do with them?' Gray asked.

'They were prepared only for the pharaohs. To be consumed. Supposedly to increase their powers of perception.'

Kat sat straighter, lowering her feet from the opposite bench.

Gray turned to her. 'What is it?'

'I've been reading some of the properties of high-spin-state metals. Specifically gold and platinum. Exposure through ingestion can stimulate endocrine systems, creating heightened senses of awareness. Remember the articles on superconductors?'

Gray nodded. High-spin atoms acted as perfect superconductors.

'The U.S. Naval Research Facility has confirmed that communication between brain cells cannot be explained by pure chemical transmission across synapses. Brain cells communicate too quickly. They've concluded that some form of superconductivity is involved, but the mechanism is still under study.'

Gray frowned. He had, of course, studied superconductivity in his doctoral program. Leading physicists believed the field would lead to the next major breakthroughs in global technologies, with applications across the board. Also, from his dual degree in biology, he was well familiar with the current theories on thought, memory, and the organic brain. But what did any of this have to do with white gold?

Kat leaned toward her laptop. She tapped up another article. 'Here. I did a search for platinum-group metals and their uses. And I found an article about calf and pig brains. A metal analysis of mammalian brains shows that four to five percent of the dry weight is rhodium and iridium.' She nodded to the sample on Gray's table. 'Rhodium and iridium in their monatomic state.'

'And you think these m-state elements might be the source of the brain's superconductivity? Its communication pathway? That the pharaohs' consumption of these powders juiced it up?'

Kat shrugged. 'Hard to say. The study of superconductivity is still in its infancy.'

'Yet the Egyptians knew about it,' Gray scoffed.

'No,' Vigor countered. 'But perhaps they learned some way of tapping into it by trial and error or by accident. However it came about, this interest and experimentation with these white powders of gold appears throughout history, passed from one civilization to the next, growing stronger.'

'How far forward can you trace it?'

'Right back to there.' Vigor pointed to the artifact on Gray's table.

Gray's interest piqued. 'Really?'

Vigor nodded, up for the challenge. 'As I said, we start first in Egypt. This white powder went by many names. The "white bread" I mentioned, but also "white nourishment" and "mfkzt." But its oldest name can be found in the Egyptian *Book of the Dead*. The substance is named hundreds of times along with its amazing properties. It is simply called "what is it."'

Gray remembered the monsignor stumbling on those same words earlier, when they first turned the powder into glass.

'But in Hebrew,' Vigor went on, '"what is it" translates to *Ma Na*.'

'Manna,' Kat said.

Vigor nodded. 'The Holy Bread of the Israelites. According to the Old Testament, it fell down from the heavens to feed the starving refugees fleeing Egypt, led by Moses.' The monsignor let that sink in and fiddled with his gathered files. 'While in Egypt, Moses showed such wisdom and skill that he was considered a potential successor to the Egyptian throne. Such esteem would entitle him to participate in the deepest level of Egyptian mysticism.'

'Are you saying Moses stole the secret to make this powder? The Egyptian white bread?'

'In the Bible, it went by many names. Manna. Holy Bread. Shrewbread. Bread of Presence. It was so precious that it was stored in the Arc of the Covenant, alongside the tablets bearing the Ten Commandments. All stored in a *golden* box.'

Gray did not miss the suggestive lift of the monsignor's eyebrow, emphasizing the parallel to the Magi's bones being preserved in a golden reliquary. 'It seems a stretch,' Gray mumbled. 'The name "manna" might just be a coincidence.'

'When was the last time you read the Bible?'

Gray didn't bother answering.

'There are many things that have perplexed historians and theologians in regards to this mysterious manna. The Bible describes how Moses set fire to the golden calf. But rather than melting into a molten slag, the gold burned down to a powder . . . which Moses then *fed* to the Israelites.'

Gray's brows pinched. Like the pharaoh's white bread.

'Also, who does Moses ask to make this Holy Bread, this manna from heaven? In the Bible, he doesn't ask a baker to prepare it. He asks Bezalel.'

Gray waited for an explanation. He was not current on his biblical names.

'Bezalel was the Israelites' *goldsmith*. He was the same

person who constructed the Arc of the Covenant. Why ask a goldsmith to bake bread unless it was something other than bread?'

Gray frowned. Could it be true?

'There are also texts from the Jewish Kabbalah that speak directly of a white powder of gold, declaring it magical, but a magic that could be used for good or evil.'

'So what became of this knowledge?' Gray asked.

'According to most Jewish sources, it was lost when the Temple of Solomon was destroyed by Nebuchadnezzar in the sixth century B.C.'

'Where did it go after that?'

'To find hints of it, we skip forward two centuries, to another famous figure in history, who also spent much of his life in Babylon, studying with scientists and mystics.' Vigor paused for emphasis. 'Alexander the Great.'

Gray sat straighter. 'The Macedonian king?'

'Alexander conquered Egypt in 332 B.C., along with a vast part of the world. The man was always interested in esoteric knowledge. Throughout his conquests, he sent Aristotle scientific gifts from around the world. He also collected a series of Heliopolitan scrolls, concerning Old Egypt's secret knowledge and magic. His successor, Ptolemy I, gathered these into the Library of Alexandria after his death. But one Alexandrian text tells a story about an object called the Paradise Stone. It was said to have mystical properties. When solid, it could surpass its own weight in gold, yet when crushed into a *powder,* it weighed less than a feather and could float.'

'Levitation,' Kat said, interrupting.

Gray turned to her.

'Such a property of superconducting material is well documented. Superconductors will float in strong magnetic fields. Even these m-state powders demonstrate superconducting levitation. In 1984, laboratory tests in both Arizona and Texas showed that rapid cooling of monatomic powders could raise their tested weight four-fold. Yet if heated again, the weight vanished to less than zero.'

'What do you mean, *less* than zero?'

'The pan weighed more *without* the substance on it, as if the pan were levitating.'

'The Paradise Stone rediscovered,' Vigor declared.

Gray began to sense the truth. A secret knowledge passed down through the generations. 'Where does the powdery trail lead next?'

'To the time of Christ,' Vigor answered. 'In the New Testament, there continue to be hints of a mysterious gold. From Revelations, chapter two: "Blessed be the man who will overcome for he shall be given the hidden manna, the white stone of the purest kind." Also the Book of Revelations describes the houses of New Jerusalem as being constructed of "gold so pure as to appear like transparent glass."'

Gray remembered Vigor mumbling that verse when the puddle of molten glass had hardened on the cathedral floor back in Cologne.

'Tell me,' Vigor continued, 'when does gold ever appear like glass? It makes no sense unless you consider the possibility of m-state gold . . . this "purest of all golds" described in the Bible.'

Vigor pointed to the table. 'Which brings us back to the biblical Magi. To a tale related by Marco Polo out of Persia. It tells the story of the Magi receiving a gift from the Christ child, and this is probably allegorical, but I think it's important. Christ gave the Magi a dull white stone, a Holy Stone. The story goes that it represented a call to the Magi to remain firm in their faith. During their journey home, the stone burst forth with fire that could not be extinguished, an eternal flame, which often symbolizes higher enlightenment.'

Vigor must have noted Gray's confusion. He continued,

'In Mesopotamia, where this story arises, the term "high fire-stone" is called *shemanna*. Or shortened to just "fire-stone" . . . *manna*.'

Vigor leaned back and crossed his arms.

Gray slowly nodded. 'So we've come full circle. Back to the manna and the biblical Magi.'

'Back to the age when the bones were crafted,' Vigor said with a nod to the table.

'And does it stop there?' Gray asked.

Vigor shook his head. 'I need to do more research, but I think it continues beyond this point. I think what I've just described is not isolated rediscoveries of this powder, but an unbroken chain of research conducted by a secret alchemical society that has been purifying this process throughout the ages. I think the mainstream scientific community is only now beginning to discover it anew.'

Gray turned to Kat, their scientific web crawler.

'The monsignor is right. There are incredible discoveries being made about these m-state superconductors. From levitation to the possibility of trans-dimensional shifting. But more-practical applications are being explored right now. Cis-platinum and carbono-platinum are already being used to treat testicular and ovarian cancers. I expect Monk, with his forensic training, could go into more detail. But there are even more intriguing discoveries just in the past few years.'

Gray motioned her to continue.

'Bristol-Meyers Squibb has reported success with monatomic ruthenium to correct cancer cells. Same with platinum and iridium, according to *Platinum Metals Review*. These atoms actually make the DNA strand correct itself, rebuilding without drugs or radiation. Iridium has been shown to stimulate the pineal gland and appears to fire up "junk DNA," leading to the possibility of increased longevity and reopening aging pathways in the brain.'

Kat leaned forward. 'Here's one from August 2004. Purdue University reports success in using rhodium to kill viruses with light from *inside* a body. Even West Nile virus.'

'Light?' Vigor asked, his eyes narrowing.

Gray glanced to him, noting the monsignor's intensified interest.

Kat nodded. 'There are a slew of articles about these m-state atoms and light. From turning DNA into superconducting strands . . . to light-wave communication between cells . . . to tapping into zero field energies.'

Rachel finally spoke up. She still kept her eyes closed. She'd been listening all along, eavesdropping. 'It makes one wonder.'

'What?' Gray turned to her.

She slowly opened her eyes. They were bright and alert. 'Here scientists are now talking about heightening awareness, levitation, transmutation, miraculous healing, anti-aging. It sounds like a list of miracles from biblical times. It makes me wonder why so many miracles happened back then, but not now. In the past few centuries, we're lucky to see an image of the Virgin Mary on a tortilla. Yet now, *science* is rediscovering these larger miracles. And much of it traces back to a white powder, a substance known better back then than today. Could such secret knowledge have been the source for the epidemic of miracles back in biblical times?'

Gray pondered this, meeting her gaze. 'And if these ancient magi knew more than we know now,' he extrapolated, 'what has this lost fraternity of wise men done with this knowledge, to what level have they refined it?'

Rachel continued the thread. 'Maybe that's what the Dragon Court is after! Maybe they found some clue, something tied to the bones that could lead them to whatever this purified end product might be. Some final plateau reached by the mages.'

'And along the way, the Court learned that murderous trick back in Cologne, a way to use the powder to kill.' He remembered the monsignor's words about the Jewish Kabbalah, that the white powder could be used for good or ill.

Rachel's face sobered. 'If they should attain even greater power, gaining access to the inner sanctum of these ancient wise men, they could change the world, remake it in their own sick image.'

Gray stared around at the others. Kat wore a calculating expression. Vigor seemed lost in his own thoughts, but the monsignor noted the sudden silence.

His eyes focused back on them.

Gray faced him. 'What do you think?'

'I think we have to stop them. But to do that, we're going to have to search for clues to these ancient alchemists. That means following in the footsteps of the Dragon Court.'

Gray shook his head. He recalled his concern that they were proceeding too cautiously, too timidly. 'I'm done following the bastards. We need to *pass* them. Let them eat our dust for a change.'

'But where do we begin?' Rachel asked.

Before anyone could answer, a programmed announcement came over the train's intercom.

'*Roma . . . Stazione Termini . . . quindici minuti!*'

Gray checked his watch. Fifteen minutes.

Rachel was staring at him.

'*Benvenuto a Roma,*' she said as he looked up. '*Lasci i giochi cominciare!*'

Gray translated, a ghost of a smile forming. It was as if she read his mind. *Welcome to Rome. . . . Let the games begin!*

Seichan slipped on a pair of black and silver Versace sunglasses.

When in Rome . . .

She stepped out onto Piazza Pia from the express bus. She wore a breezy white summer dress and nothing else except for a pair of stiletto-heeled Harley-Davidson boots with silver buckles, a match to her necklace.

The bus pulled away. Behind her, cars jammed the road, a honking, belching line of traffic, headed down Via della Conciliazone. The heat and reek of petrol struck her simultaneously. She faced to the west. Down the street, St. Peter's Basilica rose, silhouetted against the setting sun. The dome shone like gold, a masterpiece of design by Michelangelo.

Unimpressed, Seichan turned her back on Vatican City. It was not her goal.

Before her stood a structure that rivaled the great St. Peter's. The massive drum-shaped building filled the skyline, a fortress overlooking the Tiber River. Castel Sant'Angelo. Atop its roof, a mammoth bronze statue of the Archangel Michael bore aloft an unsheathed sword. The sculpture blazed in the sun. The stone structure beneath was blackened soot, stained in rivulets, like a flow of black tears.

How fitting, Seichan thought.

The place had been built in the second century as a mausoleum to Emperor Hadrian, but shortly thereafter, it had been taken over by the papacy. Still, the castle had developed an illustrious and ignoble history. Under Vatican rule, it had served as a fortress, a prison, a library, even as a brothel. It had also been a secret rendezvous spot for some of the more notorious popes, who kept concubines and mistresses within its walls, often imprisoned there.

Seichan found it amusing to make her own rendezvous

here. She crossed the gardens to the entrance and passed through the twenty-foot-thick walls to enter the first floor. It was dark and cool inside. This late in the day, tourists were dribbling out. She headed in, climbing up the wide curved Roman steps.

Off the main staircase, the castle spread out in a warren of rooms and halls. Many visitors got lost.

But Seichan was only going up to the middle level, to a terrace restaurant that overlooked the Tiber. She was to meet her contact there. After the firebombing, it was deemed too risky to meet in the Vatican itself. So her contact was going to cross down the Passetto del Borgo, a covered passageway atop an old aqueduct that connected the Apostolic Palace to the castle fortress here. The secret passage had been originally constructed in the thirteenth century as an emergency escape route for the pope, but over the centuries, it was more often used for amorous trysts.

Though today, there was nothing romantic about this meeting.

Seichan followed the signs to the terrace café. She checked her watch. She was ten minutes early. Just as well. She had a call to make.

She slipped out her cell phone, pressed the scramble feature, and tapped in the speed-dial code. A private, unlisted number. She leaned on a hip, phone to her ear, and waited for the international connection to be made.

The line buzzed, clicked, and a firm, no-nonsense voice answered.

'Good afternoon. You've reached Sigma command.'

# 8

# CRYPTOGRAPHY

'I need pen and paper,' Gray said, his satellite phone in hand.

The group waited at a sidewalk trattoria across from Rome's central train station. Upon arriving, Rachel had called for a pair of Carabinieri vehicles to collect and escort the team to Vatican City. While they waited, Gray had decided it was time to break his silence with central command. He'd been passed immediately to Director Crowe.

After a short debriefing of events in Cologne and Milan, the director had his own surprising bit of news.

'Why would she call you?' Gray asked the director as Monk fished in his pack for pad and pen.

Painter answered, 'Seichan is playing our two groups off one another to further her own end. She is not even trying to hide it. The intel she passed to us was stolen from the Dragon Court's field operative, a man named Raoul.'

Gray scowled, remembering the man's handiwork back in Milan.

'I don't think she can decipher the intel on her own,' Painter continued. 'So she passed it to us – both to solve it for her and to keep you on the tail of the Court. She's no fool. Her skill at manipulation must be masterful to be picked by the Guild to oversee this assignment . . . plus

212

you two have a past. Despite her help in Cologne and Milan, don't trust her. She will eventually turn on you and attempt to even the score.'

Gray felt the weight of the metal coin in his pocket. He didn't need the warning. The woman was ice and steel.

'Okay,' Gray said as he had pen and paper in hand, holding the phone with his shoulder. 'I'm ready.'

As Painter passed on the message, Gray wrote it down.

'And it's broken into stanzas, like a poem?' Gray asked.

'Exactly.' The director continued reciting as Gray jotted each line.

Once finished, Painter said, 'I have codebreakers working on it here and at the NSA.'

Gray frowned at the pad. 'I'll see what I can make of it. Perhaps using some of the resources at the Vatican, we can make some headway here.'

'In the meantime, keep on your toes,' Painter warned. 'This Seichan character may be more dangerous than the entire Court.'

Gray didn't argue with this last statement. With a few final clarifications, he signed off and stored the phone away. The others looked on expectantly.

'What was that all about?' Monk asked.

'The Dragon Lady called Sigma. She passed on a mystery for us to solve. It seems she has no idea what the Court is going to do next, and while they prepare, she wants us to be nipping at their heels. So she leaked some archaic passage, something discovered two months ago by the Dragon Court in Egypt. Whatever its content, she says it initiated the current operation.'

Vigor stood up from one of the trattoria's outdoor tables. With a tiny espresso cup balanced in one hand, he leaned over to read the passage along with the others.

*When the full moon mates with the sun,*
*It is born eldest.*
                    *What is it?*

*Where it drowns,*
*It floats in darkness and stares to the lost king.*
                    *What is it?*

*The Twin waits for water,*
*But will be burned to bone by bone upon the altar.*
                    *What is it?*

'Oh, that helps,' Monk grumbled.

Kat shook her head. 'What does any of this have to do with the Dragon Court, high-spin metals, and some lost society of alchemists?'

Rachel glanced along the street. 'The scholars at the Vatican may be able to help. Cardinal Spera has promised his full support.'

Gray noted Vigor had only glanced once at the sheet of paper, then turned away. He sipped his espresso.

Gray had had enough of the man's silences. He was done with polite respect of each other's boundaries. If Vigor wanted to be on this team, it was high time he acted like it.

'You know something,' Gray accused.

The others turned to them.

'So should you,' Vigor answered.

'What do you mean?'

'I already described this back on the train.' Vigor turned and tapped a finger on the pad. 'The cadence of this passage should be familiar. I described a book with a similar pattern of text. The repetition of the phrase "what is it."'

Kat remembered first. 'From the Egyptian *Book of the Dead*.'

'The Papyrus of Ani, to be exact,' Vigor continued. 'It is broken into lines of cryptic description followed by the one line repeated over and over again: "what is it." '

'Or in Hebrew, *manna*,' Gray said, remembering.

Monk rubbed a hand over the stubble poking from his shaved scalp. 'But if this passage is from some well-known Egyptian book, why would it light a fire under the Court now?'

'The passages aren't from the *Book of the Dead*,' Vigor answered. 'I'm familiar enough with the Papyrus of Ani to know these passages are not found among the others.'

'Then where did they come from?' Rachel asked.

Vigor turned to Gray. 'You said the Dragon Court discovered this in Egypt . . . only months ago.'

'Exactly.'

Vigor turned to Rachel. 'I'm sure as a part of the Carabinieri TPC that you were informed of the recent chaos at the Egyptian Museum in Cairo. The museum sent out an alert through Interpol.'

Rachel nodded and explained to the others. 'Egypt's Supreme Council of Antiquities began a painstaking process in 2004 of emptying the basement to the Egyptian Museum, prior to renovation. But upon opening the basement, they discovered over a hundred thousand pharaonic and other artifacts among its maze of corridors, an archaeological dumping ground that was all but forgotten.'

'They estimate it will take five years to catalogue it all,' Vigor said. 'But as a professor of archaeology, I've heard tidbits of discoveries. There was an entire room of crumbling parchments that scholars suspect may have come from the lost Library of Alexandria, a major bastion of Gnostic study.'

Gray recalled Vigor's discussion about Gnosticism and the pursuit of secret knowledge. 'Such a discovery would surely attract the Dragon Court.'

'Like moths to flame,' Rachel said.

Vigor continued, 'One of the items catalogued came

215

from a collection of Abd el-Latif, an esteemed fifteenth-century Egyptian physician and explorer who lived in Cairo. In his collection, preserved in a bronze chest, was a fourteenth-century illuminated copy of the Egyptian *Book of the Dead,* a complete rendering of the Papyrus of Ani.' Vigor stared hard at Gray. 'It was stolen four months ago.'

Gray felt his pulse quicken. 'By the Dragon Court.'

'Or someone in their employ. They have fingers everywhere.'

'But if the book is just a bootleg of the original,' Monk said, 'what's the significance?'

'The Papyrus of Ani has hundreds of stanzas. I wager someone forged this copy and hid *these* specific stanzas' – Vigor tapped Gray's pad – 'among the more ancient ones.'

'Our lost alchemists,' Kat said.

'Hiding needles in a haystack,' Monk said.

Gray nodded. 'Until some scholar in the Dragon Court was wise enough to pick them out, decipher the clues, and act on it. But where does that leave us?'

Vigor turned to the street. 'You mentioned on the train a desire to catch up and pass the Dragon Court. Now is our chance.'

'How so?'

'We decipher the riddle.'

'But that could take days.'

Vigor glanced over his shoulder. 'Not if I've already solved it.'

He waved for the pad of paper and flipped to a new blank page. 'Let me show you.'

Then he did the oddest thing. He wet his finger in his espresso and dampened the bottom of his tiny cup. He pressed the cup upon the paper, leaving a perfect ring of coffee stain on the blank page. He repeated it again, applying a second ring, this one overlapping the first, forming roughly a snowman shape.

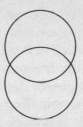

'The full moon mating with the sun.'

'What does this prove?' Gray asked.

'*Vesica Pisces*,' Rachel said, her face dawning with understanding.

Vigor grinned at her. 'Did I ever tell you how proud I am of my niece?'

7:02 p.m.

Rachel didn't like abandoning their Carabinieri escort, but she understood Uncle Vigor's excitement. Her uncle had insisted they take alternate transportation to investigate the new lead.

So she had called in to the station and recalled the patrol cars. She had left a cryptic message with General Rende that they all had an errand to run. This last was upon Gray's suggestion. He thought it best not to broadcast their destination. Not until they could investigate further.

The fewer people who knew of their discovery, the better.

So they sought alternate transportation.

Rachel followed Gray's broad back down to the rear of the public bus. Kat and Monk held a row of seats open. The air conditioning clanked, and the engine rattled the floorboards as the bus left the curb and shouldered into traffic.

Rachel climbed into a seat with Gray. Their row of seats faced Monk, Kat, and Uncle Vigor. Kat looked especially stern. She had argued for proceeding to the Vatican and securing an escort first. Gray had overruled her. She looked unsettled by this decision.

Rachel eyed Gray beside her. Some new resolve seemed to have hardened in him. It reminded her of his attitude atop the fiery spire in Cologne, a certainty of manner. His eyes shone with a determination that had disappeared after the first attack. It was back now . . . and it scared her slightly, made her heart beat faster.

The bus rumbled into traffic.

'Okay,' Gray said, 'I've taken you at your word that this side excursion is necessary. Now how about a bit of elaboration?'

Uncle Vigor raised a palm, conceding. 'If I had gone into detail, we would've missed our bus.'

He opened the pad again. 'This shape of overlapping circles can be seen throughout Christendom. In churches, cathedrals, and basilicas around the world. From this one shape, all of geometry flows. For example.' He turned the picture horizontal and shaded the lower half with the edge of his palm. He then pointed to the intersection of the two circles. 'Here you can see the geometric shape of the pointed arch. Almost all Gothic windows and archways bear this shape.'

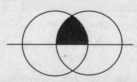

Rachel had been given the same lecture as a child. One couldn't be related to a Vatican archaeologist without knowing the importance of those two joined circles.

'It still looks like a couple of doughnuts smashed together to me,' Monk said.

Vigor righted the picture back around.

'Or like a full moon mating with the sun,' her uncle said, bringing up the stanza from the cryptic text. 'The more I consider those lines, the more layers I keep coming across, like peeling an onion.'

'What do you mean?' Gray asked.

'They buried this clue within the Egyptian *Book of the Dead*. The very first book to refer to *manna*. Later Egyptian texts begin to refer to it as 'white bread' and such. It's as if to find whatever the alchemists hid, you had to start at the beginning. Yet the very answer to this first clue also traces back to the first era of Christianity. Multiple beginnings. Even the answer itself implies multiplication. The one becoming many.'

Rachel understood what her uncle meant. 'The multiplication of the fishes.'

Vigor nodded.

'Is anyone going to explain it to us novices?' Monk asked.

'This conjoining of circles is called *Vesica Pisces,* or Vessel of the Fishes.' Vigor leaned down and shaded the intersection to reveal the fishlike shape rested between the two circles.

Gray peered closer. 'It's the fish symbol that represents Christianity.'

'It is the *first* symbol,' Vigor said. ' "When the full moon mates with the sun, it is born." ' Her uncle tapped the fish. 'Some scholars believe the fish symbol was used because the Greek for fish, *ICHTHYS,* was an acronym for *Iesous Christos Theou Yios Soter,* or Jesus Christ, the Son of God, the Savior. But the truth lies here, between these circles, locked in sacred geometry. You'll often find these locked circles in early paintings with the Christ child resting in the center junction. If you turn the form over on its side, the fish becomes a representation of female genitalia and a woman's womb, where the baby Jesus is painted.

'It is for this reason that the fish represents fertility. To be fruitful and multiply.' Vigor glanced around the group. 'As I said, there are layers upon layers of meaning here.'

Gray leaned back. 'But how does this lead us anywhere?'

Rachel was curious, too. 'There are fish symbols all over Rome.'

Vigor nodded. 'But the second line that reads, "It is born *eldest*." Plainly it's directing us to the oldest representation of the fish symbol. That would be found in the Crypt of Lucina in the Catacombs of Saint Callistus.'

'That's where we're heading?' Monk asked.

Vigor nodded.

Rachel noted Gray was not satisfied. 'What if you're wrong?' he asked.

'I'm not. The other stanzas in the text hint at it, too . . . once you solve the *Vesica Pisces* riddle. Look at the next line. "Where it drowns, it floats in darkness." A fish can't drown, not in water, but it can in earth. And the mention of darkness. It all points to a crypt.'

'But there are many crypts and catacombs throughout Rome.'

'But not many with *two* fishes, twins to each other,' Vigor said.

Gray's eyes brightened with understanding. 'Another clue, from the last stanza. "'The Twin waits for water."'

Vigor nodded. 'All three stanzas point to one place.

The Catacombs of Saint Callistus.'

Monk settled back to his seat. 'At least it's not a church this time. I'm tired of getting shot at.'

Vigor sensed they were on the right track.

Finally.

He guided the others through Porta San Sebastiano, one of the city wall's most striking gates. It also served as the gateway to the parklands that surrounded the Appian Way, a preserved section of the famous ancient Roman road. Immediately past the gates, however, stood a series of dilapidated mechanics' workshops.

Vigor dismissed the ugliness of these junkyards by directing attention ahead. At a fork in the road rose a small church. 'The Chapel of Domine Quo Vadis,' he said.

His only real audience was Kat Bryant. She strode alongside him. Kat and Gray seemed to have had a falling-out. The others followed behind. It was good to have this moment with Kat. It had been three years since they had shared a role in cataloguing evidence against a Nazi war criminal, living in rural New York. The target had been trading in stolen artwork in Brussels. It was a long, convoluted investigation, requiring subterfuge on both their parts. Vigor had been most impressed with the young woman's ability to slide into any role as easily as changing shoes.

He also knew the pain she had experienced recently. Though she was a good actress, hiding her feelings well, Vigor had spent enough time serving his flock as priest, confessor, and counselor to recognize someone still grieving. Kat had lost someone close to her heart and had not healed yet.

He pointed to the stone church, knowing there was a

message for Kat within those walls. 'The chapel here was built at the site where Saint Peter, fleeing the persecution of Nero, beheld a vision of Jesus. Christ was heading into Rome, while Peter was running out. He asked those famous words, *Domine, quo vadis*. "Lord, where are you going?" Christ replied he was heading back into Rome to be crucified again. Peter then turned back to face his own execution.'

'Ghost stories,' Kat said without malice. 'He should've run.'

'Ever the pragmatist, Kat. But you of all people should know that sometimes one's own life is less important than the cause. We all have a terminal disease. We can't escape death. But as the good works in our life celebrate our time here, so too can our deaths. To lay one's life down in sacrifice should be honored and remembered.'

Kat glanced to him. She was sharp enough to understand the tack of the conversation.

'Sacrifice is a final gift we mortals can give in life. We should not squander such a generous gift with misery, but with respectful appreciation, even joy for a life fully lived to its end.'

Kat took a deep breath. They crossed before the small chapel. Her eyes studied it – though Vigor suspected she looked just as intently inward.

'There can be lessons even in ghost stories,' Vigor finished, and guided the group down the fork to the left.

Here the road turned to cobbles of volcanic stone. Though the stones were not original to the Roman road that once led out from the gates of the city all the way to Greece, it was a romantic approximation. Slowly the way opened around them. Green swards of hillsides opened in parklands, dotted with occasional sheep and shaded by umbrella pines. Crumbling lines of walls crisscrossed the landscape, along with the occasional tomb.

At this hour, with most of the attractions closed and

the sun near to setting, they had the Appian Way to themselves. An occasional stroller or bicyclist nodded to him,
noting his collar. 'Padre,' they would mumble and continue past, glancing back at the road-weary group of
backpackers he led.

Vigor also noted a few scantily clad women lounging at
roadside spots, along with some seemlier-looking figures.
After dark, the Appian Way became a roost to prostitutes
and their ilk, and often proved dangerous to the average
tourist. Brigands and robbers still prowled the ancient
road, as they had the original Appian Way.

'It's not much farther,' Vigor promised.

He headed through an area of vineyards, green vines
tied to wood and wire, that traversed the gently sloping
hills. Ahead appeared the courtyard entrance to their destination: the Catacombs of Saint Callistus.

'Commander,' Kat asked, dropping back, 'shouldn't we
at least scout the area first?'

'Just keep your eyes open,' he answered. 'No more
delays.'

Vigor noted the firmness in the man's voice. The commander listened, but he seemed less willing to bend. Vigor
was unsure if this was good or bad.

Gray waved for them to proceed.

The subterranean cemetery had closed at five o'clock,
but Vigor had called the caretaker and arranged this special 'tour.' A petite snowy-maned gentleman in gray
coveralls stepped out of a sheltered doorway. He hobbled
over, using a wooden shepherd's crook as a cane. Vigor
knew him well. His family had been sheepherders of the
surrounding *campagna* going back generations. He held a
pipe firmly between his teeth.

'Monsignor Verona,' he said. '*Come va?*'

'*Bene grazie. E lei,* Giuseppe?'

'I'm fine, *Padre. Grazie.*' He waved toward the small
cottage that served as his homestead while watching over

the catacombs. 'I have a bottle of grappa. I know how you like a bit of the grape. From these hills.'

'Another time, Giuseppe. The day grows late and we must be about our business with much haste, I'm afraid.'

The man eyed the others as if they were to blame for the rush, then his eyes caught on Rachel. 'It cannot be! *Piccola* Rachel . . . but she is not so little anymore.'

Rachel smiled, clearly delighted to be remembered. She hadn't visited here with Vigor since she was nine years old. Rachel quickly hugged him, kissing him on the cheek. '*Ciao,* Giuseppe.'

'We must raise a cup to *piccola* Rachel, no?'

'Perhaps when we finish our business below,' Vigor pressed, knowing the man, lonely here in his cottage, only wanted a bit of company.

'*Si . . . bene . . .*' He waved his crook toward the doorway. 'It is open. I will lock after you. Knock when you come up and I will hear.'

Vigor led them to the gateway to the catacombs. He pulled open the door. He waved the others through the threshold, noting that Giuseppe had left the string of electric lights lit. The staircase descended ahead of them.

As Monk stepped through with Rachel, he glanced back to the caretaker. 'You should introduce that guy to your grandmother. They'd hit it off, I bet.'

Rachel grinned and followed the stocky man inside.

Vigor closed the door behind him and took the lead again, heading down the stairs. 'This catacomb is one of Rome's oldest. It was once a private Christian cemetery, but it spread out when some of the popes chose to be buried at this site. It now covers ninety acres and descends in four levels.'

Behind him, Vigor heard the door lock snap closed. The air grew danker as they descended, rich with the smell of loam and seeping rainwater. At the foot of the stairs, they reached a vestibule with *loculi* cut into the walls, horizontal niches for bodies to be laid to rest. Graffiti etched the walls, but it was not the work of modern vandals. Some of the inscriptions dated back from the fifteenth century: prayers, laments, testimonials.

'How far in do we have to go?' Gray asked, stepping next to Vigor. There was barely room for two to walk side by side as the way narrowed from here. The commander eyed the low ceilings.

In here, even those who didn't suffer from claustrophobia found these crumbling subterranean necropolises unnerving. Especially now. Deserted and empty.

'The Crypt of Lucina lies much deeper. It's located in the most ancient area of the catacomb.'

Galleries branched off from here, but Vigor knew the way and headed to the right. 'Stay close,' he warned. 'It's easy to get lost in here.'

The way narrowed even more.

Gray turned. 'Monk, keep a watch on our rear. Ten paces. Stay in sight.'

'Got it covered.' Monk freed his shotgun.

Ahead, a chamber opened. Its walls were pocked with larger *loculi* and elaborate *arcsololia*, arched gravesites.

'The Papal Crypt,' Vigor announced. 'It is here sixteen popes were laid to rest, from Eutychianus to Zephyrinus.'

'From E to Z,' Gray mumbled.

'The bodies were removed,' Vigor said, delving deeper, passing through the Crypt of Cecelia. 'From about the fifth century, the outskirts of Rome were plundered by a series of forces. Goths, Vandals, Lombards. Many of the most important personages buried here were moved into churches and chapels inside the city. In fact, the catacombs were so emptied out and abandoned that by the twelfth century they were completely forgotten, and were not rediscovered until the sixteenth century.'

Gray coughed. 'It seems that timeline keeps crossing itself.'

Vigor glanced back.

'Twelfth century,' Gray explained. 'That was also when the bones of the Magi were moved out of Italy into Germany. It's also when you mentioned there was a resurgence in Gnostic belief, creating a schism between emperors and the papacy.'

Vigor slowly nodded, contemplating this angle. 'It was a tumultuous time, with the papacy run out of Rome by the end of the thirteenth century. The alchemists may have sought to protect what they had learned, driven into deeper hiding as they were leaving behind clues in case of their demise, breadcrumbs for other Gnostic believers to follow.'

'Like this sect of the Dragon Court.'

'I don't think they imagined such a perverse group to be enlightened enough to seek such higher truths. An unfortunate miscalculation. Either way, I think you're right. You may have pegged the date when these clues were placed. I'd say sometime in the thirteenth century, during the height of the conflict. Few at that time knew about the catacombs. What better place to hide the clues to a secret society?'

Pondering this, Vigor piloted them through a successive series of galleries, crypts, and *cubicula*. 'It's not far. Just past the Sacramental Chapels.' He waved an arm to a gallery of six chambers. Peeling and faded frescoes displayed intricate biblical scenes interspersed with depictions of baptism and the celebration of Eucharistic meals. They were treasures of early Christian art.

After hiking through a few more galleries, their goal appeared ahead. A modest crypt. The ceiling was painted with a typical early Christian motif: the Good Shepherd, Christ with a lamb carried on his shoulders.

Turning from the ceiling, Vigor instead pointed to two neighboring walls. 'Here is what we came to find.'

Gray approached the nearest wall. A fresco of a fish had been painted against a green background. Above it, almost appearing to be carried on the back of the fish, was a basket of bread. He turned to the second wall. This fresco seemed a mirror image of the first, except the basket also bore a bottle of wine.

'It's all symbolic of the first Eucharistic meal,' Vigor said. 'Fish, bread, and wine. It also represents the miracle of the fishes, when Christ multiplied a single basket of fish and bread to feed the multitude of followers who had come to hear his sermon.'

'Again the multiplication symbolism,' Kat said. 'Like the geometry of the *Vesica Pisces*.'

'But where do we go from here?' Monk asked. He stood with his shotgun on his shoulder, facing back into the crypt.

'Follow the riddle,' Gray answered. 'The second stanza reads, "Where it drowns, it floats in darkness and stares to the lost king." We found where it floats in darkness, so we follow where it stares.' He pointed in the direction the first fish was facing.

It led further into the galleries.

Gray strode in that direction, searching around him. It did not take long to find a clear depiction of kings. Gray stopped before a fresco illustrating the adoration of the Magi. It was faded, but the details were plain enough. The Virgin Mary sat on a throne with the Christ child on her lap. Bowed before her were three robed figures, offering gifts.

'The Three Kings,' Kat said. 'The Magi again.'

'We keep running into these guys,' Monk replied from a few paces down the passage.

Rachel frowned at the wall. 'But what does it mean? Why lead us here? What did the Dragon Court learn?'

Gray let all the events of the past day trickle through his head. He didn't fight for order, but simply let his mind roam. Connections formed, dissolved, reconfigured. Slowly he began to understand.

'The real question is, *why* did these ancient alchemists lead us here?' Gray said. 'To *this* particular depiction of the Magi. As Monk mentioned, you can't turn a corner in Italy without running into these kings. So why this fresco in particular?'

No one had an answer.

Rachel offered a possible avenue to pursue. 'The Dragon Court went after the Magi bones. Maybe we need to look at it from that perspective.'

Gray nodded. He should've thought of that. They didn't need to reinvent the wheel. The Dragon Court had already solved the riddle. All they had to do was backtrack. Gray considered this and found one possible answer.

'Maybe the fish is staring toward these particular kings because they are buried. In a graveyard. Under the earth, where a fish would drown. The answer to the clue is not living Magi, but dead and buried ones, in a crypt once filled with *bones*.'

Vigor made a small sound of surprise.

'So the Dragon Court went after the bones,' Rachel said.

'I think the Dragon Court already knew the bones were not bones,' Gray said. 'They've had their nose to this trail for centuries. They must've known. Look what happened at the cathedral. They used the powder of white gold in some way to kill. They're well ahead of the game.'

'And they want more power,' Rachel said. 'The final solution of the Magi.'

Vigor's eyes narrowed in concentration. 'And if you're right, Commander – about the significance of the Magi bones being taken out of Italy to Germany – maybe the transfer was not plunder as history attests, but was done by arrangement. To safeguard the amalgam.'

Gray nodded. 'And the Dragon Court let them remain in Cologne . . . safely in sight. Knowing they were significant, but not knowing what to do with them.'

'Until now,' Monk said from a few paces away.

'But in the end,' Gray continued, 'what do all these clues ultimately point to? Right now only to relics in a church. It doesn't tell what to do with them, what they're used for.'

'We're forgetting,' Kat said. She had remained silent this entire time, focused on the fresco. 'The stanza from the passage states the fish "stares to the lost *king*." Not "kings," plural. There are three kings here. I think we're missing another layer of meaning or symbolism.' She turned to the others. 'What "lost king" is the clue hinting about?'

Gray struggled for an answer. There were riddles upon riddles.

Vigor had dropped his chin into his hand, concentrating. 'There is a fresco in a neighboring catacomb. The Catacomb of Domatilla. The fresco is painted with not three Magi, but *four*. Because the Bible was never specific on the number of Magi, early Christian artists varied the number. The lost king could mean another Magi, the one missing here.'

'A *fourth* Magi?' Gray asked.

'A figure representative of the lost knowledge of the alchemists.' Vigor nodded, raising his head. 'The second stanza's message hints that the Magi bones can be used to find this fourth Magi. Whoever he may be.'

Rachel shook her head, drawing both Gray and Vigor's attention. 'Don't forget this clue is buried in a crypt. I bet it's not the fourth Magi that we're supposed to find, but his *tomb*. One set of bones used to find another. Possibly another cache of amalgam.'

229

'Or something even greater. That would certainly excite the Dragon Court.'

'But how can the Magi bones help find this lost tomb?' Monk asked.

Gray headed back to the Crypt of Lucina. 'The answer has to be in the *third* stanza.'

2:22 p.m.
WASHINGTON, D.C.

Painter Crowe woke to a knock on his door. He had fallen asleep in his chair, tilted back. Damn ergonomics . . .

He cleared the sleep from his throat. 'Come in.'

Logan Gregory entered. His hair was wet and he wore a fresh shirt and jacket. It looked like he'd just come in for the day, rather than being here 24/7.

Logan must have noted his attention and ran a hand down his starched shirt. 'I went down to the gym for a run. I keep a second set of clothes in my locker.'

Painter had no reply, flabbergasted. Youth. He didn't think he could climb out of his chair, let alone run a few miles. But then again, Logan was only five years his junior. Painter knew it was stress more than age that weighed him down.

'Sir,' Logan continued, 'I received word from General Rende, our liaison with the Carabinieri Corps in Rome. Commander Pierce and the others have gone to ground again.'

Painter leaned forward. 'Another attack? They were supposed to be at the Vatican by now.'

'No, sir. After your call to them, they waved off the Carabinieri escort and took off on their own. General Rende wanted to know what was relayed to them. His field operative, Lieutenant Rachel Verona, informed him that you passed on some bit of intel. General Rende was not happy to be kept out of the loop.'

230

'And what did you tell him?'

Logan raised both eyebrows. 'Nothing, sir. That is official Sigma policy, is it not? We know nothing.'

Painter smiled. It sometimes felt that way.

'What about Commander Pierce, sir? What do you want to do next? Should we post an alert?'

Painter remembered Sean McKnight's earlier admonishment. Trust your agents. 'We'll wait for his next call. There's no evidence of foul play. We'll give him room to run his own game.'

Logan did not seem satisfied with this answer. 'What do you want me to do then?'

'I suggest, Logan, that you get some rest. I imagine that when Commander Pierce gets going, we're going to get very little sleep over here.'

'Yes, sir.' He headed for the door.

Painter leaned back in his chair and covered his eyes with his arm. Damn, but this chair was comfortable. He drifted away, but something troubled him, keeping him from sleep. Something nagged. Something Gray had said. Not trusting Sigma. A leak.

Could it be?

There was only one person besides himself with full intel on this operation up until now. Not even Sean McKnight knew everything. He slowly tilted forward, eyes open.

It couldn't be.

8:22 p.m. ROME, ITALY

Back at the Crypt of Lucina, Gray stood by the second fresco with the fish. They needed to solve this third riddle.

Monk asked a good question. 'Why didn't the Dragon Court just firebomb the hell out of these catacombs? Why leave them for others to find?'

Rachel stood next to him. 'With the forged copy of the

231

*Book of the Dead* still in the Court's possession, what would they have to fear? If Seichan hadn't stolen the riddle map, nobody would know to look here.'

Kat added, 'Maybe the Court wasn't so sure of their interpretation. Maybe they wanted this story in stone to be kept intact until they were certain they had the correct translation.'

Gray weighed this, sensing a greater press of time. He turned back to the fresco. 'Then let's see what they found. The third stanza has the fish waiting for water. Like the first fish, I think we're supposed to follow where it's facing.'

Gray motioned to a different gallery branching off from the crypt. The second fish pointed that way.

But Vigor continued his study of the two fishes, looking at one and then the other, mirror images. 'Twins,' he mumbled.

'What's that?'

Vigor waved a hand between the two fish. 'Whoever devised this game of riddles loved to layer it with symbolism. Choosing these two fish. Nearly identical in appearance. Referring to the second fish as 'twin' cannot be insignificant.'

'I don't see the connection,' Gray said.

'You just don't know your Greek, Commander.'

Gray frowned.

Monk, surprisingly enough, chimed in, proving his Greek heritage extended beyond a fondness for ouzo and bad dancing. ' "Twin" translates to *didymus*.'

'Very good,' Vigor said. 'And in Hebrew, "twin" translates to *Thomas*. As in Didymus Thomas. One of the twelve apostles.'

Gray remembered the discussion at Lake Como with the monsignor. 'Thomas was the apostle in conflict with John.'

'And the one who baptized the Magi,' Vigor reminded

them. 'Thomas represented Gnostic belief. I think using the word *twin* here is a tribute back to the Gospel of Thomas. By acknowledging Thomas, I wonder if these alchemists might not have been Thomas Christians themselves . . . churchgoers who followed Rome but still continued their Gnostic practices in secret. There were always whispers of such a church within the Church. A Thomas Church hiding within and alongside the canonical Church. This may be the proof.'

Gray heard the growing excitement in the other's voice.

'Perhaps this society of alchemists, which traced its roots to Moses and Egypt, merged with the Catholic Church. Continued forward in history wearing the cross and bending a knee to the Church, finding common ground with those who held sacred the secret Gospel of Thomas.'

'Hiding in plain sight,' Monk said.

Vigor nodded.

Gray followed this line of logic. It might be worth pursuing, but for now, they had another riddle to solve. He pointed down the gallery. 'Whoever left these clues, they left us a third challenge.'

*The Twin waits for water . . .*

Gray led the way down the new gallery. He searched for some fresco with water in it. He passed various biblical scenes, but none depicting water. There was a painting of a family gathered around a table, but it looked like wine was being served. Next there was a fresco with four male figures lifting their arms to heaven. None of them held a flask of water.

Vigor called behind him. He turned.

The others were gathered by one niche. He went back to them. He had searched that one already. It showed a man in a robe striking a stone with a stick. Not a drop of water.

'This is an illustration of Moses in the desert,' Vigor said.

Gray waited for elaboration.

'According to the Bible, he struck a rock in the desert and a fresh spring burst forth to quench the thirst of the fleeing Israelites.'

'Like our old fish back there,' Monk said.

'This must be the fresco indicated by the stanza,' Vigor said. 'Remember, Moses knew about manna and these miraculous white powders. It would be appropriate to acknowledge him.'

'So what clue does this crumbling painting hold?' Gray asked.

'"The Twin waits for water, but will be burned to bone by bone upon the altar,"' Vigor quoted. '"Burned to bone by bone." Think backward. Like Rachel recommended before. What did the Dragon Court do, in Cologne? The parishioners were burned somehow, a massive electrical storm in the brain. And it involved white gold. And possibly the amalgam in the Magi bones.'

'Is that the message?' Rachel asked, looking uneasy. 'To kill? To curse an altar site, like in Cologne, with blood and murder?'

'No,' Gray answered. 'The Dragon Court ignited the bones and seemingly learned nothing, since they continued on the same trail afterward. Maybe Cologne was just a test or a trial run. Maybe the Dragon Court was not sure of their interpretation of the riddle, like your uncle suggested. Either way, they were plainly aware of some of the white powder's capabilities. With their device, they proved they can activate and crudely manipulate the energy in these high-spin superconductors. They used it to kill. But I don't think that is what the alchemists originally intended.'

Rachel still looked ill at ease.

'The true answer is here,' Gray finished. 'If the Dragon Court solved it, so can we.'

'But they had months after stealing the text from

Cairo,' Monk said. 'And they know a lot more about this stuff than we do.'

Sobering nods passed around the group. Running on too little sleep, they were all razor-edged on adrenaline. The riddles were taxing what little mental reserve they still had, leaving a pall of defeat hanging over them.

Refusing to weaken, Gray closed his eyes, concentrating. He considered all he'd learned. The amalgam was composed of many different metals in the platinum group, the exact recipe of which was impossible to determine, even with current laboratory tests. The amalgam was then shaped into bones and secured in a cathedral.

Why? Did the alchemists really belong to a secret church within the Church? Is that how they managed to hide the bones during that tumultuous time, an era of antipopes and strife?

No matter the history, Gray was sure the Dragon Court's device had somehow tapped into the power in the m-state amalgam. Perhaps the tainting of the Communion wafers was only a way to test the breadth and range of that power. But what was the primary use for such a power? A tool, a weapon?

Gray mulled over the indecipherable codex of chemicals, one hidden for centuries, left behind as a series of clues to a possible storehouse of ancient power.

An indecipherable codex . . .

About to give up, the answer came to him, sudden and sharp, a pain behind the eyes.

Not a codex.

'It's a *key*,' he mumbled aloud, knowing it to be true. He faced the others. 'The amalgam is an indecipherable chemical key, impossible to duplicate. Within its unique chemistry must be the power to unlock the location of the tomb of the fourth Magi.'

Vigor started to speak, but Gray held him off with a hand.

'The Dragon Court knows how to ignite that power, to turn that key on. But where's the lock? Not in Cologne. The Dragon Court failed there. But they must have a second-best guess. The answer is here. In this fresco.'

He stared around the group.

'We've got to solve this,' he said. He turned and pointed to the fresco. 'Moses is striking a rock. Altars are usually made of stone. Does that mean anything? Are we supposed to go out to the Sinai desert and search for Moses's stone?'

'No,' Vigor said, stirring out of the fog of defeat. He reached and touched the painted rock. 'Remember the layers of symbolism in the riddle. This is not *Moses*'s stone. At least not his alone. The fresco is actually titled "Moses-Peter Striking the Rock."'

Gray frowned. 'Why two names? Moses and Peter?'

'Throughout the catacombs, Saint Peter's image was often superimposed upon Moses's acts. It was a way of glorifying the apostle.'

Rachel looked closer at the painted face. 'If this is Saint Peter's rock . . . ?'

'"Rock" in Greek is *petros*,' Vigor said. 'This is why the apostle Simon Bar-Jona took the name Peter, eventually Saint Peter. From Christ's words, "You are Peter, and on this rock I will build my Church."'

Gray attempted to put this together. 'Are you suggesting that the altar named in the riddle is the altar inside St. Peter's Basilica?'

Rachel suddenly twisted around. 'No. We've got the symbolism backward. In the stanza, the word *altar* is used, but the painting replaces it with the word *rock*. It's not an altar we're looking for, it's a rock.'

'Great,' Monk said. 'That really narrows our search parameters.'

'It does,' Rachel said. 'My uncle quoted the most significant biblical passage that connects Saint Peter to a rock. Peter would be the *rock* upon which the Church would be built. Remember where we are now. In a crypt.' She tapped the stone on the fresco. 'A rock underground.'

Rachel faced them all, her eyes so excited they almost glowed in the dark. 'What site was St. Peter's Basilica built atop? What *rock* is buried under the foundations of the church?'

Gray answered, eyes widening. 'Saint Peter's tomb.'

'The Rock of the Church,' Vigor echoed.

Gray sensed the truth. The bones were the key. The tomb was the lock.

Rachel nodded. 'That's where the Dragon Court will be heading next. We should contact Cardinal Spera immediately.'

'Oh no . . .' Vigor stiffened.

'What's wrong?' Gray asked.

'Tonight . . . at dusk . . .' Vigor checked his watch, his face ashen. He turned and headed away. 'We must hurry.'

Gray followed with the others. 'What?'

'A memorial service for the tragedy in Cologne. The mass is scheduled for sunset. Thousands will be in attendance, including the pope.'

Gray suddenly realized what Vigor feared. He pictured the massacre in the cathedral in Cologne. All eyes would be turned away from the Scavi, the necropolis below St. Peter's Basilica, where the tomb of the apostle had been excavated.

The Rock of the Church.

If the Dragon Court ignited the Magi bones down there . . .

He imagined the crowds packed inside the church, massed outside on the square.

Oh God.

# 9

# THE SCAVI

The summer day ran long.

Dusk was just settling over the Appian Way as Gray climbed out of the catacombs. He shaded his eyes with a hand. After the gloom of the catacombs, the slanting rays of the setting sun glared.

The caretaker, Giuseppe, held the door for the exiting group, then closed it behind him, locking it. 'Is everything all right, Monsignor?' The old man must have noted the strain in them as they all piled out through the doorway.

Vigor nodded. 'I just need to make a phone call.'

Gray handed Vigor his sat-phone. The Vatican needed to be alerted and the alarm raised. Gray knew the monsignor was the best person to reach someone in authority over there.

A step away, Rachel already had her cell phone out, dialing her station house.

A crack of a bullet stopped them all. It struck the flint paving of the courtyard, sparking brightly in the descending gloom.

Gray responded immediately, half surprised, half not.

'Go!' he yelled, and pointed to the caretaker's cottage that flanked one side of the courtyard. Giuseppe had left the door to his home open.

They bolted toward the shelter. Gray helped the old caretaker, supporting him, with Rachel on his other side.

238

Before they could reach the cottage, the doorway exploded with a gout of flame, throwing them all back. Gray tumbled in a pile with Giuseppe and Rachel. The rigged door, blown off its hinges, skittered across the paving stones. Glass shattered across the courtyard.

Gray dropped to a knee, sheltering Rachel and the caretaker. Kat covered Vigor in the same manner. Gray had his pistol out, pointing, but he had no target. No cloaked figures came running.

The surrounding landscape of vineyards and umbrella pines lay steeped in shadows and gloom. Silent.

'Monk,' Gray said.

His partner already had his shotgun out. He peered through the night-vision scope fixed to the top of the barrel.

'I can't pick anything out,' Monk said.

A phone rang. All eyes flicked to Vigor. He crouched with Gray's satellite phone. It rang again in his hands.

Gray motioned for him to answer it.

Vigor obeyed, raising the sat-phone to his ear.

'*Pronto*,' he said. He listened for a moment, then lowered and held out the phone toward Gray. 'It's for you.'

Gray knew they had been purposefully pinned down. No further shots were fired at them. Why? He took the phone.

Before he could speak, a voice greeted him. 'Hello, Commander Pierce.'

'Seichan.'

'I see you received my message from Sigma command.'

Seichan had somehow tracked them here, followed them and set up the ambush. And he knew the reason. 'The riddle . . .'

'From the frantic way you and your friends vacated the catacomb, I can only assume you solved the mystery.'

Gray remained silent.

'Raoul didn't wish to share his knowledge either,'

239

Seichan said calmly. 'It seems the Dragon Court wants to keep the Guild at the sidelines, only playing defensive. That won't do. So if you'd be so kind as to share what you've learned, I'll let you all live.'

Gray covered the phone's receiver. 'Monk?'

'Still nothing, Commander,' he whispered back.

Seichan had taken up a sniping position with a clear view of the courtyard. The vineyards, trees, and shadowed slopes hid her well. She must have snuck down here while they were in the catacombs, and booby-trapped the cottage, forcing them to stay in the open.

They were at her mercy.

'From your urgency,' Seichan said, 'time must be a factor. And I can wait all night, picking you off one at a time until you talk.' To emphasize this, a bullet cracked a stone at his toe, stinging him with shards. 'So be a good boy.'

Monk whispered at his side. 'She must be using an exhaust-suppression device on her rifle. I didn't even pick up a flicker out there.'

Trapped, he had no choice but to bargain. 'What do you want to know?' he asked, stalling.

'The Dragon Court is moving on a target tonight. And I believe you have discovered where that will be. Tell me and you all go free.'

'How do I know you'll keep your word?'

'Oh, you don't. You don't have much choice either. I thought that was obvious, Gray. May I call you Gray?' She continued, not missing a beat. 'As long as I find you useful, I'll keep you around, but I certainly don't need *all* of you around. I'll make an example of your companions if I must.'

Gray had no choice. 'Fine. Yes. We solved the goddamn riddle.'

'Where will the Dragon Court strike?'

'At a church,' he bluffed. 'Near the Coliseum, there is —'

240

A whistle sped by his left ear and at the same time a startled cry rose from the caretaker. Gray turned to see the old man clutching his shoulder. Blood oozed between his fingers as he fell to his backside on the stones. Rachel went immediately to his aid.

'Monk, help them,' Gray said, cursing silently.

His teammate had a med pack and the training. Still, Monk hesitated, his shotgun ready, reluctant to give up his search.

Gray waved him over more forcibly. Seichan would not make the mistake of exposing herself. Monk lowered his gun and went to the caretaker's aid.

'You get one free pass,' Seichan said in his ear. 'Another lie and it will cost more than a little blood.'

Gray's fingers tightened on the phone.

'I have my own intel,' the woman continued. 'So I'll know if your answer makes sense or not.'

Gray sought some way to throw her off track, but the caretaker's groans made it hard to focus on strategy. And he had no time – and no choice. He had to tell her the truth. She had kept him in the game up until now, and now he had to return the favor. Like it or not, he and the Guild were in bed together. This would have to be settled another time. And for that to happen, they had to live.

'If you're right about the timetable,' Gray said, 'the Dragon Court will assault the Vatican tonight.'

'Where?'

'Below the basilica. At the tomb of Saint Peter.' Gray gave a brief overview of the riddle's solution as proof of the truth.

'Clever work,' she said. 'I knew there was a reason I kept you around. Now if you'd all be so kind as to dispose of all your cellular phones. Toss them into the burning cottage. And no tomfoolery, Commander Gray. Don't assume I'm ignorant of exactly the number of phones you and your team are carrying.'

241

Gray obeyed. Kat collected all the phones, then showed each one as she tossed them through the doorway into the growing conflagration.

Except for the phone at Gray's ear.

'*Arrivederci* for now, Commander Gray.'

The phone suddenly exploded at his ear, ripped from his fingers, shot from afar. His ear rang. Blood ran down his neck.

Gray tensed, waiting for another parting shot. Instead, he heard an engine ignite with a throaty roar, then settle to a rumble. A motorbike. It headed away, staying below the ridgeline. The Dragon Lady was heading out with the information she needed.

Gray turned.

Monk had the caretaker's shoulder bandaged. 'Only a graze. Lucky.'

But Gray knew luck had nothing to do with it. The woman could've put a round through any of their eyes.

'How's your ear?' Monk asked.

Gray shook his head, angry.

Monk came forward anyway. He reached, not particularly gently, and inspected the damage on his ear. 'Just a skin lac. Hold still.' He dabbed the wound, then sprayed it from a tiny bottle.

It stung like a son of a bitch.

'Liquid bandage,' Monk explained. 'It dries in seconds. Even faster if I blow on it. But I don't want to get you too excited.'

Behind them, Rachel and Vigor helped the caretaker to his feet. Kat recovered the old man's shepherd crook. His eyes remained on his cottage. Flames now licked from the shattered windows.

Vigor placed a hand on the man's shoulder. '*Mi dispace* . . .' he apologized.

The man shrugged, his voice surprisingly firm. 'I still have my sheep. Houses can be rebuilt.'

242

'We must reach a phone,' Rachel said softly to Gray. 'General Rende and the Vatican have to be alerted.'

Gray knew that cutting their lines of communication had only been a delaying tactic, to buy the Dragon Court and thus the Guild a bit more time. He glanced to the western skies.

The sun was gone. Only a crimson glow marked its passage.

The Dragon Court was surely already on the move.

Gray spoke to the caretaker. 'Giuseppe, do you have an automobile?'

The old man slowly nodded. 'Around back.' He led the way. Behind the burning cottage stood a stone-shingle detached garage, more a shack. It had no door.

Through the opening, a shape filled the space, covered by a tarp.

Giuseppe waved his crook. 'The keys are inside. I filled it with gas last week.'

Monk and Kat went ahead to clear the car. Together they pulled the tarpaulin aside, revealing a classic '66 Maserati Sebring, black as obsidian. It reminded Gray of the early Ford Mustang fastbacks. Long hood, muscular, meaty tires, bred for speed.

Vigor glanced to Giuseppe.

He shrugged. 'My aunt's car . . . barely driven.'

Rachel walked toward it in a happy daze.

They quickly climbed inside. Giuseppe agreed to wait for the fire department, continuing his post as caretaker of the catacombs.

Rachel slid into the driver's seat. She knew the streets of Rome the best. But not all were happy with this choice of driver.

'Monk,' Rachel said as she turned the key and the engine roared.

'What?'

'Maybe you'd better close your eyes.'

243

After a brief stop at a bank of public telephones, Rachel pulled away from the curb. She sped into traffic, earning an irritated beep from an angry driver. What was his problem? A full handspan stretched between her car and the Fiat behind her. Plenty of room . . .

The Maserati's headlights speared ahead. Full night had descended. A line of brake lights wound toward the center of the city. She raced around and between the other cars, mere obstacles. She dove into the oncoming-traffic lane at times. The empty stretches on the far side were a shame to waste.

A groan echoed from the backseat.

She sped faster.

No one voiced a real complaint.

Back at the phones, Rachel had attempted to contact General Rende, while her uncle had called Cardinal Spera. Neither had been successful. Both men were at the memorial service, already under way. General Rende was personally overseeing the Carabinieri force that guarded St. Peter's Square. Cardinal Spera was in attendance at the service. Messages had been left, the alarm raised. But would it be in time?

Everyone was at the memorial mass, only steps from where the Dragon Court would strike. The crowds of people acted as the perfect cover.

'How much longer?' Gray asked from the passenger seat. He had his pack open on his lap and worked rapidly. Too busy with the road, she had no time to see what he was doing.

Rachel sped past Trajan's Market, the ancient Roman equivalent of a shopping mall. The crumbling semicircular building was set into the Quirinal Hill. It was a good landmark. 'Two miles,' she answered Gray.

'With the memorial crowds, we'll never reach the front

244

entrances,' Vigor warned, leaning forward from the back-seat. 'We should try for the railway entry into the Vatican. Aim for Via Aurelia along the south wall. We can cross the grounds behind the basilica. Go in the back way.'

Rachel nodded. Already the traffic congested as the flow bottlenecked toward the bridge over the Tiber River.

'Tell me about the excavations under the basilica,' Gray said. 'Are there any other entrances to it?'

'No,' Vigor said. 'The Scavi region is self-contained. Just under St. Peter's lies the Sacred Grottoes, accessed through the basilica. Many of the most famous crypts and papal tombs reside there. But in 1939, *sampietrini* workers were digging a tomb site for Pope Pius XI and discovered another layer beneath the Grottoes, a huge necropolis of ancient mausoleums dating back to the first century. It was named simply the *Scavi*, or Excavation.'

'How extensive is the area? What's the lay of the land?'

'Have you ever been down to the underground city in Seattle?' Vigor asked.

Gray glanced over his shoulder to the monsignor.

'I once went to an archaeological conference there,' Vigor explained. 'Beneath modern Seattle lies its past, a Wild West ghost town, where you can see intact shops, streetlamps, wooden walkways. The necropolis is like that, an ancient Roman cemetery buried beneath the Grottoes. Excavated by archaeologists, it's a maze of gravesites, shrines, and stone streets.'

Rachel finally reached the bridge and fought her way across the Tiber River. Once on the far side, she left the main flow of traffic, circled out, and headed away from St. Peter's Square. She swung to the south.

After a few serpentine turns, she found herself running alongside the towering Leonine Walls of the Vatican. It was dark here, with few streetlamps.

'Just ahead,' Vigor said, pointing an arm.

The railway spanned the road atop a stone bridge. It was here that the Vatican's railroad line exited the Holy See and joined Rome's system of tracks. Popes throughout the century had toured by train, leaving from the Vatican's own railroad depot within the walls of the papal state.

'Take that turn before the bridge,' Vigor said.

She almost missed it in the dark. Rachel yanked the wheel, fishtailing off the main avenue and onto a gravel service road that climbed steeply. Tires spat rooster tails of gravel as she fought her way to the top. The road hit a dead end at the tracks.

'That way!' Vigor pointed to the left.

There was no street, only a narrow sward of grass, weeds, and chunky rocks that paralleled the railroad tracks. Rachel twisted the wheel, bumped off the service road and onto the side of the tracks.

She shifted gears and rattled her way toward the archway through the Leonine Wall. Her headlights bobbled up and down. Reaching the wall, she manhandled the Maserati through the opening, traversing the gap between the wall and the tracks.

Ahead, her headlights splashed across the side of a midnight-blue service van that blocked the way. A pair of Swiss Guards, in blue night uniforms, flanked the van. They had rifles out, pointing at the intruder.

Rachel braked, arm already out the window, waving her Carabinieri identification. She yelled. 'Lieutenant Rachel Verona! With Monsignor Verona! We have an emergency!'

They were waved forward, but one of the guards kept his rifle at his shoulder, pointed at Rachel's face.

Her uncle quickly showed his own Vatican papers. 'We must reach Cardinal Spera.'

A flashlight searched the car, passing over the other occupants. Luckily all their weapons were hidden from direct view. It was no time for questions.

'I vouch for them,' Vigor said sternly. 'As will Cardinal Spera.'

The van was directed out of the way, clearing the path into the Vatican grounds.

Vigor still leaned his head out the window. 'Has word reached you here? Of a possible attack?'

The guard's eyes widened. He shook his head. 'No, Monsignor.'

Rachel glanced to Gray. *Oh no* . . . As they had feared, in all the confusion surrounding the memorial service, word was traveling too slowly up the chains of command. The Church was not known for its swift response . . . to change or emergency.

'Do not let anyone else through here,' Vigor ordered. 'Lock this entry down.'

The guardsman responded to the command in the monsignor's voice and nodded.

Vigor settled back into the car and pointed. 'Take the first road after the depot.'

Rachel did not have to be told to hurry. She raced through a small parking lot that fronted the quaint two-story depot and took the first right. She crossed in front of the Mosaic Studio, the Vatican's only industry, then tore between the Tribunal Palace and the Palazzo San Carlo. Here the buildings grew denser as the dome of St. Peter's filled the world ahead of them.

'Park at the Hospice of Santa Marta,' her uncle ordered.

Rachel ran her car up to the curb. The Sacristy of St. Peter rose on her left, connected to the giant basilica. The papal hospice was on her right. A covered walkway joined the sacristy to the hospice. Rachel cut her engine. They would have to continue from here on foot.

Their destination – the entrance to the Scavi – lay on the other side of the sacristy.

As they climbed out, muffled singing reached them.

The Pontifical Choir singing 'Ave Maria.' The Mass was under way.

'Follow me,' Uncle Vigor said.

He led the way through the covered archway to the open yard on the far side. The grounds were oddly deserted. All attention and focus of the Vatican had turned inward on itself, to the basilica, to the pope. Rachel had witnessed this before. Great services, like this special memorial, could empty the entire city-state, leaving few about.

On the far side of the sacristy, a low sonorous noise joined the choral singing. It came from ahead of them, through the Arch of Bells that led out to St. Peter's Square. It was the murmur of a thousand voices, rising from the crowd gathered out in the piazza. Through the arch's narrow gateway, Rachel caught a glimpse of candles glowing among the dark throng.

'Over here,' Vigor said, pulling free a large ring of keys. He led them to a nondescript door at the edge of the tiny yard. Solid steel. 'This leads down to the Scavi.'

'No guards,' Gray noted.

The only security was a pair of Swiss Guards posted by the Arch of Bells. They were armed with rifles as they studied the crowd. They didn't even glance back toward the newcomers.

'At least it's locked,' Vigor said. 'Maybe we've beat them here after all.'

'We can't count on that,' Gray warned. 'We know they have contacts inside the Vatican. They may have keys.'

'Only a few people have these keys. As head of the Pontifical Institute of Archaeology, I have a set.' He turned to Rachel and held out two other keys. 'These open the lower door . . . and the tomb site of Saint Peter.'

Rachel refused to take them. 'What – ?'

'You know the lay of the Scavi better than anyone. I must reach Cardinal Spera. The pope must be removed

248

from harm's way, and the basilica emptied without creating panic.' He touched his clerical collar. 'There's no one else who can get there fast enough.'

Rachel nodded and took the keys. It would take someone of her uncle's stature to quickly gain audience to the cardinal, especially during such an important mass. It was probably why the alarm had yet to be raised. Roadblocks of procedure. Even General Rende did not have jurisdiction upon Vatican soil.

Vigor gave Gray a sharp stare before turning away. Rachel interpreted it. *Watch after my niece.*

Rachel closed her fingers over the keys. At least her uncle was not trying to send her away. He recognized the danger. Thousands of lives hung in the balance.

Her uncle turned and headed for the sacristy's main door. It was the fastest way to reach the heart of the basilica.

Gray turned to the group and had them all don their radios, even securing an extra for her, taping the microphone to her throat himself and showing her how the barest whisper could be heard. *Subvocalizing* was the word he used. It was eerie, so quiet yet perfectly understandable.

She practiced as Monk cracked the door open. The way down to the basement was dark.

'There's a light switch just inside,' she whispered, surprised at the loudness of the audible pickup on the microphone.

'We go in dark,' Gray said.

Monk and Kat nodded. They pulled goggles over their eyes. Gray handed Rachel a pair. Night-vision. She was familiar enough with them from her military training. She donned them. The world brightened into shades of green and silver.

Gray led the way; she followed with Kat. Monk silently closed the door behind him. The way became dark, even with the scopes. Night vision required some light. Gray clicked on a handheld flashlight. It flared bright in the gloom. He secured it below his pistol.

Rachel tilted up her goggles. The way ahead went pitch dark again. Gray's flashlight must be emitting ultraviolet light, visible only through the scopes.

She reseated her goggles.

The otherworldly light illuminated an anteroom at this level. A few displays and models dotted the space, used in tours. One was a model of Constantine's first church, built on the site here in 324 B.C. The other was a model of an *aedicula*, a burial shrine shaped like a tiny two-level temple. It was such a temple that had marked Saint Peter's gravesite. According to historians, Constantine had constructed a cube made out of marble and porphyry, a rare stone imported from Egypt. He encased the *aedicula* shrine and built his original church around it.

Soon after the excavation of the necropolis began, the original Constantinian cube was rediscovered, positioned directly under the main papal altar of St. Peter's. A wall of the original temple remained, scratched and scrawled with Christian graffiti, including the Greek letters spelling out *Petros eni*, or 'Peter is within.'

And indeed, inside a cavity in that graffiti wall, bones and cloth were found that matched a man of Saint Peter's stature and age. Now they were sealed in bulletproof plastic boxes made, oddly enough, by the U.S. Department of Defense and secured back into the wall cavity.

That was their goal.

'This way,' Rachel whispered, and pointed to a steep, circular stair that led below.

Gray took the lead.

They wound down below the basement and even deeper.

A chill settled through Rachel's clothes. She felt almost naked. The goggles narrowed her vision, triggering a twinge of claustrophobia.

At the bottom of the stairs, a small door blocked the way. Rachel squeezed next to Gray, bodies touching, and noted his musky scent before she fished out the key and unlocked the door.

He held her hand against opening the door and gently but firmly pushed her behind him. He then pulled the door open a few centimeters and stared through. Rachel and the others waited.

'All clear,' he said. 'Dark as a tomb in there.'

'Funny,' Monk grumbled.

Gray pulled open the door.

Rachel readied herself for a blast, gunfire, or some sort of attack, but found only silence.

As they all pushed inside, Gray turned to the group. 'I think the monsignor was right. For once, we've got the jump on the Dragon Court. It's about time *we* set up the ambush.'

'What's the plan?' Monk asked.

'No chances. We set the trap and get the hell out of here.' Gray pointed to the door. 'Monk, stand guard at the door. It's the only way out or in. Guard our exit and our backs.'

'Not a problem.'

Gray handed what looked like two small egg cartons to Kat. 'Sonic grenades and flash bombs. I expect they'll come in dark like we did, with their ears up. Let's see if we can blind and deafen them. Distribute these as we cross to the tomb. Full coverage.'

Kat nodded.

He turned next to Rachel. 'Show me Saint Peter's tomb.'

She headed out into the dark necropolis, walking along an ancient Roman road. Family crypts and mausoleums lined the path, each six meters square. Walls were covered with ultrathin bricks, a common building material during the first century. Frescoes and mosaics decorated many of

251

the tombs, but such details were murky under night-vision. There remained a few bits of statuary, appearing to move in the eerie illumination. The dead come to life.

Rachel mapped out the route to the center of the necropolis. A metal walkway led up to a platform and rectangular window. She pointed through it.

'The tomb of Saint Peter.'

9:40 p.m.

Gray pointed his pistol and shone his UV spot into the gravesite.

Ten feet beyond the window, a brick wall rose alongside a massive cube of marble. A hole near the base of the wall had an opening in it. Bending down, he aimed his light. Within the opening, he could see a clear box with a blob of white claylike material.

Bone.

From Saint Peter.

Gray felt the hairs on his arms stand a bit on end, a shiver of awe and fear. He felt like an archaeologist, delving into a dark cave, out in some lost continent, not a couple floors below the heart of the Roman Catholic Church. Then again, maybe here was its *true* heart.

'Commander?' Kat asked. She rejoined them, having lagged a bit behind to plant her charges.

Gray straightened. 'Can we get closer?' he asked Rachel.

She pulled out the second key her uncle had given her and unlocked a gate that led into the inner sanctum.

'We must be quick,' Gray said, sensing time was running short. Then again, maybe it wasn't. Maybe the Dragon Court wouldn't strike until after midnight, like in Cologne. But he was taking no chances.

He pulled out the gear he had been calibrating on the way here. He searched the space and found an inconspicuous spot. He fixed the tiny video camera within a crevice of a neighboring mausoleum and positioned it to face Saint Peter's tomb. He took a second camera and turned it the opposite way, making sure it faced back out through the window to cover the approach.

'What are you doing?' Rachel asked.

Finished with the cameras, Gray waved them back out. 'I don't want to spring the trap too soon. I want them to get comfortable in here, set up their apparatus. Then we'll strike. I don't want to leave them any room to bolt with the Magi bones or their device.'

After they exited, Rachel relocked the gate.

'Monk,' Gray said into his radio, 'how are you doing?'

'All quiet.'

Good.

Gray crossed to a nearby crumbling mausoleum, one open at the front. The bones had long been cleared out. He freed the laptop from his pack and hid it inside the mausoleum, attaching a portable boost-transmitter to its USB port. A green light flashed a positive connection. He flicked a switch, sending the apparatus into dark mode. No light shone from computer or transmitter. Good.

Gray straightened and explained as they headed back out. 'The video cameras are not strong enough to transmit very far. The laptop will pick up the signal and boost it. It'll have enough range to reach the surface. We'll monitor it on another laptop. Once the Court is down here, trapped, we blast them with the sonic and flash charges, then sweep below with a whole barrack of Swiss Guards.'

Kat nodded and eyed him. 'If we had been too cautious back at the catacombs, delayed too long, we wouldn't have had this chance.'

Gray nodded.

Finally luck was with them. A bit of boldness had –

The explosions cut off his thought. They were not

loud, more muffled, sounding like depth charges exploding far underwater. They echoed throughout the necropolis, accompanied by a louder crash of stone.

Gray crouched as small holes were punched through the roof from above. Rock and earth blasted downward, crashing into the mausoleums and crypts below. Before the debris could even settle, ropes snaked through the smoky openings, followed by one man after another.

A full assault team.

They dropped into the necropolis and vanished.

Gray immediately recognized what was happening. The Dragon Court was entering from the floor above, the Sacred Grottoes. That level was accessed from inside the basilica. The Dragon Court must have come to the memorial service – then through their contact here, snuck below into the papal crypts of the Sacred Grotto. Their gear had probably been smuggled in over the course of a couple days and hidden among the shadowy tombs of the Grotto. Then, under the cover of the service, they regained their tools, bored specially shaped charges, and quietly punched their way down here.

The assault team would escape the same way, disappearing back among the thousands gathered here.

That must not happen.

'Kat,' Gray whispered, 'take Rachel to Monk. Don't engage. Get back above. Find the Swiss Guard.'

Kat grabbed Rachel's elbow. 'What about you?' she asked.

He was already moving, heading back toward Saint Peter's tomb. 'I'm staying here. I'll monitor from the laptop. Delay them if need be. Then signal you by radio once I spring the ambush.'

Perhaps all was not yet lost.

Monk came on over the radio. Even subvocalizing, his words were faint. 'No go here. They blasted a hole right above the exit. Practically cracked my skull with a chunk of rock. The bastards are riveting the goddamn door shut.'

Gray heard the machine-gun pops of an air gun echoing from the rear of the necropolis.

'No one's going in or out this way,' Monk finished.

'Kat?'

'Roger that, Commander.'

'Everyone go to ground,' he ordered. 'Wait for my signal.'

Gray crouched low and ran down the cemetery street. They were on their own.

9:44 p.m.

Vigor entered St. Peter's Basilica through the sacristy door, flanked by two Swiss Guards. He had shown his identification three times to gain access. But at least word was slowly filtering through the screens and checks. Maybe he hadn't been forceful enough when he'd placed the call twenty minutes ago, hedging that he didn't know for certain when the Dragon Court would assault the tomb.

But now things were moving in the right direction.

Vigor passed the monument to Pius VII and entered the nave near the middle of the church. The basilica was shaped like a giant cross, covering twenty-five thousand square meters, so cavernous two soccer teams could play a game within the confines of the nave alone.

And presently it was full. Every pew was crowded, from nave through transept. The space glowed with thousands of candles and the illumination of eight hundred chandeliers. The Pontifical Choir was in mid-song, *Exaudi Deus*, fitting for a memorial, but amplified and echoing as loud as any rock concert.

Vigor hurried, but forced himself not to run. Panic would kill. There were only a limited number of exits. He waved the two Swiss Guards to sweep right and left and alert their brothers-in-arms. Vigor had to get the pope clear first and alert the presiding clerical staff to slowly evacuate the parishioners.

Stepping into the nave, he had a clear view to the papal altar.

On the far side of the altar, Cardinal Spera was seated with the pope. The pair sat under Bernini's bronze *baldacchino,* a canopy of gilded bronze that covered the center altar. It rose eight stories, supported by four massive twisted bronze columns, decorated with gilded gold olive and laurel branches. The canopy itself was topped by a golden sphere surmounted by a cross.

Vigor worked his way surreptitiously forward. He had no time to change into proper vestments and was still shoddily attired. A few wealthy parishioners glanced at him, frowning, then noted his Roman collar. Still their glances were disdainful. A poor parish priest, they must think, awed by the spectacle.

Reaching the front, Vigor edged to the left. He would circle toward the rear of the altar, where he could speak to Cardinal Spera in private.

As he pushed past the statue of Saint Longinus, a hand reached out from a shadowed doorway. He glanced over as his elbow was gripped. It was a lanky man his own age, silver-haired, someone he knew and respected, Preffetto Alberto, the head prefect of the Archives.

'Vigor?' the prefect said. 'I heard . . .'

His words were lost to an especially loud refrain from the chorus.

Vigor leaned closer, stepping into the alcove that sheltered the doorway. It led down to the Sacred Grottoes. 'I'm sorry, Alberto. What – ?'

The grip tightened. A pistol shoved hard into his ribs. It had a silencer.

'Not another word, Vigor,' Alberto warned.

Hidden inside the crypt, Gray lay on his belly, out of view of the opening. His pistol rested beside the open laptop. He had its display turned to dark mode, glowing in UV. Two images split the screen – one feed from the camera facing Saint Peter's tomb, the other from the camera facing the main necropolis.

The assault team had divided into two groups. While one set patroled the necropolis in darkness, the other had broken out flashlights to expedite their work by the tomb. They worked quickly and efficiently, each man knowing his job. They had already opened the gate that blocked access to Saint Peter's tomb. Two men flanked the famous crypt, bent to a knee. They were fixing two large plates to either side.

The third man was immediately recognizable by his size.

Raoul.

He carried a steel case. He opened it and removed a clear plastic cylinder, full of a familiar grayish powder. The amalgam. They must have pulverized the bone down to its powdery form. Raoul slid the cylinder through the low opening into Saint Peter's tomb.

Plugging in the battery . . .

With everything in place, Gray could wait no longer. The apparatus was set. It was their one chance to catch the Court off guard, perhaps to drive them off, abandoning their gear behind.

'Ready to go blackout,' Gray whispered. His hand moved to the transmitter that controlled the sonic and flash bombs. 'Take out as many as you can while they're stunned, but don't take any needless chances. Keep moving. Stay out of sight.'

Affirmatives answered him. Monk was holed up near the door. Kat and Rachel had found another crypt to hide themselves inside. The assault team remained unaware of their presence.

Gray watched the trio of men exit the tomb area, trailing wires that led to the device. Raoul closed the gate, shielding himself from any danger. Atop the metal platform, he pressed one hand against his ear, plainly communicating the okay to proceed.

'Blackout on the count of five,' Gray whispered. 'Earplugs in place, goggles blinkered closed. Here we go.'

Gray counted down in his head. *Five, four, three* . . . Blind, he rested one hand on his pistol and the other on the laptop. *Two, one, zero.*

He hit the button on the laptop.

Though deafened by his earplugs, he could feel the deep *whump* of the sonic charges behind his sternum. He waited a three-count for the strobing flash grenades to expire. He blinkered open his goggles, then yanked out the earplugs. Shots echoed across the necropolis. Gray rolled to the entrance to the crypt.

Directly ahead, the metal platform was empty.

No one was in sight.

Raoul and his two men were gone.

Where?

The sound of gunfire intensified. A firefight waged in the dark necropolis. Gray remembered Raoul had received some communiqué just before he had ignited the sonic and flash charges. Had it been a warning? From whom?

Gray searched the vicinity. The world had receded to shades of green. He climbed the steps to the platform. He had to take the risk to secure the apparatus and the amalgam.

As he reached the top, he kept low, edging on his toes, one hand on the platform for support, his pistol swiveling to cover all directions.

Light suddenly blazed through the window ahead. It

revealed Raoul standing on the far side, a few steps from the tomb. Upon the attack, the man must have dodged back through the gate. He met Gray's eyes and lifted his arms. In his hands, he held the control device to ignite the amalgam.

Too late.

Futilely, Gray aimed and fired.

But the bulletproof glass repelled the slug.

Raoul smiled and twisted the handle on the control device.

# 10

# TOMB RAIDER

The first quake threw Vigor into the air. Or maybe it was the ground that had dropped below his feet. Either way, he went airborne.

Cries rose across the basilica.

As he fell back down, he took advantage of the moment to plant an elbow square into the nose of the traitor Alberto, who had tumbled back with the first tremor. He swung next and punched Alberto a solid blow to the Adam's apple.

The man fell heavily. The pistol tumbled from his fingers. Vigor grabbed it just as the next tremor followed the first. He was knocked to his knees. By now, screams and yells erupted all around. But beneath it all, a deep, hollow thrum vibrated, as if a bell as large as the basilica had been struck and they were all trapped inside.

Vigor remembered the description given by the witness to the Cologne survivor. A pressure as if the walls squeezed in on themselves. It was the same here. All noises – cries, pleas, prayers – were perfectly discernible but muted nevertheless.

While he climbed to his feet, the floor continued trembling. The polished marble surface seemed to ripple and shiver, appearing watery. Vigor shoved the pistol under his belt.

He turned to go to the aid of the pope and Cardinal Spera.

As he stepped forward, he felt it before he saw it. A sudden increase in pressure, deafening, squeezing inward. Then it let loose. Up from the base of the four bronze columns of Bernini's *baldacchino*, fiery cascades of electrical energy spiraled upward, spitting and crackling.

They rushed up the columns, across the canopy's roof, and met at the gold globe. A crack of thunder erupted. The ground jolted again, shattering fissures in the marble floor. From the canopy's globe, a brilliant fork of lightning erupted. It blasted upward, striking the underside of Michelangelo's dome and dancing across it. The ground bumped again, more violently.

Cracks skittered across the dome. Plates of plaster rained.

It was all coming down.


9:57 p.m.

Monk picked himself up off the floor. Blood ran into one eye. He had landed face-first into the corner of a crypt, cracking his goggles, slicing his eyebrow.

Blind now, he crouched and fished for his weapon. The shotgun's built-in night scope would help him see.

As he searched, the ground continued to vibrate under his fingertips. All gunfire had stopped after the first quake.

Monk reached forward, sweeping the ground near the crypt. His shotgun couldn't have gone far.

He felt something hard at his fingertips.

Thank God.

He reached forward and realized his mistake. It was not the butt of his weapon. It was the toe of a boot.

Behind him, he felt the hot barrel of a rifle press against the base of his skull.

Shit.

Gray heard the crack of a rifle blast across the necropolis. It was the first shot since the quakes began. He had been thrown off the metal platform and had landed near the mausoleum where he'd hid his laptop. He had rolled into a ball, taking a blow to his shoulder, keeping his goggles and pistol in place. But he had lost his radio.

Shattered shards of glass littered the stone street, blown out of the platform window with the first violent quake.

He searched around him. Up the few steps to the metal platform, the wash of light still radiated from the tomb area. He had to know what was going on in there. But he couldn't assault the gate by himself. At least not without knowing the lay of the land.

Making certain no eyes were upon him, he dove back into the mausoleum. The planted cameras should still be transmitting.

As he lay flat on his belly, one arm covering the entrance with the pistol, he engaged the laptop. The split-screen image bloomed. The camera pointing into the main necropolis revealed nothing but darkness. No further shots were heard. The necropolis had gone deathly silent again.

What had happened to the others?

With no answers, he focused on the opposite side of the screen. Nothing seemed to have changed. Gray spotted two men with rifles pointed back toward the gate, Raoul's guards. But there was no sign of the big man. The tomb seemed unchanged. But the image, the *entire* image on the screen, pulsed slightly, in tune with the vibration in the stone floor. It was as if the cameras were picking up some emanation given off by the charged device, a field of energy radiating out.

But where was Raoul?

Gray reached out and rewound the digital recorder back a full minute, stopping at the spot where Raoul stood near the tomb and twisted the control handle to his device.

On the screen, Raoul turned to watch the result. Green lights flared on the two plates fixed to either side of the tomb. Movement caught his attention. Gray used a toggle to zoom in on the tomb's small opening. The cylinder of amalgam powder vibrated – then rose off the floor.

Levitating.

Gray began to understand. He remembered Kat's description of how the m-state powders demonstrated an ability to levitate in a strong magnetic field, acting as superconductors. He recalled Monk's discovery of a magnetized cross back in Cologne. The plates with the green lights. They must be electromagnets. The Court's device apparently did nothing more than create a strong electromagnetic field around the amalgam, activating the m-state superconductor.

He now understood the energy pulsing outward.

He knew what had killed the parishioners.

Oh God . . .

Suddenly the image jolted with the first quake. The view fritzed completely for a second, then settled, the perspective slightly askew now as the camera shifted. On the screen, Raoul backed away from the tomb.

Gray didn't understand why. Nothing seemed to be happening.

Then he spotted it, half hidden in the glare of the flashlights. At the base of the tomb, a section of the stone floor slowly tilted downward, forming a narrow ramp that led beneath the tomb. From below, a cobalt light flickered. Raoul stepped in front of the camera, blocking the view. He headed down the ramp, leaving only the two guards.

That's where he had disappeared.

Gray sped up the video back to the present. He now watched a few brilliant flashes erupt from below, blinding bursts of white light. Camera flashes. Raoul was recording whatever he found down there.

A few seconds later, Raoul climbed back up the ramp. The bastard wore a grimace of satisfaction.

He had won.

9:59 p.m.

Lying flat atop the mausoleum roof, Kat had managed to get one shot off, taking out the gunman holding a rifle to Monk's head. But another quake threw off her next shot. The remaining opponent did not hesitate. From the direction his comrade's body had fallen, he must have guessed where she hid.

He dove down and clubbed Monk with the metal hilt of a hunting knife, then pulled him up as a shield. He pressed the blade to Monk's neck.

'Come out!' the man called in heavily accented English, sounding Germanic. 'Or I will remove this one's head.'

Kat closed her eyes. It was Kabul all over again. She and Captain Marshall had gone in to save two captured soldiers, teammates. Decapitation had been threatened. But they had no choice. Though the odds were stacked against them three-to-one, they had made an assault, going in quiet, with knives and bayonets. But she had missed one guard, hidden in an alcove. A crack of a rifle, and Marshall went down. She had dispatched the last guard with a fling of a dagger, but it was too late for the captain. She had held his body as he gasped his last breath, thrashing in pain, eyes on her, pleading, knowing, disbelieving . . . then nothing. Eyes gone to glass. A vital man, a tender man, gone like smoke.

'Come out now!' the man yelled across the necropolis.

'Kat?' Rachel subvocalized to her, touching her elbow.

264

The Carabinieri lieutenant lay flat next to her on the roof.

'Stay hidden,' Kat said. 'Try to make it to one of the ropes that lead out of here.' That had been their original plan, to leap from rooftop to rooftop, to gain one of the scaling ropes that still hung down from the level above, to raise the alarm and gather reinforcements. That plan must not fail.

Rachel knew this, too.

Kat had her own duty. She rolled off the mausoleum roof and landed lithely on her toes. She glided over two rows to hide her former position, leaving some room for Rachel to escape, then stepped out into the open, ten yards from the man who held Monk. Kat lifted her hands and tossed her pistol aside. She laced her fingers and put them atop her head.

'I surrender,' she said coldly.

Dazed and blind, Monk struggled, but the man restraining him had enough training to keep him subdued, on his knees, knife point digging into his neck. Kat studied Monk's eyes as she strode forward.

Three steps.

The combatant relaxed. Kat noted his knife point shift away.

Good enough.

She dove forward, pulling the dagger from her wrist sheath. She used her momentum to fling the blade. It sailed and struck the man in the eye. He fell backward, carrying Monk with him.

Kat twisted, yanking a blade from her boot. She flipped it in the direction Monk had indicated, catching the barest flicker of shadow. A third combatant. A short cry followed. A man fell out of the shadows, pierced through the neck.

Monk struggled to his feet, fingers scrabbling and finding the other's knife. But he had lost his goggles, and Kat didn't have a spare pair. She would have to guide him.

She helped Monk up and placed his hand on her shoulder.

'Stay with me,' she whispered.

She turned as a flashlight flared ahead of her. Amplified by her night-vision scopes, the sudden brightness seared into the back of her head, blinding, painful.

A fourth combatant.

Someone she missed.

Again.


10:02 p.m.

Gray had noted the bloom of light on his computer screen, deep in the necropolis. That couldn't be good. It proved not to be. On one side of the split-screen image, he watched Raoul press his radio to his ear, his smile broadening. On the other side, he watched Kat and Monk being marched out at gunpoint, arms secured behind their backs with yellow plastic fast-ties.

They were shoved up the steps to the top of the platform.

Raoul remained by the tomb. The ground continued to tremble. One of his bodyguards stood beside him; the other had gone down the ramp.

Raoul raised his voice. 'Commander Pierce! Lieutenant Verona! Show yourselves now or these two die!'

Gray remained where he was. He didn't have the force to overpower this situation. Rescue was hopeless. And if he gave in to the demands, he would just be handing his own life over. Raoul would kill them all. He closed his eyes, knowing he was dooming his teammates.

A new voice drew his eyes back open.

'I'm coming!' Rachel stepped into view on the second camera. She had her hands in the air.

Gray watched Kat shake her head. She, too, knew the foolishness of the lieutenant's act.

266

Two armed gunmen collected Rachel and drove her to join the others.

Raoul stepped forward and pointed a meaty pistol into Rachel's shoulder. He bellowed at her ear, 'This is a horse pistol, Commander Pierce! Fifty-six caliber! It will rip her arm right off! Show yourself or I'll start removing limbs! On the count of five!'

Gray saw the flash of terror in Rachel's eyes.

Could he watch his friends brutally torn apart? And if he did, what would he gain? As he hid, Raoul and his men would surely take or destroy whatever clue had been hidden here. The others' deaths would be for nothing.

'Five . . .'

He stared at the laptop, at Rachel . . .

No choice.

Suppressing a groan, he wiggled out of his pack and grabbed one item from an inner pocket, palming it.

'Four . . .'

Gray switched the laptop into dark mode and clicked it closed. If he didn't live, he would have to trust that the computer would serve as witness to the events down here.

'Three . . .'

Gray crawled out of the mausoleum but remained hidden. He circled to hide his position.

'Two . . .'

He ducked back onto the main street.

'One . . .'

He laced his hands atop his head and stepped into sight. 'I'm here. Don't shoot!'


10:04 p.m.

Rachel watched Gray march up to them at gunpoint.

From the hard look on Gray's face, she recognized her error. She had hoped her surrender would buy Gray time to act, to do something to save them, or at least himself.

She had not wanted to be the one left alone out in the necropolis, to stand by and watch the others be killed.

And while Kat had given herself up for Monk, the woman had had a rescue plan in place, botched though it may have ended. Rachel, on the other hand, had acted on faith alone, placing all her trust in Gray.

The Dragon Court leader shoved her aside, meeting Gray as he climbed atop the platform. Raoul raised the massive horse pistol, pointing it at Gray's chest.

'You've caused me a hell of a lot of trouble.' He cocked the gun. 'And no amount of body armor will stop this slug.'

Gray ignored him.

His eyes were on Monk, Kat . . . then Rachel.

He parted his fingers atop his head, revealing a matte-black egg, and said one word.

'Blackout.'


10:05 p.m.

Gray counted on the full attention of Raoul and his men as the flash grenade exploded above his head. With his eyes squeezed closed, the strobing flare still burned through his lids, a crimson explosion.

Sightless, he dropped and rolled to the side.

He heard the thunderous bark of Raoul's horse pistol.

Gray reached to his boot and pulled free his .40-caliber Glock.

As the strobe ended, Gray opened his eyes.

One of Raoul's men lay at the foot of the steps, a fist-sized hole through his chest, taking the slug meant for Gray.

Raoul roared and dove off the platform, twisting in midair, shooting blindly back at the platform.

'Down!' Gray yelled.

Major-caliber slugs tore holes through steel.

The others dropped to their knees. Monk's and Kat's hands were still secured behind their backs.

Gray rolled and clipped one dazzled gunman in the ankle, toppling him off the platform. He shot another down at the foot of the steps.

He searched for Raoul. For such a giant of a man, he moved fast. Raoul had landed out of sight, but still blasted at them from below, tearing holes through the meshed floor of the platform.

They were sitting ducks.

Gray had no way of judging how long the flash grenade's effects would last. They had to move.

'Get back!' Gray hissed to the others. 'Through the gate!'

Gray fired a volley, covering their retreat, then followed.

Raoul had stopped firing for the moment, reloading. But no doubt he would come at them again with deadly fury.

Shouts arose from deeper in the necropolis. Other gunmen. They were rushing to the aid of their compromised comrades.

What now? He had only one magazine of ammo.

A cry rose behind him.

Gray glanced back. He watched Rachel flailing backward. She must have been half dazzled by the flash bomb. In the darkness, she missed seeing the ramp in front of the tomb and back-stepped into it. She grabbed for Kat's elbow, trying to stop her fall.

But Kat was equally caught off-guard.

Both women tumbled down the ramp and rolled below.

Monk met Gray's eyes. 'Shit.'

'Down,' Gray said. It was the only shelter. And besides, they had to protect whatever clue lay below.

Monk went first, stumbling with his arms behind his back.

Gray followed as a new barrage began. Chunks of rock were torn from the surface of the tomb. Raoul had reloaded. He meant to keep them away.

Twisting around, Gray's eyes caught on the green light glowing from one of the two plates attached to the tomb. Still activated. He thought quickly and made a choice. He pointed his pistol and fired.

The slug severed the knot of wires running to the plate. The green light winked out.

Gray ran down the stone ramp, noting the immediate cessation of the trembling in the ground. Both ears popped with a sudden release of pressure. The device had shorted.

Immediately a loud grinding sounded underfoot.

Gray dove forward and landed inside a small cavern at the foot of the ramp, a natural pocket, volcanic in origin, common in the hills of Rome.

Behind him, the ramp swung back up, closing.

Gray rolled to his feet, keeping his gun pointed up. As he had hoped, the device's activation had opened the tomb, and likewise its deactivation was closing it. Outside, the barrage by Raoul continued, tearing into rock.

*Too late,* Gray thought with satisfaction.

With a final grate of stone on stone, the ramp sealed above them.

Darkness settled – but it was not complete.

Gray turned.

The others had gathered around a slab of metallic black rock that rested on the floor. It was lit by a tiny pyre of blue flame atop its surface, rising like a small flume of electrical fire.

Gray approached. There was barely room for the four of them to circle it.

'Hematite,' Kat said, identifying the rock from her background in geology. She glanced from the sealed ramp to the slab. 'An iron oxide.'

She bent down and studied the silver lines etched into its surface, tiny rivers against a black background, which were illuminated by the blue flames.

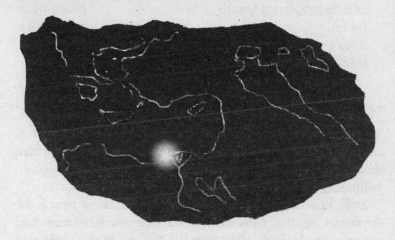

As Gray watched, the fire slowly expired, fading to a flicker, then winked out.

Monk drew their attention to a more immediate concern. Another glowing object.

'Over here,' he said.

Gray joined him. Resting in a corner of the blind cavern was a familiar silver cylinder, shaped like a barbell. An incendiary grenade. A timer counted down in the dark.

04:28.

04:27.

Gray remembered one of Raoul's bodyguards ducking down here after their leader was done taking photographs. He had been planting the bomb.

'Looks like they intended to destroy this clue,' Monk said. He dropped down to one knee, studying the device. 'Damn thing's booby-trapped.'

Gray glanced to the sealed ramp. Maybe Raoul's barrage a moment ago hadn't been meant to drive them off – but to trap them.

He stared back to the bomb.

With the fiery star on the hematite slab extinguished, the only light in the cavern glowed from the LCD timer on the incendiary grenade.

04:04.

04:03.

04:02.

Vigor had felt the sudden release. The wash of electrical fire that had been tearing plaster from the cupola dispersed in seconds. Its energy skittered away like ghostly cerulean spiders.

Still, chaos reigned inside the basilica. Few noted the cessation of the fireworks. Half the parishioners had managed to flee to safety, but the logjam at the entrances had slowed further evacuation. The Swiss Guard and Vatican Police were doing their best to assist.

Some people hid under pews. Dozens of other parishioners had been struck by falling plaster and sat with bloody fingers pressed to scalp wounds. They were being helped and consoled by a handful of brave individuals, true Christians.

The Swiss Guard had come to the rescue of the pope. But he had refused to abandon the church, acting as the captain of this sinking ship. Cardinal Spera remained at his side. They had evacuated out from under the fiery *baldacchino* and taken shelter in the Clementina Chapel off to the side.

Vigor strode over to join them. He glanced back across the basilica. The chaos was slowly subsiding. Order was being restored. Vigor stared up at the assaulted dome. It had held – whether through the mercy of God or through the engineering genius of Michelangelo.

As Vigor approached, Cardinal Spera broke through

the ranks of the Swiss Guard. 'Is it over?'

'I . . . I don't know,' Vigor said honestly. He had a larger concern.

The bones had been ignited. That was plain.

But what did that mean for Rachel and the others?

A new voice intruded, shouted with familiar command. Vigor turned to find a wide-shouldered, silver-haired man striding toward him, dressed in a black uniform, hat under his arm. General Joseph Rende, family friend and head of the local Parioli Station. Vigor now understood why order was being restored. The Carabinieri had responded in full force.

'What is His Holiness still doing here?' Rende asked Vigor, nodding to the pope, who remained ensconced among a clot of black-robed cardinals.

Vigor had no time to explain. He grabbed the general's elbow. 'We have to get below. To the Scavi.'

Rende frowned. 'I just heard word from the station . . . from Rachel . . . something about a robbery down there. Then this all happened.'

Vigor shook his head. He wanted to scream his panic, but he spoke firmly and steadily. 'Gather as many men as you can. We have to get down there. Now!'

To his credit, the general responded immediately, barking crisp commands. Black-uniformed men swiftly ran up, armed with assault weapons.

'This way!' Vigor said, heading to the sacristy door. The entrance to the Scavi was around back, not far. Still, Vigor could not move fast enough.

Rachel . . .

10:07 p.m.

Gray knelt with Monk. He had freed both his teammates' wrists with a knife hidden on Kat. Monk had borrowed Gray's night-vision scopes to aid in his study.

'Are you sure you can't defuse it?' Gray asked.

'If I had more time . . . better tools . . . some goddamn decent light . . .' Monk glanced to him and shook his head.

Gray watched the timer count down in the darkness.

02:22.

02:21.

Gray gained his feet and stepped to Kat and Rachel on the other side. Kat had been studying the ramp mechanism with the eyes of a trained engineer. She noted Gray's approach without turning.

'The mechanism is a crude pressure plate,' she said. 'Sort of like a deadman's switch. It takes weight to hold the ramp closed. But lift the weight off and the ramp opens by gears and gravity. But it doesn't make sense.'

'What do you mean?'

'As well as I can tell, the trigger plate lies under the tomb over our heads.'

'Saint Peter's tomb?'

Kat nodded and directed Gray to the side. 'Here is where they pulled the stabilizing pin after weighing down the plate with the tomb. Once set, the only way to open this ramp is to *move* Saint Peter's tomb off the plate. But that didn't happen when the Dragon Court activated their device.'

'Maybe it did. . . .' Gray pictured the cylinder containing the superconducting amalgam, how it had levitated. 'Kat, do you remember your description of the test done in Arizona – the test on these m-state powders? How, when these superconductors were charged, they weighed *less* than zero?'

She nodded. 'Because the powder was actually *levitating* the pan it held.'

'I think that's what happened here. I saw the amalgam cylinder levitate when the device was turned on. What if the field around the amalgam affected the tomb, too, like the pan in the experiment. While not actually lifting the massive structure, it simply made the stone structure *weigh* less.'

Kat's eyes widened. 'Triggering the pressure plate!'

'Exactly. Does that offer any clue on how to reopen the ramp?'

Kat stared a moment at the mechanism. She slowly shook her head. 'I'm afraid not. Not unless we can move the tomb.'

Gray glanced to the timer.

01:44.

## 10:08 p.m.

Vigor rushed down the spiral stairs that led to the Scavi. He saw no evidence of trespassing. The narrow door appeared ahead.

'Wait!' General Rende said behind him. 'Let one of my men go in first. If there are hostiles . . .'

Vigor ignored him and rushed to the door. He hit the latch. Unlocked. Thank God. He didn't have a spare key.

His weight struck the door. But it held.

He bounced back, shoulder bruised.

Flipping the latch, he shoved again.

The door refused to budge, as if blocked or bolted on the far side.

Vigor stared back at General Rende.

'Something's wrong.'

## 10:08 p.m.

Rachel stared unblinking as the timer ticked below one minute. 'There must be another way out,' she mumbled.

Gray shook his head against such wishful thinking.

Still, Rachel refused to give up. She may not know engineering, nor the art of defusing a bomb. But she *did* know Rome's history. 'No bones,' she said.

Gray stared at her as if she had slipped a gear.

'Kat,' she said, 'you mentioned that someone had to pull the stabilizing pin when the mechanism was first set, locking the ramp. Right?'

Kat nodded.

Rachel glanced at the others. 'Then he would've been trapped down here. Where are his bones?'

Kat's eyes widened.

Gray clenched a fist. 'Another way out.'

'I think I just said that.' Rachel pulled a book of matches from one of her pockets. She struck a flame. 'All we have to do is find an opening. Some secret tunnel.'

Monk joined them. 'Pass those around.'

In seconds, each member held a flickering flame. They searched for some sign of a freshening breeze, a telltale sign of a hidden exit.

Rachel spoke out of nervousness. 'Vatican Hill was named after the fortune-tellers that used to gather here. *Vates* is Latin for "seer of the future." Like many oracles of the time, they hid in caves like this and voiced prophecies.'

She studied her flame as she searched the wall.

No flicker.

Rachel tried not to glance at the timer, but failed.

00:22.

'Maybe it's sealed too tight,' Monk mumbled.

Rachel lit a fresh match.

'Of course,' she continued nervously, 'most of the oracles were charlatans. Like turn-of-the-century séances, the soothsayer usually had an accomplice hidden in a secret niche or tunnel.'

'Or under the table,' Gray said. He had squatted by the slab of hematite. He held his match low to the ground. His flame flickered, dancing shadows on the walls. 'Hurry.'

There was no need to goad them.

00:15.

That was incentive enough.

Monk and Gray grabbed the edge of the slab, bending with their knees. They heaved up, legs straining.

Kay had dropped to her hands and held a match out. 'There's a narrow tunnel,' she said with relief.

'Get inside,' Gray ordered.

Kat waved Rachel down.

Rachel slid feetfirst through the hole, discovering a stone well. She squiggled down its throat. It took no effort with the steep incline. She slid on her butt. Kat followed next, then Monk.

Rachel craned around, counting in her head. Four seconds remained.

Monk braced the slab with his back. Gray dove headfirst between the man's planted legs.

'Now, Monk!'

'Don't have to tell me twice.'

Dropping, Monk let the slab's weight push him into the chute.

'Down! Down!' Gray urged. 'Get as much –'

The explosion cut out further words.

Rachel, still half turned, saw a wash of orange flames lick around the edges of the slab, searching for them.

Monk cursed.

Rachel ignored caution and slid down the chute. It grew steeper and steeper. Soon she was bobsledding down a dank tunnel on her rear end, uncontrolled.

Distantly a new noise intruded.

A rumbling rush of water.

Oh no . . .

10:25 p.m.

Fifteen minutes later, Gray helped Rachel climb out of the Tiber River. They shivered on the bank. Her teeth chattered. He hugged her close and rubbed her shoulders

277

and back, warming her as best he could.

'I . . . I'm okay,' she said, but she didn't move away, even leaned a bit further into him.

Monk and Kat slogged out of the river, wet and muddy.

'We'd better keep moving,' Kat said. 'It'll help offset hypothermia until we can get into dry clothes.'

Gray set out, climbing the bank. Where were they? The escape chute had dumped into an underground stream. Blind, they had had no choice but to hold tight to one another's belts and follow the flow of the channel, hoping it would dump them somewhere safe.

Gray had felt some stonework as they proceeded, his arm held out to avoid obstacles. Possibly an ancient sewer line or drainage canal. It had emptied into a maze of channels. They had continued following the downward flow, until at last they had reached a glowing pool, plainly illuminated by reflected light from beyond the underground tunnel. Gray had investigated the pool and discovered a short stone passage that emptied into the Tiber River.

The others had followed, and soon they were all back under the stars with a full moon shining down on the river. They had made it.

Monk squeezed river water from his shirtsleeves, glancing back at the channel. 'If they had a goddamn back door, why all the business with the Magi bones?'

Gray had considered the same question and had an answer. 'No one could find that back door by chance. I doubt I could even find my way back through that maze. These ancient alchemists hid the next clue in such a manner that the seeker not only had to solve the riddle, but also had to have a basic understanding of the amalgam and its properties.'

'It was a test,' Rachel said, shivering in the slight breeze. Clearly she had also pondered this matter. 'A trial of passage before you could move onward.'

'I would've preferred a multiple choice test,' Monk said sourly.

Gray shook his head and climbed the bank. He kept his arm around Rachel, helping her. Her continuous shivering slowly subsided to occasional chilled shudders.

They reached the top and found themselves at the edge of a street. A park lay beyond. And farther up the hill, St. Peter's Basilica glowed golden against the night sky. Up there, sirens blared and emergency lights flickered in hues of red and blue.

'Let's find out what happened,' Gray said.

'*And* find a hot bath,' Monk grumped.

Gray didn't argue.


11:38 p.m.

An hour later, Rachel sat wrapped in a warm, dry blanket. She still wore her damp clothes, but at least the trek here and the heated arguments with a series of stubborn guards had warmed her considerably.

They were all ensconced in the offices of the Holy See's Secretary of State. The room was decorated with frescoes and outfitted with plush chairs and two long divans that faced each other. Seated around the room were Cardinal Spera, General Rende, and a very relieved uncle.

Uncle Vigor sat beside Rachel, her hand in his. He hadn't let go since they had broken through the cordon and gained access to this inner sanctum.

They had gone over a preliminary account of events.

'And the Dragon Court is gone,' Gray asked.

'Even the bodies,' Vigor said. 'It took us ten minutes to break through the lower door. All we found were some discarded weapons. They must've left the way they came in . . . through the roof.'

Gray nodded.

'At least the bones of Saint Peter are safe,' Cardinal

Spera said. 'The damage to the basilica and the necropolis can be repaired. If we had lost the relics . . .' He shook his head. 'We owe you all a large debt.'

'And no one in attendance at the memorial service died,' Rachel said, equally relieved.

General Rende held up a folder. 'Cuts and bumps, bruises, a few broken bones. More damage was done by the trampling crowd than from the series of quakes.'

Cardinal Spera absently twisted the two gold rings of his station, one on each hand, switching back and forth, a nervous gesture. 'What about the cavern below the tomb? What did you find?'

Rachel frowned. 'There was –'

'It was too dark to see clearly,' Gray said, cutting her off. He met her eyes, apologetic but firm. 'There was a large slab that had some writing on it, but I suspect that the firebomb will have scorched the surface clean. We may never know what was there.'

Rachel understood his reluctance to speak plainly. The head prefect of the Archives had vanished during the confusion, disappearing with the Dragon Court. If Preffetto Alberto worked with the Court, who else might be a part of the conspiracy? Cardinal Spera had already promised to investigate Alberto's room and private papers. Maybe it would lead somewhere.

In the meantime, discretion was important.

Gray cleared his throat. 'If this debriefing is finished, I appreciate the Vatican's hospitality in offering us a suite of rooms.'

'Certainly,' Cardinal Spera stood. 'I'll have someone show you there.'

'I'd also like to take another look around the Scavi myself. See if anything was missed.'

General Rende nodded. 'I can send you with one of my men.'

Gray turned to Monk and Kat. 'I'll see you back up in

280

the rooms.' His eyes flicked to include Rachel and Vigor.

Rachel nodded, understanding the silent command.

*Speak to no one.*

They would talk together later in private.

Gray headed out with General Rende.

Rachel watched him leave, remembering those arms around her. She tightened the blanket about her shoulders. It was not the same.

11:43 p.m.

Gray searched the mausoleum where he had hidden his gear. He found his pack where he had left it, unmolested.

Beside him, a young carabiniere stood as stiffly as his uniform was starched. The red stripes down the edges of his suit ran as straight as plumb lines, the white sash a perfect ninety-degree angle across his chest. The silver emblem on his hat looked spit-polished.

He eyed the pack as if Gray had just stolen it.

Gray did not bother to explain. He had too much on his mind. Though his backpack was still here, his laptop was gone. Someone had taken it. Only one person would steal the computer and leave the pack behind, someone conspicuously absent during the evening's events.

Seichan.

Angry, Gray stalked back up out of the necropolis. As he was escorted, he barely noted the courtyards, stairs, and hallways. His mind worked feverishly. After five minutes of hiking and climbing, he pushed inside the team's suite of rooms, leaving his escort outside.

The main room was opulent with gold leaf, embroidered furniture, and rich tapestries. A massive crystal chandelier filled a coved ceiling painted with clouds and cherubs.

Candles flickered in wall sconces and tabletop candelabras.

Kat sat in one of the chairs. Vigor in another. They had been in conversation as he entered. They had changed into thick white robes, as if this were a suite at the Ritz.

'Monk's in the bath,' Kat said, nodding to one side.

'As is Rachel,' Vigor added, pointing an arm toward the other side. All their rooms shared this common living space.

Kat noted his pack. 'You found some of our gear.'

'But not the laptop. I think Seichan nabbed it.'

Kat raised one eyebrow.

Gray felt too filthy to sit in any of the chairs, so he paced the room. 'Vigor, can you get us out of here unseen in the morning?'

'I . . . guess. If need be. Why?'

'I want us off the map again as soon as possible. The less anyone knows of our whereabouts, the better.'

Monk entered the room. 'We going somewhere?' He dug in an ear with a finger. A butterfly bandage closed the cut over his eye. He wore a white robe, too, which he had left open. At least there was a towel around his waist.

Before Gray could answer, the door on the opposite side opened. Rachel entered barefooted and robed, with her sash tied snugly. But as she strode toward the group, her robe still showed calf and much of her upper thigh. Her hair was freshly shampooed, wet and tousled. She finger-combed it into submission, but Gray liked it better wild.

'Commander?' Monk asked, dropping heavily into a chair. He kicked his legs up, adjusting his towel appropriately.

Gray took a deep swallow. *What was I saying*?

'Where are we going?' Kat prompted him.

'To find the next clue on this journey,' Gray said, clearing his throat, tightening his voice. 'After what we saw this evening, do we want the Dragon Court to gain whatever knowledge lies at the end of this treasure hunt?'

No one argued.

Monk picked at his bandage. 'What the hell *did* happen tonight?'

'I may have some idea.' Gray's words drew all their full attention. 'Is anyone familiar with Meissner fields?'

Kat raised a hand halfway. 'I've heard that term used in reference to superconductors.'

Gray nodded. 'When a charged superconductor is exposed to a strong electromagnetic field, a Meissner field develops. The strength of this field is proportional to the intensity of the magnetic field and the amount of power in the superconductor. It is a Meissner field that allows superconductors to levitate in a magnetic field. But other, stranger effects have been seen when manipulating superconductors, postulating other effects from Meissner fields. Inexplicable energy bursts, true antigravity, even distortions in space.'

'Is that what happened in the basilica?' Vigor asked.

'The activation of the amalgam, both here and in Cologne, was accomplished with nothing more than a pair of large electromagnetic plates.'

'Big magnets?' Monk asked.

'Tuned to a specific energy signature to release the power laying dormant in the m-state superconductor.'

Kat stirred. 'And the released energy – this Meissner field – levitated the tomb . . . or at least made it weigh less. But what about the electrical storm inside the basilica?'

'I can only guess. The bronze and gold canopy over the papal altar lies directly above Saint Peter's tomb. I think the metal columns of the canopy acted like giant lightning rods. They siphoned some of the energy given off below and blasted it upward.'

'But why would these ancient alchemists want to harm the basilica?' Rachel asked.

'They wouldn't,' Vigor answered. 'They didn't. Remember, we estimated that these clues were laid sometime during the thirteenth century.'

Gray nodded.

Vigor paused, then rubbed his beard. 'In fact, it would've been easy to construct the secret chamber during that same time period. The Vatican was mostly empty. It did not become the seat of papal power until 1377, when the popes returned from their century-long exile in France. Prior to that, the Lateran Palace in Rome had been the papal seat. So the Vatican was unimportant and unwatched during the thirteenth century.'

Vigor turned to Rachel. 'So the electrical storm could not be the alchemists' fault. Bernini's *baldacchino* wasn't installed until the 1600s. Centuries *after* the clues had been laid here. The storm had to be an unfortunate accident.'

'Unlike what happened in Cologne,' Gray countered. 'The Dragon Court purposefully tainted those Communion wafers with m-state gold. I think they used the parishioners as guinea pigs in some vile experiment. Their first *field* test. To judge the strength of the amalgam, to validate their theories. The ingested m-state gold acted like the bronze canopy here. It absorbed the energy of the Meissner field, electrocuting the parishioners from the inside out.'

'All those deaths,' Rachel said.

'Nothing more than an experiment.'

'We must stop them,' Vigor asserted, his voice brittle.

Gray nodded. 'But first we have to figure out where to go next. I memorized the drawing. I can sketch it out.'

Rachel glanced to him, then to her uncle.

'What?' Gray asked.

Vigor shifted and pulled forth a folded piece of paper. He leaned forward and smoothed it on the table. It was a map of Europe.

Gray frowned.

'I recognized the line drawing on the rock,' Rachel said. 'The tiny river delta gave it away, especially if you live along the Mediterranean. Watch.'

Rachel leaned forward and made a square box of her fingers, as if she were sizing up a photo shot. She laid it atop the eastern end of the map. [*See map overleaf.*]

Gray stared down, as did the others. The enclosed section of the coastline was a rough match to the etched line drawing on the hematite slab.

'It's a map,' he said.

'And the glowing star . . .' Rachel met his eyes.

'There must've been a tiny deposit of m-state gold imbedded in the slab. It absorbed the Meissner field energy and ignited.'

'Marking a spot on the map.' Rachel placed a finger on the paper.

Gray leaned closer. A city lay at her fingertip, at the mouth of the Nile, where it drained into the Mediterranean.

'Alexandria,' Gray read. 'In Egypt.'

He lifted his eyes, his face inches from Rachel's. Their eyes locked as he looked down upon her. Both froze for a heartbeat. Her lips parted slightly as if she were going to say something but forgot her words.

'The Egyptian city was a major bastion of Gnostic study,' Vigor said, breaking the spell. 'Once the home of the famed Library of Alexandria, a vast storehouse of ancient knowledge. Founded by Alexander the Great himself.'

Gray straightened. 'Alexander. You mentioned he was one of the historical figures who knew about the white powder of gold.'

Vigor nodded, eyes bright.

'Another magi,' Gray said. 'Could he be the *fourth* Magi we were instructed to seek?'

'I can't say for sure,' Vigor answered.

'I can,' Rachel replied, her voice certain. 'The verse in the riddle . . . it specifically refers to a *lost king*.'

Gray remembered the riddle about the fish. *Where it drowns, it floats in darkness and stares to the lost king.*

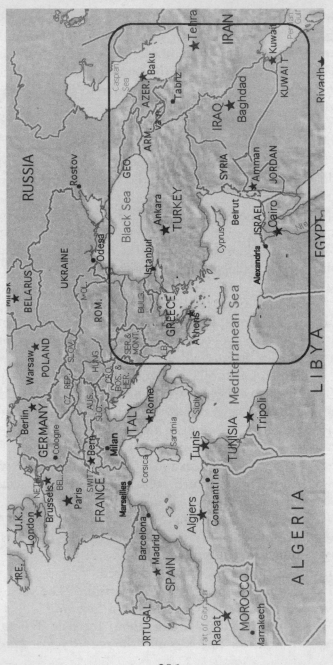

'What if it wasn't just allegorical?' Rachel insisted. 'What if it was literal?'

Gray didn't understand, but Vigor's eyes widened.

'Of course!' he said. 'I should have thought of that.'

'What?' Monk asked.

Rachel explained, 'Alexander the Great died at a young age. Thirty-three. His funeral and internment were well documented in the historical record. His body was laid in state in Alexandria.' She tapped the map. 'Only . . . only . . .'

Vigor finished for her, too excited. 'His tomb vanished.'

Gray stared down at the map. 'Making him the *lost* king,' he mumbled. His gaze swept the room. 'Then we know where we have to go next.'


11:56 P.M.

The image on the laptop played through once again, without sound, video only. From the appearance of the Dragon Court, through the escape of the Sigma team. There continued to be no answers. Whatever lay below in Saint Peter's tomb remained a mystery.

Disappointed, he closed the laptop and leaned back from his desk.

Commander Pierce had not been entirely forthcoming at the debriefing. His lie had been easy to read. The commander had discovered something in the tomb.

But what had he found? How much did he know?

Cardinal Spera leaned back, twisting the gold ring around his finger.

It was time to end all this.

# DAY
# THREE

# 11

# ALEXANDRIA

They'd be in Egypt in two hours.

Aboard the private jet, Gray inventoried his pack. Director Crowe had managed to outfit them with new supplies and weapons. Even laptops. The director had also had the foresight to move their rented Citation X plane down from Germany to Rome's Leonardo da Vinci International Airport.

Gray checked his watch. They had taken off half an hour ago. The two hours remaining until they landed in Alexandria was all the time the group had to strategize. The few hours of downtime in Rome had at least helped revive the group. They had left before dawn, sneaking out of Vatican City without alerting anyone of their departure.

Director Crowe had arranged additional cover at his end, setting up a dummy flight plan to Morocco. He had then used his contacts with National Reconnaissance Office to change their call signs in mid-flight as they turned for Egypt. It was the best they could do to cover their tracks.

Now there remained only one detail to iron out.

*Where to begin their search in Alexandria?*

To answer this, the Citation X's cabin had been turned into a research think tank. Kat, Rachel, and Vigor all hunched over workstations. Monk was up in the cockpit, coordinating transportation and logistics once on the

291

ground. The man had already taken apart and inspected his new Scattergun. He kept it with him. As he stated, 'I feel naked without it. And trust me, you wouldn't want that.'

In the meantime, Gray had his own investigation to pursue. Though it was not directly related to the immediate question, he intended to research further into the mystery of these m-state superconductors.

But first . . .

Gray stood and crossed to the trio of researchers. 'Any headway?' he asked.

Kat answered, 'We've divided our efforts. Scouring all references and documents beginning before Alexander's birth and continuing through his death and the eventual disappearance of his tomb.'

Vigor rubbed his eyes. He'd had the least sleep of any of them. A single hour nap. The monsignor had taken it upon himself to do some further research among the stacks at the Vatican Archives. He was sure that the head prefect of the libraries, the traitor Dr. Alberto Menardi, was the mastermind behind solving the riddles for the Dragon Court. Vigor had hoped to track the prefect's footsteps, to gain some additional insight. But little had been discerned.

Kat continued, 'Mystery still surrounds Alexander. Even his parentage. His mother was a woman named Olympias. His father was King Philip II of Macedonia. But there's some disagreement here. Alexander came to believe his father was a god named Zeus Ammon, and that he himself was a demigod.'

'Not exactly humble,' Gray said.

'He was a man of many contradictions,' Vigor said. 'Prone to drunken rages, but thoughtful in his strategy. Fierce in his friendships, but murderous when crossed. He dabbled with homosexuality, but married both a Persian dancer and the daughter of a Persian king, this last in an attempt to unite Persia and Greece. But back to his parentage. It was well known that his mother and father hated each other. Some historians believe Olympias may have had a hand in assassinating King Philip. And what's interesting is that one writer, Pseudo-Callisthenes, claimed Alexander was not the son of Philip, but instead was the son of an Egyptian magician to the court, named Nectanebo.'

'A magician . . . as in *magi*?' Gray understood the implication.

'Whoever his parents truly were,' Kat continued, 'he was born on July 20, 356 B.C.'

Vigor shrugged. 'But even that might not be true. On that same date, the Temple of Artemis in Ephesus burned down. One of the Seven Wonders of the ancient world. The historian Plutarch wrote that Artemis herself was "too busy taking care of the birth of Alexander to send help to her threatened temple." Some scholars believe the choice of date might be propaganda, the true date of Alexander's birth moved to match this portentous event, portraying the king as a phoenix rising from the ashes.'

'And a rise it was,' Kat said. 'Alexander lived only to thirty-three, but he conquered most of the known world during his short life. He defeated King Darius of Persia, then went on to Egypt, where he founded Alexandria, then on to Babylonia.'

Vigor finished, 'Eventually he moved east into India, to conquer the Punjab region. The same region where Saint Thomas would eventually baptize the Three Magi.'

'Uniting Egypt and India,' Gray noted.

'Connecting a line of ancient knowledge,' Rachel said, stirring from her own laptop. She didn't raise her eyes, still focused on her research, but she did work a kink from her back.

Gray liked the way she stretched, slow, unhurried.

Maybe she noticed his study. Without turning her head,

293

just her eyes flicked toward him. She stuttered a moment, glancing away. 'He . . . Alexander even sought out Indian scholars, spending a significant amount of time in philosophical discussions. He was very interested in new sciences, having been taught by Aristotle himself.'

'But his life was cut short,' Kat continued, drawing back Gray's attention. 'He died in 323 B.C. In Babylon. Under mysterious circumstances. Some say he died of natural causes, but others believe he was poisoned or contracted a plague.'

'It is also said,' Vigor added, 'that upon his deathbed in the royal palace of Babylon, he gazed out upon the city's famous Hanging Gardens, a tower of sculpted terraces, rooftop gardens, and waterfalls. Another of the Seven Wonders of the ancient world.'

'So his life began with the destruction of one and ended at another.'

'It may just be allegorical,' Vigor conceded. He scratched at the beard under his chin. 'But Alexander's history seems strangely tied to the Seven Wonders. Even the first compilation of the Seven Wonders was made by an Alexandrian librarian named Callimachus of Cyrene in the third century B.C. The towering bronze statue in Rhodes, another of the Wonders, the ten-story Colossus that spanned the island's harbor and held up a fiery torch, like your Statue of Liberty, was modeled after Alexander the Great. Then there's the Statue of Zeus in Olympia, a glowering four-story figure of gold and marble. By Alexander's own claim, possibly his real father. And there can be no doubt that Alexander visited the Pyramids of Giza. He spent a full decade in Egypt. So Alexander's fingerprints seem to be all over these masterpieces of the ancient world.'

'Can this be significant?' Gray asked.

Vigor shrugged. 'I can't say. But Alexandria itself was once home to another of the Seven Wonders, the last to be built, though it no longer stands. The Pharos Light-house of Alexandria. It rose from a spit of land extending into the harbor of Alexandria, splitting the bay into two halves. It was a three-tiered tower of limestone blocks, held together by molten lead. It rose taller than your Statue of Liberty, some forty stories. At its top, a fire burned in a brazier, amplified by a gold mirror. Its light guided boat pilots from as far away as fifty kilometers. Even today, the very name *lighthouse* harkens back to this Wonder. In French, *phare*. In Spanish and Italian, *faro*.'

'And how does this connect to our search for Alexander's tomb?' Gray asked.

'We were pointed to Alexandria,' Vigor said. 'Chasing clues left by an ancient society of magi. I can't help but think that the lighthouse, this shining symbol of a guiding light, would be significant to this group. There's also a legend surrounding the Pharos Lighthouse – that its golden light was so potent that it could burn ships at a distance. Perhaps this hints back to some unknown source of power.'

Vigor finally sighed and shook his head. 'But how this all hangs together, I don't know.'

Gray appreciated the monsignor's intellect, but he needed more concrete information, something to pursue once they arrived in Alexandria. 'Then let's go directly to the heart of the mystery. Alexander died in Babylon. What happened after that?'

Kat spoke up, leaning over her laptop. She ran a finger down a list she had compiled. 'There are many historical references to the parade of his body from Babylon to Alexandria. Once entombed in Alexandria, it became a shrine for visiting dignitaries, including Julius Caesar and the emperor Caligula.'

'During this time,' Vigor added, 'the city itself was ruled by one of Alexander's former generals, Ptolemy, and his descendants. They would go on to establish the Library of Alexandria, turning the city into a major site of intellectual and philosophical study, bringing scholars from around the known world.'

'And what happened to the tomb?'

'That's what's intriguing,' Kat said. 'The tomb was supposedly a massive sarcophagus made of gold. But in other references, including the major historian of the time, Strabo, the tomb is described as being made of *glass*.'

'Perhaps golden glass,' Gray said. 'One of the states of the m-state powder.'

Kat nodded. 'In the early third century A.D.; Septimus Severus closed the tomb from viewing, out of concern for its safety. It's also interesting to note that he placed many secret books into the vault. Here's a quote.' She leaned forward to the laptop. '"So none could read the books nor see the body."' She pushed back and glanced to Gray. 'This plainly supports that *something* of great importance was hidden at this tomb site. Some storehouse of secret arcana that Septimus feared would be lost or stolen.'

Vigor elaborated, 'There were many attacks upon Alexandria from the first through third centuries. They grew worse and worse. Julius Caesar himself burned a large portion of the Alexandrian library to ward off attack at the harbor. These attacks would continue, leading to the eventual destruction and dissolution of the library by the seventh century. I can understand why Septimus would want to protect a portion of the library by hiding it. He must have hidden the most important scrolls there.'

'It wasn't just military aggressors that threatened the city,' Kat added. 'A series of plagues struck. Frequent earthquakes damaged significant parts of Alexandria. A whole section of the city fell into the bay in the fourth century, destroying the Ptolemaic Royal Quarters, including Cleopatra's palace, and much of the Royal Cemetery.

In 1996, a French explorer, Franck Goddio, discovered sections of this lost city in the East Harbor of Alexandria. Another archaeologist, Honor Frost, believes that perhaps this might be the fate of Alexander's tomb, sunk into a watery grave.'

'I'm not convinced of that,' Vigor said. 'Rumors abound on the location of that tomb, but most historical documents place the tomb in the center of the city, away from the coastline.'

'Until, like I said, Septimus Severus closed it off,' Kat argued. 'Maybe he moved it.'

Vigor frowned. 'Either way, throughout the subsequent centuries, treasure hunters and archaeologists scoured Alexandria and its vicinity. Even today, there's a gold-rush-like fervor to find this lost tomb. A couple of years ago, a German geophysics team used ground-penetrating radar to show that the subsoil throughout Alexandria is riddled with anomalies and cavities. There are plenty of places to hide a tomb. It could take decades to search them all.'

'We don't have decades,' Gray said. 'I don't know if we have twenty-four hours.'

Frustrated, Gray paced the narrow cabin. He knew the Dragon Court had the same intel as they did. It would not take them long to realize the hematite slab under Saint Peter's tomb was a map with Alexandria marked on it.

He faced the trio. 'So where do we look first?'

'I may have one hint,' Rachel said, speaking for the first time in a while. She had been furiously typing at her keyboard and squinting at the screen periodically. 'Or two.'

All attention turned to her.

'There is a reference back in the ninth century, testimony from the emperor of Constantinople, that some, and I quote, "fabulous treasure" was hidden within or under the Pharos Lighthouse. In fact, the caliph who ruled Alexandria at the time dismantled half of the lighthouse searching for it.'

Gray noted that Vigor stirred at her words. He remembered the monsignor's interest in the lighthouse. Rachel must have been swayed by her uncle and gone in search of clues.

'Others periodically continued the search, but the lighthouse served a strategic role for the harbor.'

Vigor nodded, his eyes glowing with excitement. 'What better place to hide something you don't want dug up than under a structure too important to tear down?'

'Then it all ended on August 8, 1303, when a massive quake shook the eastern Mediterranean. The lighthouse was destroyed, toppling into the same harbor where the Ptolemaic ruins fell.'

'What became of the original site?' Gray asked.

'It varied over the centuries. But in the fifteenth century, a Mamluk sultan built a fort on the peninsula. It still stands today, the Fort of Qait Bey. Some of its construction includes the original limestone blocks that made up the lighthouse.'

'And if the treasure was never found,' Vigor continued, 'then it must still be there . . . *beneath* the fort.'

'If it ever existed,' Gray warned.

'It's a place to start looking,' Vigor said.

'And what do we do? Knock on the door and ask them if it's okay to dig under their fort?'

Kat offered a more practical solution. 'We contact NRO. They have access to satellites with ground-penetrating radar capability. Have them do a pass over the site. We can look for any abnormalities or cavities like the German geophysicists did in the city. It might help pinpoint our search.'

Gray nodded. It wasn't a bad idea. But it would take time. He had already checked. It would be eight hours until the next pass of a surveillance satellite.

Rachel offered an alternative. 'Remember the back door into the cavern under Saint Peter's tomb? Maybe we don't have to go in the front door of the Fort of Qait Bey. Maybe there's a back entrance. One underwater like in Rome.'

Gray liked her idea.

Rachel seemed to take strength from the approval in his face. 'There are tour groups that dive on the sites near Qait Bey and the Ptolemaic ruins. We could easily blend in and search the underwater coastline of the harbor.'

'It might not lead to anything,' Kat said, 'but it would allow us to do something until a GPR satellite could make a pass over there.'

Gray nodded slowly. It was a start.

Monk pushed into the cabin from the cockpit. 'I have a van and a hotel already booked under our aliases, and customs has already been cleared through some cooperation with Washington. I think that should take care of everything.'

'No.' Gray turned to him. 'We're also going to need a boat. Preferably something fast.'

Monk's eyes widened. 'Okay,' he dragged out. His gaze settled on Rachel. 'But she's not going to be driving the damn thing, is she?'

8:55 a.m.
ROME, ITALY

The heat of the morning did not help Raoul's mood. It was only midmorning and already the temperature spiked. Sunlight baked the stone square outside and glared too brightly. His naked body gleamed with sweat as he stood at the doors out to his room's balcony. The doors were open but no breeze moved.

He hated Rome.

He despised the stupefying herds of tourists, the black-

299

draped locals smoking continually, the constant chatter, yells, the honking cars. The air reeked of petrol.

Even the whore he had picked up in Travastere, her hair smelled of cigarettes and sweat. She stank of Rome. He rubbed his raw knuckles. At least the sex had been satisfactory. No one had heard her screams through the ball gag. He had enjoyed the way she squirmed under his knife as he dragged the tip around the wide brown nipples and corkscrewed down her breast. But he had found greater satisfaction pounding her face with his fist, flesh to flesh, as he rutted into her.

Upon her body, he beat out his frustration with Rome, with the bastard American who had nearly blinded him, ruining his chance to make their deaths slow. And now he had learned that the others had somehow again escaped certain doom.

He turned from the window. The whore's body was already wrapped in the bedsheets. His men would dispose of the corpse. It meant nothing to him.

At the bedside table, the phone rang. He had been expecting this call. It was what had really soured his mood.

He crossed and picked up the cell phone.

'Raoul,' he said.

'I received the report from last night's mission.' As expected, it was the Imperator of his Order. His voice was stiff with fury.

'Sir –'

He was cut off. 'I won't accept any excuse. Failure is one thing, but insubordination will not be tolerated.'

Raoul frowned at this last. 'I would never disobey.'

'Then what about the woman, Rachel Verona?'

'Sir?' He pictured the black-haired bitch. He remembered the smell of the nape of her neck as he clutched her and threatened her with a knife. He had felt her heartbeat in her throat as he squeezed and lifted her to her toes.

'You were instructed to capture her . . . not kill her. The others were to be eliminated. Those were your orders.'

'Yes, sir. Understood. But three times now, I've been restrained from using full brutal force against the American team because of this caution. They are still in this matter only because of such restraint.' He hadn't been planning on excusing his failures, but here was one handed to him. 'I need better clarification. Which is more important: the mission or the woman?'

A long silence stretched. Raoul smiled. He poked the dead body on the bed with the tip of his finger.

'You do make a good point.' The edge of fury had faded from the other's voice. 'The woman is important, but the mission must not be jeopardized. The wealth and power at the end of this trail must be ours.'

And Raoul knew why. It had been drilled into him since childhood. The ultimate goal of their sect. To bring about a New World Order, one led by their Court, descendants of kings and emperors, genetically pure and superior. It was their birthright. For generations, going back centuries, their Court had hunted for the treasure and arcane knowledge of this lost society of mages. Whoever possessed it would hold the 'keys to the world,' or so it was written in an ancient text in the Court's library.

Now they were so close.

Raoul spoke, 'Then I have the go-ahead to proceed forward without concern for the woman's security?'

A sigh came through. Raoul wondered if the Imperator was even aware of it. 'There will be disappointment in her loss,' he answered. 'But the mission must not fail. Not after so long. So to clarify, the opposition must be destroyed by any and all means. Is that plain enough?'

'Yes, sir.'

'Good. But I will also ask that if the opportunity *should* arise where the woman could be captured, all the better. Still, take no needless risks.'

Raoul tightened a fist. He had a question that had been bothering him. He had never asked it before. He had learned it best to keep such curiosities to himself, to obey without question. Still, he asked it now. 'Why is she so important?'

'The Dragon blood runs strongly through her. Back all the way to our Austrian Hapsburg roots. In fact, she had been chosen for you, Raoul. To be your mate. The Court sees great value in strengthening our lines through such a blood tie.'

Raoul stood straighter. He had been denied offspring until now. The few women who took his seed were forced to abort or were killed. It was forbidden to sully their royal bloodlines by producing mud children.

'I hope this information encourages you to seek out an opportunity to secure her. But as I stated, even her blood is expendable if the mission is threatened. Is that understood?'

'Yes, sir.' Raoul found his breath shortened. He again pictured the woman clutched in his arms, held at knifepoint. The smell of her fear. She *would* make a good baroness . . . and if not that, then at least an excellent brood mare. The Dragon Court hid a few such women across Europe, caged away, kept alive only to produce children.

Raoul grew hard thinking about such an opportunity.

'Everything has been arranged in Alexandria,' the Imperator finished. 'The endgame nears. Get what we need. Slay all who stand in your way.'

Raoul slowly nodded, though the Imperator could not see it.

He pictured the black-haired bitch . . . and what he would do to her.

302

Rachel stood behind the wheel of the speedboat, one knee on the bucket seat behind her to support her. Once past the No Wake buoy, she gunned the throttle and shot across the bay. The boat skimmed the flat water, bucking over the occasional wake of another boat.

Wind whipped her hair. Spray cooled her face. Sunlight glinted brightly off the sapphire blue waters of the Mediterranean. Her every sense rang and tingled.

It helped awaken her after the plane ride and the hours spent in front of the computer. They had landed forty minutes ago. They had breezed through customs, greased by Monk's calls, and had found the boat and gear already waiting for them at the pier to the East Harbor.

Rachel glanced behind her.

The city of Alexandria rose from the arc of the blue bay, a modern sprawl of high-rise apartments, hotels, and time-share properties. Palm trees dotted the garden median dividing the city from the water. There was little evidence of the city's ancient past. Even the famed Alexandrian library, lost centuries ago, had arisen anew as a massive complex of glass, steel, and concrete, decorated with reflecting pools and serviced by a light-rail station.

But now, out in the water, some of the past came alive again. Old wooden fishing boats dotted the bay, painted in vibrant jeweled hues: ruby reds, sapphire blues, emerald greens. Some sails were raised, square-shaped, the skiff's direction guided by two oars, an ancient Egyptian design.

And ahead rose a citadel right out of the Middle Ages, the Fort of Qait Bey. It crested a spit of land that divided the bay into halves. A stone causeway joined the fortress to the mainland. Along its length, fishermen with long poles relaxed and shouted among themselves, as their ancestors probably had for centuries into the past.

Rachel studied the Fort of Qait Bey. Built solely of white

limestone and marble, it shone starkly against the deep-blue waters of the bay. The main citadel was built atop a foundation of stone, raised twenty feet. There, towering walls, topped with arched parapets, were guarded by four towers and circled a central higher keep. A flagpole jutted from the inner castle, flapping the Egyptian colors, striped bands of red, white, and black, along with the golden eagle of Saladin.

Squinting, Rachel pictured what had once stood atop this foundation: the forty-story-tall Pharos Lighthouse, built in tiers like a wedding cake, decorated with a giant statue of Poseidon, and tipped by a giant fiery brazier, flaming and smoking.

Nothing remained of this Wonder of the ancient world, except perhaps for a few limestone blocks, rebuilt into the citadel here. French archaeologists had also discovered a tumble of blocks in the East Harbor, along with a twenty-foot section of statue, believed to be the sculpture of Poseidon. It was all that was left of the Wonder since the earthquake devastated the region.

Or was it? Could there be another treasure, one dating even further back in time, hidden below the foundations?

The lost tomb of Alexander the Great.

That's what they had come to find out.

Behind her, the others were gathered over the pile of scuba gear, checking tanks, regulators, and weight belts.

'Do we really need all this gear?' Gray asked. He picked up a full-face mask. 'Thick dry suits and all this special head gear?'

'You'll need it all,' Vigor said. Her uncle was an experienced diver. Being an archaeologist in the Mediterranean, there was no way not to be. Many of the region's most exciting discoveries were found underwater, including here in Alexandria, where the lost palace of Cleopatra had recently been discovered, sunk under the waves of this same bay.

But there was a reason these underwater treasures had remained hidden for so long.

Her uncle explained. 'The pollution here in the East Harbor, coupled with the sewage, has made these waters dangerous to explore without proper protection. The Egyptian tourist board has floated concepts for opening a marine archaeological park here, serviced by glass-bottomed boats. Some unscrupulous tour operators already offer dive trips. But exposure to heavy-metal toxins and the risk of typhoid is real for those entering the water.'

'Great,' Monk said. He already looked a tad green around the gills. He clutched the starboard rail, teeth clenched. He kept his head a bit over the side, like a dog hanging his head out a window. 'If I don't drown, I'll end up catching some flesh-melting disease. You know, there's a reason I joined the Army Special Forces versus the Navy or Air Force. Solid ground.'

'You could stay on the boat,' Kat said.

Monk scowled at her.

If they were going to find some underwater tunnel leading to a secret treasure chamber under the fort, they would need everybody. They were all certified divers. They would search in shifts, rotating one person out to rest and guard both boat and gear.

Monk had insisted on the first shift.

Rachel sped their boat along the eastern edge of the spit of land. Ahead, the citadel of Qait Bey grew in size, filling the horizon. It hadn't looked so massive from the pier. It would be a daunting task to explore the depths surrounding the fort.

A worry began to nag her. It had been her idea to attempt this search. What if she was wrong? Maybe she had missed a clue pointing somewhere else.

She slowed the boat, nervous energy growing.

They had mapped out the regions into quadrants for a

systematic exploration of the bay around the fort. She throttled down, approaching the first dive spot.

Gray stepped next to her. He rested one hand on the seatback. His fingertips brushed her shoulder. 'This is quadrant A.'

She nodded. 'I'll drop anchor here and raise the orange flag warning of divers in the water.'

'Are you all right?' he asked, leaning down.

'I just hope this isn't a wild-goose chase, as you Americans say.'

He smiled, determination warming into reassurance. 'You gave us a start. It was more than we had going into the matter. And I'd rather be chasing wild geese, as we Americans say, than doing nothing.'

Without realizing it, she shifted her shoulder so it pressed against his hand. He didn't pull away.

'It's a good plan,' he said, his voice softer.

She nodded, at a loss for words, and glanced away from those damn eyes of his. She cut the engine and thumbed the release for the anchor. She felt the shudder under her seat as the chained rope dropped.

Gray turned to the others. 'Let's suit up. We'll drop here, check our marine radios, then begin the search.'

Rachel noted that he kept his hand at her shoulder.

It felt good there.


10:14 a.m.

Gray fell backward into the sea.

Water swamped over him. Not an inch of skin was exposed to the potential pollution and sewage. The seams of the full-body suit were double-taped and double-sewed. The neck and wrist seals were heavy-duty latex. Even his AGA mask completely covered his face, sealing the Viking hood over his head. The regulator was built into its faceplate, freeing his mouth.

306

Gray found the spread of peripheral vision through the mask worth the extra time it took to suit up, especially since visibility was poor here in the harbor. Silt and sediment clouded the view to a range of ten to fifteen feet.

Not bad. It could be worse.

His BC buoyancy vest bobbed him back to the surface, full of air, compensating for the weight belt. He watched Rachel and Vigor drop into the sea on the other side of the boat. Kat was already in the water on his side.

He tried the radio, a Buddy Phone, ultrasonically transmitting on an upper single sideband. 'Can everyone hear me?' he asked. 'Check in.'

He got positive responses all around, even from Monk, who was taking up the first guard shift on the boat. Monk also had an Aqua-Vu marine infrared video system to monitor the group below.

'We'll drop to the bottom here and sweep toward shore in a wide spread. Everyone knows their positions.'

Affirmatives answered.

'Down we go,' he said.

He vented the air in his BC vest and lowered into the water, dragged down by his weight vest. This was the point where many novice divers experienced a panicked claustrophobia. Gray never had. Instead, he felt the opposite, a total freedom. He was weightless, flying, capable of all sorts of aerial acrobatics.

He spotted Rachel dropping on the opposite side of the boat. She was easy to spot by the broad red stripe across the chest of her black suit. They each had a different color for ease of identification. His was blue, Kat's pink, Vigor's green. Monk had already climbed into his suit, too, ready for his shift. His stripe was yellow, somehow fitting considering his attitude toward diving.

Gray watched Rachel. Like him, she seemed to enjoy the freedom below the waves. She twisted and flew, spiraling down with a minimal flicker of fins. He took a moment to enjoy the curves of her form, then concentrated on his own descent.

The sandy bottom rose up, cluttered with debris.

Gray adjusted his buoyancy to keep him drifting just above the seabed. He searched right and left. The others settled into similar postures.

'Can everyone see each other?' he asked.

Nods and affirmatives all around.

'Monk, how's the underwater video camera working?'

'You look like a bunch of ghosts. Visibility is crap. I'll lose you once you head out.'

'Keep in radio contact. Any problems, you raise the alarm and haul ass over to us.' Gray was pretty confident that they had the jump on the Dragon Court, but he was not taking any chances with Raoul. He didn't know how much of a head start they had gained. But there were plenty of other boats about. It was broad daylight.

Still, they needed to act quickly.

Gray pointed an arm. 'Okay, we'll head to shore, keep no greater distance than fifteen feet apart. Visual contact with each other at all times.'

The four of them could sweep a swath of about twenty-five yards across. Once at shore, if nothing was detected, they would shift down the coastline another twenty-five yards and swim back toward the waiting boat. Back and forth, quadrant by quadrant, they would comb the entire coastline around the fort.

Gray set out. He had a dive knife attached to a sheath on the back of his wrist and a flashlight on the other. With the sun directly overhead and the water only forty feet deep, there was no need for the extra illumination, but it would come in handy to explore nooks and crannies. He had no doubt that the passage they sought would not be plain or it would have already been discovered.

It was another riddle to solve.

As he swam, he pondered what they had missed. There

must have been more of a clue to the map drawn on the stone than merely pointing to Alexandria. It must have also held some clue embedded about the location here. Had they missed something? Had Raoul stolen a clue out of the cave below Saint Peter's tomb? Did the Dragon Court already have the answer?

Unconsciously he had begun to swim faster. He lost sight of Kat on his right. He was last in line on this side. He slowed and she reappeared. Satisfied, he moved onward. A shape appeared ahead, jutting from the sandy bottom. A rock? A ridge of reef?

He kicked forward.

Out of the silty gloom, it appeared.

What the hell . . . ?

The stone face stared back at him, human, worn by the sea and time, but its features were surprisingly clear, the expression stoic. Its upper torso rode atop the squat form of a lion.

Kat had noted his attention and swept slightly closer. 'A sphinx?'

'Another one over here,' Vigor announced. 'Broken, on its side. Divers have reported dozens of them littered around the seabed in the shadow of the fort. Some of the decorations from the original lighthouse.'

Despite the urgency, Gray stared at the statue, amazed. He studied the face, sculpted by hands two thousand years old. He reached one arm out and touched it, sensing the immense breadth of time between himself and that sculptor.

Vigor spoke out of nowhere. 'Fitting that these masters of riddles should be guarding this mystery.'

Gray pulled back his hand. 'What do you mean?'

A chuckle. 'Don't you know the story of the Sphinx? The monster terrorized the people of Thebe, eating them if they couldn't solve its riddle. "What has one voice, and is four-footed, two-footed, and three-footed?"'

309

'And the answer?' Gray asked.

'Mankind,' Kat said next to him. 'We crawl on all fours as babes, then upright on two feet as adults, and lean upon a staff in old age.'

Vigor continued. 'Oedipus solved the riddle and the Sphinx threw herself off a cliff and died.'

'Toppling from a height,' Gray said. 'Like these sphinxes.'

He pushed away from the stone statue and swam onward. They had their own riddle to solve. After another ten minutes of silent searching, they reached the rocky coastline. Gray had come across a tumble of giant blocks, but no passage, no opening, no clues.

'Back again,' he said.

They shifted down the coast and set out again, swimming away from the shoreline toward the boat.

'Everything quiet up there, Monk?' Gray asked.

'Getting a nice suntan.'

'Make sure you use SPF 30. We'll be down here a while.'

'Aye, aye, Captain.'

Gray continued for another forty minutes, sweeping to the boat, then back again. He came across a sunken husk of a rusted ship, more chunks of stone blocks, a broken pillar, even an inscribed chunk of obelisk. Fish in a rainbow of hues danced away.

He checked his air gauge. He was breathing conservatively. He still had half a tank left. 'How's everyone's air holding up?'

After comparing, it was decided to go topside in twenty minutes. They'd take a half-hour break, then back into the water.

As he swam, he went back to his original pondering. He kept sensing they had missed something critical. What if the Dragon Court had taken some object from the cave, a second clue? He kicked harder. He had to let that fear go. He had to proceed as though he had the same intel as the Court, an equal playing field.

The silence of the deep pressed on him. 'This just doesn't seem right,' he mumbled.

The radio transmitted his voice.

'Did you find something?' Kat asked. Her shadowy form drifted closer.

'No. That's just it. The longer I'm down here, the more I'm convinced we're doing this wrong.'

'I'm sorry,' Rachel said from out of nowhere, sounding hopeless. 'I probably put too much emphasis – '

'No.' Gray remembered her worry topside. He kicked himself for rekindling it. 'Rachel, I think you've targeted the correct place to search. The problem is *my* plan. This whole searching quadrant by quadrant. It just doesn't feel right.'

'What do you mean, Commander?' Kat asked. 'It may take some time, but we'll get the area covered.'

That was just it. Kat had clarified it for him. He wasn't one for systematic, dogged methodology. While some problems were best solved that way, this mystery wasn't one of them.

'We've missed a clue,' he said. 'I know it. We recognized the map in the tomb, realized it pointed to Alexander's tomb, then flew here. We searched records, books, and files, trying to solve a riddle that has baffled historians for more than a millennium. Who are we to solve it in one day?'

'So what do you want us to do?' Kat asked.

Gray settled to a stop. 'We go back to square one. We've based our search on historical records available to anyone. The only advantage we have over all the treasure hunters of the past centuries is what was discovered under Saint Peter's tomb. We missed a clue down there.'

*Or one was stolen,* Gray thought. But he did not speak this worry aloud.

'Maybe we didn't miss a clue at the tomb,' Vigor said. 'Maybe we didn't look deep enough. Remember the

311

catacombs. The riddles were multilayered, multifathomed. Could there be another layer to this riddle?'

Silence answered him . . . until an unexpected voice solved it all.

'That goddamn fiery star,' Monk swore. 'It wasn't just pointing down at the city of Alexandria . . . it was pointing down at the stone slab.'

Gray felt the ring of truth in Monk's words. They had been so focused on the inscribed map, the fiery star, the implication of it all, but they had ignored the unusual medium of the artist.

'Hematite,' Kat said.

'What do you know about it?' Gray asked, trusting her background in geology.

'It's an iron oxide. Large deposits have been found throughout Europe. It is mostly iron, but sometimes it contains a fair amount of iridium and titanium.'

'Iridium?' Rachel said. 'Isn't that one of the elements in the amalgam? In the Magi bones?'

'Yes,' Kat said, voice suddenly sounding strained over the radio. 'But I don't think that's the significant part.'

'What?' Gray asked.

'I'm sorry, Commander. I should have thought of it. The iron in hematite is often weakly *magnetic,* not as strongly as magnetite, but it's sometimes used as a lodestone.'

Gray realized the implication. Magnetism had also opened the first tomb. 'So the star wasn't just pointing to Alexandria, it was pointing to a magnetized stone, something we're supposed to find.'

'And what did the ancient world do with lodestones?' Vigor asked, excitement growing in his voice.

Gray knew the answer. 'They made compasses!' He fed air into his BC vest and rose toward the surface. 'Everyone topside!'

312

In a matter of minutes, they were shedding tanks, vests, and weight belts. Rachel climbed into the pilot's seat, glad to sit down. She pressed the button to raise the anchor. It chugged upward.

'Go slow,' Gray said. He had taken up a post at her shoulder.

'I second that,' Monk said.

'I'll watch the compass,' Gray continued. 'You keep us on a snail-paced circuit around the fort. Any twitch on the compass needle and we drop anchor and search below.'

Rachel nodded. She prayed that whatever magnetized stone lay down there, it was strong enough for their shipboard compass to detect.

With the anchor retracted, she eased the throttle to the barest chop of her propellers. Motion forward was barely detectable.

'Perfect,' Gray whispered.

Onward they glided. The sun slowly rose into the sky overhead. They pulled up the boat's canopy to shade the group as the day's heat climbed. Monk lay sprawled on the portside bench, slightly snoring. No one spoke.

Worry grew in Rachel with each slow turn of the boat's propeller.

'What if the stone isn't out here?' she whispered to Gray, who kept a vigil on the compass. 'What if it's inside the fort?'

'Then we'll search there next,' Gray said, squinting toward the stone citadel. 'But I think you're right about a secret entrance. The hematite slab sat over a secret tunnel to the cavern that led down to a river channel. Water. Perhaps that's another layer of the riddle.'

Kat heard them, a book open on her lap. 'Or we're reading too much into it,' she said. 'Trying to force what we want to match the riddle.'

313

Up in the bow end, Vigor massaged a sore calf muscle from the swim. 'I think the ultimate question of where the stone might lie – on land or in the water – depends on *when* the alchemists hid the clue. We estimated the clues were hidden sometime around the thirteenth century, maybe a little before or a little after, but that's the critical era of conflict between Gnosticism and orthodoxy. So, did the alchemists hide their next clue before or after the Pharos Lighthouse collapsed in 1303?'

No one had an answer.

But a few minutes later, the compass needle gave a shaky twitch.

'Hold it!' Gray hissed.

The needle steadied again. Kat and Vigor glanced to them.

Gray placed a hand on Rachel's shoulder. 'Go back.'

Rachel tweaked the throttle into neutral. Forward momentum stopped. She let the waves bob them backward.

The needle pitched again, swinging a full quarter turn.

'Drop anchor,' Gray ordered.

She pressed the release, hardly breathing.

'Something's down there,' Gray said.

Everyone began to move at once, grabbing for fresh tanks.

Monk woke with a start, sitting up. 'What?' he asked blearily.

'Looks like you're going on guard duty again,' Gray said. 'Unless you want to take a dip?'

Monk scowled his answer.

Once the boat was secure and the orange flag raised, the same four divers fell back into the water.

Rachel bubbled out her buoyancy and sank under the waves.

Gray's voice reached her through the radio. 'Watch your wrist compasses. Zero in on the anomaly.'

Rachel studied her compass as she descended. The

314

water was fairly shallow here. Less than ten meters. She reached the sandy bottom quickly. The others dropped around her, hovering like birds.

'Nothing's here,' Kat said.

The seabed was a flat expanse of sand.

Rachel stared at her compass. She kicked a body length away, then back again. 'The anomaly is right here.'

Gray lowered to the bottom and swept his wrist over the floor. 'She's right.'

He reached to his other wrist and unsheathed his knife. With the blade in hand, he began stabbing into the soft sand. The blade sank to the hilt each time. Silt stirred up, clouding the view.

On his seventh stab, the knife plainly jarred, failing to penetrate more than a few centimeters.

'Got something,' Gray said.

He sheathed the knife and began digging in the sand. The view grew quickly murky, and Rachel lost sight of him.

Then she heard him gasp.

Rachel moved closer. Gray swept back. The disturbed sand dispersed and settled.

Protruding from the sand was a dark bust of a man.

'I think that's magnetite,' Kat said, studying the stone of the sculpture. She swept her wrist compass over the bust. The needle twirled. 'Lodestone.'

Rachel edged closer, staring at the face. There was no mistaking the features. She had seen the same countenance a couple of times today.

Gray recognized it, too.

'It's another sphinx.'

12:14 p.m.

Gray spent ten minutes clearing the shoulders and upper torso, reaching the lion's shape below. There was no doubt

315

it was one of the sphinxes, like the others littered on the seabed.

'Hiding it among the others,' Vigor said. 'I guess that answers the question of when the alchemists hid their treasure here.'

'*After* the lighthouse collapsed,' Gray said.

'Exactly.'

They hovered around the magnetic sphinx, waiting for the disturbed silt and sand to settle.

Vigor continued, 'This ancient society of mages must have known the location of Alexander's tomb after Septimus Severus hid it in the third century. They left it undisturbed, letting it safeguard the most valuable scrolls from the lost library. Then perhaps the quake in 1303 not only brought down the lighthouse, but exposed the tomb. They took the opportunity to hide more down there, using the chaotic time after the earthquake to plant their next clue, bury it, and allow the centuries to cover it up again.'

'And if you're right,' Gray said, 'that pinpoints the date when these clues were planted. Remember, we'd already estimated that the clues were laid around the thirteenth century. We were off by only a few years. It was 1303. The first decade of the fourteenth century.'

'Hmm . . .' Vigor drifted closer to the statue.

'What?'

'It makes me wonder. In that same decade, the true papacy was chased out of Rome and exiled in France. The antipopes ruled Rome for the next century.'

'So?'

'Similarly, the Magi bones were moved from Italy to Germany in 1162, another time when the true pope was chased out of Rome and an antipope sat on the papal seat.'

Gray followed this train of thought. 'So these alchemists hid their stuff whenever the papacy was in jeopardy.'

'So it would seem. This would suggest that this society of mages had ties to the papacy. Perhaps the alchemists did indeed join the Gnostic Christians of those turbulent times, Christians open to the quest for arcane knowledge, the *Thomas* Christians.'

'And this secret society merged with the orthodox church?'

Vigor nodded in the murky water. 'When the overall church came under threat, so did the secret church. So they sought safeguards. First moving the bones to safety in Germany during the twelfth century. Then during the embattled years of the exile, they hid the true heart of their knowledge.'

'Even if this is true, how does this help us find Alexander's tomb?' Kat asked.

'Just as the clues that led to Saint Peter's tomb were buried in the stories of Catholicism, the clues here might be tied to the mythologies of Alexander. Greek mythologies.' Vigor ran a gloved finger down the face of the statue. 'Why else mark the gateway with a sphinx?'

'The riddle masters of the Greeks,' Gray mumbled.

'And the monsters killed you outright if you didn't answer them correctly,' Vigor reminded them. 'Perhaps choosing this symbol is a warning.'

Gray studied the sphinx as the sand cleared, its expression enigmatic. 'Then we'd better solve this riddle.'


12:32 p.m.
FINAL DESCENT INTO ALEXANDRIA

The Gulfstream IV private jet received clearance from the tower to land. Seichan listened to the chatter of the cockpit crew through the open doorway. She sat in the seat nearest the door. Sunlight blazed through the window on her right.

A large form stepped to her left.

317

Raoul.

She continued to stare out the window as the jet tilted on a wing over the violet-blue of the Mediterranean and lined up for the final approach to the runway.

'What's the word from your contact on the ground?' Raoul asked, biting off each word.

He must have noted her using the jet's air-phone. She fingered the dragon charm on her necklace. 'The others are still in the water. If you're lucky, they may solve this mystery for you.'

'We won't need them for that.' Raoul stepped back to join his men, a team of sixteen, including the Court's master adept.

Seichan had already met the esteemed Vatican biblio-phile, Dr. Alberto Menardi, a lanky silver-haired man with a pocked complexion, thick lips, narrow eyes. He sat in the back of the plane, nursing a broken nose. She had a full dossier on him. His ties to a certain Sicilian criminal organization ran deep. It seemed even the Vatican could not keep such weeds from taking root in their soil. Then again, she could not discount the keen edge to the man's mind. He had an IQ three points above Einstein.

It had been Dr. Alberto Menardi who, fifteen years ago, had discerned from the Dragon Court's library of Gnostic texts the ability of electromagnetism to unlock the energy of these superconducting metals. He had over-seen the research project in Lausanne, Switzerland, and tested the effects on animal, vegetable, and mineral. And who would miss the occasional lone Swiss backpacker? These last experiments would turn the stomach of even the worst Nazi scientists.

The man also had a disturbing fetish for young girls.

But not for sex.

For sport.

She had seen some of the pictures and wished she hadn't. If she hadn't already been instructed by the Guild to eliminate the man, she would have done so on her own.

The plane began its final descent.

Somewhere far below, the Sigma team labored.

They were no threat.

It would be as easy as shooting fish in a barrel.

# 12

# RIDDLE OF THE SPHINX

'Remember that damn fish,' Monk radioed from the boat above.

Twelve feet down, Gray frowned up at the bobbing keel overhead. They had spent the last five minutes ruling out various options. Maybe the sphinx sat atop a tunnel. But how would they move a ton of stone? Levitation was discussed, using the amalgam, like back at St. Peter's. Gray had a test tube of the powder from his research on the Milan bones. But to activate it would require electricity of some sort . . . not wise in water.

'What fish are you talking about, Monk?' Gray asked. He had seen enough fish down here to turn him off seafood.

'From the first riddle,' Monk answered. 'You know. The painted fish in the catacombs.'

'What about it?'

'I can see you guys and the statue through the Aqua-Vu camera. The sphinx is facing *toward* that big fort.'

Gray stared at the statue. From here, where visibility was no greater than five yards, it was hard to get the bigger picture. Monk had the better perspective. And the bigger picture was his area of expertise, seeing the forest through the trees.

'The catacombs . . .' Gray mumbled, understanding Monk's intent.

320

*Could it be that easy?*

'Remember,' Monk continued, 'how we had to follow the direction the fish was facing to find our next clue? Maybe the sphinx is facing toward the tunnel opening.'

'Monk could be right,' Vigor said. 'These clues were planted in the early fourteenth century. We should be considering the problem from the perspective of that era's level of technology. They didn't have scuba gear at the time. But they did have compasses. The sphinx may be nothing but a magnetic road marker. You use your compass to find it. Swim down to take a peek at where it's facing and move onto shore.'

'There's only one way to find out,' Gray said. 'Monk, keep the boat anchored here until we're sure. We'll swim toward shore.'

Gray kicked away from the statue. He waited until he was far enough away to get a good compass fix without the magnetic interference of the lodestone. 'Okay, let's see where this leads.'

He set off. The others trailed behind him. They stuck close together.

The shore was not far. The spit of land rose steeply. The sandy bottom ended abruptly at a tumbled maze of stone blocks. Man-made.

'Must have once been a section of the Pharos Lighthouse,' Vigor said.

Barnacles and anemones had taken over the area, forming it into their own reef. Crabs scrabbled and tiny fish darted.

'We should spread out,' Kat said. 'Search the area.'

'No.' Gray intuitively understood what needed to be done. 'It's like the magnetic sphinx hidden among the other sphinxes.' He kicked off the bottom, traveling up the reefscape. He kept one arm fixed in front of him, watching the wrist compass.

It didn't take long.

Passing over one block, his compass needle pitched and rolled. He was only four yards from the surface. The front of the block was about two feet square.

'Here,' he said.

The others joined him.

Kat took a blade and scraped off the accumulation of sealife. 'Hematite again. Less strongly magnetic. You'd never notice it unless you were looking for it.'

'Monk,' Gray said.

'Yeah, boss.'

'Bring the boat over here and drop anchor.'

'On my way.'

Gray searched the edges of the block. It was cemented to its neighbors – above, below, and to the sides – by coral, sand, and dense accumulations of rough-shelled mussels.

'Everyone pick a side and dig the edges clear,' he ordered. He pictured the hematite slab under Saint Peter's tomb. It had covered a secret tunnel. He had no doubt that they were on the right track.

For once.

In a couple of minutes, the block was cleared.

The beat of a propeller echoed leadenly through the water.

Monk approached the shoreline slowly. 'I can see you guys,' he said. 'A bunch of striped frogs sitting on a rock.'

'Lower the anchor,' Gray said. 'Slowly.'

'Here it comes.'

As the prong of heavy steel dropped from the keel, Gray swam over and helped guide it to the hematite block. He jammed a corner into a gap between the block and its neighbor.

'Winch it up,' Gray ordered.

Monk retracted the anchor line. It grew taut.

'Everybody back,' Gray warned.

The block rocked. Sand billowed from it. Then the

chunk of stone tipped loose. It had only been about a foot thick. It rolled down the cliff face, bouncing with muffled crashes, then landed heavily on the sandy floor.

Gray waited for the silt to clear. Pebbles continued to rain down the wall of rock. He moved forward. In the gap-toothed opening left by the dislodged stone, a dark space loomed.

Gray flicked on the flashlight on his wrist. He pointed it into the opening. The light illuminated a straight tunnel, angled slightly upward. It was a tight squeeze. No room for air tanks.

Where did it lead?

There was only one way to find out.

Gray reached to the buckles securing his air tank. He shimmied out of them.

'What are you doing?' Rachel asked.

'Someone's got to go take a look.'

'We could unrig the boat's Aqua-Vu camera,' Kat said. 'Use a fishing pole or an oar to push the camera inside.'

It wasn't a bad plan – but it would take time.

Time they didn't have.

Gray settled his tank to a shelf of rock. 'I'll be right back.' He took a deep breath, unhooked the regulator hose from his mask, then turned to face the tunnel.

It would be snug.

He remembered the riddle of the Sphinx. How it described the first stage of man. Crawling on all fours. It was a fitting way to enter.

Gray ducked his head, arms forward, flashlight leading. He kicked off and sailed into the cramped tunnel.

As the tunnel swallowed him up, he remembered Vigor's earlier warning about the riddle of the Sphinx.

Get it wrong . . . and you were dead.

As Gray's flippers vanished into the tunnel, Rachel held her breath.

It was foolhardy madness. What if he got stuck? What if a section of the tunnel collapsed? One of the most dangerous forms of scuba diving was cave diving. Only those with a death wish enjoyed that sport.

And they had air tanks.

She clutched the edge of the rockface with her gloved fingers. Uncle Vigor shifted to her side. He placed his hand over hers, urging confidence.

Kat crouched by the opening. The woman's flashlight pierced the dark tunnel. 'I can't see him.'

Rachel's grip on the rock tightened.

Her uncle felt her flinch. 'He knows what he's doing. He knows his limits.'

*Does he?*

Rachel had recognized the edge of wildness about him in the last few hours. It both thrilled her and scared her. She had spent enough time with him. Gray did not think like other people. He operated at the fringes of common sense, trusting his quick thinking and reflexes to pull him out of tight scrapes. But the sharpest mind and fastest reflexes would not help you if a wall of rock dropped on top of your head.

A chop of words reached her. ' – can – clear – okay –'

It was Gray.

'Commander,' Kat said loudly, 'you're breaking up.'

'Hang –'

Kat glanced at them. Through her mask, her frown was clear.

'Is this better?' Gray said, the reception steadier.

'Yes, Commander.'

'I was out of water. Had to duck my head back down.' His voice sounded excited. 'The tunnel is short,' he said.

'A straight shot angled up. If you take a deep breath and kick a bit with your fins, you'll pop right up here.'

'What did you find?' Uncle Vigor asked.

'Some stone tunnels. Looks solid enough. I'm going to push forward and explore.'

'I'm going with you,' Rachel blurted out. She struggled with the buckles on her vest.

'First let me make sure it's safe.'

Rachel shrugged out of her air tank and vest and propped them into a crevice. Gray wasn't the only bold one. 'I'm coming up.'

'Me too,' her uncle said.

Rachel took a breath and undid her hose. Free, she swam to the tunnel opening and ducked through. It was pitch dark. In her haste, she had forgotten to turn on her flashlight. But as she flicked her legs and pushed deeper, a ripple of light appeared only three meters ahead. Her buoyancy helped propel her. The light grew. The tunnel widened to either side.

In a matter of moments, she popped out into small pool.

Gray frowned at her. He stood on the stone bank that lipped the circular pool. A drum-shaped chamber opened around her. A man-made cave. The roof was corbeled in narrowing rings, giving it the appearance of being inside a tiny step pyramid.

Gray held out an arm for her. She didn't refuse, gawking at the chamber. He helped haul her out.

'You shouldn't have come,' he said.

'And you shouldn't have gone,' she countered, but her eyes were still on the blocks of stone around her. 'Besides, if this place has withstood an earthquake that toppled the Pharos Lighthouse, I think it can handle my footsteps.'

At least, she hoped so.

A moment later, Vigor appeared, splashing up into the pool

Gray sighed. He should've known better than to try to keep these two away.

Rachel shed her mask and pushed back her hood. She shook loose her hair, then bent to help the monsignor out of the water.

Gray kept his mask in place and ducked his head under the water. The radio worked best with water contact.

'Kat, maintain a post by the tunnel exit. Once we're out of the water, we'll lose communication pretty quickly. Monk, if there's any trouble, relay it to Kat, so she can fetch us.'

He received affirmatives from both. Kat sounded irritated.

Monk was glad to stay where he was. 'You go ahead. I've pretty much had my fill of crawling around in tombs.'

Gray straightened and finally pulled away his own mask. The air smelled surprisingly fresh, if not a tad crusty with algae and salt. There must be a few crevices to the surface.

'A tumulus,' Vigor said, free of his own mask. He eyed the stone ceiling. 'An Etruscan tomb design.'

Two tunnels led out from here, angled apart. Gray was anxious to explore. One was taller than the other, but narrower, barely wide enough for one man to pass through. The other was low, requiring one to hunch a bit, but it was wider.

Vigor touched the blocks that made up one wall. 'Limestone. Cut and fitted tightly, but feel . . . the blocks are cemented with lead.' He turned to Gray. 'According to the historical record, this is the same design as the Pharos Lighthouse.'

Rachel stared around her. 'This might be part of the

original lighthouse, perhaps a subfloor or basement cellar.'

Vigor headed for the closest tunnel, the shorter of the two. 'Let's see where this leads.'

Gray blocked him with an arm. 'Me first.'

The monsignor nodded his head, a bit apologetic. 'Of course.'

Gray leaned down, pointed his flashlight. 'Conserve your flashlight's batteries for now,' he instructed. 'We don't know how long we'll be down here.'

Gray took a step forward, hunched beneath the low roof. A twinge pricked his back from one of the bruising slugs he had taken back in Milan. He felt like an old man.

He froze.

Crap.

Vigor bumped into him from behind.

'Back, back, back . . .' he urged.

'What?' Vigor asked but obeyed.

Gray retreated into the pool chamber.

Rachel eyed him oddly. 'What's wrong?'

'You ever hear of the story about the man who had to choose between two doors, behind one hid a tiger, the other a lady?'

Rachel and Vigor nodded.

'I could be wrong, but I think we're faced with a similar dilemma. Two doors.' Gray pointed to each dark tunnel. 'Remember the riddle of the Sphinx, marking the ages of man? Crawling, upright, and bent over. It took crawling to get into here.' Gray recalled thinking that when he entered the tunnel.

'Now two ways lead forward,' he continued. 'One where you can walk upright, another which requires you to hunch. Like I said, I could be wrong, but I'd prefer we take that other tunnel first. The one where you walk upright, the *second* stage of man.'

Vigor eyed the tunnel they had been about to enter. In

his profession as an archaeologist, he must know all about booby-trapped tombs. He nodded. 'No reason to be hasty.'

'No reason at all.' Gray circled the pool to the other tunnel.

He shone his flashlight and led the way. It took about ten steps until he breathed again.

The air grew a bit musty. The tunnel must be leading into the depths of the peninsula. Gray could almost sense the weight of the fort above him.

The passage made a series of sharp jags, but eventually his light revealed the tunnel's end. A larger space opened ahead. The glow of his flashlight reflected off something beyond.

Gray continued more slowly.

The others crowded behind him.

'What do you see?' Rachel asked at the end of the line.

'Amazing . . .'


1:08 p.m.

On the monitor of the Aqua-Vu camera, Monk watched Kat cooling her heels by the tunnel entrance. She sat perfectly still, hovering with minimal effort, a conservation of energy. As he spied, she shifted ever so subtly, underwater tai chi. She stretched a leg, turning a thigh, accentuating the long curve of her body.

He trailed a finger down the screen of a monitor.

A perfect S.

Perfect.

He shook his head and turned away. Who was he fooling?

He searched the flat expanse of blue water. He wore polarized sunglasses, but by now, the constant noonday glare made his eyes ache.

And the heat . . .

Even in the shade, it had to be over a hundred degrees. His dry suit chafed. He had unzipped and peeled down the upper section of suit, and stood bare-chested. But all the sweat seemed to have pooled in his crotch.

And now he had to take a leak.

He'd better cut off the diet Cokes.

Motion caught his eye. Coming around the far side of the peninsula. A large sleek ship, midnight blue. Thirty-footer. He read the lines. Not an ordinary ship. Hydrofoil. It raced over the waters, slightly raised on its surface-piercing skids. It flew unimpeded over the slight waves, skimming like a sled on ice.

Crap, it was fast.

He followed its curve around the spit of land, a quarter klick out. It aimed toward the East Harbor. It was too small for a ferry shuttle. Maybe some rich A-rab's private yacht. He raised a pair of binoculars and searched for the ship. It took an extra moment to pin down the boat.

In the bow, he spotted a pair of girls in bikinis. No burka-wrapped modesty here. Monk had already surveyed a few of the other boats around the harbor, fixing them in place in his mental chessboard. One mini-yacht had a party in full swing, champagne flowing. Another houseboat-like craft had an older couple lounging about buck naked. Apparently Alexandria was the Fort Lauderdale of Egypt.

'Monk,' Kat called from the radio.

He wore a headset connected to the underwater transceiver. 'What is it, Kat?'

'I'm picking up a pulsing note of static over the radio. Is that you?'

He lowered the binoculars. 'It's not me. I'll run a diagnostic on the transceiver. You might be picking up someone's fish finder.'

'Roger that.'

Monk glanced across the water. The hydrofoil slowed

and settled deeper into the water. It had drifted to the far side of the harbor.

Good.

Monk fixed its berth among the other boats in his head, one more piece to the chessboard. He turned his attention to the Buddy Phone transceiver. He twisted the amplitude control, earning a feedback whine in his ear, then reset the channel.

'How's that?' he asked.

Kat answered. 'Better. It's gone now.'

Monk shook his head. *Damn rental equipment . . .*

'Let me know if it returns,' he said.

'Will do. Thanks.'

Monk eyed the length of her form on the camera screen and sighed. What was the use? He picked up his binoculars. Where were those two bikini-clad girls?

1:10 p.m.

Rachel stepped last into the chamber. The two men parted to either side in front of her. Despite Gray's warning to conserve their batteries, Uncle Vigor had flicked on his own flashlight.

The spears of light illuminated another drum-shaped room, domed above. The ceiling plaster had been painted black. Silver stars glowed brightly against the dark background. But the stars had not been painted onto the ceiling. They were metallic inlays.

The ceiling was reflected in a still pool of water that covered the entire floor. It looked knee-deep. The effect of the mirrored image in the water created a mirage of a perfect sphere of stars, above and below.

But that still wasn't the most amazing sight.

Resting in the middle of the chamber, rising from the pool of water, stood a giant pyramid of glass, as tall as a man. It seemed to float in the center of the phantom sphere.

The glass pyramid glinted with a familiar golden hue. 'Could it be . . . ?' Uncle Vigor muttered.

'Gold glass,' Gray said. 'A giant superconductor.'

They spread out along the narrow lip of stone that surrounded the pool. Four copper pots rested in the water at the edges of the pools. Her uncle inspected one, then moved on. Ancient lamps, Rachel guessed. But they had brought their own illumination.

She studied the structure in the middle of the pool. The pyramid was square-bottomed, four-sided, like the pyramids of Giza.

'Something's inside it,' Rachel said.

The reflection off the glass surfaces of the pyramid made details inside difficult to discern. Rachel hopped into the water. It was a little deeper than her knees.

'Careful,' Gray said.

'Like you'd take that advice,' she shot back, wading toward the pyramid.

Splashes behind her announced the others were following. They crossed to the glass structure. Her uncle and Gray repositioned their lamps to penetrate the pyramid.

Two shapes appeared.

One stood in the exact center of the pyramid. It was a bronze sculpture of a giant finger, raised and pointing up. So large, she doubted she could get her arms around it. The detail work was masterful, from the trimmed fingernail down to the wrinkles at the knuckles.

But it was the shape below the raised finger that drew most of her attention. A figure, crowned and masked in gold, robed in a flow of white gown, lay atop a stone altar. The arms outstretched to either side, Christlike. But the golden face was distinctly Greek.

Rachel turned to her uncle. 'Alexander the Great.'

Her uncle stepped slowly around, getting a view from all angles. His eyes glistened with tears. 'His tomb . . . the historical record mentioned his last resting place was in glass.' He reached to touch one of the outstretched hands, buried only a few centimeters into the glass, then thought better of it and lowered his arm.

'What's with the bronze finger?' Gray asked.

Uncle Vigor stepped back to them. 'I . . . I think it's from the Colossus of Rhodes, the giant statue that spanned the island's harbor. It represented the god Helios but was modeled after Alexander the Great. No part of the statue was thought to still exist.'

'Now this last remnant has become Alexander's headstone,' Rachel said.

'I think *all* of this is a testament to Alexander,' her uncle said. 'And to the science and knowledge he helped foster. It was at the Library of Alexandria that Euclid discovered the rules of geometry. All around here are triangles, pyramids, circles.'

Uncle Vigor then pointed up and down. 'The reflected sphere split by water harkens to Eratosthenes, who at Alexandria calculated the diameter of the Earth. Even the water here . . . it must be fed through small channels to keep this pool full. It was at the library that Archimedes designed the first screw-shaped water pump, which is still in use today.'

Her uncle shook his head at the wonder. 'All of this is a monument to Alexander and the lost Library of Alexandria.'

That reminded Rachel of something. 'Weren't there supposed to be books down here? Didn't Septimus bury the most important scrolls of the library down here?'

Vigor searched around. 'They must have been cleared out after the quake. When the clues were planted here. The knowledge must've been taken and sent to whatever hidden vault we seek. We must be close.'

Rachel heard the quaver in her uncle's voice. What else might they discover?

'But before we move on,' Gray said, 'we first must solve this riddle.'

'No,' Uncle Vigor said. 'The riddle is not even exposed yet. Remember at St. Peter's. We must pass some test. Prove our knowledge, like the Dragon Court did with their understanding of magnetism. Only after that was the secret revealed.'

'Then what are we supposed to do?' Gray asked.

Uncle Vigor stepped back, his eyes on the pyramid. 'We have to activate this pyramid.'

'And how do we go about doing that?' Gray asked.

Vigor turned to Gray. 'I need some soda.'

**1:16 p.m.**

Gray waited for Kat to ferry up the last of the cans of Coke. They needed two more six-packs. 'Does it matter if it's diet Coke or regular?' Gray asked

'No,' Vigor said. 'I just need something acidic. Even citrus juice would work, or vinegar.'

Gray glanced to Rachel. She just shook her head and shrugged.

'Would you care to explain now?' Gray asked.

'Remember how magnetism opened the first tomb,' Vigor said. 'We know that the ancients were well aware of magnetism. Lodestones were widely distributed and used. Chinese compasses date back to 200 B.C. To move forward, we had to prove our understanding of magnetism. It even led us here. A magnetic marker left underwater.'

Gray nodded.

'So another scientific wonder must be demonstrated here.'

Vigor was interrupted by the arrival of Kat. She rose up into the entry pool, bearing aloft two more six-packs, making it a total of four.

'We're going to need Kat's help for a few minutes,' Vigor said. 'It'll take four people.'

'How are things topside?' Gray asked Kat.

She shrugged. 'Quiet. Monk fixed a radio glitch. That was the extent of any excitement.'

'Let him know you'll be off the air for a couple minutes,' Gray said, uneasy, but they needed whatever was hidden here.

Kat dunked under, passing on the message. She then quickly climbed out and they all returned to Alexander's tomb.

Vigor waved for them to disperse. He pointed to a copper urn at the pool's edge. There were four of the pots. 'Each of you take a six-pack of soda and take up a post by the jars.'

They spread out.

'Care to tell us what we're doing?' Gray asked as he reached his copper jar.

Vigor nodded. 'Demonstrating another scientific wonder. What we must show here is the knowledge of a force known even to the Greeks. They called it *electrikus*. A name for the static charge of a cloth rubbed over amber. They witnessed it in the form of lightning and along the masts of their sailing ships as Saint Elmo's fire.'

'Electricity,' Gray said.

Vigor nodded. 'In 1938, a German archaeologist named Wilhelm Koenig discovered a number of curious clay jars in the National Museum of Iraq. They were only fifteen centimeters tall. They were attributed to the Persians, the homeland of our biblical Magi. The odd thing about the tiny jars was that they were plugged with asphalt, and from the top protruded a copper cylinder with an iron rod inside. The conformation was familiar to anyone with knowledge of voltaic sciences.'

Gray frowned. 'And for those not familiar?'

'The jars . . . they were the exact conformation of battery cells, even earning the name "the Baghdad Batteries."'

Gray shook his head. 'Ancient batteries?'

'Both General Electric and *Science Digest* magazine in

1957 replicated these jars. They primed them with vinegar, and the jars gave off significant volts of electricity.'

Gray stared down at the jars at his feet, remembering the monsignor's request for soda, another acidic solution. He noted the iron rod sticking out of the top of the solid copper jar. 'Are you saying these are batteries? Ancient Duracell Coppertops?'

He stared at the pool. If the monsignor was correct, Gray understood now why jars were resting in the seawater pool. Whatever shock was generated by the batteries would flow through the water to the pyramid.

'Why don't we just jump-start the pyramid?' Kat said. 'Bring down a marine battery from the boat?'

Vigor shook his head. 'I think the activation is tied to the amount of current and the position of the batteries. When it comes to the magnitude of power in these superconductors – especially one this size – I think we should stick to the original design.'

Gray agreed. He remembered the quake and the destruction inside the basilica. That had been with only a single cylinder of m-state powder. He eyed the giant pyramid and knew they'd better heed the monsignor's recommendation.

'So what do we do?' Gray asked.

Vigor popped the top to one of his sodas. 'On my count, we fill up the empty batteries.' He stared around the group. 'Oh, and I suggest we stand well back.'

1:20 p.m.

Monk sat behind the boat's wheel, tapping an empty can of soda on the starboard rail. He was tired of all this waiting. Maybe scuba diving wasn't so bad. The water looked inviting as the day's heat rose.

The loud rumble of an engine drew a glance across the harbor.

The hydrofoil, which had seemed to drop anchor, was on the move again. He listened to the engine throttle up. There seemed to be a bit of commotion on the deck.

He reached for his binoculars. Better safe than sorry.

As he raised the binoculars, he glanced to the monitor of the Aqua-Vu camera. The tunnel continued to be unmanned.

What was taking Kat so long?

**1:21 p.m.**

Gray emptied his third can into the cylinder core of his jar. Soon Coke was bubbling down the copper side of the battery. Full.

He stood up and took the last swig from his soda can. *Ugh . . . diet . . .*

The others finished about the same time, standing and moving back.

A bit of carbonation frothed out the tops of all the cylinders. Nothing else happened. Maybe they had done it wrong, or the soda wouldn't work – or even more likely, the monsignor's idea was simply full of crap.

Then a spark danced from the tip of the iron rod of Gray's jar and cascaded down the copper surface to fizzle out in the seawater.

Similar weak pyrotechnics drizzled from the other batteries.

'It may take a few minutes for the batteries to build and discharge a proper voltage.' Vigor's voice had lost its confident edge.

Gray frowned. 'I don't think this is going to –'

Simultaneously from all four batteries, brilliant arcs of electricity crackled through the water, fire in the deep. They struck the four sides of the pyramid.

'Back against the wall!' Gray yelled.

His warning was not needed. A blast of force thumped

outward from the pyramid, throwing him bodily against the wall. The pressure made it feel like Gray was on his back, the drum-shaped chamber circling over him, the pyramid above him, a topsy-turvy amusement ride.

Yet Gray knew what held him.

A Meissner field, a force that could levitate tombs.

Then the true fireworks began.

From all surfaces of the pyramid, crackling bursts of lightning shattered to the ceiling, seeming to strike the silver stars imbedded there. Jolts also lanced into the pool, as if attempting to attack the reflected stars in the water.

Gray felt the image burning into his retina, but he refused to close his eyes. It was worth the risk of blindness. Where the lightning struck the water, flames erupted and danced across the pool's surface.

Fire from water!

He knew what he was witnessing.

The electrolysis of water into hydrogen gas and oxygen. The released gas then ignited, set to flame by the play of energies here.

Trapped by force, Gray watched the fire above and below. He could barely comprehend the power being unleashed here.

He had read theoretical studies on how a superconductor could store energy, even light, within its matrix for an infinite span of time. And in a *perfect* superconductor even the quantity of energy or light could be infinite.

Was that what he was witnessing?

Before he could grasp it fully, the energies suddenly died away, a lightning storm in a bottle, brilliant but brief.

The world swung back upright as the Meissner field expired and his body was released. Gray stumbled a step forward. He caught himself from falling into the pool. Fires died back into the water. Whatever energy had been trapped inside the pyramid had been expended.

No one spoke.

They silently gathered together, needing the company of others, the physicality of one another.

Vigor was the first to make coherent motion. He pointed to the ceiling. 'Look.'

Gray craned. The black paint and stars persisted, but now strange letters glowed in a fiery script across the dome of the roof.

όπως είναι ανωτέρω, έτσι είναι κατωτέρω

'It's the clue,' Rachel said.

As they stared, the letters faded rapidly. Like the fiery pyre atop the black hematite slab at St. Peter's, the revelation only lasted a brief time.

Gray hurried to free his underwater camera. They needed a record.

Vigor stayed his hand. 'I know what it says. It's Greek.'

'You can translate?'

The monsignor nodded. 'It's not difficult. It's a phrase attributed to Plato, describing how the stars affect us and are in fact a reflection of us. It became the foundation for astrology and the cornerstone for Gnostic belief.'

'What's the phrase?' Gray asked.

'"As it is above, so it is below."'

Gray stared at the starry ceiling and at the reflection in the water. Above and below. Here was the same sentiment expressed visually. 'But what does it mean?'

Rachel had wandered from the group. She slowly made a complete circuit of the room. She called from the far side of the pyramid. 'Over here!'

Gray heard a splash.

They hurried over to her. Rachel waded toward the pyramid.

'Careful,' Gray warned.

'Look,' she said, and pointed.

Gray made it around the edge of the pyramid and saw

338

what had excited her. A tiny section of the pyramid, six inches square, had vanished midway up one face, dissolved away, consumed during the firestorm. Resting inside the hollow lay one of Alexander the Great's outstretched hands, closed in a fist.

Rachel reached for it, but Gray motioned her away.

'Let me,' he said.

He reached to touch the hand, glad he was still wearing his diving gloves. The brittle flesh felt like stone. Between the clenched fingers, a bit of gold glinted.

Teeth gritted, Gray broke off one of the fingers, earning a gasp from Vigor.

It couldn't be helped.

From the fist, Gray removed a three-inch-long gold key, thick toothed, one end forged into a cross. It was surprisingly heavy.

'A key,' Kat said.

'But to what lock?' Vigor asked.

Gray stepped away. 'To wherever we must go next.' His eyes wandered to the ceiling to where the letters had faded away.

'As it is above, so it is below,' Vigor repeated, noting the direction of his gaze.

'But what is the significance?' Gray mumbled. He pocketed the key into his thigh pouch. 'Where does it tell us to go?'

Rachel had moved a step away. She slowly turned in a circle, surveying the room. She stopped, her gaze fixed on Gray. Her eyes shone brightly. He knew that look by now.

'I know where to start.'

1:24 p.m.

In the raised pilot compartment of the hydrofoil, Raoul zipped into his wet suit. The boat was owned by the Guild. It had cost the Dragon Court a small fortune to rent it, but there could be no mistakes today.

'Bring us in along a sweeping curve as near as possible without raising suspicion,' he ordered the captain, a dark-skinned Afrikaner with a pattern of pinpoint scars over his cheeks.

Two young women, one black, one white, flanked the man. They were dressed in bikinis, their equivalent of camouflage gear, but their eyes glinted with the promise of deadly force.

The captain didn't acknowledge Raoul, but he shifted the wheel and the craft angled to the side.

Raoul turned away from the captain and his women. He headed out to the ladder to the lower deck.

He hated being aboard a craft not directly under his authority. He clambered down the ladder to join the twelve-man team that would undertake the dive. His other three men would operate the strafing guns cleverly engineered into the bow and both flanks of the stern. The last member of his team, Dr. Alberto Menardi, was ensconced in one of the cabins, preparing to unravel the riddles here.

And there was one unwelcome addition to the team.

The woman.

Seichan stood with her wet suit half-unzipped, down to her belly button. Her breasts were barely concealed behind the neoprene. She stood by her tanks and her Aquanaut sled. The tiny one-person sleds were propelled by twin propulsion jets. They would skim a diver through the water at breakneck speeds.

The Eurasian woman glanced up to him. Raoul found her mixed heritage repellent, but she served her purpose. His eyes traveled along the length of her bare midriff and chest. Two minutes alone with her, and he'd have that constant disdainful smirk smashed off her face.

But for now, the bitch had to be tolerated.

This was Guild territory.

340

Seichan had insisted on accompanying the assault team. 'Only to observe and offer advice,' she had purred. 'Nothing more.'

Still, he spotted the speargun among her stack of diving gear.

'We evac in three minutes,' Raoul said.

They would go overboard as the hydrofoil slowed to turn around the peninsula, just sightseers getting a closer look at the old fort. They would swim into position from there. The hydrofoil would hang back, ready to intercede with its guns if necessary.

Seichan tugged on her zipper. 'I've had our radio man intermittently jamming their communications. So when their radios go fully out, they'll be less suspicious.'

Raoul nodded. She had her uses. He'd give her that much respect.

With a final check of his watch, he lifted an arm and made a circling gesture with a finger. 'Mount up,' he said.


1:26 p.m.

Back in the tunnel entrance to Alexander's tomb, Rachel knelt down on the stone floor. She worked on her project, preparing to prove her point.

Gray spoke to Kat. 'You'd better get back out in the water. Check in with Monk. It's been longer than the couple minutes we had told him. He'll be getting edgy.'

Kat nodded, but her eyes glanced around the room, settled on the tomb pyramid. Reluctantly, she turned and headed back down the tunnel toward the entry pool.

Vigor finished his own inspection of the tomb chamber. His face was still aglow with wonder. 'I don't think it will fire like that again.'

Gray nodded at Rachel's side. 'The gold pyramid must have acted like a capacitor. It stored its energy, perfectly preserved within its superconducting matrix . . . until the

341

charge was released by the shock, creating a cascade reaction that emptied the pyramid.'

'That means,' Vigor said, 'that even if the Dragon Court discovers this chamber, they'll never be able to raise the riddle.'

'Or gain the gold key,' Gray said, patting his thigh pouch. 'We're finally a full step ahead of them.'

Rachel heard the relief and satisfaction in his voice.

'But first we have to solve this riddle,' she reminded him. 'I have an inkling of where to begin, but no answer yet.'

Gray came over to her. 'What are you working on?'

She had a Mediterranean map spread on the stones, the same map she had used to demonstrate that the inscription on the hematite slab depicted the coastline of the eastern Mediterranean. With a black felt marker, she had carefully drawn spots on the map and assigned names to each.

Sitting back, she waved an arm to the tomb chamber. 'The phrase – "as it is above, so it is below" – was originally meant to bring the star's positions into our own lives.'

'Astrology,' Gray said.

'Not exactly,' Vigor argued. 'The stars truly ruled ancient civilizations. Constellations were the timekeepers of seasons, the guideposts for travel, the home of the gods. Civilizations honored them by building their monuments as a reflection of the starry night. A new theory about the three pyramids of Giza is that they were aligned as such to match the three stars of Orion's belt. Even in more modern times, every Catholic cathedral or basilica is built along an east-west axis, to mark the rising and setting of the sun. We still honor that tradition.'

'So we're supposed to look for patterns,' Gray said. 'Significant positions of something in the sky or on the Earth.'

'And the tomb is telling us what to pay attention to,' Rachel said.

'Then I must be deaf,' Gray said.

Her uncle had figured it out by now, too. 'The bronze finger of the Colossus,' he said, staring out at the tomb. 'The giant pyramid, perhaps representative of the one at Giza. The remnants of the Pharos Lighthouse above us. Even the drum-shaped tomb might hearken back to the Mausoleum of Halicarnassus.'

'I'm sorry,' Gray said with a frown. 'The mausoleum of what?'

'It was one of the Seven Wonders,' Rachel said. 'Remember how closely Alexander was tied to them all.'

'Right,' Gray said. 'Something about his birth coinciding with one and his death another.'

'The Temple of Artemis,' Vigor said with a nod. 'And the Hanging Gardens of Babylon. They're all connected to Alexander . . . to here.'

Rachel pointed to the map she was working on. 'I've marked all their locations. They are spread throughout the eastern Mediterranean. They are all localized in the same region mapped out on the hematite slab.' [*See map overleaf.*]

Gray studied the map. 'Are you saying we're supposed to be looking for a pattern among the seven of them?'

'"As it is above, so it is below,"' Vigor quoted.

'Where do we even begin?' Gray asked.

'Time,' Rachel said. 'Or rather the progression of time, as hinted at by the Sphinx's riddle. Moving from birth to death.'

Gray's eyes narrowed, then widened with understanding. 'Chronological order. When the Wonders were built.'

Rachel nodded. 'But I don't know the order.'

'I do,' Vigor said. 'What archaeologist in the region wouldn't?'

He knelt down and took the felt marker. 'I think Rachel is right. The first clue that started this all was hidden in a book in Cairo, near Giza. The pyramids are also the oldest of the Seven Wonders.' He placed the tip of the

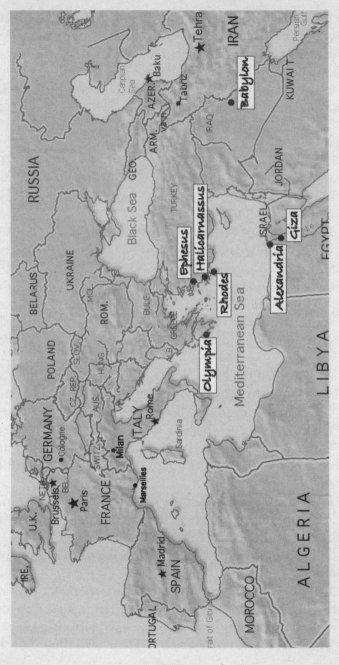

marker on Giza. 'I find it interesting that this tomb lies under the Pharos Lighthouse.'

'Why's that?' Gray asked.

'Because the lighthouse was the *last* of the Wonders to be built. From first to last. This might also indicate that wherever we go next might be the end of the road. The last stop.'

Uncle Vigor leaned down and carefully drew lines, connecting the Seven Wonders in order of their construction. 'From Giza to Babylon, then on to Olympia, where the statue of Zeus towered.'

'Alexander's supposed real father,' Rachel reminded.

'From there, we go to Artemis's Temple at Ephesus, then Halicarnassus, then the island of Rhodes . . . until at last we reach our own spot on the map. Alexandria and its famous lighthouse.'

Her uncle leaned back. 'Is anyone still wondering if we're not on the right track?'

Rachel and Gray stared at his handiwork.

'Christ . . .' Gray swore. [*See map overleaf.*]

'It forms a perfect hourglass,' Rachel said.

Vigor nodded. 'The symbol for the passage of time itself. Formed by two triangles. Remember that the Egyptian symbol for the white powder fed to the pharaohs was a triangle. As a matter of fact, triangles were also symbolic for the *benben* stone of the Egyptians, a symbol of sacred knowledge.'

'What's a *benben* stone?' Gray asked.

Rachel answered. 'They're the caps placed over the tips of Egyptian obelisks and pyramids.'

'But they're mostly represented by triangles in art,' her uncle added. 'In fact, you can see one on the back of your own dollar bill. American currency shows a pyramid with a triangle hovering over it.'

'The one with the eye inside it,' Gray said.

'An *all-seeing* eye,' Vigor corrected. 'Symbolic of that

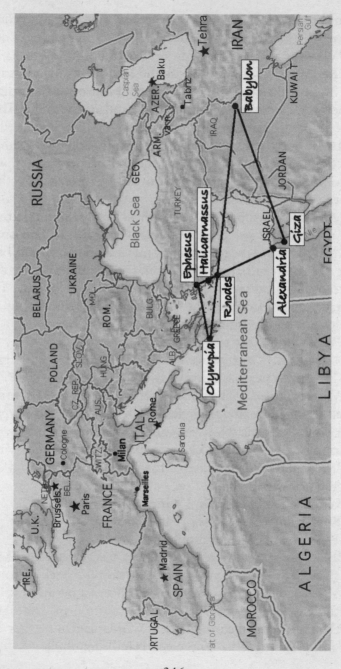

sacred knowledge I was talking about. It makes one wonder if this society of ancient mages didn't have some influence on the early fraternities of your forefathers.' This last was said with a smile. 'But certainly for the Egyptians, there seems to be an underlying theme of triangles, sacred knowledge, all tying back to the mysterious white powder. Even the name *benben* makes this connection.'

'What do you mean?' Rachel said, intrigued.

'The Egyptians implied significance to the spelling of their words. For instance, *a-i-s* in ancient Egyptian translates to "brain," but if you reversed the spelling to *s-i-a*, that word means "consciousness." They used the very spelling of the words to connect the two: consciousness to the brain. Now back to *benben*. The letters *b-e-n* translate to "sacred stone," as I mentioned, but do you know what you get if you spell it backward?'

Rachel and Gray shrugged at the same time.

'*N-e-b* translates to "gold."'

Gray let out a breath of surprise. 'So gold is connected to sacred stone and sacred knowledge.'

Vigor nodded. 'Egypt is where it all began.'

'But where does it end?' Rachel asked, staring down at her map. 'What is the significance of the hourglass? How does it point to the next location?'

They all stared out at the pyramidal tomb.

Vigor shook his head.

Gray knelt down. 'It's my turn at the map.'

'You have an idea?' Vigor said.

'You don't have to sound so shocked.'

1:37 p.m.

Gray set to work, using the back of his knife as a straight edge. He had to get this right. With the felt marker in hand, he spoke as he worked, not looking up.

'That big bronze finger,' he said. 'See how it's in the exact center of the room, positioned under the dome?'

The others glanced out to the tomb. The water had settled to a flat sheen again. The arched starscape on the ceiling was again reflected perfectly in the water, creating an illusion of a starry sphere.

'The finger is positioned like the north-south pole of that spherical mirage. The axis around which the world spins. And now look at the map. What spot marks the center of the hourglass?'

Rachel leaned closer and read the name there. 'The island of Rhodes,' she said. 'Where the finger came from.'

Gray smiled at the wonder in her voice. Was it from the revelation or the fact that *he* had discovered it?

'I think we're supposed to find the axis through the hourglass,' he said. He took the felt marker and drew a line bisecting the hourglass vertically. 'And that bronze finger points toward the north pole.' He continued, using his knife blade as a guide, and extended the line north.

His marker stopped at a well-known and significant city. [*See map opposite.*]

'Rome,' Rachel read off the map.

Gray sat back. 'The fact that all this geometry points right back to Rome must be significant. It must be where we have to go next. But where in Rome? The Vatican again?'

He stared around at the others.

Rachel's brow had bunched up.

Vigor slowly knelt down. 'I think, Commander, that you're both right and wrong. Can I see your knife?'

Gray handed it over, glad to let the monsignor usurp his position.

He played with the knife's edge on the map. 'Hmm . . . two triangles.' He tapped the hourglass pattern.

'What about it?'

Vigor shook his head, eyes focused. 'You were right

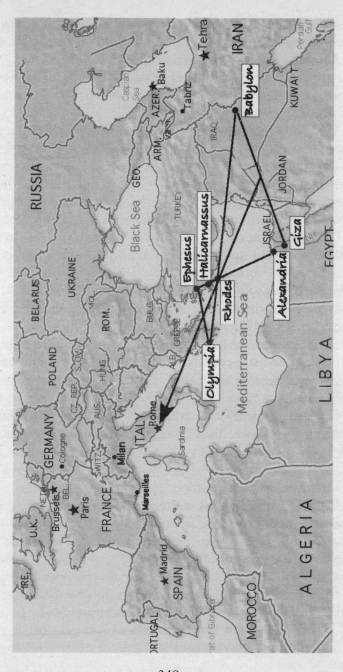

about the fact that this line hits Rome. But it's not where we're supposed to go.'

'How do you know that?'

'Remember the multiple layers of riddles here. We have to look deeper.'

'To where?'

Vigor dragged his finger along the edge of the blade, extending the line past Rome. 'Rome was only the first stop.' He continued the imaginary line farther north, into France. He halted at a spot just a bit north of Marseilles. [*See map opposite.*]

Vigor nodded and smiled. 'Clever.'

'What?'

Vigor passed back the knife and tapped the spot. 'Avignon.'

A gasp arose from Rachel.

Gray failed to see the significance. His confused expression made that plain.

Rachel turned to him. 'Avignon is the place in France to which the papacy was exiled in the early fourteenth century. It became the papal seat of power for almost a full century.'

'The *second* seat of papal power,' Vigor stressed. 'First Rome, then France. Two triangles, two symbols of power and knowledge.'

'But how can we be sure?' Gray said. 'Maybe we're reading too much into it.'

Vigor waved away his concern. 'Remember, we already had pinpointed the date when we thought the clues were planted, when the papacy left Rome. The first decade of the fourteenth century.'

Gray nodded, but he was not totally convinced.

'And these crafty alchemists left us another layer to the riddle to help firmly establish this location.' Vigor pointed to the shape on the map. 'When do you think the hourglass was first invented?'

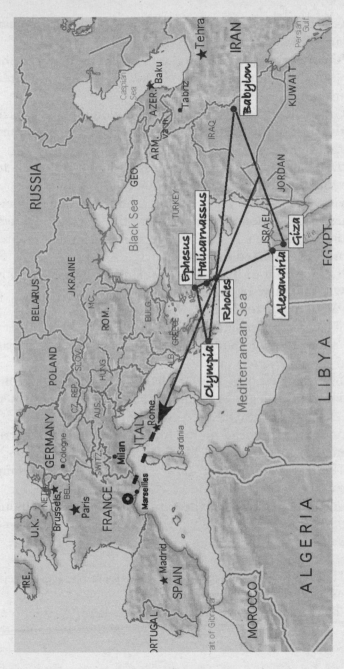

Gray shook his head. 'I assumed it was at least a couple thousand years . . . maybe older.'

'Oddly enough, the hourglass's invention matched the time of the first mechanical clocks. Only seven hundred years ago.'

Gray calculated in his head. 'That would place it back to the start of the thirteen hundreds again. The beginning of the fourteenth century.'

'Marking time, as all hourglasses should do, back to the founding of the French papacy.'

Gray felt a thrill chase through him. Now they knew where they needed to go next. With the gold key. To Avignon, to the French Vatican. He sensed a similar excitement in Rachel and her uncle.

'Let's get out of here,' Gray said, and led them quickly down the tunnel to the entry pool.

'What about the tomb?' Vigor said.

'The announcement of the discovery will have to wait for another day. If the Dragon Court comes calling, they'll find out they're too late.'

Gray hurried into the far chamber. He knelt, slid his mask over his features, and ducked his head underwater, preparing to let the others know the good news.

As soon as his head hit the water, his radio buzzed, irritating and loud. 'Kat . . . Monk . . . can anyone hear me?'

There was no answer. Gray recalled Kat mentioning some glitch with the Buddy Phones. He listened for a moment longer. His heartbeat thudded more loudly in his chest.

Shit.

He shoved out of the water.

That white noise wasn't static. They were being jammed.

'What?' Rachel asked.

'The Dragon Court. They're already here.'

# 13

## BLOOD IN THE WATER

JULY 26, 1:45 p.m.
ALEXANDRIA, EGYPT

Kat bobbed in the gentle waves.

Her radio had completely died ten seconds ago. She had popped up to check with Monk. She found him with binoculars fixed to his face.

'The radio –' she started.

'Something's fucked,' he said, cutting her off. 'Get the others.'

She reacted instantly, flipping down, kicking her legs high. The weight shoved her in a vertical dive. She emergency-flushed the air from her BC vest and plummeted straight down.

Diving for the tunnel, she reached her other hand to free the buckle straps that held her vest and tank. Movement at the entrance stayed her fingers.

The sleek form of a diver jettisoned out of the tunnel. A streak of blue across the black suit identified the swimmer as Commander Pierce. A perpetual whine filled her ears. No way to communicate the urgency.

But there proved to be no need.

On the commander's heels, two other forms fled the tunnel.

Vigor and Rachel.

Kat twisted back upright. Clicking off her Buddy Phone to end the whine, she kicked toward Gray. He must have realized the radio fritz meant trouble. He simply stared hard at her through his face mask and pointed an arm up questioningly.

*Was it clear above?*

She gave him an okay signal. No hostiles above. At least not yet.

Gray did not bother with securing their abandoned tanks. He waved the others up. They kicked off the rocks and aimed for the keel of the boat.

To the side, Kat noted the anchor being raised.

Monk was readying for an immediate departure.

Kat filled the buoyancy vest and kicked upward, fighting the drag of her tank and weight belt. Above, the others were already breaching the surface.

A new humming whine filled her hearing.

It wasn't the radio this time.

She searched the waters for the source, but the visibility in the polluted harbor was poor. Something was coming . . . coming fast.

As a Navy intelligence officer, she had spent plenty of time aboard all manner of watercraft, including submarines. She recognized the steady hum.

Torpedo.

Locked on the speedboat.

She thrashed upward, but knew she'd never reach them in time.

1:46 p.m.

Monk engaged the boat's engine while maintaining a watch for the hydrofoil through his binoculars. It had just vanished behind the tip of the peninsula. But he had watched it slow suspiciously a few seconds ago, two hundred yards out. There had been no telltale activity on the stern deck, but he had noted a rippling line of bubbles in the craft's wake as it glided slowly away.

Then he'd heard the whine over the radio.

Kat appeared a few seconds after that.

They needed to get out of here. He knew it in his gut.

'Monk!' a voice called. It was Gray, surfacing to the port side.

Thank God.

He began to lower his binoculars when he spotted a streaking object racing through the water. A fin cleaved through the waves. A metal fin.

'Fuck . . .'

Dropping the binoculars, Monk shoved the throttle to full. The boat bucked forward with a scream of the engine. He twisted the wheel to starboard. Away from Gray.

'Everybody down!' he screamed, and shoved his mask over his face. He had no time to zip his suit.

With the boat canting away under him, he ran for the stern, stepped on the back seat, and catapulted into the water.

The torpedo struck behind him. The force of the explosion flipped him feet over head. Something punched him in the hip, rattling all the way to his teeth. He struck the water, rolling across the surface, chased by a wash of flames.

Before it could reach him, he sank into the cool embrace of the sea.

Rachel had surfaced just as Monk yelled. She watched him run for the stern of the boat. Reacting to his panic, she shoved back down and twisted to dive.

Then the explosion hit.

The concussion through the water stabbed her ears, even through her thick neoprene hood. All the air slammed out of her. Her mask's seals broke. Seawater rushed in.

She scrambled back to the surface, blind, eyes stinging. With her head out of water, she emptied her mask,

355

coughing and gagging. Debris continued to rain down into the water. Smoking flotsam steamed and rocked. Flaming rivers of gasoline skimmed the waves.

She searched the waters.

No one.

Then to her left, a flailing shape burst out of the water. It was Monk, dazed and choking.

She paddled over to him and grabbed an arm. His face mask had been turned half around his head. She steadied him as he gagged.

'Goddamn,' he wheezed out, and tugged his mask around.

A new noise traveled over the water. Both turned.

Rachel watched a large hydrofoil swing around the fort, tilted up on skids. It circled out toward them.

'Down!' Monk urged.

They fled together under the water. The explosion had stirred the sand, closing visibility down to a few feet.

Rachel pointed in the general direction of the tunnel entrance, lost in the murk. They needed to reach the abandoned scuba tanks, a source of much-needed air.

Reaching the pile of rocks, she searched around her for the tunnel entrance, for the others. Where was everyone else?

She scrambled along the tumble of boulders. Monk kept with her, but he struggled with his suit. He had only been half zipped up. The upper section flapped and tangled.

Where were the tanks? Had she gotten turned around?

A dark shape passed overhead, further away from shore. The hydrofoil. From Monk's reaction, it was the source of their trouble.

A burning pressure built in Rachel's lungs.

Illumination bloomed in the gloom ahead. She moved instinctually toward it, hoping to find her uncle or Gray. Out of the murk, a pair of divers swept into view, leaning on motorized sleds. Silt spiraled behind them.

The divers swung out to trap them against the shore.

Lit by their lamps, steel arrowheads glinted. Spearguns.

To emphasize the threat, a popping *zip* sounded. A lance of steel streaked at Monk. He jerked aside. The spear pierced the loose half of his suit, shredding through.

Rachel held her palms up, toward the divers.

One of them pointed a thumb, ordering them to the surface.

Caught.

Gray helped Vigor.

The monsignor had knocked into him when the boat had exploded. He had taken a chunk of fiberglass to the side of his head, slicing through his neoprene suit. Blood flowed from the cut. Gray had no way of judging the damage, but the older man was dazed.

Gray had managed to reach the air tanks and now helped hook the monsignor up. Vigor waved him off as the air flowed. Gray swung to a second tank and rapidly reconnected his regulator.

He took several deep breaths.

He eyed the tunnel opening. There was no refuge to be found in there. The Dragon Court would certainly come here. Gray would not be trapped in another tomb.

Grabbing up his tank, Gray pointed away.

Vigor nodded, but his face searched the clouded waters.

Gray read his fear.

Rachel.

They had to survive to be of any help. Gray headed out, leading Vigor. They would find a niche among the fall of boulders and debris to hide in. Earlier, he had noted a sunken rusted skiff about ten yards off, over-turned and tilted against the rocks.

He guided Vigor along the cliff. The scuttled boat appeared. He settled the monsignor in its shadow. He motioned for Vigor to stay, then slipped on his tank, freeing his arms.

Gray pointed outward and made a circling motion.

*I'm going to search for the others.*

Vigor nodded, trying, it seemed, to look hopeful.

Gray headed back toward the tunnel, but he kept close to the seabed. The others, if able, would make for the air tanks. He glided from shadow to shadow, keeping to the boulders.

As he neared the tunnel entrance, a glow grew. He slowed. Individual lights differentiated, splashing over the rocks and pointed outward.

He moved into the darkness behind a chunk of stone and spied.

Black-suited divers clustered around the tunnel opening. They wore mini-tanks, containing less than twenty minutes of air, made for short dives.

Gray watched one diver duck through the opening and vanish.

After a few seconds, some confirmation must have been passed along. Another five divers swept one after the other into the tunnel. Gray recognized the last sleek shape to disappear into the tomb shaft.

Seichan.

Gray swung away. None of his teammates would come here now.

As he moved out of hiding, a shape welled up in front of him, appearing from nowhere. Large. The razored tip of a speargun pressed into the flesh of his belly.

Lights flared around him.

Behind the mask, Gray recognized the heavy countenance of Raoul.

Rachel helped free Monk. The spear shaft had pinned a flap of his suit to the seabed. She tugged him loose.

Two yards away, the two divers hovered on their sleds,

like surfers on broken surfboards. One motioned them to the surface. Now.

Rachel didn't need the urging.

As she obeyed, a dark shadow swept up and behind the pair of divers.

*What . . . ?*

Two flashes of silver flickered.

One diver clutched his air hose. Too late. Through the man's mask, Rachel saw his gasped breath draw in a wash of seawater. The second was even less lucky. He was ripped clean off his sled, torn away by a knife lodged in his throat.

Blood spread in a cloud.

The attacker wrenched the blade free and the cloud thickened.

Rachel spotted the pink stripe against the attacker's black suit.

Kat.

The first diver choked and writhed, drowning in his mask. He attempted to flee to the surface, but Kat was there. Knives in both hands dispatched him with brutal efficiency.

Kat kicked his form away. Weighted down by tank and belt, his body drifted into the depths.

Finished, Kat dragged his sled to Rachel and Monk. She pointed up to the surface and motioned to the sled.

To make a fast getaway.

Rachel had no idea how to operate the vehicle – but Monk did. He mounted the half-board and grabbed the handlebar-like controls. He waved for Rachel to climb atop him and ride piggyback.

She did so, throwing her arms around his shoulders. Lights now danced across the edges of her vision.

Kat swam for the other sled, a speargun in hand.

Monk twisted the throttle, and the sled dragged them away, upward, toward safety, toward fresh air.

They burst from the surf like a breaching whale, then slammed back down. Rachel was jarred, but she kept her grip tight. Monk raced them across the smooth waters, zigzagging through the flaming debris field. Oil lay thick over the water.

Rachel risked freeing a hand to rip up her mask, sucking in air.

She tugged Monk's mask up, too.

'Ow,' he said. 'Watch the nose.'

They passed the overturned bulk of their speedboat – only to find the long form of the hydrofoil waiting for them on the left.

'Maybe they haven't seen us,' Monk whispered.

Gunfire chattered, strafing across the water, aiming right for them.

'Hang on!' Monk yelled.

The point of Raoul's spear dug Gray out of his hiding place. Another diver raised a second spear to the side of Gray's throat.

As Gray moved, a knife slashed at him, wielded by Raoul.

He flinched, but the blade only cut the straps to his tank. The heavy cylinder dropped toward the bottom. Raoul waved for him to unhook the regulator. Did they mean to drown him?

Raoul pointed to the nearby tunnel entrance.

Apparently they meant to interrogate him first.

He had no choice.

Gray swam to the entrance, flanked by guards. He dove through, trying to think of some plan. He sailed up to the entry pool and found the chamber ringed with other men in wet suits. Their mini-tanks were small enough to allow them to traverse the tunnel. Some were shedding out of their vests and tanks. Others pointed spearguns, alerted by Raoul.

Gray climbed out of the pool and removed his mask. Every move was tracked by the point of a spear.

He noted Seichan leaning against one wall, seeming oddly relaxed. Her only acknowledgment was the raise of a single finger.

*Hello.*

At Gray's other side, a shape plowed upward into the entry pool. Raoul. In a single movement, the large man one-armed his way out of the pool and to his feet, a gymnastic demonstration of power. His frame must have barely fit through the tunnel. He had abandoned his mini-tanks outside.

Dragging off his mask and peeling back his hood, he strode to Gray.

It was the first time Gray had a good look at the man. His features were craggy, nose long and thin, aquiline. His coal black hair hung to his shoulders. His arms were massed with muscle, as thick around as Gray's thigh, plainly grown from steroids and too much time spent in the gym, not from real-world labor.

*Eurotrash,* Gray thought.

Raoul towered over him, trying to intimidate.

Gray just lifted an eyebrow quizzically. 'What?'

'You're going to tell us everything you know,' Raoul said. His English was fluent, but it was heavily accented with disdain and something Germanic.

'And if I don't?'

Raoul waved an arm as another form splashed up into the entry pool. Gray immediately recognized Vigor. The monsignor had been found.

'There's not much a side-scanning radar can't detect,' Raoul said.

Vigor was dragged bodily from the pool, not gently. Blood from his scalp wound dribbled down one side of his face. He was shoved toward them, but he tripped from exhaustion and fell hard to his knees.

Gray bent down to go to his aid, but a spearhead drove him back.

Another diver surfaced in the pool. He was clearly weighted down. Raoul stepped over and unburdened the man. It was another of those barbell-shaped charges. An incendiary grenade.

Raoul slung the device over a shoulder and stepped back to them. He raised his own speargun and pointed it at Vigor's crotch. 'As the monsignor has sworn off using this part of his anatomy anyway, we'll start here. Any missteps and the monsignor will be able to join the castrato choir of his church.'

Gray straightened. 'What do you want to know?'

'Everything . . . but first, show us what you found.'

Gray lifted an arm toward the tunnel to Alexander's tomb, then swung it around to the other tunnel, the shorter of the two, the one that required one to hunch over to traverse it. 'It's that way,' he said.

Vigor's eyes widened.

Raoul grinned and lifted his speargun. He waved a group of men into the tunnel. 'Check it out.'

Five darted away, leaving three men with Raoul.

Seichan, leaning near the tunnel entrance, watched the group disappear. She stepped to follow.

'Not you,' Raoul said.

Seichan glanced over a shoulder. 'Do you and your men want to leave this harbor?'

Raoul's face reddened.

'The escape boat is ours,' she reminded him, and ducked away.

Raoul clenched a fist but stayed silent.

Trouble in paradise . . .

Gray turned. Vigor's gaze was hard upon him. Gray motioned with his eyes. *Dive away at the first opportunity.*

He faced the tunnel again. He prayed he was correct about the Sphinx's riddle. It was death to solve it wrongly.

And that certainly was about to be proven here, one way or the other.

That left only one mystery to be answered.

Who would die?

Monk raced the bullets. His jet sled skidded across the water. Rachel clung to him from behind, half choking his airway.

The harbor was in chaos. Other watercraft fled from the fighting, scattering like a school of fish. Monk hit the wake of a crabbing boat and sailed high into the air.

Gunfire chewed into the wave below.

'Grab tight!' he cried.

He flipped the sled on its side just as they hit the water. Under they went. He straightened their course and dove deeper, speeding through the water at a depth of three feet.

At least that's what he hoped.

Monk had squeezed his eyes closed. Without his mask, he couldn't have seen much anyway. But before diving under, he caught a glimpse of an anchored sailboat directly ahead.

If he could get under it . . . put it between him and the hydrofoil . . .

He counted in his head, estimating, praying.

The world went momentarily darker through his eyelids. They were under the shadow of the sailboat. He did an additional four-count and canted back upward toward the surface.

They burst back into sunlight and air.

Monk craned back. They had more than cleared the sailboat. 'Fuck, yeah!' The hydrofoil had to swing around the obstacle, losing ground.

'Monk!' Rachel yelled in his ear.

He faced forward to see a boxy wall of boat in front of him, the naked houseboat couple's. Crap! They were flying right toward its port side. There was no shying from it.

Monk slammed his weight forward and tipped the nose of the sled straight down. They dove in a steep dive . . . but was it steep enough to duck under the houseboat, like he had the sailboat?

The answer was no.

Monk slammed into the keel with the tip of his sled. The sled flipped ass-end up. Monk clutched an iron grip to the handles. The sled skittered against the wood side, barnacles ripping at his shoulder. He gunned the throttle and shot deeper.

He finally cleared the underside of the boat and sped back into clear water.

He jetted upward, knowing he had little time.

Rachel was gone, knocked off with the first collision.

Gray held his breath.

A commotion immediately sounded from down the low tunnel. The first of the men must have reached the end of the passage. It must have been short.

'*Eine Goldtür!*' he heard shouted. *A gold door.*

Raoul hurried forward, dragging Gray with him. Vigor was kept pinned at the pool's edge by a diver with a speargun.

The tunnel, lit up by the explorers' flashlights, extended only some thirty yards and was slightly curved. The end could not be seen, but the last two men in line – and Seichan – were limned against the glow, all focused forward.

Gray had a sudden fear that perhaps they'd been wrong about the gold key they had found. Maybe it was meant for this door.

'*Es wird entriegelt!*' a shout called. *Unlocked!*

From where Gray stood, he heard the click as the door was opened.

It was too loud.

Seichan must have noted it, too. She spun around and leaped back toward them. She was too late.

From all walls, sharpened poles of steel shot out of crevices and shadowed nooks. They skewered across the passage, piercing through flesh and bone, and embedded into holes drilled on the opposite side. The deadly tangle started deep and swept outward in a matter of two seconds.

Lights bobbled. Men screamed, impaled and pinned.

Seichan made it within two steps of the exit, but the tail end of the booby trap caught her. A single sharpened pole lanced out and impaled through her shoulder. She jerked to a stop, legs going out from under her.

A pained gasp was the only sound she made, hung up and skewered on the bar.

Shocked, Raoul weakened his grip on Gray.

Taking advantage, Gray wrested free and flung himself toward the pool. 'Go!' he shouted to Vigor.

Before he could take a second step, something struck the back of his head. Hard. He went down on one knee. He was clubbed again, on the side of the head, pistol-whipped with the butt of a speargun.

He had underestimated the speed of the giant.

A mistake.

Raoul kicked Gray onto his face and pressed a boot on his neck, bearing down with full weight.

Gasping, Gray watched Vigor fished back out of the pool. The monsignor had been caught by the ankle and denied escape.

Raoul leaned down, leering into Gray's view.

'A nasty little trick,' he said.

'I didn't know –'

The boot pressed harder, squeezing off his words.

'But you have eliminated a bit of a problem for me,' he continued. 'Taking that bitch out of the picture. But now we have some work to do . . . the two of us.'

Rachel clawed back to the surface of the water, hitting her head again on the side of the boat. She choked on a mouthful of water and broke through to open air. She coughed and gagged repeatedly, reflexively, unable to stop. Her limbs floundered.

A gate suddenly dropped and she saw a naked middle-aged man standing there, bare-assed to the world. '*Tudo bem, Menina?*'

Portuguese. Asking if she was okay.

She shook her head, still coughing.

He bent down and offered an arm. Taking it, she allowed herself to be hauled up and stood shakily. Where was Monk?

She watched the hydrofoil banking away, heading out toward deeper waters. The reason soon became apparent. A pair of Egyptian police cruisers sped out from the far pier, revving up, gaining speed, finally responding. The chaos in the harbor must have delayed them, but better late than never.

Relief flooded through her.

Rachel turned to find the man's wife or companion, equally naked.

Except for the gun.

Monk surfed around the stern of the houseboat, searching for Rachel. Further out in the harbor, a police cruiser wailed across the waters. Lights flashed an angry red and white. The hydrofoil raced away, picking up speed, lifting to the full extent of its skids.

Escaping.

There was no way for the police to catch it. The hydrofoil headed out . . . to international waters or to some other hidden berth.

Monk turned his full attention to his search for Rachel. He feared to find her floating facedown, drowned in the polluted water. He edged around the stern, staying close to the boat.

He spotted motion on the rear deck of the houseboat.

Rachel . . . she had her back to him, but looked unsteady. The naked middle-aged man supported her with one arm.

He slowed. 'Rachel . . . are you o – '

She glanced back, eyes panicked. The man raised his other arm. He held a snub-nosed automatic rifle, pointed at Monk's face.

'Oh . . . I guess not,' Monk muttered.

Gray's neck was about to break.

Raoul knelt atop him, one knee square on the middle of his back, the other on the back of his neck. One hand twisted into Gray's hair, yanking his head back. The man's other hand held the speargun straight-armed toward Vigor's left eye.

The monsignor was on his knees, flanked by two divers with additional guns. A third looked on, scowling with a knife balanced in his hand. All eyes were narrowed with raw hatred. Gray's trick had slain five of their men, comrades-in-arms.

Moans still echoed from the bloody tunnel, but there would be no rescue for them. Only revenge.

Raoul leaned closer. 'Enough games. What did you learn in – '

A zinging *thwack* cut off his words.

The speargun clattered from Raoul's grip. A roaring howl erupted from him as he fell off Gray.

Released, Gray rolled across the floor, snatched up the abandoned speargun, and shot one of the men holding Vigor.

The shaft pierced through the diver's neck, knocking him back.

The other man straightened, turning his weapon on

Gray, but before he could fire, a spear flashed through the air from the pool and spitted the man through the belly.

His weapon fired reflexively, but the shot went wild as he tumbled backward.

Vigor slapped the one unfired speargun toward Gray, then flung himself low.

Gray grabbed it and swung it toward Raoul.

The giant ran for the nearby tunnel, the one that led to Alexander's tomb. Raoul clutched a hand to his other wrist, his palm pierced through by a length of steel spear.

Kat's shot had been precise, disarming and disabling.

The last of the Court's men, the one with the dagger, was the first into the tunnel and led the way. Raoul followed.

Gray gained his feet, took aim at Raoul's back, and fired.

The spear flew down the tunnel. Raoul would not reach the first turn in time. The shaft struck the large man in the back and clanged.

The spear clattered harmlessly to the stone floor.

Gray cursed his luck. He had hit the incendiary grenade still slung over Raoul's shoulder. Saved by his own damn bomb.

The giant vanished around the first turn of the passage.

'We have to go,' Kat said. 'I killed the two guards outside, slipping in on one of their own sleds, caught them by surprise. But I don't know how many more are out there.'

Gray eyed the tunnel, hesitating.

Vigor was already in the water. 'Rachel . . . ?'

'I sent her off with Monk on another sled. They should be at shore by now.'

Vigor hugged Kat quickly, his eyes bright with tears of relief. He pulled down his mask.

'Commander?'

Gray considered going after Raoul, but a cornered dog

was the most dangerous. He didn't know if Raoul had a dry-wrapped pistol or some other weapon stashed, but the bastard definitely had a bomb. Raoul could lob it here on a short fuse and take them all out.

He turned away.

They had what they needed.

One hand patted the thigh pouch and the hidden gold key.

It was time to go.

Gray pulled on his mask and joined the others. On the stone floor, the man he'd shot through the throat was already dead. The other moaned, pierced fully through the belly. Blood pooled under him. Shot through the kidney. Or maybe his aorta had been nicked. He'd be dead in minutes.

Gray felt no pity. He remembered the atrocities in Cologne and Milan. 'Let's get the hell out of here.'

Raoul yanked the spear from his hand. Steel ground on bone. Fire lanced through his arm to his chest, emptying his breath in an angry hiss. Blood poured. He pulled his glove off and tied the neoprene around his palm, stanching and putting pressure on the wound.

No broken bones.

Dr. Alberto Menardi had the medical background to patch him up.

Raoul stared across the room, illuminated by his flashlight on the floor. What the hell was this place?

The glass pyramid, the water, the starry dome . . .

The last surviving man, Kurt, returned from the passageway. He had gone to reconnoiter the entry pool. 'They left,' he reported. 'Bernard and Pelz are dead.'

Raoul finished his first aid and considered the next step. They would have to evacuate quickly. The Americans could send the Egyptian police straight here. The original plan had been to lure the local authorities away with the hydrofoil, leaving Raoul and his team to do a full investigation down here in secret, then make their escape in the clunky, nondescript houseboat.

Now matters had changed.

Cursing, Raoul bent to his pack on the ground. It held a digital camera. He would get a visual record, get it to Alberto, and hunt down the Americans.

It wasn't over yet.

As Raoul dug out his camera, his foot nudged the sling holding the incendiary grenade. A fold of sealcloth fell away. He ignored it until he noted a slight red glow on the neighboring wall.

Fuck . . .

Dropping to a knee, he snatched the bomb and rolled it digital face forward.

00:33.

He spotted the deep ding in the casing near the timer. Where the American bastard had struck it with the speargun.

00:32.

The impact must have shorted something, activated the timer.

Raoul tapped the abort code. Nothing.

He shoved up, the sudden motion making his hand ache. 'Go,' he ordered Kurt.

The man's eyes were fixed on the bomb. But he glanced up, nodded, and ran for the tunnel.

Raoul retrieved his digital camera, took several rapid flash pictures, sealed the camera in a pocket, then strode away.

00:19.

He retreated back to the entry room. Kurt was already gone.

'Raoul!' a voice called to him.

He spun, startled, but it was only Seichan. The bitch was still trapped in the other tunnel.

Raoul waved to her. 'It was nice doing business with you.'

He pulled down his mask and dove cleanly into the pool. He snaked down the tunnel and found Kurt waiting beyond. The diver was examining two other bodies, two more of their men. Kurt shook his head.

A savage fury swelled inside Raoul.

Then a rumbling reverberation trembled through the water, sounding like a passing freight train. The tunnel behind him flashed with a dull orange glow. He glanced back as it rapidly subsided. The trembling faded.

All gone.

Raoul closed his eyes. He had nothing to show. The Court would have his balls . . . and probably more. He considered simply swimming away, disappearing. He had money stashed in three different Swiss bank accounts.

But he'd still be hunted.

Raoul's radio buzzed in his ear. 'Seal One, this is Slow Tug.'

He opened his eyes. It was his pick-up boat. 'Seal One here,' he responded leadenly.

'We report two additional passengers aboard.'

Raoul frowned. 'Please clarify.'

'A woman you know and an American.'

Raoul clenched his wounded fist. Saltwater burned with a cleansing agony. The fire spread through him.

Perfect.


3:22 p.m.

Gray stalked across the length of the hotel suite, the one Monk had prebooked for the group. They were on the top floor of the Corniche Hotel, having arrived twenty-five minutes ago. The balcony windows overlooked the glass-and-steel sweep of the new Alexandria Library. The harbor beyond shone like dark blue ice. Boats and yachts seemed imbedded in place. Calm had quickly returned to the harbor.

Vigor had watched the local news station and listened as an Egyptian newsman reported on a confrontation among a group of drug smugglers. The police had failed to subdue them. The Court had escaped.

Gray also knew the tomb had been destroyed. He and the others had used air tanks and two of the abandoned sleds to flee to the far side of the harbor, where they shed their gear under a pier. But while crossing, Gray had heard a muffled thump through the water behind him.

The incendiary grenade.

Raoul must have blown it as he made his escape.

Once Gray, Kat, and Vigor had climbed out of the harbor, stripped to trunks and swimsuits, they had blended into a crowd of sunbathers and crossed a seaside park to their hotel. Gray had expected to find Monk and Rachel already here.

But there continued to be no sign of the pair.

No messages, no calls.

'Where could they be?' Vigor asked.

Gray turned to Kat. 'And you saw them leave with one of the motorized sleds?'

She nodded, face taut with guilt. 'I should've made sure . . .'

'And we'd both be dead,' Gray said. 'You made a choice.'

He couldn't fault her.

Gray rubbed his eyes. 'And she has Monk with her.' He took a measure of comfort in that.

'What do we do?' Vigor asked.

Gray lowered his arms and stared out the window. 'We have to assume they've been captured. We can't count on our security here lasting much longer. We'll have to evacuate.'

'Leave?' Vigor said, standing up.

Gray felt the full weight of his responsibility. He faced Vigor, refusing to look away. 'We have no choice.'

4:05 p.m.

Rachel climbed into the terry-cloth robe. She snugged it around her naked form while glaring at the cabin's other occupant.

The tall, muscular blonde woman ignored her and stepped to the cabin doorway. 'All finished in here!' she called out to the passageway.

The door opened to reveal a second woman, a twin to the first but auburn-haired. She entered and held the door for Raoul. The large man ducked through the hatch.

'She's clean,' the blonde reported, peeling off a pair of latex gloves. She had performed a full body-cavity search on Rachel. 'Nothing hidden.'

*Certainly not any longer,* Rachel thought angrily. She turned her back slightly and knotted the robe's sash, tight, under her breasts. Her fingers trembled. She squeezed her fingers on the knot. Tears threatened, but she resisted, refusing to give Raoul the satisfaction.

Rachel stared out the tiny porthole, attempting to discern some landmark, something to pinpoint where she was. But all she saw was featureless sea.

She and Monk had been transferred from the houseboat. The ponderous craft had trundled out of the harbor, met a speedboat, and the pair were tied, hooded, and gagged by a foursome of thick-necked men. They were shoved into the smaller boat, then whisked away, bouncing over the waves. They had traveled for what seemed like half a day but was probably only a little more than an hour. Once the hood was tugged off her face, Rachel had found the sun had hardly moved across the sky.

In a small cove, hidden by a tumble of rock, the familiar hydrofoil waited like a midnight-blue shark. Men

373

worked the ropes, preparing to ship out. She'd spotted Raoul at the stern, arms crossed over his chest.

Manhandled aboard, Rachel and Monk were separated.

Raoul had taken charge of Monk.

Rachel still didn't know what had become of her team-mate. She had been hustled below deck to a cabin, guarded by the two Amazon women. The hydrofoil had imme-diately edged out of the cove and sped away, heading straight out into the Mediterranean.

That had been more than half an hour ago.

Raoul came forward and grabbed her upper arm. His other hand was bandaged. 'Come with me.' His fingers dug hard, to bone.

She allowed herself to be led out into the wood-paneled hallway, lit by sconces. The passageway crossed from stern to bow, lined by doors to private cabins. There was only one steep stairway, more like a ladder, to the main deck.

Instead of going up, Raoul marched her toward the bow.

Raoul knocked on the door to the last cabin.

'*Entri*,' a muffled voice said.

Raoul pulled the door open and dragged Rachel inside. The cabin was larger than her prison cell. It held not only a bed and chair, but also a desk, sidetable, and book-shelves. On every flat surface, texts, magazines, even scrolls were stacked. One corner of the desk supported a laptop computer.

The room's occupant straightened and turned. He had been leaning over his desk, glasses perched on the tip of his nose.

'Rachel,' the man said warmly, as if they were the best of friends.

She recognized the older man from the days when she had accompanied Uncle Vigor to the Vatican Libraries. He had been the head prefect of the Archives, Dr. Alberto

Menardi. The traitor stood a few inches taller than she, but he had a perpetual hunch to his posture, making him seem shorter.

He tapped a sheet on his desk. 'From this fresh handwriting – a woman's, if I'm not mistaken – this map must have been embellished by your own hand.'

He waved her over.

Rachel had no choice. Raoul shoved her forward.

She tripped over a stack of books and had to grab the edge of the desk to keep from falling. She stared down at the map of the Mediterranean. The hourglass was drawn upon it, as were the names of the Seven Wonders.

She kept her face stoic.

They had found her map. She had sealed it in a pouch of her dry suit. Now she wished she'd burned it.

Alberto leaned closer. His breath reeked of olives and sour wine. He drew a fingernail along the axis line that Gray had scribed. It stopped at Rome. 'Tell me about this.'

'It's where we're supposed to go next,' Rachel lied. She was relieved her uncle had not drawn on the map in ink himself. He had simply extended the line with his finger and the straight edge of Gray's knife.

Alberto turned his head. 'Now, why is that? I'd like to hear all about what went down in that tomb. In great detail. Raoul has been good enough to supply digital snapshots, but I think a firsthand account would be of more value.'

Rachel kept silent.

Raoul's fingers tightened on her arm. She winced.

Alberto waved Raoul away. 'There's no need for that.'

The pressure relented, but Raoul did not let go.

'You have the American for that, don't you?' Alberto asked. 'Maybe you'd better show her. We could all use a little fresh air, no?'

Raoul grinned.

Rachel felt a knot of terror tighten around her heart.

She was led out of the cabin and forced up the steps. As she climbed, Raoul reached and slid a palm up her robe, along her thigh, fingers kneading. She scrambled upward.

The stairs led to the open stern of the hydrofoil. Sunlight glared off the white decking. Three men lounged on side benches, casually carrying assault rifles.

They eyed her.

She cinched her robe tighter, shuddering, still feeling Raoul's fingers on her. The large man climbed up, followed by Alberto.

She stepped around a short wall that separated the stairwell from the deck. She found Monk.

He was lying on his stomach, naked except for boxers, his wrists bound behind him and his legs hog-tied at the ankle. It looked like two of his fingers had been broken on his left hand, bent back at impossible angles. Blood smeared the deck. He opened one swollen eye when she stepped out.

He had no quip for her.

That scared her more than anything.

Raoul and his men must have taken their anger out on Monk, the only target.

'Untie his arms,' Raoul ordered. 'Get him on his back.'

The men responded quickly. Monk groaned as his arms were freed. He was flipped onto his back. One of the guards held a rifle at Monk's ear.

Raoul grabbed a fire-ax from a stanchion.

'What are you doing?' Rachel hurried to stand between the large man and Monk.

'That depends on you,' Raoul said. He hefted the ax to his shoulder.

One of the men responded to some discreet signal. Rachel's elbows were grabbed and pinned behind her back. She was carted backward.

Raoul pointed his ax, one-armed, at the third man. 'Sit

on his chest, hold his left arm down at the elbow.' Raoul strode forward as the man obeyed. He glanced back to Rachel. 'I believe the *professore* asked you a question.'

Alberto stepped forward. 'And don't leave out any details.'

Rachel was too horrified to respond.

'He has five fingers on this side,' Raoul added. 'We'll start with the broken ones. They're not of much use anyway.' He raised the ax.

'No!' Rachel choked out.

'Don't . . .' Monk groaned to her.

The guard with the rifle kicked Monk in the head.

'I'll tell you!' Rachel blurted out.

She spoke rapidly, explaining all that had happened, from the discovery of Alexander's body to the activation of the ancient batteries. She left out nothing, except for the truth. 'It took us some time, but we solved the riddle . . . the map . . . the Seven Wonders . . . it all points back to the beginning. A complete circle. Back to Rome.'

Alberto's eyes glowed with the telling, asking a few pertinent questions, nodding every now and then. 'Yes, yes . . .'

Rachel finished. 'That's all we know.'

Alberto turned to Raoul. 'She's lying.'

'I thought so.' He swung the ax down.

4:16 p.m.

Raoul enjoyed the woman's scream.

He pulled his ax head from where it had embedded in the deck. He had missed the captive's fingertips by the breadth of a hair. He yanked the ax to his shoulder and turned to the woman. Her face had paled to a shiny translucency.

'Next time, it's for real,' he warned.

Dr. Alberto stepped forward. 'Our large friend here

377

was good enough to get an angled flash on that center pyramid. It shows a square hole in its surface. Something you failed to mention. And a sin of omission is as good as a lie. Is that not so, Raoul?'

He raised the ax. 'Shall we try again?'

Alberto leaned closer to Rachel. 'There's no need for your friend to come to harm. I know something must have been taken from the tomb. It makes no sense to blindly point to Rome without an additional clue. What did you take from the pyramid?'

Tears rolled down her face.

Raoul read the tortured agony in every line of her face. He grew hard, remembering a few moments ago. Through a one-way mirror, he had spied as one of the captain's bitches had fingered through all the woman's private places. He had wanted to perform the body-cavity search himself, but the captain had refused. His boat, his rule. Raoul hadn't pressed. The captain was in a sour enough mood upon learning of Seichan's demise, lost with so many of Raoul's men.

Besides, he would soon be performing his own private inspection of the woman . . . but he planned on being much less gentle.

'What was taken?' Alberto pressed.

Raoul widened his stance, hefting the ax higher over his head. His freshly sutured hand ached, but he ignored it. Maybe she wouldn't tell . . . maybe this could be stretched out. . . .

But the woman cracked. 'A key . . . a gold key,' she whimpered, then sank to her knees on the deck. 'Gray . . . Commander Pierce has it.'

Behind her tears, Raoul heard a trace of hope in her voice.

He knew a way to squash that.

He brought the ax down in a steady hard swing. The ax severed the man's hand at the wrist.

'It's time to go,' Gray said.

He had given Vigor and Kat an additional forty-five minutes to call all the local hospitals and medical centers, even discreet calls to the municipal police. Maybe they had been injured, unable to contact them. Or they were cooling their heels in a jail cell.

Gray stood up as his sat-phone rang from his pack.

All eyes turned.

'Thank God,' Vigor gasped.

Only a handful of people had the phone's number: Director Crowe and his teammates.

Gray grabbed his phone and swung up its antenna. He moved closer to the window. 'Commander Pierce,' he said.

'I will keep this brief, so there's no confusion.'

Gray stiffened. It was Raoul. That could only mean one thing . . .

'We have the woman and your teammate. You'll do exactly as we say or we'll be mailing their heads to Washington and Rome . . . after we're done playing with their bodies, of course.'

'How do I know they're still – ?'

A shuffle sounded at the other end. A new voice gasped. He heard the tears behind the words. 'They . . . I . . . they cut off Monk's hand. He –'

The phone was taken away.

Gray tried not to react. Now was not the time. Still, his fingers clenched hard to the phone. His heart climbed into his throat, constricting his words.

'What do you want?'

'The gold key from the tomb,' Raoul said.

So they knew about it. Gray understood why Rachel had revealed the secret. How could she not? She must have traded the information for Monk's life. They were

379

safe as long as the Court knew Gray retained the key. But that didn't mean worse mutilations would not be performed if he didn't cooperate. He remembered the condition of the tortured priests in Milan.

'You want a trade,' he said coldly.

'There is an EgyptAir flight leaving Alexandria at 2100 hours for Geneva, Switzerland. You will be on that flight. You alone. We will have false papers and tickets in a locker, so no computer searches will trace your flight.' Directions to the locker followed. 'You will not contact your superiors . . . either in Washington or Rome. If you do, we'll know. Is that understood?'

'Yes,' he bit off. 'But how do I know you'll stick to your end of the bargain?'

'You don't. But as a gesture of goodwill, when you land in Geneva, I'll contact you again. If you follow our directions precisely, I'll free your man. He'll be sent to a local Swiss hospital. We will pass on satisfactory confirmation of this for you. But the woman will remain in custody until you give over the gold key.'

Gray knew the offer to free Monk was probably sincere, but not out of goodwill. Monk's life was an advance on the deal, a token to lure Gray into cooperating. He tried to shut out Rachel's earlier words. They had cut off Monk's hand.

He had no choice.

'I'll be on the flight,' he said.

Raoul was not done. 'The others on the team . . . the bitch and the monsignor . . . are free to go as long as they stay quiet and out of the way. If either sets foot in Italy or Switzerland, the deal is off.'

Gray frowned. He understood keeping the others out of Switzerland . . . but why Italy? Then it struck him. He pictured Rachel's map. The line he had drawn. Pointing to Rome. Rachel had revealed much – but not all.

Good girl.

'Agreed,' Gray said, his mind already wheeling out in various scenarios.

'Any sign of subterfuge and you'll never see the woman or your teammate again . . . except for body parts mailed out daily.' The connection ended.

Gray lowered the phone and turned to the others. He repeated the conversation verbatim, so all would understand. 'I will be on that flight.'

Vigor's face had drained of blood, his worst fears realized.

'They could ambush you at any point,' Kat said.

He nodded. 'But I believe as long as I keep moving toward them, they'll let me. They'll not risk losing the key in a failed attempt.'

'And what about us?' Vigor asked.

'I need you both in Avignon. Working on the mystery there.'

'I . , . I can't,' Vigor said. 'Rachel . . .' He sank to the bed.

Gray firmed his voice. 'Rachel has bought us a slim chance in Avignon, some leeway. Paid with Monk's blood and body. I won't let their efforts be squandered.'

Vigor looked up at him.

'You have to trust me.' Gray's demeanor hardened. 'I'll get Rachel. You have my word.'

Vigor stared at him, attempting to read something there. Whatever he found, he seemed to gain some resolve from it.

Gray hoped it was enough.

'How do you – ?' Kat began.

Gray shook his head, stepping away. 'The less we know of each other's movements from here, the better.' He crossed and gathered up his pack. 'I'll contact you when I have Rachel.'

He headed out.

With one hope.

Seichan sat in the dark, holding a broken bit of knife.

The spear through her shoulder still held her pinned to the wall. The inch-thick lance had sheared up under her collarbone and out the top of her shoulder, missing major blood vessels and her scapula. But she remained hooked in place. Blood seeped continually down the inside of her wetsuit.

Every movement was agony.

But she was alive.

The last of Raoul's men had gone quiet about the time the last flashlight had died. The firebomb Raoul had set to destroy the far chamber had barely reached this room. The heat had come close to parboiling her, though, but now she wished for that heat again.

A chill had set in, even through her suit. The stone surfaces leached the warmth from her. The blood loss didn't help.

Seichan refused to give up. She fingered the broken blade in her hand. She had been picking at the stone block, where the sharpened end of the spear had embedded. If she could dig it free, loosen the shaft . . .

Rock chips littered the floor. Down there was also the broken hilt to her dagger. It had shattered shortly after she'd started.

All she had left was a three-inch remnant of blade. Her fingers were bloody from the blade and the coarse rock. It was a futile effort.

Cold sweat oiled her face.

Off to the side, a glow grew. She thought it was her imagination. She turned her head. The entry pool was shining. The illumination grew.

The water stirred. Someone was coming.

Seichan clutched the bit of knife – both fearful and hopeful.

Who?

A dark shape splashed up. A diver. The flashlight blinded her as the figure climbed out.

She shadowed her eyes against the sudden brightness and glare.

The diver lowered the flashlight.

Seichan recognized a familiar face as he yanked back his mask and approached. Commander Gray Pierce.

He stepped toward her and lifted a hacksaw. 'Let's talk.'

# DAY
# FOUR

# 14

## GOTHIC

Director Painter Crowe knew he was in for another sleepless night. He had heard the reports out of Egypt of an attack at the East Harbor of Alexandria. Had Gray's team been involved? With no eyes in the sky, they had been unable to investigate through satellite surveillance.

And still no word had been passed from the field. The last messages had been exchanged twelve hours ago.

Painter regretted not relating his suspicions to Gray Pierce. But at that point, they had only been suspicions. Painter had needed time to finesse some further intelligence. And still he wasn't certain. If he proceeded more boldly, the conspirator would know he'd been discovered. It would put Gray and his teammates in further jeopardy.

So Painter worked his end alone.

A knock on his office door drew his eyes from the computer screen.

He turned off his computer monitor to hide his work. He buzzed the lock. His secretary was gone for the day.

Logan Gregory entered. 'Their jet is in final approach.'

'Still headed into Marseilles?' Painter asked.

Logan nodded. 'Due to land in eighteen minutes. Just after midnight local time.'

'Why France?' Painter rubbed his tired eyes. 'And they're still maintaining a communication blackout?'

'The pilot will confirm their destination, but nothing else. I was able to worm out a manifest through French customs. There are two passengers aboard.'

'Only two?' Painter sat straighter, frowning.

'Flying under diplomatic vouchers. Anonymous. I can attempt to dig through that.'

Painter had to work carefully from here. 'No,' he said. 'That might raise some alarm bells. The team wants to keep their activity cloaked. We'll give them some room. For now.'

'Yes, sir. I also have requests from Rome. The Vatican and the Carabinieri have not heard anything and are getting anxious.'

Painter had to offer them something or the EU authorities might react harshly. He considered his options. It would not take long for the authorities in Europe to ascertain the jet's destination. It would have to do.

'Be cooperative,' he finally said. 'Let them know of the flight to Marseilles, and that we'll pass on further intel as we learn more.'

'Yes, sir.'

Painter stared at his blank computer screen. He had a narrow window of opportunity. 'Once you contact them, I'll need you to run an errand for me. Out to DARPA.'

Logan frowned.

'I have something that I need personally couriered over to Dr. Sean McKnight.' Painter slid over a sealed letter in a red pouch. 'But no one must know you're headed over there.'

Logan's eyes narrowed quizzically, but he nodded. 'I'll take care of it.' He took the pouch, tucked it under his arm, and turned away.

Painter spoke to him. 'Absolute discretion.'

'You can trust me,' Logan said firmly, and closed the door with a click of the lock.

Painter switched back on his computer. It showed a

map of the Mediterranean basin with swaths of yellow and blue crisscrossing it. Satellite paths. He laid his pointer over one. NRO's newest satellite, nicknamed Hawkeye. He double-clicked and brought up trajectory details and search parameters.

He typed in Marseilles. Times came up. He cross-referenced with NOAA's weather map. A storm front swept toward southern France. Heavy cloud cover would block surveillance. The window of opportunity was narrow.

Painter checked his watch. He picked up the phone and spoke to security. 'Let me know when Logan Gregory has left the command center.'

'Yes, sir.'

Painter hung up the phone. Timing would be critical. He waited out another fifteen minutes, watching the storm front track over Western Europe.

'C'mon,' he mumbled.

The phone finally rang. Painter confirmed that Logan was gone, then stood up and left his office. The sat-recon was down one floor, neighboring Logan's office. Painter rushed down there to find a lone technician jotting in a logbook, nestled in the arced bank of monitors and computers.

The man was surprised by the sudden appearance of his boss and jerked to his feet. 'Director Crowe, sir . . . how can I help you?'

'I need a tap feed into NRO's H-E Four satellite.'

'Hawkeye?'

Painter nodded.

'That clearance is beyond my – '

Painter placed a long alphanumeric sequence in front of him. It was valid for only the next half hour, obtained by Sean McKnight.

The technician's eyes widened, and he set to work. 'There was no need to come down here yourself. Dr. Gregory could've patched the feed to your office.'

'Logan is gone.' Painter placed a palm on the technician's shoulder. 'Also I need all record of this tap erased. No recording. No word that this tap ever occurred. Even here in Sigma.'

'Yes, sir.'

The technician pointed to a screen. 'It'll come up on this monitor. I'll need GPS coordinates to zero in on.'

Painter gave them.

After a long minute, the dark airfield bloomed onto the screen.

Marseilles Airport.

Painter directed the feed to zoom down onto a certain gate. The image jittered, then smoothly swelled. A small plane appeared, a Citation X. It sat near the gate, door open. Painter leaned forward, obscuring the view from the technician.

Was he too late?

Movement pixilated. One figure, then another stepped into view. They hurried down the stairs. Painter didn't need to magnify their faces.

Monsignor Verona and Kat Bryant.

Painter waited. Maybe the manifest had been false. Maybe they all were aboard.

The screen shuddered with a wave of blocky pixels.

'Bad weather coming in,' the technician said.

Painter stared. No other passengers left the jet. Kat and the monsignor vanished through the gate. With a worried frown, Painter waved for the feed to be cut. He thanked the technician and stepped away.

Where the hell was Gray?

1:04 a.m.
GENEVA, SWITZERLAND

Gray sat in the first-class cabin of the EgyptAir jet. He had to give the Dragon Court credit. They didn't spare expense. He glanced around the small cabin. Eight seats. Six passengers. One or more were probably spies for the Court, keeping an eye on him.

It didn't matter. He was cooperating fully . . . for now.

He had picked up his plane tickets and false ID from a bus locker, then proceeded to the airport. The four-hour flight was interminable. He ate the gourmet meal, drank two glasses of red wine, watched some movie with Julia Roberts, even power-napped for forty-two minutes.

He turned to the window. The gold key shifted against his chest. It rested on a chain around his neck. His body heat had warmed the metal, but it still hung heavy and cold. Two people's lives weighted it down. He pictured Monk, easy mannered, sharp-eyed, bighearted. And Rachel. A mix of steel and silk, intriguing and complicated. But the woman's last call haunted him, so full of pain and panic. He ached to the marrow, knowing she had been captured under his watch.

Gray stared out the window as the jet made a steep approach, necessary for landing in the city nestled among the towering Alps.

The lights of Geneva glittered. Moonlight silvered the peaks and lake.

The plane swept over a section of the Rhône River that split the city. Landing gear engaged with a whine. Moments later they were touching down at the Geneva International Airport.

They taxied to their gate, and Gray waited for the cabin to empty before gathering up his one carefully packed bag. He hoped he had everything he would need. Slinging his bag over his shoulder, he headed out.

As he exited the first-class cabin, he searched for any sign of danger.

And one other. His traveling companion.

She had been in the coach seats. She wore a blonde wig, a conservative navy blue business suit, and heavy black eyeglasses. She carried herself with a subdued demeanor, her left arm in a sling, half hidden under her jacket. The disguise would not pass close inspection. But no one was expecting her.

Seichan was dead to the world.

She exited ahead of him without a glance.

Gray followed a few passengers behind her. Once in the terminal, he queued up for customs, showed his false papers, had them stamped, and was on his way. He hadn't checked any baggage.

He strode out to the well-lit street, which was still crowded. Late travelers scurried for cars and taxies. He had no idea what was expected of him from here. He had to wait for some contact from Raoul. He shifted closer to the taxi line.

Seichan had vanished, but Gray sensed she was near.

He had needed an ally. Cut off from Washington, from his own teammates, he had made a pact with the devil. He had freed her with his hacksaw after exacting a promise from her. They would work together. In return for her freedom, she would help Gray free Rachel. Afterward, they would part ways. All debts forgiven, past and present.

She had agreed.

As he treated and bandaged her wound, she had looked on him most oddly, stripped to the waist, breasts bared, unabashed. She studied him like a curiosity, a strange bug, with an intensity of focus. She said little, exhausted, perhaps in slight shock. But she recovered smoothly, a lioness slowly waking, cunning and amusement lighting her eyes.

Gray knew that her cooperation was less out of obligation than fury at Raoul. Cooperation suited her immediate need. She had been left for dead, a slow agonizing end. She wanted to make Raoul pay. Whatever contract had been agreed upon between the Court and the Guild was over for her. All that was left was vengeance.

But was that all?

Gray remembered her eyes upon him and her dark curiosity. But he also remembered Painter's earlier warning about her. It must have been plain on his face.

'Yes, I am going to betray you,' Seichan had said plainly as she pulled on her shirt. 'But only after this is over. You will attempt the same. We both know this. Mutual distrust. Is there a better form of honesty?'

Gray's sat-phone finally rang. He freed it from his bag. 'Commander Pierce,' he said tersely.

'Welcome to Switzerland,' Raoul said. 'There are train tickets waiting for you at the city-center terminal, under your false name, headed to Lausanne. It leaves in thirty-five minutes. You'll be on it.'

'What about my teammate?' Gray said.

'As arranged, he's on his way to the hospital in Geneva. You'll have confirmation by the time you board the train.'

Gray headed to the taxis. 'Lieutenant Verona?' he asked.

'The woman is being well accommodated. For now. Don't miss your train.'

The line went dead.

Gray climbed into a taxi. He didn't bother searching for Seichan. He had piggybacked a chip on his phone, tied to her cell phone. She had overheard the conversation. He trusted her skill to keep up with him.

'Central train station,' he told the driver.

With a curt nod, the cabby sailed out into traffic and headed toward downtown Geneva. Gray sank back into his seat. Seichan had been right. Upon learning of his summons to Switzerland, she had told him where she suspected Rachel was being kept. Some castle up in the Savoy Alps.

After ten minutes, the taxi swept alongside the lake. Out in the water, a giant fountain sprayed more than a hundred yards into the air. The famous Jet d'Eau. It was lit up by lamps, a fairy-tale sight. Some festival was under way near the piers.

Gray heard an echo of singing and laughter.

It sounded like it was coming from another world.

In another couple of minutes, the taxi offloaded him in front of the train terminal. He crossed to the ticket counter, gave his false name, and showed his papers. He was given tickets to the lakeside city of Lausanne.

He strode toward his gate, keeping a wary watch for anyone nearby. He saw no sign of Seichan. A worry nagged. What if she simply took off? What if she double-crossed him to Raoul? Gray drove down such worries. He had made a choice. It was a calculated risk.

His phone rang again.

He pulled it free and adjusted the antenna.

'Commander Pierce,' he said.

'Two minutes to satisfy yourself.' Raoul again. A click and hiss of a transfer sounded. The next voice was more distant, echoing a bit, but familiar.

'Commander?'

'I'm here, Monk. Where are you?' Gray was sure the conversation was being eavesdropped on by more than just Seichan. He had to be careful.

'They dumped me at some hospital with this cell phone. Told me to expect your call. I'm in the emergency room. Doctors are all speaking goddamn French.'

'You're in Geneva,' Gray said. 'How are you doing?'

A long pause.

'I know about your hand,' Gray said.

'Goddamn bastards,' Monk said with an edge of fury. 'They had a doctor on board their ship. Drugged me, IVs, sutured my . . . my stump. The docs here want X-rays and such, but they seem satisfied with the other doctor's umm . . . handiwork, so to speak.'

Gray appreciated Monk's attempt at levity. But his voice was hard-edged.

'Rachel?'

Pain intensified his words. 'I haven't seen her since they drugged me. I have no idea where she's at. But . . . but, Gray . . .'

'What?'

'You have to get her away from them.'

'I'm working on that. But what about you? Are you safe?'

'Seem to be,' he said. 'I was told to keep my mouth shut. That I've done, playing dumb. The doctors, though, have called the local police. Security is posted.'

'For now, do as they ordered you,' Gray said. 'I'll get you out of there as soon as I can.'

'Gray,' Monk said, voice strained. Gray recognized his tone. He wanted to communicate something, but he also knew the others were eavesdropping. 'They . . they let me go.'

The connection fritzed again. Raoul came back on the line.

'Time's up. As you can see, we honor our word. If you want the woman freed, you'll bring the key.'

'Understood. What then?'

'I'll have a car waiting for you at the Lausanne station.'

'No,' Gray said. 'I won't put myself into your custody until I know Rachel is safe. When I arrive in Lausanne, I want confirmation that she is alive. Then we'll make arrangements.'

'Don't press your hand,' Raoul growled. 'I'd hate to have to chop it off, like your friend's. We'll continue this conversation when you're here.'

The connection ended.

Gray lowered the phone. *So Raoul was in Lausanne.*

He waited for the train. It was the last train heading out. The deck was sparsely crowded. He studied his fellow travelers. No sign of Seichan. Were any spies for the Court here?

Finally the train arrived, clattering up the track. It glided to a stop with a piercing sigh of air. Gray climbed into the middle car, then hurriedly moved between cars toward the rear, hoping to shake any tail.

In the gap between the last two cars, Seichan waited.

She did not acknowledge him, except to hand him a long leather duster. She turned and shouldered out an emergency exit that opened on the opposite side of the track, away from the deck.

He followed, dropping down. He tugged on the jacket and pulled up the collar.

Seichan hurried across another track and up onto a neighboring deck. They left the station, and Gray found himself at the edge of a parking lot.

A BMW motorcycle, black and yellow, stood a step away.

'Climb on,' Seichan said. 'You'll have to drive. My shoulder . . .' She had abandoned the sling to ride here from the rental office, but it was another fifty miles to Lausanne.

Gray hopped in front, kicking back the tail of his jacket. The bike was still warm.

She climbed behind him and put her good arm around his waist.

Gray gunned the engine. He had already memorized the roads from here to Lausanne. He raced out of the parking lot and throttled up once out on the street. He zipped toward the highway that led out of Geneva and into the mountains.

His headlights speared ahead.

He chased the light, faster and faster, winds whipping his jacket edge. Seichan leaned tighter against him, arm around him, hand under his jacket. Fingers clutched his belt.

He resisted the urge to force her arm away. Wise or not, he had made this bed. He blasted up the narrow highway. They needed to reach Lausanne a half hour ahead of the train. Would it be enough time?

As he wound up into the heights that bordered the lake, Gray's mind drifted back to his conversation with Monk. What had Monk been trying to tell him? *They let me go.* That was plain enough. But what had Monk been implying?

He considered his earlier assessment, back in Egypt. He had known the Court would let Monk go. The release was done to ensure and lure Gray's cooperation. And Raoul still had Rachel as a bargaining chip.

*They let me go.*

Was there more to his release? The Court was ruthless. They were not known to give away potential assets. They had used Monk's torture to ply Rachel into talking. Would they give up such an asset so readily? Monk was right. Not unless the Court had an even better hold on Rachel.

But what?

2:02 a.m.
LAUSANNE, SWITZERLAND

Rachel sat in her cell, numb and exhausted.

Any time she closed her eyes, she again relived the horror. She saw the ax swinging down. Monk's body jerking up. His chopped hand flopping across the deck like a landed fish. Blood spraying.

Alberto had yelled at Raoul for his action – not for his brutality, but because he wanted the man still alive. Raoul had waved away his concern. A tourniquet had been applied. Alberto had Raoul's men drag Monk down to the ship's galley.

Later, she had been informed by one of the Guild women that he still lived. Two hours later, the hydrofoil had sailed up to an island in the Mediterranean. They were transferred to a small private jet.

Rachel had spotted Monk, groggy, his severed wrist

bandaged to the elbow, strapped to a stretcher. She was then locked in a back compartment. Alone. No windows. Over the course of another five hours, they landed twice. She was finally let out.

Monk was gone.

Raoul had blindfolded and gagged her. She was transferred from plane to truck. Another half hour of twisty driving and they arrived at their final destination. She heard the wheels bumping over wooden planks. A bridge. The truck braked to a stop.

Dragged out, she heard a cacophony of growling and barking, loud, angry, large. A kennel of some sort.

She was led by the elbow through an opening and down steps. A door closed behind her, shutting off the barking. She smelled cold stone and dampness. She had also felt the pressure elevation as the truck drove up here.

Mountains.

Finally she was shoved forward and tripped over a sill. She landed hard on hands and knees.

Raoul grabbed her rear with both hands and laughed. 'Already begging for it.'

Rachel leapt away and crashed her shoulder into something solid. Her soggy gag and hood were pulled off. Rubbing her shoulder, she stared around the small stone cell. Again no windows. Her sense of time was beginning to slip. The only furniture in the cell was a steel cot. A thin mattress rolled up on one end. A pillow rested on top. No sheets.

The cell had no bars. One wall was a solid sheet of glass, except for a rubber-sealed door and fist-sized ventilation holes. But even the holes had tiny lids that could be swung over the openings, for soundproofing or a way to slowly suffocate the prisoner.

She had been left down here for over an hour.

Not even any guards. Though she did hear voices down the hall, probably posted at the stairwell.

A commotion sounded. She lifted her face and stood. She heard Raoul's coarse voice, orders barked. She backed from the glass wall. Her clothes had been returned to her on the boat, but she had no weapons.

Raoul appeared, flanked by two men.

He did not look happy.

'Get her out of there,' he spat.

A key opened the door. She was dragged out.

'This way,' Raoul said. He led her down the hallway.

She spotted other cells, some sealed like hers, others open and stacked with wine bottles.

Raoul marched her to the stairs and up to a dark moonlit courtyard. Stone walls towered on all sides. An archway, sealed by a portcullis, led out to a narrow bridge that spanned a gorge.

She was in a castle.

A row of trucks lined the wall nearest the gateway.

Along a neighboring wall, a long row of twenty chain-link cages stretched. Low grumbles rose from that corner. Large shadows shifted, muscular, powerful.

Raoul must have noted her attention. 'Perro de Presa Canario,' he said with a note of savage pride. 'Fighting dogs, an ancestral line from the 1800s. Perfection of breeding. Pure pit fighter. All muscle, jaws, and teeth.'

Rachel wondered if he was also describing himself.

Raoul led her away from the gate and toward the central keep. Two tiers of stairs led up to a thick oak door. It was brightly lit by sconces, almost inviting. But they didn't go that way. A side door led to a level beneath the stairs.

Using a touchpad, he unlocked the lower door.

As the door swung open, Rachel caught a whiff of antiseptic and something darker, more fetid. She was forced into a square room, brightly lit with fluorescent bulbs. Stone walls, linoleum floor. A single guard stood before the one door that led away.

Raoul crossed and opened it.

Beyond stretched a long, sterile hallway. A series of rooms opened off it. She glanced into a few as she was marched down the passage. Stainless-steel cages filled one. Banks of computers tied to rows of plates occupied another. Electromagnets, she guessed, used to experiment with the m-state compounds. A third chamber held a single steel table, shaped in a rough X. Leather straps indicated that the table was meant to hold a man or woman spread-eagled. A surgical lamp hung above it.

The sight chilled her to the bone.

Another six rooms stretched beyond. She had seen enough and was happy to stop alongside a door on the opposite wall.

Raoul knocked and pushed inside.

Rachel was surprised by the contrast. It was like stepping into the turn-of-the-century parlor of a distinguished Royal Society scholar. The room here was all polished mahogany and walnut. Underfoot spread a thick Turkish rug patterned in crimson and emerald.

Bookshelves and display cabinets lined all the walls, filled with neatly arranged texts. Behind glass, she noted first-edition copies of *Principia* by Sir Isaac Newton, and beside it, Darwin's *Origin of Species*. There was also an illuminated Egyptian manuscript spread open in one case. Rachel wondered if it was the one that had been stolen from the Cairo museum, the forged text with the encrypted stanzas that had started this whole murderous adventure.

Everywhere she looked there was artwork. Etruscan and Roman statuary decorated the shelves, including a two-foot-tall Persian horse, the head broken off, a masterpiece stolen from Iran a decade ago, supposedly representing Alexander the Great's famous horse, Bucephalus. Paintings stood above cabinets. She knew one was a Rembrandt, another a Raphael.

But resting in the center of the room was a massive

carved mahogany desk. It rested near a stacked-stone, floor-to-ceiling fireplace. Small flames flickered in the hearth.

*'Professore!'* Raoul called, closing the door behind them.

Through a back door leading to other private rooms, Dr. Alberto Menardi entered. He wore a black smoking jacket trimmed in crimson. He had the gall to be still wearing his clerical Roman collar above a black shirt.

He carried a book under one arm and shook a finger at Rachel. 'You haven't been totally honest with us.'

Rachel felt her heart stop beating, her breath became trapped.

Alberto turned to Raoul. 'And if you hadn't distracted me with the need to mend that American's wrist, I would've discovered this sooner. Both of you, come here.'

They were waved to the cluttered desk.

Rachel noted her map of the Mediterranean spread out on the top. New lines had been added, circles, meridians, degree marks. Tiny arcane numbers were inscribed along one edge of the map. A compass and T square rested beside it, along with a sextant. Plainly, Alberto had been working on this puzzle, either not trusting Rachel or figuring she and her uncle were too obtuse.

The prefect tapped the map. 'Rome is *not* the next place.'

Rachel forced herself not to flinch.

Alberto continued, 'All the subtext to this geometric design signifies forward motion in time. Even this hourglass, it segments time, marching forward one grain at a time, to the inevitable end. For this reason, the symbol of the hourglass has always represented death, the end of time. To have an hourglass show up here can only mean one thing.'

Raoul's frown deepened, indicating his lack of understanding.

Alberto sighed. 'Obviously, it signifies the end of this journey. I'm sure that wherever this clue points, it marks the last stop.'

Rachel felt Raoul stir beside her. They were close to their end goal. But they didn't have the gold key, and for all Alberto's intelligence, he hadn't solved the complete riddle yet. But he would.

'It can't be Rome,' Alberto said. 'That's moving backward, not forward. There is another mystery to solve here.'

Rachel shook her head, feigning exhausted disinterest. 'That's all we could calculate before we were attacked.' She waved around his room. 'We didn't have your resources.'

Alberto studied her as she spoke. She stared, unflinching.

'I . . . I believe you,' he said slowly. 'Monsignor Vigor is quite sharp, but this riddle is layered in mystery.'

Rachel kept her features dull, allowing some fear to show, acting cowed. Alberto worked alone. He'd plainly ensconced himself in here to solve the Court's mysteries. Trusting no one else, conceited in his own superiority. He would not understand the value of the wider perspective, a diversification of viewpoint. It had taken the entire team's expertise to piece the mystery together, not the work of one man.

But the prefect was no fool. 'Still,' he said, 'we should be sure. You kept hidden the discovery of the gold key. Maybe there's more you kept hidden.'

Fear edged higher. 'I've told you everything,' she swore with mustered conviction. Would they believe her? Would they torture her?

She swallowed hard, trying to hide it. She would never talk. Too much was at stake. She had seen the power displayed in Rome and Alexandria. The Dragon Court must never possess it.

Even Monk's life would be forfeit from here. They

were both soldiers. Back on the hydrofoil, she had given the information about the gold key not only to spare Monk, but also to engage Gray, to give him a chance to do something. It had seemed a reasonable risk. Like now, the Court had still been missing a vital piece of the puzzle. She had to hold on to the discovery of Avignon and the French papacy.

Or all would be lost.

Alberto shrugged. 'There's only one way to find out if you know more. It's time we ensured the complete truth from you. Take her next door. We should be ready.'

Rachel's breathing grew quicker, but she could not seem to get enough air. She was manhandled by Raoul back out the door. Alberto followed, shedding his jacket, ready to get down to work.

Rachel pictured again Monk's hand flopping on the ship's deck. She had to gird herself for worse. They must not know. Not ever. No reason would be good enough for her to reveal the truth.

As Rachel stepped out into the hall, she saw that the far room, the one that held the strange X-shaped table, was lit up much brighter. Someone had turned on the overhead surgical lamp.

Raoul partially blocked the view. She spotted an IV bottle on a stand. A tray of long surgical instruments, sharp-edged, corkscrewed, and razor-toothed. A figure was strapped to the table.

Oh God . . . Monk . . . ?

'We can stretch this interrogation all night long,' Alberto promised, stepping past to enter the room first. He crossed and donned a pair of sterile latex gloves.

Raoul finally dragged her forward into the suite of surgical horrors.

Rachel finally saw who was strapped to the table, pinioned, limbs stretched and tied, nose already dripping blood.

'Someone came snooping where they shouldn't have,' Raoul said with a hungry smile.

The captive's face turned toward her. Their eyes met with recognition. And at that moment, all will left her.

Rachel lunged forward. 'No!'

Raoul grabbed a fistful of her hair and dragged Rachel to her knees. 'You'll watch from here.'

Alberto picked up a silver scalpel. 'We'll start with the left ear.'

'No!' Rachel screamed. 'I'll tell you! I'll tell you everything!'

Alberto lowered the blade and turned to her.

'Avignon,' she sobbed. 'It's Avignon.'

She felt no guilt in the telling. She had to trust Gray from here. All hope rested on him. Rachel stared into the terrified eyes of the bound prisoner.

'*Nonna* . . .' Rachel moaned.

It was her grandmother.


2:22 a.m.
AVIGNON, FRANCE

The city of Avignon glowed, shouted, sang, and danced.

The annual Summer Theater Festival ran each July, the world's largest showcase of music, drama, and art. Youth crowded into the city, camping in parks, flooding hotels and youth hostels. It was an around-the-clock party. Even the lowering skies did not discourage the festival-goers.

Vigor turned from a couple in full fellatio on a secluded park bench. The woman's long hair hid most of her effort at pleasuring her male companion. Vigor hurried past with Kat at his side. They had chosen to pass through the high park to reach the Place du Palais, the Palace Square. The pope's castle sat atop a spur of rock overlooking the river.

As they passed a lookout spot, a curve of the river appeared below. Jutting out into it was the famous bridge of French nursery rhymes, Le Pont d'Avignon, or St. Benezet Bridge. Built in the late twelfth century, it was the only bridge to span the Rhône River . . . though after so many centuries, only four of its original twenty-two arches remained. The partial span was lit up brilliantly. Partiers danced atop it, traditional folk dancers from the look of it. Music trailed up to them.

In Avignon, the past and present mingled as they did in few other cities.

'Where do we begin?' Kat asked.

Vigor had spent the flight here in research, trying to answer that exact question. He spoke as he led them away from the river and toward the city. 'Avignon is one of the oldest townships of Europe. It can trace its roots back to Neolithic times. It was settled by the Celts, then the Romans. But what Avignon is most famous for today is its Gothic heritage, which flourished during the century of the French papacy. Avignon boasts one of the largest ensembles of Gothic architecture in all of Europe. A true Gothic town.'

'And the significance of that would be what?' Kat asked.

Vigor recognized the stiffness in her voice. She was worried about her teammates, cut off from them, sent here. He knew she felt a deep-seated responsibility for the capture of his niece and Monk. She carried that burden despite her own commander's insistence that she had done the right thing.

Vigor felt an echo of her concern. He had dragged Rachel into this adventure. Now she was in the hands of the Dragon Court. But he knew that guilt would do them no good. He had grown up with faith. It was the cornerstone of his being. He found some solace in placing his faith in Rachel's safety into the hands of God – and Gray.

But that didn't mean he couldn't be proactive himself.

405

*God helps those who help themselves.* He and Kat had their own duty here.

Vigor answered her question. 'The word "Gothic" comes from the Greek word "goetic." Which translates to "magic." And such architecture was considered magical. It was like none seen at the time: the thin ribbing, the flying buttresses, the impossible heights. It gave an impression of *weightlessness.*'

As Vigor stressed this last word, Kat understood. 'Levitation,' she said.

Vigor nodded. 'The cathedrals and other Gothic structures were almost exclusively built by a group of masons who named themselves the Children of Solomon, a mix of Knights Templar and monks of the Cistercian Order. They retained the mathematical mysteries to build these structures, supposedly gained when the Knights Templar discovered the lost Temple of Solomon during the Crusades. The Knights grew rich . . . or rather *richer*, as it was said they had already discovered King Solomon's vast treasure, possibly even the Ark of the Covenant, which was said to have been hidden at the Temple of Solomon.'

'And supposedly the Ark is where Moses stored his pots of manna,' Kat said. 'His recipe for m-state metals.'

'Don't discount that possibility,' Vigor said. 'In the Bible, there are many references to strange powers emanating from the Ark. References to it levitating. Even the word *levitate* is derived from the caretakers of the Ark, the Levite priests. And the Ark was well known for being deadly, killing with bolts of light. One fellow, a carter named Uzzah, sought to stabilize the Ark when it tipped a bit. He touched it with his hand and was struck down. Scared poor King David enough that he at first refused to take the Ark into his city. But the Levite priests showed him how to approach it safely. With gloves, aprons, and divesting oneself of all metal objects.'

'To keep from getting shocked.' Kat's voice had lost some of its stiffness, the mystery drawing her out.

'Maybe the Ark, with the m-state powders stored inside, acted like an electrical capacitor. The superconducting material absorbed ambient environmental energy and stored it like the gold pyramid had. Until someone mishandled it.'

'And got electrocuted.'

Vigor nodded.

'Okay,' Kat said. 'Let's say these Knights Templar rediscovered the Ark and possibly these m-state superconductors. But can we know if they understood its secrets?'

'I may have an answer. Commander Gray originally challenged me to trace historical references for these strange monatomic powders.'

'From Egypt to the biblical Magi,' Kat said.

Vigor nodded. 'But I wondered if it stretched further. Past the age of Christ. Were there more clues left to find?'

'And you found them,' Kat said, reading his excitement.

'These m-state powders went by many names: white bread, the powder of projection, the Paradise Stone, the Magi Stone. To my surprise, looking forward from biblical times, I found another mysterious stone of alchemical history. The famous Philosopher's Stone.'

Kat frowned. 'The stone that could turn lead into gold?'

'That is a common misconception. A seventeenth-century philosopher, Eiranaeus Philalethes, a well-respected Royal Society Fellow, set the record straight in his treatises. To quote him, the Philosopher's Stone was "nothing but gold digested to its highest degree of purity . . . called a stone by virtue of its fixed nature . . . gold, more pure than the purest . . . but its appearance is that of a very fine powder."'

'The gold powder again,' Kat said, surprised.

'Can there be any clearer reference? And it wasn't only

Eiranaeus; a fifteenth-century French chemist, Nicolas Flamel, described a similar alchemical process with the final words, and I quote, "It made a fine powder of gold, which is the Philosopher's Stone.'"

Vigor took a breath. 'So clearly some scientists at the time were experimenting with a strange form of gold. In fact, the entire Royal Society of scientists was fascinated by it. Including Sir Isaac Newton. Many don't know that Newton was a fervent alchemist and also a colleague of Eiranaeus.'

'Then what became of all their work?' Kat asked.

'I don't know. Many probably reached dead ends. But another colleague of Newton, Robert Boyle, also researched alchemical gold. But something disturbed him, something he discovered. He stopped his research and declared such studies dangerous. So dangerous, in fact, that he said its misuse could "disorder the affairs of mankind, turning the world topsy-turvy." It makes one wonder what scared him. Could he have touched upon something that drove our lost alchemical society deep underground?'

Kat shook her head. 'But what does the Philosopher's Stone have to do with Gothic architecture?'

'More than you'd think. An early-twentieth-century Frenchman named Fulcanelli wrote a best-selling treatise titled *Le Mystère des Cathédrales*. It elaborated on how the Gothic cathedrals of Europe were coded with arcane messages, pointing to a vein of lost knowledge, including how to prepare the Philosopher's Stone and other alchemical secrets.'

'A code in stone?'

'Don't be surprised. It was what the Church was doing already. Most of the populace at the time was illiterate. The decorations of the cathedrals were both instructional and informative, biblical storytelling in stonework. And remember who I said built these massive Gothic storybooks.'

'The Knights Templar,' Kat said.

'A group known to have gained secret knowledge from the Temple of Solomon. So perhaps, besides telling biblical stories, they incorporated some additional coded messages, meant for their fellow Masonic alchemists.'

Kat wore a doubtful expression.

'One only has to look closely at some of the Gothic artwork to raise an eyebrow or two. The iconography is full of zodiac symbols, mathematical riddles, geometric mazes right out of alchemical texts of the time. Even the author of *The Hunchback of Notre Dame*, Victor Hugo, spent a whole chapter decrying how the artwork of Notre Dame was contrary to the Catholic Church. Describing its Gothic art as "seditious pages" in stone.'

Vigor pointed ahead, through the trees. The park ended as they neared the Palace Square. 'And Fulcanelli and Hugo weren't the only ones who believed something heretical was involved with the Knights Templar's artwork. Do you know why Friday the thirteenth is considered unlucky?'

Kat glanced to him and shook her head.

'October 13, 1307. A Friday. The king of France, along with the pope, declared the Knights Templar to be heretics, sentencing them to death, and crucifying and burning their leader. It is well believed that the real reason the Knights were outlawed was to wrest power from them and gain control of their riches, including the secret knowledge they possessed. The king of France tortured thousands of Knights, but their storehouse of riches was never discovered. Still, it marked the end of the Knights Templar.'

'Truly an unlucky day for them.'

'The end of an unlucky *century,* really.' Vigor led the way out of the park and along the tree-lined street that led toward the center of town. 'The division between the Church and the Knights started a hundred years earlier when Pope Innocent III brutally wiped out the Cathars, a sect of Gnostic Christians with ties to the Knights Templar. It was really a century-long war between orthodoxy and Gnostic belief.'

'And we know who won that,' Kat said.

'Do we? I'm wondering if it wasn't so much a victory as an assimilation. If you can't beat them, join them. An interesting paper turned up in September 2001, titled the Chinon Parchment. It was a scroll dated a year after that bloody Friday the thirteenth, signed by Pope Clement V, absolving and exonerating the Knights Templar. Unfortunately, King Philippe of France ignored this and continued his country-wide massacre of the Knights. But why this change of heart by the Church? Why did Pope Clement build his Avignon palace here in the Gothic tradition, constructed by the same heretical masons? And why did Avignon become in fact the Gothic center of Europe?'

'Are you suggesting the Church did an about-face and took the Knights into their fold?'

'Remember how we'd already come to conclude that some aspects of the Thomas Christians, Christians of Gnostic leanings, were already hidden inside the Church. Perhaps they convinced Pope Clement to intervene to protect the Knights from King Philippe's rampage.'

'To what end?'

'To hide something of great value – to the Church, to the world. During the century of the Avignon papacy, a great surge of building occurred here, much of it overseen by the Children of Solomon. They could have easily buried away something of considerable size.'

'But where do we begin looking?' Kat said.

'To the work commissioned by that wayward pope, built by the hands of the Knights, one of the largest masterworks of Gothic architecture.'

Vigor waved forward, where the street emptied into a large square, populated by merrymakers from the festival. Colored lights framed a dancing area, a rock band on a

410

makeshift stage pounded out a riff, and young people writhed, laughed, and yelled. Along the fringes, tables had been set up, crowded with more festival participants. A juggler tossed flaming brands into the night sky. Clapping encouraged him. Beer flowed, along with paper cups of coffee. Cigarette smoke billowed, along with special hand-rolled herbs.

But backdropped against this party rose an immense, dark, and looming structure, framed by square towers, fronted by massive archways of stone, and set off by a pair of conical spires. Its stone face was a sober contrast to the merriment below. History weighed it down . . . and an ancient secret.

The Palace of the Popes.

'Somewhere within its structure lies some seditious page of stone,' Vigor said, stepping closer to Kat. 'I'm sure of it. We must find it and decode it.'

'But where do we begin looking?'

Vigor shook his head. 'Whatever had frightened Robert Boyle, whatever terrible secret finally forged an alliance between heretical Knights and the orthodox church, whatever mystery required a Mediterranean-wide treasure hunt to solve . . . the answer is hidden here.'

Vigor felt a sharp wind blow up from the river. Avignon was named after the constant breezes off the river, but he sensed the true storm to come. Overhead, the stars were gone. Dark clouds lowered.

How much time did they have left?

2:48 a.m.
LAUSANNE, SWITZERLAND

That's how we calculated it was Avignon,' Rachel finished. 'The French Vatican. That's the next and last stop.'

She was still on her knees on the linoleum. Her grandmother remained strapped to the table. Rachel had told

411

them everything, leaving out no detail. She had answered every one of Alberto's questions. She had attempted no prevarication. She could not risk the prefect testing her veracity upon the flesh of her grandmother.

Monk and Rachel were soldiers. Her *nonna* was not.

Rachel would not let any harm come to the old woman. It was up to Gray now to keep the gold key from the Court. She had turned all hope and trust over to him. She had no other choice.

During her dissertation, Alberto had jotted notes, stepping back into his office to get pen and pad, along with Rachel's map. He nodded once she was done, obviously convinced.

'Of course,' he said. 'So simple, so elegant. I would've eventually figured this out, but now my efforts can best be put to unraveling the next mystery . . . in Avignon.'

Alberto turned to Raoul.

Rachel stiffened. She remembered what had happened last time. Even though she had told them the truth about the gold key, Raoul had still chopped off Monk's hand.

'Where are Monsignor Verona and the other American now?' Alberto asked.

'Last I heard, they were heading to Marseilles,' Raoul said. 'In their private jet. I thought they were following orders. Staying close, but clear of Italy.'

'Marseilles is only twenty minutes from Avignon,' Alberto said with a scowl. 'Monsignor Verona must already be en route to work on the mystery. Find out if his plane has landed.'

Raoul nodded and passed the order to one of his men, who ran down the hall.

Rachel slowly gained her feet. 'My grandmother . . .' she said. 'Can you let her go now?'

Alberto waved a hand, as if he had forgotten about the old woman. Clearly he had grander things on his mind.

Another of the men stepped forward and ripped free

412

the leather straps that held her grandmother. With tears streaming down her face, Rachel helped her *nonna* from the table.

Rachel silently sent out a prayer to Gray. Not just for herself and Monk, but now also for her grandmother.

Her *nonna* shakily gained her feet, leaning one hand on the table for support. She reached out and wiped Rachel's tears. 'There, there, child . . . enough with the crying. It was not all that awful. I've been through worse.'

Rachel almost laughed. Her grandmother was attempting to console her.

Waving Rachel aside, her grandmother stalked toward the prefect. 'Alberto, you should be ashamed of yourself,' she scolded, as if speaking to a child.

'*Nonna* . . . no . . .' Rachel warned, reaching out an arm.

'Not believing my granddaughter was capable of keeping secrets from you.' She hobbled over and gave Alberto a kiss on the cheek. 'I told you Rachel was too clever for even you.'

Rachel's outstretched arm froze. The blood iced in her veins.

'You must trust an old lady sometimes, no?'

'You are right as ever, Camilla.'

Rachel could not breathe.

Her grandmother motioned for Raoul to give her his arm. 'And you, young man, maybe now you see why such strong Dragon's blood is worth protecting.' She reached up and patted the bastard's cheek. 'You and my granddaughter . . . you two will make *bellissimo bambini*. Many beautiful babies.'

Raoul turned and weighed Rachel with those cold, dead eyes.

'I will do my best,' he promised.

# 15

## HUNTING

Gray followed Seichan up the pine-studded mountainside. They had abandoned the motorbike at the bottom of a narrow gorge, hiding it among some flowering Alpine rose shrubs. Prior to that, they had ridden the last half-mile in the dark, headlamp off. The extra caution had slowed them down, but it couldn't be helped.

Seichan led the way now on foot, no lights, climbing up a slope of loose scree toward a sheer rockface. Gray tried to pierce the weave of pine branches. Earlier, he had caught a glimpse of the castle as they rode up out of Lausanne and into the surrounding mountains. The chateau had sat like a hulking granite gargoyle, square faced, eyes glowing with lamplight. Then it had disappeared as they passed under a bridge that spanned far overhead.

Gray stepped up beside Seichan. She held a GPS device before her as she climbed. 'Are you sure you can find this back entrance?'

'They had me hooded the first time here. But I had a GPS tracker hidden' – she glanced to Gray – 'somewhere private. I recorded the approach's position and elevation. It should lead us to the entrance.'

They continued to the towering cliff face.

Gray studied Seichan. What was he doing trusting her? In the dark forest, worries mounted. And not just about

414

his choice of teammate. He began to doubt his own judgment. Was this the action of a true leader? He was risking everything in this rescue attempt. Any tactician would have weighed the odds and gone straight to Avignon with the key. He was placing the entire mission in jeopardy.

And if the Dragon Court won . . .

Gray pictured the dead in Cologne, the tortured priests in Milan. Many more would die if he failed.

And for what?

At least he knew the answer to that.

Gray continued up the hillside, lost in his own thoughts. Seichan checked her GPS unit, then moved to the left. A crack in the cliff appeared, half hidden by a tilted slab of granite, covered in moss and tiny white snowbell flowers.

She ducked under it and led the way up into a narrow tunnel. She clicked on a penlight. A short way inside, an old grate blocked the way. Seichan quickly picked the lock.

'Any alarms?' Gray asked.

Seichan shrugged and pushed open the gate. 'We'll find out.'

Gray searched the walls as they entered. Solid granite. No wires.

Ten yards past the gate, a set of crude stairs led upward. Gray took the lead from here. He checked his watch. The train from Geneva should be pulling into the Lausanne station in another few minutes. His absence would be noted. Time was running out.

He sped faster up the stairs, but he kept a watch for any surveillance or alarm devices. He climbed the equivalent of fifteen stories, tension mounting with each step.

Finally the tunnel dumped into a wider room, a domed cavity in the rock. At the back wall, a natural spring spattered and flowed down into a cut in the rock, flowing toward the roots of the mountain. But in front of the spring stood a large slab of cut stone. An altar. Stars were painted on the ceiling. It was the Roman temple Seichan had described. So far, her intel was spot-on accurate.

Seichan stepped into the room behind him. 'The stairs up into the castle are over there,' she said and pointed an arm toward another tunnel leading out.

He took a step toward it when the darkness at the mouth of the tunnel shifted. A large shape stepped into the meager light.

Raoul.

He bore a submachine gun in his hands.

Light flared to his left. Two other gunmen rose from hiding behind the slab. Behind Gray, a steel door slammed shut across the lower passageway.

But worse, he felt the cold barrel of a gun at the base of his skull.

'He's carrying the gold key around his neck,' Seichan said.

Raoul strode forward. He stopped in front of Gray. 'You should be wiser in your choice of companions.'

Before Gray could respond, a meaty fist slammed into his belly.

Gray coughed out his air and fell to his knees.

Raoul reached to his throat and grabbed the chain. He yanked the key free, ripping the pendant from Gray's neck with a snap. He held it up to the light.

'Thank you for delivering this to us,' Raoul said. 'And yourself. We have a few questions for you before we leave for Avignon.'

Gray stared up into Raoul's face. He could not hide his shock. The Court knew about Avignon. How . . . ?

But he knew.

'Rachel . . .' he mumbled.

'Oh, don't worry. She's alive and well. Catching up with family at the moment.'

Gray didn't understand.

'Don't forget about his teammate at the hospital,' Seichan said. 'We don't want to leave any loose ends.'

Raoul nodded. 'That's already being taken care of.'

Unable to sleep, Monk watched television. It was in French. He didn't speak French, so he was not really paying attention. It was white noise as he thought. The morphine fogged the edges of his mind.

He kept his eyes off his bandaged stump.

Fury kept the pain reliever's sedation at bay. Not only for his mutilation, but for being the fall guy in this operation. Pulled out of the fight. Used as a goddamn bargaining chip. The others were in danger, and he was locked down in a private room, guarded by hospital security.

Still, he couldn't deny a hollow pain deep inside him, one that morphine could not touch. He had no right to feel sorry for himself. He lived. He was a soldier. He had seen buddies pulled off the field in far worse condition than him. But the ache persisted. He felt violated, abused, less a man, certainly less a soldier.

Logic would not soothe his heart.

The television droned on.

A commotion outside his door drew his eye. Arguing. Raised voices. He shifted higher in his bed. What was going on?

Then the door burst open.

He stared in shock as a figure strode past the security guards.

A familiar figure.

Monk could not keep the shock from his voice. 'Cardinal Spera?'

Rachel had been returned to her cell, but she was not alone.

A guard stood outside the bulletproof glass.

Inside, her grandmother sank to the cot with a sigh. 'You may not understand now, but you will.'

Rachel shook her head. She stood against the far wall, confused, dazed. 'How . . . how could you?'

Her grandmother stared up at her with those sharp eyes of hers. 'I was once like you. Only sixteen when I first came to this castle from Austria, escaping as the war ended.'

Rachel remembered her grandmother's tales of her family's flight to Switzerland, then eventually Italy. She and her father were the only members of her family to survive. 'You were escaping from the Nazis.'

'No, child, we *were* Nazis,' her *nonna* corrected her.

Rachel closed her eyes. *Oh God . . .*

Her grandmother continued, 'Papa was a party leader in Salzburg, but he also had ties to the Imperial Dragon Court of Austria. A very powerful man. It was through that fraternity that we made our escape, underground through Switzerland, through the generosity of the Baron of Sauvage, Raoul's grandfather.'

Rachel listened with growing horror, though she wanted to cover her ears and deny it.

'But such safe passage required a payment. My father granted it. My virginity . . . to the baron. Like you, I resisted, not understanding. My father held me down the first time, for my own good. But it would not be the last. We were hidden here at the castle for four months. The baron bedded me many nights, until I was heavy with his bastard child.'

Rachel found herself sinking down the wall, settling to the cold stone floor.

'But bastard or not, it was a good crossing, mixing a noble Austrian line of Hapsburgs with a Swiss Bernese line. I grew to understand as the child grew in my belly. It was the way of the Court, strengthening pure lines. My father pressed it upon me. I grew to understand that I carried a noble bloodline back to emperors and kings.'

Sitting on the floor, Rachel tried to comprehend the brutality done to the young girl who would become her grandmother. Had her grandmother validated that cruelty and abuse by couching it in a grander scheme? Brainwashed at that fragile age by her father. Rachel sought to find sympathy for the old woman but failed.

'My father took me to Italy, to Castel Gondolfo, the home of the pope's summer palace. I gave birth to your mother there. A shame. I was beaten for it. A male child had been hoped for.'

Her grandmother shook her head sadly. She continued, relating an alternate history of their family. How she was married off to another member of the Dragon Court, one with ties to the Church in Castel Gondolfo. It was a marriage of convenience and deceit. Their family had been assigned to seed their children and grandchildren into the Church, as unwitting spies for the Court, blind moles. To maintain their secrecy, Rachel's mother and Uncle Vigor were kept unaware of their blasted heritage.

'But you were meant for so much more,' her grandmother said with hard pride. 'You proved your Dragon blood. You were noticed and chosen to be drawn back into the full fold of the Court. Your blood was too valuable to waste. The Imperator chose you personally to cross our family line back upon the ancient Sauvage line. Your children will be kings among kings.'

Her *nonna*'s eyes shone with the wonder of it. '*Molti bellissimo bambini*. All kings of the Court.'

Rachel had no strength now to even raise her head. She covered her face with her hands. Every moment of her life flashed past her. What was real? Who was she? She thought back on the number of times she had taken her grandmother's side over her mother, even her *nonna*'s advice on her love life. She had revered and emulated the old woman, respecting her hard, no-nonsense edge. But did such solidity come from toughness or psychosis? What did that imply about herself? She shared this bloodline . . . with the grandmother . . . dear God, with that bastard Raoul.

Who was she?

Another concern arose. Fear pushed her to speak. 'What . . . what about Uncle Vigor . . . your son?'

Her grandmother sighed. 'He has served his role in the Church. Celibacy ended his bloodline. Now he is no longer needed. Our family's legacy will carry forth through you, gloriously into the future.'

Rachel heard a trace of pain behind these last words and glanced up. She knew her grandmother loved Vigor . . . in fact, more than Rachel's own mother. She wondered if her grandmother had resented that daughter she had given birth to, a child of rape. And was that same trauma carried down to the next generation? Rachel and her own mother had always had a strained relationship, an unspoken pain that neither could surmount, neither understood.

And where would it stop?

A shout drew her attention to the door. Men were coming. Rachel climbed to her feet, as did her grandmother. So alike . . .

Down the hall, a troop of guards marched past. Rachel stared in despair at the second in line. Gray, hands bound behind his back, trudged past. He glanced into her cell. Spotting her, his eyes widened in surprise. He tripped a step.

'Rachel . . .'

Gray was shoved forward by Raoul, who leered into

the cell and held up something on a chain as he passed.

A gold key.

Despair settled completely over Rachel.

Nothing now stood between the Court and the treasure at Avignon. After centuries of manipulation and machination, the Dragon Court had won.

It was over.

3:12 a.m.
AVIGNON, FRANCE

Kat did not like any of this. There were too many civilians around. She marched up the steps toward the main entrance to the Pope's Palace. There was a flow of people into and out of the gateway.

'It's a tradition to hold the play inside the palace,' Vigor said. 'Last year, they did Shakespeare's *The Life and Death of King John*. This year it's a four-hour production of *Hamlet*. The play and party lasts well into the morning. They hold it in the Courtyard of Honor.' He pointed ahead.

They fought their way through a group of German tourists exiting the palace and crossed through the arched entry. Coming from ahead, voices echoed off the stone wall in a mix of languages.

'It will be hard to conduct a thorough search with all these people,' Kat said with a frown.

Vigor nodded as a snare-beat of thunder rumbled across the sky.

Laughter and clapping echoed.

'The play should be nearly over,' Vigor said.

The long gateway ended at an open-air courtyard. It was dark, except for the large stage on the far side, framed by curtains and decorated like the throne room to a great castle. The backdrop was in fact the very wall of the far courtyard. To either side rose lighting towers, casting spots upon the actors, and towering speakers.

A crowd gathered below the stage in seats or sprawled on blankets on the stone floor. From the stage, a few figures stood amid a pile of bodies. An actor spoke in French, but Kat was fluent.

'I am dead, Horatio. Wretched queen, adieu!'

Kat recognized one of the last lines of *Hamlet*. The play was indeed rounding toward the end.

Vigor drew her to the side. 'The courtyard here divides two different sections of the palace – the new and the old. The back wall and the one to the left are a part of the Palais Vieux, the old palace. Where we stand and to the right is the Palais Neuf, the section built later.'

Kat leaned closer to Vigor. 'Where do we begin?'

Vigor pointed to the older section. 'There is a mysterious story connected to the Pope's Palace. Many historians of the time report that at dawn on September 20, 1348, a great column of fire was seen above the old section of the palace. It was noted by the entire town. Many of the superstitious believed the flame heralded the Great Plague, the Black Death, which started about the same time. But what if it wasn't? What if it was some manifestation of the Meissner field, a flux of energy being released when whatever secret was sealed here? The appearance of the flame might mark the exact date the treasure was buried.'

Kat nodded. It was something to follow.

'I pulled down a detailed map from the Internet,' Vigor said. 'There's an entrance into the old palace near the Gate of Our Lady. One seldom used.'

Vigor led the way to the left. An archway opened. They ducked inside as a great peal of lightning split the sky overhead. Thunder boomed. The actor on the stage stopped in mid-soliloquy. Nervous laughter tinkled through the audience. The storm might end the play early.

Vigor motioned to a stout door off to the side.

Kat dropped and set to work with her lockpicks, while

Vigor shielded her work with his body. It did not take long to free the latch. Kat clicked it open.

Another flash of lightning drew Kat's eye back to the courtyard. Thunder cracked and the skies opened. Rain fell heavily from the low clouds. Cries and cheers erupted from the audience. A mass exodus began.

Kat shouldered open the door, held it for Vigor, then closed it behind them.

It bumped closed with a solid snap of the latch. Kat relocked it.

'Do we have to be worried about security?' she asked.

'Sadly, no. As you'll see, there's nothing really to steal. Vandalism is the greater concern. There might be a night watchman. So we should be cautious.'

Nodding, Kat kept her flashlight off. Enough light filtered through the high windows to illuminate a ramp leading up toward the next level of the castle.

Vigor led the way up. 'The private apartments of the pope lie in the Tower of Angels. The rooms were always the most secured area of the palace. If something was hidden, we should probably wind our way there.'

Kat pulled out a compass and kept it fixed in front of her. A magnetic marker had led them to Alexander's tomb. It might here, too.

They traversed several rooms and halls. Their footsteps echoed hollowly through the vaulted spaces. Kat now understood the lack of real security. The place was a stone tomb. Denuded of almost any decoration or furniture. There was no evidence of the opulence that must have once frilled the palace. She tried to picture the flow of velvet and fur, the rich tapestries, the lavish banquets, the gilt and the silver. Nothing remained but stone and timbered rafters.

'After the popes left,' Vigor whispered, 'the place fell into disrepair. It was ransacked during the French Revolution, serving eventually as a garrison and barracks for

Napoleon's troops. Much of the place was whitewashed and destroyed. Only a few areas still retain some of the original frescoes, such as the papal apartments.'

As Kat walked, she also sensed a strange conformation to the place: halls that ended too abruptly, rooms that seemed oddly small, staircases that dropped to levels without doors. The thickness of walls varied from a few feet to some eighteen feet thick. The palace was a true fortress, but Kat sensed hidden spaces, passages, rooms – features common among medieval castles.

This was confirmed when they entered a room Vigor designated as the treasury. He pointed to four places. 'They buried their gold under the floor. In subterranean rooms. It was always rumored that other such vaults were yet to be discovered.'

They crossed other rooms: a large wardrobe, a former library, an empty kitchen whose square walls narrowed down to an octagonal chimney over a central firepit.

Vigor finally led them into the Tower of Angels.

Kat's compass had not twitched a beat, but she concentrated more fully now. Worry mounted. What if they didn't find the entrance? What if she failed? Again. The hand holding the compass began to shake. First her failure with Monk and Rachel . . .

And now this.

She gripped her compass tighter and willed her hand steady. She and Vigor would solve this. They must. Or all the sacrifice by the others would be for nothing.

Determined, she climbed from one level to the next of the papal apartments. With no sign of any caretaker, Kat risked switching on a small penlight to help illuminate their search.

'The pope's living room,' Vigor said at the entrance to one room.

Kat crisscrossed the length of it, studying her compass. The walls here were decorated with swirls of peeling paint, and a large corner fireplace dominated the room. Thunder echoed through the thick walls.

Once finished with her pass, she shook her head.

Nothing.

They moved on. One of the most spectacular rooms came next: the Room of the Stag. Its frescoes depicted elaborate hunting scenes, from falconry, to bird nesters, to frolicking dogs, to even a rectangular fish-breeding pond.

'A *piscarium*,' Vigor said. 'Fish again.'

Kat nodded, remembering the significance of fish to their own hunt. She searched this room with an even tighter pattern of surveillance. Her compass refused to budge. With no clue, she waved Vigor onward.

They climbed another level.

'The pope's bedroom,' Vigor said, sounding disappointed and worried now, too. 'This is the last of the rooms in the apartments.'

Kat entered the chamber. No furniture. Its walls were painted a brilliant blue.

'Lapis lazuli,' Vigor said. 'Prized for its luster.'

The rich decoration depicted a nighttime forest, hung with birdcages of every shape and size. A few squirrels scrambled among the limbs.

Kat searched the room, from one end to the other.

Still nothing.

She lowered her compass. She turned to find the same understanding in Vigor's eyes. They had failed.


3:36 a.m.
LAUSANNE, SWITZERLAND

Gray was shoved into a stone cell. It was sealed with Lexan glass, bulletproof and an inch thick. The door slammed shut. He had spotted Rachel in a cell two spaces down . . . along with her grandmother.

It made no sense.

Raoul growled at his men and headed away, gold key in hand.

Seichan stood at the door, smiling at him. With his hands still bound behind his back by plastic ties, he threw himself bodily at her, crashing into the glass wall.

'You goddamn bitch!'

She only smiled, kissed her fingertips, and pressed them to the glass. 'Bye, loverboy. Thanks for the ride here.'

Gray fell away from the door, turning his back, cursing under his breath, calculating. Raoul had confiscated his pack, given it to one of his underlings. He'd been patted down, his weapons taken from his shoulder and ankle holsters.

He overheard talk by Rachel's cell. A door was opened.

Raoul growled to one of his guards, 'Take Madame Camilla up to the trucks. Have all the men ready. We'll be leaving for the airport in a few minutes.'

'*Ciao*, Rachel, my *bambina*.'

No response to her grandmother. What was going on?

Footsteps marched away.

Gray still sensed a presence by the other door.

Raoul's voice spoke again. 'If only I had more time,' Raoul whispered icily. 'But orders are orders. It all comes to an end in Avignon. The Imperator will be returning here with me. He wants to watch as I take you for the first time. After that, it's just the two of us . . . for the rest of your life.'

'Fuck you,' Rachel spat back at him.

'Exactly right.' Raoul laughed. 'I'm going to teach you how to scream and properly pleasure your superior. And if you don't bend to everything I demand, you won't be the first bitch Alberto lobotomized for the Court. I don't need your mind to fuck you.'

He stalked away with a final order to a guard. 'Keep a watch down here. I'll radio when I'm ready for the

American. We'll have a short bit of fun before we leave.'

Gray listened as Raoul's footsteps faded.

He didn't wait any longer. He kicked the toe of his boot hard against the solid rock wall. A three-inch blade sprang from the heel. He crouched and sliced free the ties that bound his wrist. He moved quickly. Timing was everything.

He reached into the front of his pants. Seichan had shoved a thin canister past his belt buckle when he'd thrust himself against the glass wall. Her left hand had passed through an air vent, while her other hand distracted with her feigned kiss of good-bye.

Gray pulled the canister free, stepped to the door, and sprayed the hinges. The steel bolts began to dissolve. He had to give it to the Guild. They had cool toys. While Gray could not contact his superiors, nothing had stopped Seichan from coordinating equipment from hers.

Gray waited a full minute, then yelled to the guard stationed a few steps down the hall. 'Hey! You! Something's wrong over here.'

Footsteps approached.

Gray retreated back from the door.

The guard came forward.

Gray pointed to the smoky sizzle billowing by the door. 'What the hell?' he yelled. 'Are you assholes trying to gas me?'

With a crinkled brow, the guard stepped closer to the door.

Good enough.

Gray leapt forward, slammed into the door, popping the hinges. The plate of hard glass slammed into the guard. He crashed against the far wall, striking his head hard. As he slumped, he tried to free his pistol.

Gray shoved aside the door and pivoted off it to swing around. He planted his boot-heel blade into the man's throat, then ripped it free, taking out most of the man's neck.

427

Bending, he liberated the pistol from the guard's holster and a set of keys. He ran to Rachel's cell.

She was already up and at the door. 'Gray . . . !'

He keyed the lock. 'We don't have much time.'

He yanked the door open – and she was in his arms. She wrapped tight to him, lips at his ears, breath on his neck.

'Thank God,' she whispered.

'Actually, thank Seichan,' he said. Despite the urgency to keep moving, he held the embrace a bit longer, sensing she needed it.

And maybe he did, too.

But finally they both separated. Gray pointed his pistol toward the end of the hall. He checked his watch. Two minutes.

3:42 a.m.

Seichan stood at the foot of the stairs that led up to the main keep. She knew the only escape was out the front door. Steel blast doors sealed the back exit under the castle.

In the brilliantly lit courtyard, a caravan of five SUVs was being loaded. Men yelled orders. Crates were shoved into the backs of the trucks. Dogs barked in kennels.

Seichan studied it all from the corner of her eye, tracking one man among the throng. Maximum mayhem would be needed. She had already confiscated a set of keys to the last Mercedes SUV. A silver one. Her favorite color.

Behind her, a door opened. Raoul stepped out, along with an old woman.

'We'll take you as far as the airport. A plane will get you back to Rome.'

'My granddaughter . . .'

'She'll be taken care of. I promise.' This last was said with an icy smile.

Raoul noted Seichan. 'I don't believe we'll be needing the Guild's services any longer.'

Seichan shrugged. 'Then I'll head out with you and be on my way.' She nodded to the silver SUV.

Raoul helped the old woman down the steps and strode toward the lead vehicle, where Dr. Alberto Menardi waited. Seichan continued to track her target. Motion along one wall of the courtyard drew her eye.

A door opened. She spotted Gray. He had a pistol. Good.

Across the courtyard, Raoul lifted a radio to his mouth. Most likely calling down to the cells. She could wait no longer. The man she'd been tracking wasn't as close to Raoul as she'd hoped – but he was still in the thick of things.

She fixed her eyes on the soldier who still carried Gray's pack over one shoulder. It was always easy to count on avarice among the foot soldiers. The fellow was not letting his booty out of his sight. The pack was stuffed with weapons and expensive electronic gear.

Unfortunately for the soldier, the bottom lining of the pack also had a quarter kilo of C4 sewn into it. Seichan pressed the transmitter in her pocket, hopping over the balustrade of the front staircase.

The explosion blew out the center of the caravan.

Men and body parts flew into the dark sky. Gas tanks ignited on two of the cars. A ball of fire rolled upward. Flaming debris scattered to all corners of the courtyard.

Seichan moved quickly. Waving to Gray, she pointed her pistol at the silver SUV. Its windshield was cracked, but it was otherwise intact. Gray and the woman dashed out. The three zeroed in on the vehicle.

A pair of soldiers tried to stop them. Gray took out one, Seichan the other. They reached the SUV.

The rev of an engine drew her eye toward the castle gate. The lead truck jumped forward. Raoul was making his escape. Gunfire pelted toward them as soldiers tumbled into a second truck. Its engine was already running.

Raoul popped up out of the sunroof of the lead truck, facing back toward them. He raised a massive horse pistol in his fist.

'Down!' Seichan barked, dropping flat.

The gun sounded like a cannon. She heard the windshield collapse and the back window blow out. The thick slug passed completely through the vehicle. In plain sight, she rolled toward the rear, keeping the truck between her and Raoul.

Gunfire spat from the other side. Gray, on his belly, in a better position to snipe, shot at Raoul as the lead truck fishtailed toward the exit. The second truck followed.

Raoul continued to shoot, fearless of the hostile fire.

A slug slammed through the front grille of the SUV.

Shit.

The bastard was taking out their truck.

The front headlamp exploded. From her viewpoint on the ground, Seichan watched a stream of oil flow out of the engine compartment and pool on the stones.

The slide of Gray's pistol popped open. Out of ammo.

Seichan crab-crawled to join him, but it was too late.

One truck, then the other, shot out of the gate. Raoul's laughter carried back to them. The portcullis gate dropped behind the last vehicle, its teeth slamming into the stone notches, sealed tight.

A trundling noise penetrated the echo in her ears.

She rose to a crouch. Steel shutters dropped over all the windows and doors to the castle. Modern fortification. The Court took their security seriously. They were trapped in the courtyard.

A new sound followed.

The click of a series of heavy latches.

Seichan turned along with Gray and Rachel. She now understood the trailing laughter by the escaping bastard.

430

The gates to the line of twenty kennels rose up on motorized wheels.

Monsters of muscle, leather, and teeth stalked out, snarling, frothing, driven mad by the thunder and blood. Each pit-dog stood chest-high, massing close to a hundred kilos, twice the weight of most men.

And the dinner bell had just rung.

3:48 a.m.
AVIGNON, FRANCE

Kat refused to concede defeat. Holding despair at bay, she stalked the length of the blue bedroom atop the Tower of Angels. 'We're looking at this the wrong way,' she said.

Unlike her, Vigor remained stock-still in the room's center. His eyes were somewhere else, calculating. Or was it worry for his niece? How focused was he on the task at hand?

'What do you mean?' he mumbled.

'Maybe there's not a magnetic marker.' She held up the compass, drawing his eye, attempting to engage him fully.

'Then what?'

'What about all that talk earlier? The Gothic history of the town and this place?'

Vigor nodded. 'Something built into the structure of the building. But without a magnetic marker, how are we to find it? The palace is huge. And considering the state of disrepair, the clue might have been destroyed or removed.'

'You don't believe that,' Kat said more firmly. 'This secret society of alchemists would've found a way to preserve it.'

'Still, how do we find it?' Vigor asked.

Lightning crackled out the nearby window. It lit up the gardens below the tower and the spread of city below the hill. The dark river snaked past below. The rain had begun

431

to fall harder. Another fork of lightning scintillated across the belly of the black clouds.

Kat watched the display and slowly turned to Vigor, conviction firming with sudden insight. She pocketed her compass, knowing it was no longer needed.

'*Magnetism* opened Saint Peter's tomb,' she said, stepping back to him. 'And it was magnetism that led us to Alexander's tomb. But once there, it was *electricity* that ignited the pyramid. The same might lead us to the treasure here.' She waved a hand at the dazzle of the storm. 'Lightning. The palace was built atop the largest hill, the *Rocher des Doms*, the Rock Dome.'

'Attracting lightning strikes. A flash of light that illuminates darkness.'

'Is there some depiction of lightning that we missed?'

'I don't recall.' Vigor rubbed his chin. 'But I think you've struck a significant chord. Light is symbolic of knowledge. Enlightenment. It was the primary goal of Gnostic faith, to seek the primordial light mentioned in Genesis, to reach out for this ancient font of knowledge and power that flows everywhere.'

Vigor ticked off on his fingertips. 'Electricity, lightning, light, knowledge, power. They're all related. And somewhere there is a symbol of this, built into the design of the palace.'

Kat shook her head, at a loss.

Vigor suddenly stiffened.

'What?' She stepped closer.

Vigor quickly knelt and drew in the dust. 'Alexander's tomb was in Egypt. We can't forget to carry that forward, one riddle to the next. The Egyptian symbol for light is a circle with a dot in the center. Representing the sun.

'But sometimes it's flattened into an oval, forming an eye. Representing not only the sun and light, but also knowledge. The burning eye of insight. The *all-seeing eye* of Masonic and Templar iconography.'

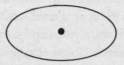

Kat frowned at the drawings. She had seen no such markings. 'Okay, but where do we begin looking for it?'

'It's not going to be found – but *formed*,' Vigor said, standing up. 'Why didn't I think of this before? A feature of Gothic architecture is the mischievous play of light and shadow. The Templar architects were masters of this manipulation.'

'But where can we – ?'

Vigor cut her off, already heading out the door. 'We have to go back down to the first floor. To where we already saw the potential for a flaming eye within a circle of light.'

Kat followed Vigor. She didn't recall any such depiction. They hurried down the stairs and out of the Tower of Angels. Vigor led the way across a banquet hall and ended up in a room they'd already explored.

'The kitchen?' she asked, surprised.

Kat stared again at the square walls, the central raised hearth, and overhead, the octagonal chimneypiece. She didn't understand and began to say so.

Vigor reached out a hand and cupped it over her penlight. 'Wait.'

A brilliant bolt of lightning shattered outside. Enough illumination traveled down the open chimney to shine a perfect oval upon the fire pit. The silver light flickered, then went dark.

'As it is above, so it is below,' Vigor said in a hushed

voice. 'The effect is probably more evident when the noon sun climbs directly overhead or lies at some precise angle.'

Kat pictured the firepit ablaze, bright with flames. A fire within a circle of sunlight. 'But how can we be sure this is the right place?' Kat asked, circling the hearth.

He frowned. 'I'm *not* entirely sure, but Alexander's tomb was under a lighthouse topped by a fiery flame. And considering the usefulness of both a lighthouse and a kitchen, it makes sense to bury something beneath a location that serves a good function. Successive generations would preserve it for its utility.'

Unconvinced, Kat bent down and slipped a knife free to examine the central hearth. She dug at the rock that lined the firepit, exposing an orange-hued stone at the base. 'It's not hematite or magnetite.' If it had been either one, she might be convinced. 'It's just bauxite, an aluminum hydroxide ore. A good thermal conductor. Makes sense for a fireplace. Nothing unusual.'

She glanced over to Vigor. He wore a large grin.

'What?'

'I walked right past it,' Vigor said, joining her. 'I should have considered that another stone would point the way. First hematite, then magnetite, now bauxite.'

Kat stood, confused.

'Bauxite is mined right here in this area. In fact, it's named after the Lords of Baux, whose castle lies only ten miles from here. It sits atop a hill of bauxite. This stone points a finger back at them.'

'So?'

'The Lords of Baux had an uneasy relationship with the French popes, their new neighbors. But they were best known for an odd claim they asserted most vehemently. They claimed to be descended from a famous biblical figure.'

'Who?' Kat asked.

'Balthazar. One of the Magi.'

Kat's eyes widened. She turned back to the hearth. 'They sealed the opening with stones from the Magi's descendants.'

'Do you still doubt we've found the right spot?' Vigor asked.

Kat shook her head. 'But how do we open it? I don't see any keyhole.'

'You already told us. Electricity.'

As if emphasizing the point, thunder boomed through the thick walls.

Kat shed out of her pack. It was worth a try. 'We don't have any of those ancient batteries.' She pulled out a larger flashlight. 'But I have some modern Duracell Coppertops.'

She cracked open her flashlight and used the tip of a knife to tease loose the positive and negative wires. With the power switch off, she twisted them together, then lifted her handiwork.

'You'd better stand back,' Kat warned.

Reaching out, she brought the flashlight's wires into contact with the bauxite stone, a weakly conductive ore. She flicked the flashlight's switch.

An arc of electricity stabbed to the stone. A deep bass tone responded as if a large drum had been struck.

Kat darted back as the tone faded. She joined Vigor by the wall.

Along the edges of the stone hearth, a fiery glow spread, scribing the entire firepit.

'I think they've cemented the blocks with molten m-state glass,' Kat mumbled.

'Like the ancient Egyptian builders used molten lead to cement the Pharos Lighthouse.'

'And now the electricity is releasing the stored power in the glass.'

Other traceries of fire jittered across the face of the hearth, outlining each and every stone. It flared brighter,

435

searing a crisscrossed pattern onto her retina. Heat washed out toward them.

Kat shielded her eyes. But the effect didn't last long. As the glow faded, the stone blocks of bauxite began to fall away, no longer cemented, tumbling down into a pit hidden below the hearth.

Kat heard the crash of stone on stone. A rattling continued as the blocks tumbled deeper. No longer able to restrain her curiosity, she stepped forward and shone her penlight. The edges of the hearth now outlined a dark staircase leading down.

She turned to Vigor. 'We've done it.'

'Heaven help us,' he said.

3:52 a.m.
LAUSANNE, SWITZERLAND

A quarter mile from his castle, Raoul lowered his cell phone and stalked away from his truck. Fury narrowed his vision to pinpoints. Blood dripped from a scalp wound. That Asian bitch had betrayed him. But he would get his satisfaction. His dogs would make short work of all of them.

And if not . . .

He crossed to the second truck. He pointed to two men. 'You and you. Return to the chateau. On foot. Stand guard at the portcullis. Shoot anyone you see move. No one leaves that courtyard alive.'

The pair piled out of the truck and set a fast pace back to the castle.

Raoul returned to the lead vehicle.

Alberto waited for him. 'What did the Imperator say?' he asked as Raoul climbed into the front passenger seat.

Raoul pocketed his cell phone. The Guild betrayal had surprised their leader as much as it did Raoul. But Raoul had left out his own treachery back in Alexandria, leaving

436

the bitch to die and lying about it. He should've expected something. He pounded a fist on his knee. When she handed the American to him, he had let his guard down.

Stupid.

But matters would be rectified.

In Avignon.

Raoul answered Alberto, 'The Imperator will be joining us in France, along with more forces. We push ahead as planned.'

'And the others?' Alberto glanced back toward the chateau.

'They no longer matter. There's nothing they can do to stop us.'

Raoul waved the driver forward. The truck headed for the Yverdon airfield. He shook his head at his losses here. Not the men. The bitch. Rachel Verona. He had such bloody plans for her. . . .

But at least he had left her a little parting gift.


3:55 a.m.

Rachel gathered with Gray and Seichan on the steps to the main castle, their backs to the metal shutters over the doors. Moving stealthily, they had retreated from the pack of dogs to this relative shelter.

They still only had the one gun. Six bullets.

Gray had attempted to scrounge another weapon amidst the fiery carnage in the courtyard, but all he found were two damaged rifles. Gray carried Seichan's weapon. She was busy with a GPS unit, concentrating fully, trusting Gray to watch her back.

What was she doing?

Rachel kept a step away from the woman, closer to Gray. One hand clutched his shirttail. She didn't know when she had grabbed it, but she didn't let go. It was all that was keeping her on her feet.

One of the pit-dogs padded silently past the bottom of the stairs. It dragged a limb of one of the dead soldiers. Twenty of the monsters roamed the yard, tearing at bodies, snarling and spitting at one another. A few fights broke out, savage, lightning-fast tussles.

It wouldn't be long before their pig-eyed attention turned to them.

Any noise drew the beasts. The moaning injured died first. They all knew that once the first shot was fired, the entire pack would be upon them.

Six bullets. Twenty dogs.

Off to the side, movement . . .

Through the oily smoke, a thin figure rose among the debris, wobbly, unsteady. A breeze blew the haze away, and Rachel recognized the shape, teetering on thin legs.

'*Nonna* . . .' she whispered.

Blood caked the old woman's hair on the left side.

Rachel had thought her grandmother had escaped with Raoul.

Had the explosion knocked her down?

But Rachel supposed otherwise. Raoul must have pistol-whipped her out of the way, leaving her behind, useless baggage.

A moan rose from the old woman. She lifted a hand to the side of her head. 'Papa!' she called feebly in a strained voice.

The blow, the confusion, the looming castle must have dislocated her grandmother, drawing her into the past.

'Papa . . .' Pain beyond her head injury keened in her voice.

But Rachel wasn't the only one to hear the pain.

A few meters away, a dark shape rose from behind a flaming tire, stalking out of the smoke, drawn by the frail cry.

Rachel let go of Gray's belt and stumbled a step down.

'I see it,' Gray said, stopping her with a hand.

438

He raised his gun, aimed, and squeezed the gun. The *pop* was explosive in the silent yard, but the yelp of the target was louder as the dog pitched over and rolled. Howls rose from it. It gnashed at its wounded back leg, attacking the pain. Other dogs swooped down upon it. Drawn by the blood. Lions on a wounded gazelle.

Rachel's grandmother, startled by the beast, had fallen on her backside, mouth frozen in an O of surprise.

'I have to get to her,' Rachel whispered. It was an instinctive reaction. Despite the treachery, her *nonna* still had a place in her heart. She didn't deserve to die like this.

'I'll go with you,' Gray said.

'She's dead already,' Seichan said with a sigh, lowering her GPS unit. But she followed them down the stairs, sticking close to the only gun.

In a tight knot, they traversed the edge of the courtyard. Pools of flaming oil lit the way.

Rachel wanted to run, but one massive brindled beast eyed them, hunched over a headless body, hackles raised, teeth bared, guarding its catch. But Rachel knew if she ran, the brute would be upon her in seconds.

Gray covered it with his pistol.

Her grandmother scooted away from the trio of dogs fighting over their injured brethren, ripping and tearing at each other to the point it was impossible to tell which beast Gray had shot. Her movement was tracked by another two beasts, coming at her from opposite sides.

They would be too late.

Another two shots and one beast collapsed, sliding on its face. The other bullet only grazed the second dog. The injury seemed to pique its bloodlust. It lunged at the fallen woman.

Rachel ran forward.

Gray's gunshots had drawn more dogs. But committed now, there was no choice. He shot as he ran, dropping another two dogs, the last from only a yard away.

Before Rachel could reach her grandmother, the lunging dog struck. It snatched her grandmother's arm, raised in defense. It bit clean through thin bone and withered flesh and tugged the old woman to the ground.

There was no cry.

The dog slammed on top of her, striking for the throat.

Gray fired near Rachel's ear, half deafening her. The impact knocked the beast aside, off the old woman's chest. The dog's body writhed and convulsed, a clean head shot . . . also their last.

The slide on Gray's pistol jacked open.

Rachel dropped to her knees, reaching her grandmother. Blood pumped from the old woman's severed arm. Rachel cradled the body.

Gray crouched with her. Seichan dropped too, lowering their silhouette.

Dogs fought all around them, and they were out of bullets.

Her grandmother stared up at her and spoke weakly in Italian, eyes glazed. 'Mama . . . I'm sorry . . . hold me . . .'

A crack of a rifle and her grandmother jerked in her arms, shot through the chest. Rachel felt the bullet exit, grazing a line of fire under her own arm.

She stared up.

Thirty yards away, two gunmen stood beyond the iron portcullis gate.

The new blast drew off a few of the dogs.

Gray sought to use the distraction to retreat to the castle wall. Rachel followed, not letting go of her grandmother, dragging her along.

'Leave her,' Gray urged.

Rachel ignored him, tears flowing, angry. Another rifle blast and a slug sparked off the stone a few feet away. Seichan reached down and helped carry her grandmother. Working together, they retreated faster.

At the gate, a pair of dogs struck the bars, gnashing at

the gunmen, blocking their aim. But it wouldn't last for long.

Reaching the relative shelter of the castle's wall, Rachel collapsed over her grandmother's body. They were still in direct view of the gate . . . but the entire courtyard was exposed. One of the dogs was blasted away from the portcullis. Another bullet pinged off the metal shutter of a window overhead.

Rachel, bent over her grandmother, finally freed the purse still hooked over her *nonna*'s shoulder, a permanent fixture to the old woman. Rachel snapped the clasp, reached inside, and felt the butt of cold steel.

She pulled out her grandmother's heirloom.

The Nazi P-08 Luger.

'*Grazie, Nonna.*'

Rachel aimed toward the gate. She fixed her stand and let cold anger steady her grip. She squeezed the trigger . . . followed the recoil and fired again.

Both men fell.

Her focus widened – too late to stop the slavering beast leaping out of the smoke, muzzle snarled, teeth bared, going for her throat.

## 4:00 a.m.

Gray stiff-armed Rachel to the side, knocking her down. He faced the monster and lifted his other arm. In his hand, he clutched a tiny silver canister.

'Bad dog . . .'

He sprayed the beast point-blank in the nose and eyes.

The dog's weight struck him, flattening him on his back.

The beast howled – not in bloodlust, but searing agony. It rolled off Gray and writhed across the stone, grinding its face into the cobbles, pawing at its eyes.

But its sockets were already empty. Eaten away by the acid.

It rolled another two times, mewling.

Gray felt a twinge of discomfort. The dogs had been tortured into this savage state. It wasn't their fault. Then again, perhaps any death was better than being under the thumb of Raoul.

The dog finally quieted and collapsed to the pavement.

But its tumult drew the eyes of a dozen others.

Gray glanced to Rachel.

'Six more shots,' she answered.

Gray shook his canister. Not much left.

Seichan had her eyes on the skies. Then Gray heard it, too.

The *thump-thump* of a helicopter.

It winged up over the ridge and castle walls. Lights blazed down. Rotorwash stirred a whirlwind.

Dogs scattered in fear.

Seichan spoke above the roar. 'Our ride's here!'

A nylon ladder tumbled out an open door and struck the stones only a few yards off.

Gray didn't care who it was as long as they were free of this bloody courtyard. He raced forward and waved Rachel up the ladder. One hand held the flailing ladder steady, the other took Rachel's Luger.

'Up!' he ordered, leaning close to her. 'I'll hold 'em off.'

Rachel's fingers trembled as he freed her gun. His eyes met hers. He recognized a well of horror and sorrow that went beyond the bloodshed here.

'You'll be okay,' he said, making it sound like a promise. One he meant to keep.

She nodded, seeming to draw strength, and mounted the ladder.

Seichan went next, scrambling up behind her like a trapeze artist, even with her injured shoulder.

Gray followed last. He hadn't needed to use the gun again. He shoved the Luger into the back of his belt and fled up the rope ladder. In moments, he was clambering into the cabin of the helicopter.

As the door was slammed behind him, Gray straightened to thank the person who had given him an arm and helped him inside.

The man wore a shit-eating grin. 'Hi, boss.'

'Monk!'

Gray grabbed him in a bear hug.

'Watch the arm,' his partner said.

Gray let him loose. Monk's left arm was strapped to his body, and a leather guard sheathed the bandaged stump of his wrist. He looked well enough, but paler. Dark circles shadowed his eyes.

'I'm fine,' Monk said, motioning him to sit and strap in as the helicopter sped away. 'Just try keeping me out of the action.'

'How . . . ?'

'We locked on to your emergency GPS signal,' he explained.

Gray pulled his seat harness over his shoulder and snapped it in place.

He stared at the other occupant of the cabin.

'Cardinal Spera?' Gray said, confusion in his voice.

Seichan sat next to him and answered, 'Who do you think hired me?'

# 16

## THE DAEDALUS MAZE

As thunder boomed beyond the palace, Kat waited for Vigor. The monsignor had gone down the firepit's dark stairs fifteen minutes ago.

*To take a peek,* he had said.

She shone her light down the stairs.

*Where was he?*

She considered following him, but caution kept her at her post. If he was in trouble, he would've yelled. She remembered the ramp sealing and trapping them under Saint Peter's tomb. What if that happened here? Who would know where to look for them?

She maintained her post, but she dropped to a knee and called below, trying to keep her voice soft at the same time. 'Vigor!'

Footsteps answered her, hurried, coming up from below. A glow suffused, then focused down into a flashlight. Vigor climbed to within a half-dozen stairs. He waved to her.

'You must see this!'

Kat took a deep breath. 'We should wait for Gray and the others to call.'

Vigor climbed another stair with a frown. 'I'm as concerned as you, but there are surely other mysteries to solve down here. That is our purpose in being sent as an advance team. That is how *we* help the others. The

444

Dragon Court, Gray, and the others are all in Switzerland. It will be hours before they can get here. We should put the time to good use and not squander it.'

Kat considered his argument. She checked her watch again. She also remembered Gray's admonishment about being *too* cautious. But she was also damn curious.

She nodded. 'But we check back up here every quarter hour for any contact from Gray.'

'Of course.'

Kat shouldered her pack and waved him down. She left one of her cell phones by the firepit, to pick up any call coming in – and to leave at least one breadcrumb to follow if they became sealed and trapped below.

While she'd bend about being too cautious, she wasn't foolhardy.

She left that to Gray.

Kat ducked below, following Vigor. The stairs led straight down for a fair shot, then turned upon themselves and headed even deeper. Oddly, the air smelled dry, rather than dank.

The steps ended at a short tunnel.

Vigor's pace hurried.

From the hollow echo of the monsignor's footsteps, Kat sensed that a larger cavern lay beyond. It was confirmed a moment later.

She stepped out onto a three-meter stone ledge. Their two lights cast wide swaths across the domed and vaulted space, stretching above and below. It must have once been a natural cavity in the granite, but a great undertaking had transformed it.

Kneeling, Kat ran her fingers along the stonework underfoot, precisely fitted blocks of raw marble. Straightening, Kat shone her flashlight to the sides and down.

Skilled craftsmen and engineers had built a series of twelve bricked tiers, descending from their perch and on down toward the distant floor. The space was roughly circular in shape. Each level below was smaller than the next, like a vast amphitheater . . . or an upside-down step pyramid.

She shone her light across the yawning space contained within these tiers.

It wasn't empty.

Thick arches of granite spanned out from the tiered footings in a corkscrew pattern, supported by giant columns. Kat recognized the arches. Flying buttresses. Like those that supported Gothic cathedrals. In fact, the entire interior space had that lofty, weightless feeling of a church.

'This had to have been built by the Knights Templar,' Vigor said, moving along the tier. 'Nothing like this has ever been seen. A sonata of geometry and engineering. A poem in stone. Gothic architecture at its most perfect.'

'A cathedral underground,' Kat mumbled, awed, reverential.

Vigor nodded. 'But one built to worship history, art, and knowledge.' He swept his arm out.

But there was no need.

The stone framework served only one purpose, to support a convoluted maze of timber scaffolding. Shelves, rooms, ladders, and stairs. Glass glittered. Gold shone. It all held a storehouse of books, scrolls, texts, artifacts, statuary, and strange brass contraptions. Each step around seemed to open new vistas, like some vast M. C. Escher painting, impossible angles, dimensional contradictions supported by stone and timber.

'It's a huge library,' Kat said.

'And museum, and storehouse, and gallery,' Vigor finished. He hurried to the side.

A stone table, like an altar, sat not far from the entry tunnel.

A leather-bound book spread open under glass . . . gold glass.

446

'I was afraid to touch it,' Vigor said. 'But you can see fairly well through it.' He shone his light down upon the exposed pages.

Kat peered at the book. It was heavily decorated in oils. An illuminated manuscript. Tiny script flowed down the page. It appeared to be a list.

'I think this is the codex for the entire library,' Vigor said. 'A ledger and filing system. But I can't be sure.'

The monsignor's palms hovered over the glass case, plainly fearful of touching it. They had seen the effects of such superconducting material. Kat stepped back. She noted that the entire complex glittered with similar glass. Even the walls of the tiers had plates of the glass dotted along them, embedded like windows, set like jewels.

What did it mean?

Vigor still bent over the book. 'Here it lists in Latin "the Holy Stone of Saint Trophimus."'

Kat glanced back to him for explanation.

'He was the saint who first brought Christianity to this area of France. It is said he had a visitation of Christ during a secret meeting of early Christians in a necropolis. Christ knelt on a sarcophagus and his imprint remained. The sarcophagus lid became a treasure, supposedly invoking the knowledge of Christ upon those who beheld it.' Vigor stared out at the vaulted cathedral of history. 'It was thought lost forever. But it's here. Like so much else.'

He waved back to the book. 'Complete texts of forbidden gospels, not just the tattered fragments of those found near the Dead Sea. I saw four gospels listed. One I had never even heard before. The Brown Gospel of the Golden Hills. What might it contain? But most of all . . .' Vigor lifted his flashlight. 'According to the codex, somewhere out there is stored the Mandylion.'

Kat frowned. 'What's that?'

'The true burial shroud of Christ, an artifact that predates the controversial Turin Shroud. It was taken from

447

Edessa to Constantinople in the tenth century, but during periods of marauding, it vanished. Many suspected it ended up in the treasury of the Knights Templar.' Vigor nodded. 'Out there lies the proof. And possibly the true face of Christ.'

Kat felt the weight of ages . . . all suspended in perfect geometry.

'One page,' Vigor mumbled.

Kat knew the monsignor was referring to the fact that all these wonders were listed on just one page of the leather-bound book – which appeared to have close to a thousand pages.

'What else might be found here?' Vigor said in a hushed voice.

'Have you explored all the way to the bottom?' Kat asked.

'Not yet. I went back up to fetch you.'

Kat headed to the narrow stairs that led from one tier to the next. 'We should at least get a general layout of the space, then head back up.'

Vigor nodded, but he seemed reluctant to leave the book's side.

Still, he followed Kat as she wound back and forth down the switchbacking stairs. She gazed up at one point. The entire edifice hung above her, suspended as much in time as space.

At last they reached the top of the last tier. A final set of stairs led to a flat floor, hemmed in by the last tier. The library did not extend below. All the treasure piled above, held suspended by a pair of giant arches, footed on the last tier.

Kat recognized the stone of these arches.

Not granite or marble.

Magnetite again.

Also, directly beneath the crossing of the arches, rising from the center of the floor, stood a waist-high column of magnetite, like a stone finger pointing up.

Kat descended more cautiously to the floor below. A lip of natural granite surrounded a thick glass floor. Gold glass. She didn't step out on it. The brick walls around it also were embedded with mirrored plates of gold glass. Twelve she counted, the same as the number of tiers.

Vigor joined her.

Like Kat, he took in all these details, but both their focuses fixed to the lines of silver – probably pure platinum – that etched the floor. The image somehow fit as an ending to this long hunt. It depicted a twisted maze leading to a central rosette. The stubby pillar of magnetite rose from its center.

Kat studied the space: the maze, the arches of magnetite, the glass floor. It all reminded her of the tomb of Alexander, with its pyramid and reflective pool.

'It looks like another mystery to solve.' She stared at the treasures hanging above her head. 'But if we already opened this ancient storehouse of the mages, what's left to find?'

Vigor stepped closer. 'Don't forget Alexander's gold key. We didn't need it to open anything here.'

'That means . . .'

'There's more than just this library.'

'But what?'

'I don't know,' Vigor said. 'But I recognize this maze pattern.'

Kat turned to him.

'It's the Labyrinth of Daedalus.'

Gray waited to interrogate the others until they were airborne again. The helicopter had flown them all to the Geneva International Airport, where Cardinal Spera had a private Gulfstream jet fueled and cleared for immediate takeoff to Avignon. It was surprising what a high-ranking official in the Vatican could accomplish.

Which posed Gray's first question.

'What is the Vatican doing hiring a Guild operative?' he asked.

The five of them had swung their seats around to face one another.

Cardinal Spera acknowledged the question with a nod. 'It was *not* the Holy See itself that hired Seichan.' He motioned to the woman seated beside him. 'It was a smaller group, acting independently. We heard of the Dragon Court's interest and activity. We had already used the Guild to investigate the group peripherally.'

'You hired mercenaries?' Gray accused.

'What we sought to protect required less-than-official means. To fight fire with fire. The Guild's reputation might be ruthless, but they're also efficient, honor their contracts, and get the job accomplished by any means.'

'Yet they didn't stop the massacre in Cologne.'

'It was an oversight on my part, I'm afraid. We were unaware of the significance of their theft of the Cairo text. Or that they would act so swiftly.'

The cardinal sighed and twisted one of his gold rings, then another, back and forth, a nervous gesture. 'So much bloodshed. After the murders, I approached the Guild again, to directly plant an operative among them. It was easy to do once Sigma had been called into play. The Guild offered its services, Seichan had had a run-in with you already, and the Court took the bite.'

Seichan spoke up. 'My orders were to discover what the Court knew, how far their operation had progressed, and to thwart them however I saw fit.'

'Like standing by while they tortured priests,' Rachel said.

Seichan shrugged. 'I came late to that little party. And once under way, there's no discouraging Raoul.'

Gray nodded. He still had her coin from Milan. 'And you helped us escape then, too.'

'It suited my purpose. By helping you, I was serving my mission to keep the Court challenged.'

Gray studied Seichan as she spoke. Whose side was she really playing on? With all her double and triple crosses, was there more she kept hidden? Her explanation sounded good, but all her efforts could merely be a ruse to serve the Guild.

The Vatican was naive to trust them . . . or her.

But either way, Gray owed Seichan another debt.

As planned, she had arranged to have Monk whisked out of the hospital before Raoul's goons struck. Gray had assumed she would employ some of her Guild operatives – not call Spera, her employer. But the cardinal had got the job done, declaring Monk a Vatican ambassador and shuffling him out of there.

And now they were on their way to Avignon.

Still, one thing bothered Gray.

'Your group at the Vatican,' he said, eyeing Spera. 'What's their interest in all this?'

Spera had folded his hands on the table. Clearly he was reluctant to speak further, but Rachel reached across to him. She took his hands and splayed them out. She leaned forward to study them.

'You have two gold rings with the papal seal,' she said.

The cardinal pulled his hands back, covering one hand over the other. 'One for my station as cardinal,' he explained. 'And one for my position as secretary of state. Matching rings. Its traditional.'

'But they don't match,' she said. 'I hadn't noticed until you folded your fingers together like that. With the rings on each hand side by side. They aren't the same ring. They're mirror images of the other. Exact reflected copies.'

Gray frowned.

'They're *twins*,' Rachel said.

Gray asked to see the rings himself. She was right. Reverse images of the papal seal. 'And Thomas means "twin,"' Gray mumbled, staring up at the cardinal. He remembered Spera's comment about how only a small group within the Vatican had hired the Guild. Gray now knew which group.

'You're a part of the Thomas Church,' he said. 'That's why you've been trying to stop the Court in secret.'

Spera stared for a long breath, then slowly nodded. 'Our group has been an accepted, if not promoted, part of the Apostolic Church. Despite beliefs to the contrary, the Church is not beyond science or research. Catholic universities, hospitals, and research facilities advocate forward thinking, new concepts and ideas. And yes, a certain part is steadfast and slow to respond, but it also contains members who do challenge and keep the Church malleable. That is a role we still serve.'

'And what about in the past?' Gray asked. 'This ancient society of alchemists we're hunting? The clues we've been following?'

Cardinal Spera shook his head. 'The Thomas Church of today is not the same as before. That church vanished during the French papacy, disappearing along with the Knights Templar. Mortality, conflict, and secrecy separated it even further, leaving only shadows and

452

rumors. The true fate of that Gnostic church and its ancient lineage remains unknown to us.'

'So you're as in the dark about all this as we are,' Monk said.

'I'm afraid so. Except we knew that the old church existed. It was not mythology.'

'So did the Dragon Court,' Gray said.

'Yes. But we've sought to preserve the mystery, trusting in the wisdom of our forefathers, believing it was hidden for a reason and that such knowledge would reveal itself when the time was right. The Dragon Court, on the other hand, has sought to uncover its secrets through bloodshed, corruption, and torture, seeking nothing more than a power to dominate and rule all. We've opposed them for generations.'

'And now they are so close,' Gray said.

'And they have the gold key,' Rachel reminded them, shaking her head.

Gray rubbed his face in exhaustion. He had handed it over himself. He'd needed the key to convince Raoul of Seichan's renewed loyalty. It had been a gamble certainly, but so had the whole rescue plan. Raoul was supposed to have been captured or killed at the castle – but the bastard had escaped.

Gray stared at Rachel. Feeling guilty, he wanted to say something, to explain everything, but he was saved as the pilot came over the radio.

'You all might want to secure your seatbelts. We're coming up onto some bumpy weather ahead.'

Lightning flashed across the clouds below.

Thunderclouds stacked higher ahead, lit up momentarily by the crackling bolts, then vanishing into darkness. They were flying into the teeth of a real storm.

Vigor walked along the stone lip that circled the glass floor – and its etched labyrinth. He had been studying it for a full minute in silence, fascinated by the mystery here.

'Notice how it's not truly a maze,' he finally said. 'No blind corners or dead ends. It's just one long, continuous, sinuous path. You can find this exact same maze done in blue and white stones at the Chartres Cathedral outside Paris.'

'But what's it doing down here?' Kat asked. 'And why did you call it the Labyrinth of Daedalus?'

'The Chartres labyrinth went by many names. One was *le Dedale*. Or "The Daedalus." Named after the mythological architect who constructed the maze for King Minos of Crete. The labyrinth was the home of the Minotaur, a bull-like beast that the warrior Theseus eventually defeated.'

'But why put such a maze inside the Chartres cathedral?'

'It wasn't just Chartres. During the height of church-building in the thirteenth century, when Gothic construction was at its most ardent, different mazes were placed in many cathedrals. Amiens, Rheims, Arras, Auxerre . . . all had mazes as you entered their naves. But centuries later the Church destroyed them all, deeming them pagan artifacts, except for the one at Chartres.'

'Why spare Chartres?'

Vigor shook his head. 'That cathedral has always been the exception to the rule. Its roots in fact are pagan, built atop the Grotte des Druides, a famous pagan pilgrimage site. And to this day, unlike any other cathedral, not a single king, pope, or famous personage is buried beneath its stones.'

'But that doesn't answer why the maze was repeated down here,' Kat said.

'I can imagine a few explanations. First, the Chartres

454

maze was based on a drawing from a second-century Greek text of alchemy. Fitting symbol for our lost alchemists. But the labyrinth at Chartres was also representative of journeying from this world to paradise. Worshippers in Chartres would crawl on hands and knees along this tortuous path from the outside until they reached the center rosette, representing symbolically a pilgrimage from here to Jerusalem, or from this world to the next. Hence the maze's other names. *Le Chemin de Jerusalem.* "The Road to Jerusalem." Or *le Chemin du Paradis.* "The Road to Paradise." It was a spiritual journey.'

'Do you think it's hinting that we must make this journey ourselves, follow the alchemists to solve their last great mystery?'

'Exactly.'

'But how do we do that?'

Vigor shook his head. He had an idea, but he needed more time to think about it. Kat seemed to recognize that he was not speaking freely, but she respected him enough and didn't press.

Instead, she checked her watch.

'We should head back up. See if Gray has attempted to make any contact.'

Vigor nodded. He stared back one more time, pointed his flashlight across the space. It reflected off the glass surfaces: the floor and the embedded plates in the wall. He pointed it up. More reflections glittered, jeweled ornaments in a giant tree of knowledge.

There was an answer here.

He needed to find it before it was too late.


5:28 a.m.
OVER FRANCE

*Why aren't they answering?*

Gray sat with the jet's air-phone fixed to his ear. He

455

was trying to raise Kat. But so far with no luck. Maybe it was the storm, interfering with the signal. The plane bucked and rolled through spats of lightning and sonorous rumbles of thunder.

He sat near the back of the cabin for privacy. The others, strapped to their seats, were still deep in discussion.

Only Rachel glanced back periodically, concerned to hear about her uncle. But maybe it was more. Since their rescue in Lausanne, she'd never been more than a step away from him. She still refused to discuss in detail what had happened at the castle. A haunted quality hung about her. And since then, it was as if she sought some solidity from him. Not to cling to – that wasn't her. It was more simple reassurance, grounding herself in the moment. No words were needed.

And while Monk had also been severely traumatized, Gray knew they'd eventually talk. They were soldiers-in-arms, best friends. They would work through it.

But Gray didn't have that patience with Rachel. A part of him wanted an immediate solution and answer to what troubled her. Any attempt to discuss what had happened at Lausanne had so far been rebuffed, gently but firmly. Still, he read the pain in her eyes. And as much as his heart ached, all he could do was stand beside her, wait until she was ready to speak.

At his ear, the phone's incessant ring finally stopped as the other line was picked up. 'Bryant here.'

Thank God. Gray sat straighter. 'Kat, it's Gray.'

The others in the cabin turned toward him.

'We have Rachel and Monk,' he said. 'How is everything over there?'

Kat's voice, usually so stoic, rang with relief. 'We're fine. We've found the secret entry.' She went on to briefly explain all they'd discovered. Occasionally the transmission broke up and he missed a word here and there, due to the storm.

Gray noted Rachel's intense stare at him and nodded his head to her. Her uncle was fine.

She closed her eyes in gratitude and sank back to her seat.

Once Kat was finished, Gray gave a short account of events in Lausanne. 'Barring any delay from the storm, we'll be landing at Avignon Caumont Airport in about thirty minutes. But we don't have much lead time on the Court. Maybe half an hour if we're lucky.'

Seichan had given them intel on the Court's means of transportation. Raoul had a pair of planes stored in a small airfield half an hour outside of Lausanne. Calculating the airspeed of the Court's planes, Gray knew they had a small lead on the Court. One he meant to keep.

'With all teammates secure again,' Gray told Kat, 'I'm going to break the silence with central command. Contact Director Crowe. I'll have him coordinate ground support with the local authorities. I'll call again as soon as we land. In the meantime, watch your back.'

'Roger that, Commander. We'll be waiting for you.'

Gray hung up. He dialed the access number to Sigma command. It rang through a series of scrambled switchboards and finally connected.

'Logan Gregory.'

'Dr. Gregory, it's Commander Pierce.'

'Commander –' The irritation rang in the one word.

Gray cut off an official scolding for his lack of communication. 'I must speak to Painter Crowe immediately.'

'I'm afraid that's not possible, Commander. It's nearly midnight here. The director left command about five hours ago. But no one knows where he went.' Aggravation clipped his words again, even harder-edged than his irritation at Gray.

At least Gray understood the man's frustration. What was the director doing leaving central command at a time like this?

'He may have gone over to DARPA, to coordinate with Dr. McKnight,' Logan continued. 'But I'm still ops leader for this mission. I want a full debriefing on your whereabouts.'

Gray suddenly felt uncomfortable speaking. Where had Painter Crowe gone? Or was he even gone? Ice chilled through him. Was Gregory blocking him from reaching the director? Somewhere there was a leak at Sigma. Who could he believe?

He weighed the odds – and did the only thing he could. Perhaps it was rash, but he had to go with his gut.

He hung up the phone, disconnecting the line.

He couldn't risk it.

He had a jump on Dragon Court. He wouldn't give it away.

5:35 a.m.

Eighty air miles away, Raoul listened to his contact's report over his plane's radio. A grin slowly spread. 'And they're still in the Pope's Palace?'

'Yes, sir,' his spy said.

'And you know where they are inside.'

'Yes, sir.'

Raoul had called from his castle upon learning of Avignon. He had coordinated with some local talent on the ground in Marseilles. They had been sent to Avignon to hunt down the two operatives: the monsignor and that Sigma bitch who had speared his hand. They had been successful.

Raoul checked the plane's clock. They would be landing in forty-four minutes.

'We can take them out anytime,' his spy said.

Raoul saw no need to delay. 'Do it.'

458

Kat's life was saved by a penny.

Standing beside the firepit, she had been using the coin to pry open the battery compartment on her penlight. It flipped out of her fingers and to her toes. She bent to pick it up.

The crack of the pistol coincided with a shatter of stone from the wall beside her head.

Sniper.

Still bent over, Kat shoulder-rolled to the floor, pulling out her holstered Glock. She landed on her back and fired between her knees toward the dark doorway where the shots had come from.

She shot four times, a splay of fire to cover all angles.

She heard a satisfying grunt and the clatter of a gun to stone. Something heavy followed with a thud.

Rolling across the floor, she reached Vigor. The monsignor crouched near the top of the firepit tunnel. She handed him her gun. 'Down,' she ordered. 'Shoot anybody that comes into view.'

'What about you?'

'No, don't shoot me.'

'I mean where are you going?'

'Hunting.' Kat had already extinguished their flashlights. She unhooked her night-vision goggles and pulled them over her eyes. 'There might be more.' She freed a long steel blade from her belt.

With Vigor tucked down his hole, Kat moved to the door and checked the passage. The world was all shades of green. Even the blood. It was the only movement in the hallway, spreading in a pool from the prone body.

She sidled up to the man dressed in camouflage gear.

Mercenary.

Her shot had been lucky, clipping the man through the

throat. She didn't bother checking for a pulse. She grabbed his gun and crammed it into her own holster.

Staying low, she worked from passage to hall to room, circling the kitchen area. If there were any others, they'd be near. The aborted gunplay would've sent them into hiding. Foolish. They placed too much faith in firepower, counting on the sniper to do the work for them.

Kat worked the circuit efficiently. She came across no one.

Right.

She reached behind to the side pocket of her pack and removed the heavy plastic-wrapped package. She broke the seal with her thumb and lowered her hand to her hip.

Twisting around a corner, she stepped into the single hallway that funneled back to the kitchen. She stood taller and strode confidently, marching ahead.

Bait.

She balanced the blade in her right hand. Her left emptied the contents of the package across the floor behind her.

Rubberized ball bearings, coated with NPL Super Black.

Invisible to night-vision.

They littered the floor behind her, bouncing and rolling silently.

She headed to the kitchen, her back to the bulk of the palace. She didn't hear the second man's approach, but she heard his tumbled step behind her.

Dropping and twisting, she pivoted on a knee and threw her dagger with all the strength of her shoulder and skill of her wrist. It flew with deadly accuracy, piercing straight through the man's mouth, open in surprise as his right heel slipped on one of the rubber bearings. His gun went off, the shot high, digging into the timbered rafters.

Then he was on his back, convulsing, pithed through the base of his skull.

Kat crossed to him, staying low, skating through the ball bearings.

By the time she reached him, he lay still. She yanked out her knife, confiscated his weapon, and retreated back to the kitchen. She waited another two full minutes for any sign of a third or fourth assassin.

The palace remained quiet.

Thunder rumbled in greater intensity beyond the walls. A series of blinding lightning flashes came through the high windows. The full brunt of the storm crashed across the high hill.

Finally confident they were alone, Kat called the all-clear to Vigor. He climbed back into view.

'Stay there,' she warned in case she was wrong.

She crossed back to the first body and searched it. As she feared, she found a cell phone.

Damn.

She sat there a moment, his cell phone in her hand. If the kill order had been given to the assassins, she knew for sure that their position in the palace must have been already relayed.

Kat returned to Vigor. She checked her watch.

'The Court knows where we are,' Vigor said, also assessing the situation.

Kat saw no reason to acknowledge the obvious. She freed her own cell phone. Commander Pierce needed to know. She dialed the number he had left, but she failed to pick up a signal. She tried closer to the window. No luck.

The storm had knocked out reception.

At least to the jet in the air.

She pocketed the phone.

'Maybe once they land,' Vigor said, recognizing her failed attempt. 'But if the Dragon Court knows we're here, our headway just got narrower.'

'What do you propose?' Kat asked.

'We gain it back.'

'How?'

Vigor pointed to the dark stairs. 'We still have twenty

461

minutes until Gray and the others get here. Let's put it to use. We'll solve the riddle below, so once they arrive, we're ready to act.'

Kat nodded at the logic. Plus it was the only way to make up for her lapse. She should never have allowed the spies to get so close.

'Let's do it.'


6:02 a.m.

Gray hurried with the others across the storm-swept tarmac. They had landed at the Avignon Caumont Airport only five minutes ago. He had to give Cardinal Spera credit . . . or at least his Vatican influence. Customs was cleared in the air, and a BMW sedan waited to ferry them to the Pope's Palace. The cardinal had also left and gone into the terminal, to raise the local authorities. The Pope's Palace had to be locked down.

That is, after they reached there, of course.

Gray ran with his cell phone, attempting to reach Kat and Vigor.

No answer.

He checked his signal strength. Free of the plane, the reception was another bar stronger. So what was the problem?

He let it ring and ring.

Finally he gave up. The only answer lay at the palace. Drenched, they all climbed into the waiting sedan as a brilliant display cracked across the sky, illuminating Avignon, nestled along a silver stretch of the Rhône. The Pope's Palace was visible, the highest point in the city.

'Any luck?' Monk asked, nodding to the cell phone.

'No.'

'It could be the storm,' Seichan said.

No one was convinced.

Gray had attempted to get Seichan to stay behind at

the airport. He wanted only those he fully trusted at his side. But Cardinal Spera had insisted she go, placing full faith in his contract with the Guild. And Seichan reminded Gray of his own contract between them. She had agreed to rescue Monk and Rachel in order to exact her revenge upon Raoul. She had met her end of the bargain. Gray had to meet his.

Rachel took the driver's seat.

Not even Monk objected.

But his partner kept his shotgun on his lap, pointed at Seichan. Taking no chances either. The weapon had been recovered by Cardinal Spera in the *Scavi* below St. Peter's. Monk seemed relieved to have it returned, more than his own hand.

With everyone seated, Rachel whipped the car around and headed away from the airport, aiming for the city. She took the narrow streets at breakneck speeds. At this early hour with a fierce storm blowing, there was little other traffic. They flew up some steep grades that had become rivers and planed around corners.

A few minutes later, Rachel wheeled them into the square before the palace. She side-swiped into a pile of chairs. Streamers of lights, now dark, draped the plaza. It looked like an abandoned party, waterlogged and deserted.

They piled out of the vehicle.

Rachel led the way to the main entrance, having been here before. She rushed them through a gateway, to a courtyard, then to a side door, the one Kat had mentioned.

Gray found the latch sawed off and the locking mechanism ripped out.

Not the fine handiwork of a former intelligence officer.

Someone else had broken inside.

Gray waved everyone back. 'Stay here. I'll check it out.'

'Not to be insubordinate,' Monk said. 'But I'm not into the whole separating thing again. That didn't work out so well last time.'

'I'm coming,' Rachel said.

'And I don't believe you have authority over my comings and goings,' Seichan said.

Gray didn't have time to argue – especially if he couldn't win.

They set off into the palace. Gray had memorized the layout. He scouted ahead in a series of steps, cautious but swift. After coming upon the first body, he slowed. Dead. Already cooling.

He checked. Okay, *this* was the handiwork of a former intelligence officer. He moved on and almost landed on his face as his heel slipped on a rubber ball bearing. He caught himself with a hand against the wall.

Definitely Kat toys.

They continued, shuffling through the bearings.

Another body lay near the entrance to the kitchen. They had to step through the pool of blood to get inside.

Voices reached him. He held the others to the hallway and eavesdropped.

'We're already late,' a voice said.

'I'm sorry. I had to be sure. All the angles needed to be checked.'

Kat and Vigor. In mid-argument. Their voices echoed up from a hole in the center of the kitchen. A glow grew brighter, bobbling a bit.

'Kat,' Gray called out, not wanting to startle his teammate. He had seen enough of her skill splayed in the halls here. 'It's Gray.'

The light went out.

Kat appeared a moment later, gun ready, pointed toward him.

'It's safe,' Gray said.

Kat climbed out. Gray waved the others into the room. Vigor emerged next from the hole.

Rachel rushed to him. He opened his arms and hugged her tight.

Kat spoke first and nodded to the bloody hallway. 'The Dragon Court knows about this location.'

Gray agreed. 'Cardinal Spera is rousing the local authorities right now. They should be here soon.'

Vigor kept one arm around his niece. 'Then we may have just enough time.'

'For what?' Gray asked.

'To unlock the true treasure below.'

Kat nodded. 'We solved the riddle here.'

'And what's the answer?' Gray asked.

Vigor's eyes brightened. 'Light.'


6:14 A.M.

He couldn't wait any longer.

From the terminal concourse of the tiny airport, Cardinal Spera had spied on the group as they departed in the BMW sedan. He waited five minutes as the commander had requested, giving the team time to reach the palace. He stood up and crossed to one of the armed security personnel, a blond young man in uniform.

In French, he asked to be taken to the man's on-duty superior. He showed him his Vatican identification. 'It is a matter of utmost urgency.'

The guard's eyes widened, recognizing who stood before him.

'Of course, Cardinal Spera. Right away.'

The young man led him off the concourse and through a card-coded security gate. Down at the end of a hall lay the office of the head of airport security. The guard knocked and was gruffly called inside.

He pushed the door, holding it open. Looking back to the cardinal, the guard failed to see the pistol with a silencer raised toward the back of his head.

Cardinal Spera lifted a hand. 'No . . .'

The gunshot sounded like a firm cough. The guard's

head snapped forward, followed by his body. Blood sprayed into the hallway.

A door off to the side opened.

Another gunman appeared. A pistol jabbed into Cardinal Spera's stomach. He was forced into the office. The guard's body was dragged inside behind him. Another man scooted a towel over the floor with his foot, sopping up the gore.

The door shut.

Another body already decorated the room, lying crumpled on its side.

The former security chief.

Behind his desk, a familiar figure stood.

Cardinal Spera shook his head in disbelief. 'You're part of the Dragon Court.'

'Its leader in fact.' A pistol rose into sight. 'Clearing the way here for the rest of my men to arrive.'

The gun lifted higher.

The muzzle flashed.

Cardinal Spera felt a kick to his forehead – then nothing.


6:18 a.m.

Rachel stood with the other four around the etched glass floor.

Kat stood guard up above, equipped with a radio.

They had descended the tiers to the bottom level in almost reverential silence. Her uncle had offered commentary about the massive museum nested within this subterranean cathedral, but few questions were posed.

It truly felt like a church, engendering whispers and awe.

As they had climbed down, Rachel gaped at the myriad wonders that must be stored here. She had spent all of her adult life protecting and collecting stolen art and antiquities. Here was a collection that dwarfed any museum's. To catalogue it would take decades and a university full of scholars. The immensity of age contained within this space made her life feel small and insignificant.

Even her recent trauma, the revelation of her family's dark past, seemed trivial, a minor blotch against the long history held suspended here.

As she descended deeper, her burden grew lighter. Its hold loosened around her heart. A certain weightlessness enveloped her.

Gray dropped to a knee to stare at the glass floor and the labyrinth drawn in platinum upon it.

'It's Daedalus's maze,' her uncle said, and briefly explained its history and ties to Chartres Cathedral.

'So what are we supposed to do here?' Gray asked.

Vigor walked around the circular floor. He had cautioned them to remain on the lip of granite that surrounded the glass labyrinth. 'Plainly this is another riddle,' he said. 'Besides the maze, we have a double arch of lodestone above us. A pillar of the same in the center. And these twelve m state gold plates.' He indicated the windows of glass that pocked the wall around them, formed by the last tier.

'They are positioned along the periphery like the markings on a clock,' Vigor said. 'Another timepiece. Like the hourglass that led us here.'

'So it would seem,' Gray said. 'But you mentioned light.'

Vigor nodded. 'It's always been about light. A quest for the primordial light of the Bible, the light that formed the universe and everything in it. That is what we must prove here. Like magnetism and electricity before, now we must demonstrate an understanding of light . . . and not just any light. Light with *power*. Or as Kat described it, *coherent* light.'

Gray frowned, standing up. 'You mean a laser.'

Vigor nodded. He pulled free an object from his pocket. Rachel recognized it as a laser-targeting scope from one of the Sigma weapons. 'With the power of these super-conducting amalgams coupled with jewels like diamonds and rubies, the ancients might have developed some crude form of projecting coherent light, some type of ancient laser. I believe knowledge of that craft is neces-sary to open the final level.'

'How can you be sure?' Gray said.

'Kat and I measured these twelve plates of mirrored glass. They are very subtly angled to reflect and bounce light from one to the other in a set pattern. But it would take a powerful light to complete the entire circuit.'

'Like a laser,' Monk said, eyeing the plates with concern.

'I don't think it would take a strong amount of coher-ent light,' Vigor said. 'Like the weak Baghdad batteries used to ignite the gold pyramid in Alexandria, only some small force is necessary, some indication of an under-standing of coherence. I think the energy stored in the plates will do the rest.'

'And it might not even be *energy*,' Gray said. 'If you're right about light being the base of the mystery here, superconductors not only have the capability of storing energy for an infinite period of time, they can also store *light*.'

Vigor's eyes widened. 'So a little coherent light might free the rest?'

'Possibly, but how do we go about starting this chain reaction?' Gray asked. 'Point the laser at one of the glass plates?'

468

Vigor stepped around and motioned to the lodestone pillar, about two feet thick, resting in the middle of the floor. 'The pedestal out there stands the same height as the plate windows. I suspect whatever device the ancients used was meant to rest atop it while aimed at one particular window. Our proverbial twelve o'clock marker.'

'And which one's that?' Monk asked.

Vigor stopped beside the far window. 'True north,' he said. 'It took a bit of fancy footwork to calculate with all this lodestone around. But this is the one. I think you set the laser down, point it at this plate, then get clear.'

'Seems simple enough,' Monk said.

Gray began to step out toward the central pedestal when his radio buzzed. He placed a hand over his ear, listening. Everyone stared at him.

'Kat, be careful,' Gray said into his radio. 'Approach cautiously. Let them know you're not hostile. Keep silent about us until you're sure.'

He ended the call.

'What's the matter?' Monk asked.

'Kat's spotted a patrol of French police. They've entered the palace. She's going to investigate.' Gray waved the group toward the stairs. 'This will have to wait till later. We'd better head back up.'

They filed out from around the glass pool. Rachel waited for her uncle. He looked reluctantly toward the glass floor.

'Maybe it's best,' she said. 'Maybe we shouldn't fool with what we barely understand. What if we did it wrong?' Rachel nodded to the massive library of ancient knowledge already contained here. 'If we're too greedy, we could lose it all.'

Her uncle nodded, put an arm around her as they climbed up, but his eyes still occasionally glanced below.

They worked their way up four tiers when a commanding voice bullhorned down to them from above.

*'TOUT LE MONDE EN LE BAS LÀ! SORTEZ AVEC VOS MAINS SUR LA TÊTE!'*

Everyone froze.

Rachel translated. 'They're calling for us to exit with our hands on our heads.'

A new voice bellowed through the bullhorn in English. It was Kat. 'COMMANDER! THEY CONFISCATED MY RADIO, BUT IT IS THE FRENCH POLICE. I'VE VERIFIED THEIR LEADER'S IDENTIFICATION.'

'Must be the guard sent by Cardinal Spera,' Monk said.

'Or someone called in a burglary, noting the lights in here,' Rachel added. 'Or the broken door lock.'

*'SORTEZ TOUT DE SUITE! C'EST VOTRE DERNIER AVERTISSEMENT!'*

'They certainly don't sound happy,' Monk said.

'What do you expect with all the dead bodies upstairs?' Seichan said.

'Okay,' Gray ordered. 'Up we go. We need to prepare them for the arrival of Raoul and his buddies.'

They all marched up the remaining tiers. Gray had them holster or set aside their weapons. Not wanting to spook the police, they obeyed the command and went upstairs with their hands on their heads.

The kitchen, empty before, was now crowded with uniformed men. Rachel spotted Kat, back to one wall, hands on her head, too. The French police were taking no chances. Guns were raised.

Gray attempted to explain in stilted French, but they were separated and made to stand against the wall. The leader shone his light down the passageway, nose crinkled with distaste.

A commotion by the hallway marked the arrival of a newcomer, someone with authority. Rachel watched a familiar family friend enter the kitchen, out of place here, but welcome. Had Cardinal Spera called him?

Her uncle brightened, too. 'General Rende! Thank God!'

It was Rachel's boss, the head of her Carabinieri unit. He cut a striking figure, even out of uniform.

Uncle Vigor tried to step forward but was forced back. 'You must get the *gendarmes* to listen. Before it's too late.'

General Rende eyed her uncle with an uncharacteristic sneer of disdain. 'It's already too late.'

Out from behind him marched Raoul.

# 17

# THE GOLD KEY

Gray seethed as his wrists were secured behind his back and snugged tight with plastic fast-ties. The other mercenaries, masquerading as French police, stripped weapons and secured the rest of them. Even the bastard Raoul wore a policeman's uniform.

The giant stepped in front of Gray. 'You're damn tough to kill,' Raoul said. 'But that's going to end. And don't hope for a rescue call from the cardinal. He ran into an old friend at the airport.' He nodded to General Rende. 'It seemed our leader here decided the poor cardinal was of no further use to the Court.'

Gray's heart clenched.

Raoul grinned, a savage and bloody expression.

General Rende marched up to them, dressed in civilian clothes, an expensive black suit and tie, polished Italian shoes. He had been in discussion with another man, one wearing a clerical collar. It had to be the prefect, Alberto Menardi, the Court's resident Rasputin. He had a book tucked under one arm and a satchel in hand.

The general stepped to Raoul. 'Enough.'

'Yes, Imperator.' Raoul backed a step.

Rende pointed down to the tunnel. 'We don't have time to gloat. Take them below. Find out what they've learned. Then kill them.' Rende stared around the room, his blue eyes icy, his silver hair slicked back. 'I will make no

472

pretensions of your survival. Your only choice is to make your deaths slow or quick. So make your peace in whatever manner you see fit.'

Vigor spoke by the far wall. 'How could you?'

Rende strode over to him. 'Fear not, my old friend, we will spare your niece,' he said. 'That I promise you. You've both served your duty by keeping the Court abreast of archaeological and art history treasures. You've served the Court well these many years.'

Vigor's face went cold, realizing how he'd been used and manipulated.

'Now that role comes to an end,' Rende said. 'But your niece's bloodline goes back to kings and will produce kings to come.'

'By mating me with that bastard?' Rachel spat back.

'It is not the man or the woman,' Raoul answered. 'It's always been the blood and the future. The purity of our lineage is as much a treasure as what we seek.'

Gray stared at Rachel, trussed up next to her uncle. Her face was pale, but her eyes flashed with fury. Especially when Raoul grabbed her by the elbow. She spat in his face.

He cuffed her hard across the mouth, knocking her head back and splitting her lip.

Gray lunged forward, but a pair of rifles shoved him back.

Raoul leaned closer to her. 'I like a little fire in my bed.' He dragged her forward. 'And this time, I'm not letting you out of my sight.'

'Get what we came here for,' Rende said, his face unperturbed by the violence. 'Then we'll start unloading as much as we can before the storm ends. The trucks will be arriving in another fifteen minutes.'

Gray now understood the uniforms. The masquerade would buy them time to clear a good section of the treasure below. He didn't fail to note the barrow full of silver incendiary grenades wheeled into the room as they were

473

tied up. Anything that the Court couldn't carry away would be destroyed.

Alberto joined Raoul.

'Bring the axes, the electric drills, and the acid,' Raoul said, and waved his men forward.

Gray knew the tools were not meant for heavy construction.

They were tools of a true sadist.

Prodded by guns, separated by soldiers, the group was led back down into the tunnel. Once below, even the guards, smirking and hard-edged, grew quiet, eyes widening.

Raoul stared at the spread of Gothic arches and the treasure. 'We'll need more trucks.'

Alberto walked in a daze. 'Amazing . . . simply amazing. And according to the *Arcadium*, this is just the dregs left at the true doorstep to a greater treasure.'

Despite the danger, Vigor glanced over to the prefect in shock. 'You have Jacques de Molay's last testament?'

Alberto clutched his book tighter to his chest. 'A seventeenth-century copy. The last known to exist.'

Gray stared at Vigor, meeting his eyes questioningly.

'Jacques de Molay was the last Grand Master of the Knights Templar, tortured by the Inquisition for his refusal to reveal the location of their treasure. He was burned at the stake. But there were rumors of a Templar text, a final treatise by de Molay before he was captured.'

'The *Arcadium*,' Alberto said. 'In the possession of the Dragon Court for centuries. It hinted at a treasure. One independent of the mass of gold and jewels of Knights Templar. A greater treasure. One that would put the very keys to the world into its discoverer's hand.'

'The lost secret of the mages,' Vigor said.

'It's here,' Alberto said, eyes almost aglow.

They descended the tiers toward the glass floor.

Upon reaching the bottommost tier, the soldiers spread

out atop it, taking up positions all along the rim. Gray and the others were forced to their knees. Alberto went down alone to the glass floor, studying its labyrinth.

'One last riddle,' he mumbled.

Raoul stood with Rachel near the top of the last terrace's stairs. He turned to face the group on their knees. 'I think we'll start with the women,' Raoul said. 'But which one?'

Swinging to the side, he grabbed a fistful of Rachel's hair, at the back of her neck. He bent over her and kissed her hard on the mouth. Rachel squirmed, gasping, but tied up, there was little she could do.

Fire narrowed Gray's vision. He knelt down and stamped the toe of his boot against the stone. He felt the hidden blade *snick* out of the heel, the same one he had used to free himself in the castle cell. He hid the knife behind his tied wrists. With minimal movement, he cut the ties on the razored edge. Though free, he kept his hands behind his back.

Raoul pulled back from his embrace. His lower lip bled. Rachel had bitten him, but he simply grinned. He shoved her hard in the center of her chest. Off balance, she fell to her backside with a teeth-jarring impact.

'Stay,' Raoul said, palm out, as if commanding a dog.

A rifle at Rachel's skull firmed the order.

Raoul turned back to the group. 'I'll save my fun for her later. So we'll need another woman to start with.' He strode over to Seichan, stared down at her, then shook his head. 'You'd probably enjoy it too much.'

He turned next to Kat and waved to the guards that flanked her to drag her in front of the others. Raoul bent down and picked up the ax and a power drill. He stared between the two, then lowered the ax. 'Already did that.'

He lifted the drill and pressed the trigger. The buzz of its motor echoed across the chamber, hungry with the promise of pain.

'We'll start with an eye,' Raoul said.

One of the guards yanked Kat's head back. She tried to fight, but the other kicked her hard in the belly, knocking out her breath. As they held her in place, Gray saw the tear roll from the corner of Kat's eye. Not scared. Angry.

Raoul lowered the drill toward her face.

'Don't!' Gray yelled. 'There's no need for this. I'll tell you what we know.'

'No,' Kat said, and was punched in the face by one of the guards.

Gray understood her warning. If the Dragon Court gained the power here, the 'keys to the world,' it would mean Armageddon. Their own lives here, their own blood, were not worth that price.

'I'll tell you,' Gray repeated.

Raoul straightened a bit.

Gray hoped to lure him closer.

But Raoul remained where he was. 'I don't seem to recall asking any questions yet.' He bent over again. 'This is only a demonstration. When it comes to the question-and-answer period of this conversation, we'll get more serious.'

The drill growled louder.

Gray could wait no longer. He would not sit idle as another teammate was maimed by this madman. Better to die in a firefight. He leapt to his feet, driving an elbow into the groin of the soldier guarding him. With the man's attention fixed to the torture, Gray caught his rifle, pointed it at Raoul, and pulled the trigger.

*Click.*

Nothing happened.


7:22 a.m.

Rachel watched Gray be clubbed to the ground by a soldier behind him, using the butt of a rifle.

Raoul laughed, revving his drill.

'Take his boots off,' Raoul ordered. He stalked up to Gray as he was manhandled around. 'You don't think I failed to have the security tapes reviewed after your escape, do you? When I didn't hear from the two men I sent back to assassinate you at the castle, I sent another team to investigate. Nothing but dogs in the yard. They found out how you escaped and radioed it to me.'

Gray's laces were sliced and the boots tugged off.

'So I let you have your little hope,' Raoul said. 'It's always best to know an enemy's secret. Keeps surprises to a minimum. I figured you'd eventually go for a gun . . . but I'd hoped you'd have a bit more stomach. Waited until things got really bloody.' Raoul lifted the drill and turned away. 'Now, where were we?'

Rachel stared as Gray was trussed up again. His face was hollow and hopeless. This scared her more than the threat of torture.

'Leave the others alone,' Gray said. He struggled to his feet. 'You're wasting time. We know how to open the gate. Harm a single one of us and you'll learn nothing.'

Raoul eyed him. 'Explain and I'll consider your offer.'

Gray searched the others, looking forlorn. 'It's light,' he said.

Kat groaned. Vigor hung his head.

'He's right,' a voice called up from the floor below. Alberto climbed a few steps. 'The mirrors on the wall are reflective and angled.'

'It takes laser light,' Gray continued, revealing all. He went on to explain what Vigor had related.

Alberto joined them. 'Yes, yes . . . it makes perfect sense.'

'Well, we'll just see,' Raoul said. 'If he's wrong, we'll start chopping limbs.'

Gray turned to Rachel and the others. 'They would've found out eventually. They already have the gold key.'

Raoul ordered his men: 'Bring the prisoners down below. I don't want to take any chances. Stand them against the lower wall. The rest of you' – he eyed the ring of soldiers that stood guard atop the tier – 'keep a constant bead on each of them. Shoot anyone that moves.'

Rachel and the other five were led below and forced to separate, to spread out along the wall. Gray stood only three steps from her side. She longed to reach out to him, to hold his hand, but he seemed lost in his own misery.

And she dared not move.

Soldiers lay flat on the tier above, rifles aimed at them.

Gray mumbled, staring at the glass floor. His words reached only her own ears. 'The Minotaur's maze.'

Her brow crinkled. Standing in place, he glanced at her, then back to the floor. What was he trying to indicate?

*The Minotaur's maze.*

Gray was referring to one of the names for the labyrinth. Daedalus's maze. The mythic labyrinth that was home to the bullish Minotaur, a deadly monster in a deadly maze.

*Deadly.*

Rachel remembered the trap at Alexander's tomb. The deadly passageway. To solve these riddles didn't require just the technology. You had to know your history and mythology. Gray was trying to warn her. They may have solved the technology, but not the entire mystery.

She now understood Gray's hope. He had only told Raoul enough to hopefully get the man killed.

Raoul freed a laser scope and stepped toward the central pedestal. Then he seemed to think better of it. He pointed the scope to Gray.

'You,' he said, plainly suspicious. 'You take it out there.'

Gray was forced away from the wall, away from her side. His arms were cut free. But he was hardly free. Rifles tracked his every step.

Raoul shoved the laser into Gray's hand. 'Set it up. Like you described.'

Gray glanced to Rachel, then headed across the glass floor in his socks.

He had no choice.

He had to enter the Minotaur's maze.

7:32 a.m.

General Rende checked his watch. Thunder rumbled beyond the walls of the palace. What he had sought for so long was about to come true. Even if they failed to open whatever secret vault lay below, he had taken a brief look. That storehouse alone was a treasure to dwarf all others.

They would escape with as much as they could and destroy the rest.

His demolition expert was already going over the incendiary charges.

All that was left was to wait for the trucks.

He had arranged for a caravan of three heavy-duty Peugeot trucks. They would run in shifts to a huge warehouse at the outskirts of town near the river, unhooking their load, mounting an empty container, and returning.

Back and forth for as long as they could.

The general frowned at his watch. They were running late. He had had a call from the lead driver five minutes ago. The roads were a mess, and even though dawn had already broken, it remained a perpetual twilight under the thunderclouds and torrents of rain.

Despite the delay, the storm served to shelter them, to cover their actions, to keep any interest here to a minimum. Outlying guards were ready to eliminate anyone who became too curious. Bribes had been paid.

They should have half a day.

A call came through on the radio. He answered it.

'First truck is climbing the hill now,' the driver reported.

Thunder boomed in the distance.

Now it began.

Scope in hand, Gray crossed to the short pillar of magnetite. Overhead, double arches of the same stone stretched. Even without touching anything, Gray sensed the power that lay dormant.

'Hurry up!' Raoul called from the edge.

Gray stepped to the pedestal. He placed the scope atop the pillar, balanced it, and pointed it toward the twelve o'clock window. He paused to take a deep breath. He had tried to warn Rachel to be ready for anything. Once this was activated, they were all in danger.

'Turn on the laser!' Raoul barked. 'Or we begin shooting out kneecaps.'

Gray reached to the power switch and thumbed it on.

A fine beam of red light shot out and struck the gold glass plate.

Gray remembered the batteries at Alexander's tomb. It took a moment for whatever charge or electrical capacitance to build, then the fireworks began.

He had no intention of standing here when that happened.

He turned and strode rapidly back to the wall. He didn't run, no rash actions, or he'd be shot in the back. He regained his spot on the wall.

Raoul and Alberto stood at the base of the stairs.

All eyes were on the single strand of red fire that linked scope to mirror.

'Nothing's happening,' Raoul growled.

Vigor spoke from the other side. 'It may take a few seconds to build enough energy to activate the mirror.'

Raoul raised a pistol. 'If it doesn't – '

It did.

A deep tonal note sounded and a new ray of laser shot out from the twelve o'clock plate and struck the five o'clock one. There was a half-second dazzle.

480

No one spoke.

Then another beam of red fire blazed out, slamming into the ten-o'clock marker. It reflected immediately, springing from mirror to mirror.

Gray stared at the spread before him, forming a fiery star, waist high. He and the others stood between points of the display, knowing better than to move.

The symbolism was plain.

The Star of Bethlehem.

The light that had guided the Magi.

The humming note grew louder. The star's fire blazed brighter.

Gray turned his head, squinting.

Then he felt it, some threshold crossed. Pressure slammed outward, shoving him to the wall.

The Meissner field again.

The star seemed to bow upward from the center as if shoved up from the floor. It reached the cross of magnetite arches overhead.

A burst of energy crackled across the vaulted archways.

Gray felt a tug on the metal buttons of his shirt.

The magnetic charge of the arches had grown tenfold.

The star's energy was repelled by the new field and slammed back down, striking the glass floor with a loud metallic chime, the strike of a giant bell.

The central pillar blasted upward as if jarred by the collision. It struck the center of the crossed arches – and stuck there, two electromagnets clinging tight.

As the chime faded, Gray felt a pop in his ears as the field broke. The star winked out, though a ghost of its blaze still shone across his vision. He blinked away the afterburn.

Overhead, the short column still clung to the intersection of the archways, pointing downward now. Gray followed the stone finger.

In the middle of the floor, where the column had stood before, lay a perfect circle of solid gold. A match to the key. At its center – *the center of everything* – was a black slot.

'The keyhole!' Alberto said. He dropped his book, opened his satchel, and pulled out the gold key.

Gray caught a hard glance from across the floor, from Vigor. At that moment, Gray had handed them not just the gold key, but the key to the world.

Alberto must have suspected the same. In his excitement, he stepped out onto the glass floor.

Bolts of electricity shot upward from the surface, piercing through the man, lifting him off his feet and holding him suspended. He screamed and writhed as fire licked into him. Skin blackened; his hair and clothes caught fire.

Raoul tripped back to the stairs in horror, landing on his backside.

Gray turned to Rachel. 'Get ready to run.'

Now might be their only chance.

But she didn't seem to hear him, transfixed like the others.

Alberto's cry finally cut out. As if knowing its prey was dead, a final bolt of energy tossed the man's corpse to the shoreline of the glass pool.

No one moved. The smell of burnt flesh wafted.

Everyone stared at the deadly labyrinth.

The Minotaur had arrived.

General Rende retreated back up the steps to the kitchen. He had been called down by one of his soldiers when the brilliant star had ignited below. He wanted to see what was happening – but from a safe distance away.

Then the light had expired.

Disappointed, he had turned away as a tortured wail erupted.

It stood the small hairs on his neck on end.

He fled back up to the kitchen. One of his men, wearing a French uniform, rushed up to him. 'The first truck is here!' he said hurriedly.

Rende shook off the momentary anxiety.

He had a job to do.

'Radio everyone who's not on guard duty. It's time to empty the vault.'

Rachel knew they were in trouble.

Raoul roared back to his feet, swinging toward Gray. 'You knew this!'

Gray backed a step down the wall. 'How could I know he'd be fried?'

Raoul lifted his pistol and pointed it. 'Time to learn a lesson.'

But the gun was not pointed at Gray.

'No!' Rachel moaned.

The pistol blasted. Across the floor, Uncle Vigor clutched his belly with a shocked groan. His feet slid out from under him, and he sank to the floor.

Seichan moved to his side, slipping to him like a black cat. She kept Vigor's feet from touching the glass.

But Raoul wasn't done with them. He pointed his pistol next toward Kat. She was only three meters away.

The gun pointed at her head.

'Don't!' Gray said. 'I had no idea that would happen! But I now know the mistake Alberto made!'

Raoul turned to him, anger in every muscle. But Rachel recognized his fury was not at the loss of Alberto, but due to the fact that the sudden and dramatic death had frightened him. And he didn't like being scared.

'What?' Raoul growled.

Gray pointed to the labyrinth. 'You can't just walk out to the keyhole. You have to follow the path.' He waved to the twisted maze.

Raoul's eyes narrowed, the fire ebbed. Understanding lessened the fear.

'Makes sense,' Raoul said. He crossed to the corpse, bent down and broke the fire-contorted fingers, still clutched around the key. He freed the length of gold and wiped the charred flesh from its surface.

He waved one of his men down from above. He pointed out to the center. 'Take this out there,' he ordered, and held out the gold key.

The young soldier balked. He had seen what had happened to Alberto.

Raoul pointed his pistol at the man's forehead. 'Or die here. Your choice.'

The man reached out and took the key.

'Get going,' Raoul said. 'We're on a timetable here.' He kept his pistol pointed at the man's back.

The soldier crossed to the entry point of the maze. Leaning back, he placed one toe on the glass, then yanked it back. Nothing happened. More confident, but wary, he reached again and placed his foot down on the surface.

Still no electrical display.

Clenching his teeth, the soldier stepped fully out onto the glass floor.

'Stay away from the platinum etchings,' Gray warned.

The soldier nodded, glancing appreciatively toward Gray. He took another step.

Without warning, a stab of crimson fire jetted out of a pair of windows. The star flickered into existence, then died again.

The soldier had frozen in place. Then his legs sagged under him. He fell backward out of the maze. As he struck the ground, his body split in halves, sheared across the waist by the laser. A tangled nest of intestines snaked out from the upper half.

Raoul backed away, eyes flashing fire. The pistol again lifted. 'Any more bright ideas?'

Gray remained stock-still. 'I . . . I don't know.'

'Maybe it's a timing thing,' Monk called over. 'Maybe you have to keep moving. Like that movie *Speed*.'

Gray glanced to his teammate, then back again, unconvinced.

'I've had enough with losing my own men,' Raoul said, fury building. 'And I'm done waiting while you piece this puzzle together. So you'll have to simply *show* me how it's done.'

He motioned Gray forward.

Gray stood in place, obviously attempting to find some answer.

'I can always begin shooting your friends again. I know it helps my stress.' Raoul pointed the gun again at Kat.

Gray finally moved, stepping over the prone body.

'Don't forget the key,' Raoul said.

Gray bent to pick it up.

It then struck Rachel. *Of course.*

Gray straightened and moved to the entry point of the maze. He began to step out, bunching up a bit to run, ready to follow Monk's advice.

'No!' Rachel called out. She hated to help Raoul reach his goal. She had been prepared to die to keep the Court from gaining what lay hidden here. But she couldn't watch Gray die either, cut in half or electrocuted.

She remembered Gray's whisper about the Minotaur. He refused to give up. As long as they still lived, there was hope. She believed him. And more importantly, she trusted him.

Gray turned to her.

In his eyes, she saw the same trust shining there.

For her.

The weight of it silenced her.

'What?' Raoul barked.

'It's not speed,' Rachel said, startled. 'Time is valued by these alchemists. They left clues, from an hourglass to this mirrored clockface. They would not use time to kill.'

'Then what?' Gray asked, eyes still heavy upon her. But it was a burden she was willing to bear.

Rachel spoke quickly. 'The mazes in all the cathedrals. They represented symbolic journeys. From this world to the next. To spiritual enlightenment in the center.' She pointed to the dead body, cut in half at the waist, the height of the mirrored windows. 'But to reach there, pilgrims crawled. On hands and knees.'

Gray nodded. 'Below the level of these windows.'

Across the floor, her uncle groaned, seated on the floor, blood seeping between his fingers. Seichan sat with him. Rachel knew it wasn't the pain that elicited the moaned response. She saw it in her uncle's eyes. He had already figured out this last riddle, too. But he had kept silent.

By speaking, Rachel had betrayed the future, risking the world.

Her eyes found Gray. She had made her choice. With no regret.

Even Raoul believed her.

He waved for Gray to hand over the key. 'I'll take it there myself – but you're going first.'

Plainly Raoul did not have *full* trust in her idea. Gray passed him the key.

'As a matter of fact,' Raoul said, pointing his gun at

Rachel, 'since it's your idea, why don't you come along, too? To help keep your man honest.'

Rachel stumbled forward. Her hands were cut free. She crouched down with Gray. He nodded to her, transmitting a silent message.

*We'll be okay.*

She had little reason to feel confident, but she nodded back.

'Let's get going,' Raoul said.

Gray went first, crawling out onto the maze without hesitation, fully trusting in Rachel's assessment.

She was held back by Raoul until Gray was a full body-length away.

The glass floor remained quiet.

'Okay, now you,' she was ordered.

Rachel set out, following Gray's path. She felt a vibration through her palms. The face of the glass was warm. As she moved, she heard a distant hum, not mechanical or electric, more like the murmur of a vast crowd across a distance. Maybe it was the blood rushing through her ears, pounded by her worried heart.

Raoul yelled behind her to his men. 'Shoot any of the others if they move! The same goes for the two out here. Upon my orders, take them out.'

So if the maze didn't kill them, Raoul would.

Rachel continued onward. With only one hope.

Gray.

7:49 a.m.

Rende placed a hand on the demolition expert's shoulder. 'Are the charges primed?'

'All sixteen of them,' the man answered. 'Just tap this button three times. The grenades are daisy-chained on a ten-minute fuse.'

*Perfect.*

He turned to the row of sixteen men. Other wheelbarrows stood out in the hall, waiting to be loaded. Five handtrucks also stood ready. The first truck had been carefully backed to the main gate, and the second was on its way. It was time to empty the vault.

'Get to work, men. Double time.'

7:50 a.m.

Gray's knees ached.

Three-quarters around the maze, it became torture on his kneecaps. The smooth glass now felt like rough concrete. But he dared not stop. Not until he reached the center.

As he made his turns around the circuit, he crossed alongside the neighboring paths with Rachel and Raoul. It would only take a hip check to knock Raoul off his path. Even Raoul suspected this, pointing his gun at Gray's face as they passed.

But there was no need for the caution. Gray knew if he crossed the platinum etched lines with even a hand or a hip, he'd be killed as quickly as Raoul. And with the glass face activated, Rachel would probably be electrocuted, too.

So he let Raoul pass unmolested.

When he crossed paths with Rachel, their eyes remained fixed upon each other. Neither spoke. A bond had grown between them, one built on danger and trust. Gray's heart ached with every pass: to hold her, to comfort her. But there was no stopping.

Around and around they went.

A droning grew inside his head, vibrating up the bones of his arms and legs. He also heard a commotion above. In the cathedral. Soldiers involved in some activity up there.

He ignored it all and crawled onward.

After a final turn, a straight shot led to the center rosette. Gray hurried forward, glad to reach home base at last. With his knees on fire, he lunged the last distance and sprawled onto his back.

The droning grew into a murmuring just beyond the range of the audible. He sat up, his hairs vibrating with the noise. *What the hell . . . ?*

Rachel appeared and crawled toward him. Staying low, he helped her into the center. She slipped into his arms. 'Gray . . . what are we – ?'

He knelt with her and squeezed her silent.

There was only one hope.

A slim one.

Raoul appeared and crawled over to them. He wore a huge grin. 'The Dragon Court owes you both for your generous service.' He pointed his gun. 'Now stand up.'

'What?' Gray asked.

'You heard me. Stand up. Both of you.'

With no choice, Gray tried to pull himself out of Rachel's arms, but she clung to him. 'Let me first,' he whispered.

'Together,' she answered.

Gray met her eyes and saw her determination.

'Trust me,' she said.

Gray took a deep breath, and the two of them stood up. Gray expected to be cut in half, but the floor remained quiet.

'A safe zone,' Rachel said. 'In the center of the star. The lasers never crossed this part.'

Gray kept his arm around Rachel. It fit like it belonged there.

'Keep back or you'll be shot,' Raoul warned. He stood up next, stretched a kink, and reached into a pocket. 'Now to see what prize you delivered to us.'

Raoul pulled out the key, bent down, and shoved it into the keyhole.

'A perfect fit,' Raoul mumbled.

Gray pulled Rachel tighter into his arms, fearful of what would happen next, certain of only one thing.

In her ear, he whispered the secret he had been holding from everyone since Alexandria.

'The key's a fake.'

## 7:54 a.m.

General Rende had come down to oversee the first load of treasure. They could not take everything, so someone had to perform triage, pick the choicest bits of antiquity, art, and ancient texts. He stood near the landing with inventory pad in hand. His men crawled along the topmost tier of the massive structure.

Then a strange rumble vibrated through the cavern.

It wasn't an earthquake.

More like something shook all his senses at once. His balance shifted a few degrees off kilter. His hearing roared. His skin chilled like someone had just walked over his grave. But worst of all, his vision shimmered. It was like the world became a bad television picture tube, fritzing the screen image, playing with perspective. Three dimensions dissolved to a flat two.

Rende fell back to the stairwell.

Something was happening. Something wrong.

He felt it down to his bones.

He fled up the stairs.

## 7:55 a.m.

Rachel clung to Gray as the vibration worsened. The floor under them pulsed with white light. With each beat, arcs of electricity raced outward along the lines of platinum, crackling and flaring. In seconds, the entire labyrinth shone with an inner fire.

Gray's words echoed in her ears. *The key's a fake.*

And the labyrinth responded.

A deep tone chimed beneath them, ominous and foreboding.

Pressure again built, closing and squeezing.

A new Meissner field grew, strangely skewing perception.

Overhead, the entire complex seemed to vibrate, like a flickering filament of a lightbulb.

Reality bent.

A meter away, Raoul straightened from where he crouched over the inserted key, unsure of what was happening. But he must have sensed it, too. An overwhelming sense of wrongness. It nauseated the senses.

Rachel clung to Gray, glad for the support.

Raoul swung toward them and brought his pistol up. He came to the truth too late. 'Back at the castle. You gave us the wrong goddamn key.'

Gray stared at him. 'And you lose.'

Raoul pointed his gun.

Around them, the fiery star shattered back into existence, blasting forth from all the windows simultaneously. Raoul crouched lower, fearful of being cut in half.

Overhead the stone pedestal broke free from its magnetic attachment to the lodestone arches. It plummeted back to the ground. Raoul looked up too late. The edge of the stone caught him in the shoulder and crushed him to the floor.

As the pillar struck, the glass shattered like ice under them, skittering out in all directions. From the cracks, a blinding brilliance erupted.

Gray and Rachel remained standing.

'Hold tight,' Gray whispered.

Rachel sensed it, too. A rising vibration of power, under them, around them, through them. She needed to be closer. He responded, turning her to face him, arms crushing her to his chest, leaving no space. She pulled

491

hard to him, feeling his heart beat through his rib cage.

Something was rushing up from below.

A bubble of black energy. It was about to strike.

She closed her eyes as the world exploded with light.


On the floor, Raoul's shoulder flamed with white-hot agony. Crushed bones ground together. He fought to escape, panicked.

Then a supernova exploded under and through him, so bright it penetrated to the back of his skull. It spread through his brain. He fought its penetration, knowing it would undo him.

He felt violated, splayed open, every thought, action, desire bared.

No . . .

He could not shut it out. It was larger than him, more than him, undeniable. All his being was drawn out along a shining white thread. Stretched to the point of breaking, agonized, but it left no room for anger, self-hatred, shame, loathing, fear, or recrimination. Only a purity. An unadulterated essence of being. This is who he could be, who he was born to be.

No . . .

He didn't want to see this. But he could not turn away. Time stretched toward the infinite. He was trapped, aflame in a cleansing light, far more painful than any Hell.

He faced himself, his life, his possibility, his ruin, his salvation . . .

He saw the truth – and it burned.

No more . . .

But the worst was still to come.


Seichan clutched the old man to her chest. Both kept their heads bowed from the blinding eruption of light, but Seichan caught glimpses from the corner of her eyes.

492

The fiery star blasted skyward on a fountain of light, rising from the center of the labyrinth and spinning upward into the dark cathedral above. Other glass mirrors, embedded in the vast library, caught the starshine and reflected it back a hundredfold, feeding the rising maelstrom. A cascade reaction spread through the entire complex. In a heartbeat, the two-dimensional star unfolded into a giant three-dimensional sphere of laser light, spinning within and around the subterranean cathedral.

Energy scintillated and crackled out from it, sweeping the tiers.

Screams bellowed and rang.

Over her head, one soldier leapt from the tier above, trying to get to the floor below. But there was no sanctuary for him. Bolts struck him before he even hit the ground, burning him to bone by the time he crashed to the labyrinth floor.

But most disturbing of all, something had happened to the arched cathedral itself. The view seemed to flatten, losing all sense of depth. And even this image shimmered, as if what hung above her was merely a reflection in water, not real, a mirage.

Seichan closed her eyes, afraid to watch, terrified to the core.

Gray held Rachel. The world was pure light. He sensed the chaos beyond, but here it was just the two of them. The droning hum again rose around them, coming from within the light, a threshold he could not cross or comprehend.

He remembered Vigor's words.

*Primordial light.*

Rachel lifted her face. Her eyes were so bright in the reflected light that he could almost sense her thoughts. She seemed to read him, too.

Something in the character of the light, a permanence

that could not be denied, an agelessness that made everything small.

Except for one thing.

Gray leaned down, lips brushing hers, breaths shared. It wasn't love. Not yet. Just a promise.

The light flared brighter as Gray deepened his kiss, tasting her. What once droned, now sang. His eyes closed, but he still saw her. Her smile, her flash of eye, the angle of her neck, the curve of her breast. He felt that permanence again, that ageless presence.

Was it the light? Was it the two of them?

Only time would tell.

General Rende fled with the first screams. He didn't need to investigate further. As he clambered out of the stairwell into the kitchen, he had seen the sheen of energies reflected up from below.

He had not gotten this far in the Court from being foolhardy.

That he left to lieutenants like Raoul.

Flanked by two soldiers, he retreated out of the palace, winding toward the main courtyard. He would commandeer the truck, return to the warehouse, regroup there, and strategize a new plan.

He needed to be back in Rome before noon.

As he exited the door, he noted that the exterior guard, still in police uniforms, maintained the gate. He also noted the rain had slowed to a drizzling mist.

Good.

It would hasten his retreat.

Near the truck, the driver and another four uniformed guards noticed his approach and came forward to meet him.

'We must leave immediately,' Rende ordered in Italian.

'Somehow I don't see that happening,' the driver said in English, pulling back his cap.

The four uniformed guards raised weapons at his group. General Rende took a step back.

These were *real* French police . . . except for the driver. From his accent, he was obviously an American.

Rende glanced back to the gateway. More French policemen stood guard. He'd been betrayed by his own ruse.

'If you're looking for *your* men,' the American said, 'they're already secured in the back of the truck.'

General Rende stared at the driver. Black hair, blue eyes. He didn't recognize him, but he knew the voice from conversations over the phone.

'Painter Crowe,' he said.

Painter spotted a flash of muzzle fire. From the second-story window of the palace. A lone sniper. Someone they had missed.

'Back!' he yelled to the patrol around him.

Bullets chewed across the wet pavement, strafing between Painter and the general. The police scattered to the side.

Rende fled back, yanking out his pistol.

Ignoring the automatic fire, Painter dropped to one knee, lifting two weapons, one in each fist. Aiming instinctively, Painter pointed one pistol toward the upper window.

*Pop, pop, pop . . .*

The general dropped to the ground.

A cry sounded from the second story. A body tumbled out.

But Painter noted it only from the corner of his eye. His full focus was on General Rende. They both pointed guns at the other, both kneeling, weapons almost touching.

'Back away from the truck!' Rende said. 'All of you!'

Painter stared hard at the man, judging him. He read the raw fury in the other's eyes, everything falling apart around him. Rende would shoot, even if it meant forfeiting his life.

The man offered him no choice.

Painter dropped his first pistol, then lowered the second gun away from Rende's face, pointing it at the ground.

The general grinned triumphantly.

Painter squeezed the trigger. An arc of brilliance shot out from the tip of the second pistol. The taser barbs struck the puddle at the general's knee. The jolt of electricity blew Rende off his legs, slamming him onto his back, gun flying.

He screamed.

'Hurts, doesn't it?' Painter said, snatching up his regular pistol and covering the general.

The police swarmed around the fallen man.

'Are you all right?' one of the patrolman asked Painter.

'Fine.' He stood. 'But damn . . . I really miss fieldwork.'


7:57 a.m.

Down in the cavern, the fireworks had only lasted a little over a minute.

Vigor lay on his back, staring up. The screaming had stopped. He had opened his eyes, sensing at the primitive level of his brain that it was over. He caught the last spin of the sphere of coherent light, then watched it collapse inward on itself like a dying sun.

Above stretched empty space.

The entire cathedral had flickered and vanished with the star.

Seichan stirred from where she had sheltered beside him. Her eyes were also fixed above. 'It's all gone.'

'If it was ever there,' Vigor said, weak from blood loss.

Gray broke the embrace with Rachel, the acuity of his senses fading with the light. But he still tasted her on his lips. That was enough.

For now.

Some of the shine remained in her eyes as she searched around. The others were stirring from where they had flattened themselves against the ground. Rachel spotted Vigor, struggling to sit up.

'Oh God . . .' she said.

She slipped out of Gray's arm to check on her uncle. Monk headed in the same direction, ready to employ his medical training.

Gray kept guard, staring at the heights around him.

No shots rang out. The soldiers were gone . . . along with the library. It was as if something had cored out the center, leaving only the amphitheater-like rings of ascending tiers.

Where had it all gone?

A moan drew his attention to the floor.

Raoul lay crumpled nearby, curled around his trapped arm, crushed under the fallen pillar. Gray stepped over and kicked his pistol aside. It skittered across the glass floor, now a cracked and scattered jigsaw.

Kat came over.

'Leave him for now,' Gray said. 'He's not going anywhere. We'd best collect as many weapons as we can. There's no telling how many others might be up there.'

She nodded.

Raoul rolled onto his back, stirred by Gray's voice.

Gray expected some final curse or threat, but Raoul's face was twisted in agony. Tears rolled down his cheeks. But Gray suspected it wasn't the crushed arm that was triggering this misery. Something had changed in Raoul's face. The perpetual hard edge and glint of disdain had

497

vanished, replaced with something softer, more human.

'I didn't ask to be forgiven,' he keened out in anguish.

Gray frowned at this statement. *Forgiven by whom?* He remembered his own exposure to the light a moment ago. *Primordial light.* Something beyond comprehension, beyond the dawn of creation. Something had transformed Raoul.

He recalled the naval research done on superconductors, how the brain communicated via superconductivity, even maintained memory that way, stored as energy or possibly light.

Gray glanced to the shattered floor. Was there more than light stored in the superconducting glass? He remembered his own sensation during that moment. A sense of something greater.

On the floor, Raoul covered his face with one hand.

Had something rewired the man's soul? Could there be hope for him?

Movement drew Gray's eye. He saw the danger immediately.

He moved to stop her.

Ignoring him, Seichan lifted Raoul's gun. She pointed it at the trapped man.

Raoul turned to face the barrel. His expression remained anguished, but now a flicker of raw fear lit his eyes. Gray recognized that shine of black terror in the man – not for the gun, nor for the pain of death, but for what lay beyond.

'No!' Gray called.

Seichan pulled the trigger. Raoul's head snapped back to the glass with a crack as loud as the pistol shot.

The others froze in shock.

'Why?' Gray asked, stunned, stepping forward.

Seichan rubbed her wounded shoulder with the butt of her pistol. 'Payback. Remember we had a deal, Gray.' She nodded to Raoul's body. 'Besides, like the man said, he wasn't looking for forgiveness.'

Painter heard the echo of the gunshot through the palace. He motioned the French patrol to pause. Someone was still fighting in here.

Was it his team?

'Slowly,' he warned, waving them forward. 'Be ready.'

He continued deeper into the palace. He had come to France on his own. Not even Sean McKnight knew he had undertaken this assignment, but Painter's Europol credentials had gotten him the field support he needed in Marseilles. It had taken the entire length of a transatlantic trip to track General Rende, first to a warehouse outside Avignon, then to the Pope's Palace. Painter remembered his mentor's warning that a director's position was behind a desk, not out in the field.

But that was Sean.

Not Painter.

Sigma was now his organization, and he had his own way of solving problems. He gripped his gun and led the way.

Upon first hearing of a possible leak from Gray, Painter made one decision. To trust his own organization. He had put the new Sigma together from the ground up. If there was a leak, it had to be an unintentional one.

So he had done the next logical thing: followed the trail of intel.

From Gray . . . to Sigma . . . to their Carabinieri liaison out in Rome.

General Rende had been kept abreast of every detail of the operation.

It had taken some careful prying to follow the man's tracks, which included suspicious trips to Switzerland and back. Eventually Painter had discovered one thin tie back to the Dragon Court. A distant relative of Rende who had been arrested two years ago for trafficking in stolen antiquities, in Oman of all places. The thief had gained his freedom from pressure by the Imperial Dragon Court.

As he'd investigated deeper, Painter had kept Logan Gregory out of the loop, so the man could continue his role as Sigma liaison. He hadn't wanted to spook Rende, not until he could be sure.

Now that his suspicions had been verified, Painter had another concern.

Was he too late?

**8:00 a.m.**

Rachel and Monk secured her uncle's temporary belly wrap, using Gray's shirt. Uncle Vigor had lost a fair amount of blood, but the bullet had passed clean through. According to Monk, nothing major seemed to have been hit, but he needed immediate medical attention.

Uncle Vigor patted her hand once she was finished, then Monk helped him to his feet and half carried him.

Rachel hovered alongside them. Gray joined her, putting an arm around her waist. She leaned a bit into him, drawing strength from him.

'Vigor will be fine,' Gray promised. 'He's tough. He's come this far.'

She smiled up at him, but she was too tired to put much emotion behind it.

Before they even reached the first tier, a booming voice echoed down to them, using a bullhorn again. '*SORTEZ AVEC VOS MAINS SUR LA TÊTE!*' The command echoed away, to come out with their hands up.

'*Déjà vu,*' Monk sighed. 'Pardon my French.'

Rachel lifted her rifle.

A second command in English followed. 'COMMANDER PIERCE, WHAT'S YOUR STATUS?'

Gray turned to the others.

'Impossible,' Kat said.

'It's Director Crowe,' Gray confirmed, shock in his voice.

He turned and cupped his mouth and yelled back.

'ALL CLEAR DOWN HERE! WE'RE COMING UP!'

Gray then turned to Rachel, eyes bright.

'Is it over?' she asked.

As answer, he pulled her to him and kissed her. There was no mysterious light this time, only the strength of his arms and sweetness of his lips. She sank into him.

Here was all the magic she needed.


8:02 a.m.

Gray led the way up.

Monk helped Vigor, carrying him under his good arm. Gray kept an arm around Rachel. She leaned heavily against him, but she was a burden he was happy to bear.

Though relieved, Gray kept them armed this time. He was not walking into another ambush. Rifles and pistols in hand, they began the long trek up to the kitchen. Bodies, burned or electrocuted, littered the tiers.

'Why were we spared?' Monk asked.

'Maybe that lower level sheltered us,' Kat said.

Gray didn't argue with her, but he suspected it was something more than that. He remembered the suffusing glow of the light. He sensed something more than random photons. Maybe not an intelligence. But something beyond raw power.

'And what happened to the treasure house?' Seichan asked, staring out at the empty expanse. 'Was it all a hologram of some sort?'

'No,' Gray answered as they climbed. He had a theory. 'Under powerful conditions, flux tubes can be generated within a Meissner field. Affecting not only gravity, like the levitation we've already seen, but also distorting

501

space. Einstein showed that gravity actually *curves* space. The flux tubes create such a vortex in gravity that it *bends* space, possibly even folding it on itself, allowing movement across.'

Gray noted the looks of disbelief. 'Research is already being done on this at NASA,' he pressed.

'Smoke and mirrors,' Monk grumbled. 'That's what I think it was.'

'But where did it all go?' Seichan asked.

Vigor coughed. Rachel stepped toward him. He waved her away, only clearing his throat. 'Gone where we can't follow,' he said hoarsely. 'We were judged and found wanting.'

Gray felt Rachel begin to speak, to mention the false key. He squeezed her and nodded to her uncle, urging her to let him speak. Maybe it wasn't all the fake key. Could Vigor be right? Had they brushed against something they weren't ready for?

The monsignor continued, 'The ancients sought the source of primordial light, the spark of all existence. Maybe they found a doorway into or a way to ascend up to it. The white bread of the Pharaohs was said to have helped these Egyptian kings shed mortal flesh and rise as a being of light. Maybe the ancient alchemists finally achieved this, moving out of this world and into the next.'

'Like traveling along the labyrinth,' Kat said.

'Exactly. The maze may be symbolic for their ascension. They left this gateway here for others to follow, but we came – '

'Too early,' Rachel suddenly blurted, interrupting.

'Or too late,' Gray added. The words had just popped into his head, like the flash of a camera bulb, leaving him dazed.

Rachel glanced to him. She lifted a hand to rub her forehead.

He saw a similar confusion in her eyes, as if the words

had come unbidden to her, too. He glanced over the lip of the tier down to the shattered glass floor, then back to her.

Perhaps Raoul was not the only one affected by the light.

Had an echo been left inside them? An understanding, a final message?

'Too late . . . or too early,' Vigor continued with a shake of his head, drawing back Gray's attention. 'Wherever the ancients fled with their treasures – into the past, into the future – they have left us with only the present.'

'To create our own heaven or hell,' Monk said.

They continued in silence, climbing tier after tier. Reaching the top level, a group of French police waited, along with a familiar face.

'Commander,' Painter said. 'It's good to see you.'

Gray shook his hand. 'You have no idea.'

'Let's get all of you topside.'

Before they could move, Vigor stirred from Monk's arm. 'Wait.' He stumbled away, one hand on the wall.

Gray and Rachel stepped after him.

'Uncle . . .' she said, concerned.

A short distance away stood a stone table. It seemed everything had not vanished with the library. A leather-bound book rested on the table. Its glass case, though, was gone.

'The ledger,' Vigor said, tears welling. 'They left the ledger!'

He attempted to pick it up, but Rachel motioned him aside and collected it herself. She shut it and tucked it under an arm.

'Why leave that behind?' Monk asked, helping the monsignor again.

Vigor answered, 'To let us know what awaits us. To give us something to seek.'

'Dangling the proverbial carrot before the mule,' Monk

said. 'Great. They couldn't leave a chest of gold . . . okay, maybe not *gold* . . . I'm damn sick of gold. Diamonds, a chest of diamonds would be fine.'

They hobbled toward the stairs.

Gray glanced back one more time. With the space empty, he noted the cavern's shape, a cone-shaped pyramid balanced on its tip. Or the upper half of an hourglass, pointing down toward the glass floor.

But where was the lower half?

As he stared, he suddenly knew.

'As it is above, so it is below,' he mumbled.

Vigor glanced back to him, rather sharply. Gray saw the understanding and knowledge in the old man's eyes. He had already figured it out, too.

The gold key was meant to open a gateway. To the lower half of the hourglass. But where? Was there a cavern directly beneath this one? Gray didn't think so. But somewhere the cathedral of knowledge waited. What had hung here was a mere reflection from another place.

Like Monk said. Smoke and mirrors.

Vigor stared at him. Gray remembered Cardinal Spera's mission: to preserve the secret of the Magi, trusting that the knowledge would reveal itself when the time was right.

Maybe that's what life's journey was all about.

The quest.

To seek the truth.

Gray placed a hand on Vigor's shoulder. 'Let's go home.'

With Rachel under his arm, Gray climbed the stairs.

Out of darkness and toward the light.

# EPILOGUE

Gray pedaled down Cedar Street, passing by the Takoma Park Library. It felt good to feel the rush of air and the bright sunshine on his face. It seemed like the last three weeks had been spent underground at Sigma command, in meeting after meeting.

He had just come from a final debriefing with Painter Crowe. The meeting had centered on Seichan. The Guild operative had vanished like a ghost as they'd left the Pope's Palace, stepping around a dark corner and disappearing. But Gray had found a token from her in his pocket.

Her dragon pendant.

Again.

And while the first pendant left at Fort Detrick had plainly been meant as a threat, this one felt different to Gray. A promise. Until they met again.

Kat and Monk had been at the debriefing, too. Monk had sat fiddling with his new state-of-the-art prosthesis, not so much uncomfortable with his new hand as he was anxious about the coming evening. Kat and Monk were going out on their first real date. The two had grown close after returning to the States. And oddly enough, it was Kat who had moved things forward and asked Monk out on tonight's dinner date.

Afterward, alone, Monk had pulled Gray aside, half giddy. 'It's got to be the mechanical hand. Comes with a

505

two-stroke vibration mode. What woman wouldn't want to date me?'

Despite the flippancy, Gray saw the genuine affection and hope in his friend's eyes. And also a little terror. Gray knew that Monk still bore some trauma from his mutilation, some insecurity.

Gray hoped that Monk would call him tomorrow, tell him how everything had turned out.

He shifted his weight to one pedal, knee out, and skimmed low around the corner onto Sixth Street. His mother had asked him to come to lunch.

And while he could've refused, he had been putting off something for too long. He glided past the rows of Victorian and Queen Anne cottages, dapple-shaded by a canopy of elms and maples.

He made a final turn onto Butternut Avenue, hopped the curb, and braked into the driveway of his parents' Craftsman bungalow. He snapped off his helmet and carried his bike onto the porch.

He called through the screen door. 'Mom, I'm home!'

He leaned the bike against the railing and opened the door.

'I'm in the kitchen!' his mother said.

Gray smelled something burning. A bit of smoke hung about the rafters.

'Is everything all right?' he asked, crossing down the short hall.

His mother wore jeans, a checkered blouse, and an apron snugged around her waist. She had dropped her hours at the university to part-time, two days a week. To help care for things at home.

Smoke filled the kitchen.

'I was making grilled cheese sandwiches,' she said, fluttering her hands. 'I got a phone call from my TA. Left them on the griddle too long.'

Gray eyed the pile of sandwiches on a plate. Each was

charred on one side. He fingered one. The cheese hadn't even melted. How did his mother do that? Burn the sandwiches yet still keep them cold. It had to be a skill.

'They look fine,' Gray said.

'Call your father.' She waved her dishtowel, trying to waft out the smoke. 'He's out back.'

'More birdhouses?'

His mother rolled her eyes.

Gray crossed to the open back door and leaned out. 'Pop! Lunch is ready.'

'Be right there!'

Gray returned as his mother set out some plates.

'Could you pour some orange juice?' she asked. 'I need to get a fan.'

Gray stepped to the refrigerator, found the carton of Minute Maid, and began filling the tumblers. With his mother gone, he set the carton down and removed a small glass vial from his back pocket.

A gray-white powder filled it halfway. The last of the amalgam.

With Monk's assistance, he had done some research into the m-state powders, how the compounds stimulated endocrine systems and seemed to have a strong ameliorative affect on the brain, increasing perception, acuity . . . *and memory.*

Gray dumped the contents of the vial into one of the glasses of orange juice and used a teaspoon to stir it.

His father entered through the back door. Sawdust speckled his hair. He wiped his boots on the rug, nodded to Gray, and dropped heavily into a chair.

'Your mother tells me you're heading back to Italy.'

'Only for five days,' Gray answered, nesting all three glasses between his palms and carrying them over. 'Another business trip.'

'Right . . .' His father eyed him. 'So who's the girl?'

Gray startled at the question and bobbled some of the

507

orange juice. He hadn't told his father anything about Rachel. He wasn't sure what to say. After their rescue, the two had spent a night in Avignon together as matters were sorted out, curled in front of a small fire while the storm exhausted itself. They hadn't made love that night, but they had talked. Rachel had explained about her family's history, haltingly, with some tears. She still could not balance her feelings about her grandmother.

Finally, they had fallen asleep in each other's arms.

In the morning, circumstance and duty had pulled them apart.

Where would it lead now?

He was heading back to Rome to find out.

He still called daily, sometimes twice daily. Vigor was healing well. Following the funeral for Cardinal Spera, he had been promoted to the position of prefect at the Archives, to oversee the repair of the damage done by the Court. Last week, Gray had received a note of thanks from Vigor but also discovered a message hidden within the text. Below the monsignor's signature lay two inked seals, papal insignia, mirror images of each other, the twin symbols of the Thomas Church.

It seemed the secret church had found a new member to replace the lost cardinal.

Upon learning this, Gray had shipped Alexander's gold key to Vigor, the *real* gold key, from a safe deposit box in Egypt. For safekeeping. Who better to secure it? The fake key, the one used to trick Raoul, had been fashioned at one of the many shops in Alexandria known for their skill at counterfeiting antiquities. It had taken less than an hour, performed while Gray had freed Seichan from Alexander's watery tomb. He hadn't dared transport the real key to France, to the Dragon Court.

General Rende's testimony and confession while in custody proved how dangerous that would have been. The litany of atrocities and deaths stretched back decades.

With Rende's confession, his sect of the Dragon Court was slowly being rooted out. But how thoroughly or completely would never be known.

Meanwhile, closer to Gray's heart and mind, Rachel continued to sort out her life. With Raoul's death, she and her family had inherited Chateau Sauvage, a bloody inheritance to be sure. But at least the curse had died along with Rachel's grandmother. No other Verona family members had been aware of the grandmother's dark secret. To settle matters further, plans were already under way to sell the chateau. The proceeds would go to the families of those killed in Cologne and Milan.

So lives slowly healed and moved forward.

Toward hope.

And possibly more . . .

Gray's father sighed and tipped back in his kitchen chair. 'Son, you've been in an awfully good mood lately. Ever since your return from that business trip last month. Only a woman puts that kind of shine on a man.'

Gray settled the tumblers of orange juice on the table.

'I may be losing my memory,' his father continued. 'But not my eyesight. So tell me about her.'

Gray stared at his father. He heard the unspoken addendum.

*While I can still remember.*

His father's casual manner hid a deeper vein. Not sorrow or loss. He was reaching out for something now. In the present. Some connection to a son he'd perhaps lost in the past.

Gray froze by the table. He felt a flare of old anger, older resentment. He didn't deny it, but he let the heat wash through him.

His father must have sensed something, because he settled his chair to the floor and changed the subject. 'So, where are those sandwiches?'

Words echoed in Gray's head. *Too early . . . too late.* A

last message to live in the present. To accept the past and not rush the future.

His father reached for the spiked glass of orange juice.

Gray blocked him, covering the cup with his hand. He lifted the tumbler away. 'How about a beer? I think I saw a Bud in the fridge.'

His father nodded. 'That's why I love you, son.'

Gray stepped to the sink, dumped the orange juice down the drain, and watched it swirl away.

*Too early . . . too late.*

It was time he lived in the present. He didn't know how much time he had with his father, but he would take what he could get and make the very best of it.

He crossed to the fridge, grabbed *two* beers, popped the lids on the way back, pulled out one of the kitchen chairs, sat down, and placed a bottle in front of his father.

'Her name is Rachel.'

# AUTHOR'S NOTE

Thanks for following me on this latest journey. As before, I wanted to take this last moment to separate fact from fiction. I also hope this spurs some further investigation by readers. To aid in this, I've listed some of the books below that inspired this storyline.

So let's start at the beginning. The Prologue. The Magi relics are indeed stored in a golden sarcophagus at the Cologne Cathedral, and the caravan that transported the bones from Milan to Cologne was indeed ambushed in the twelfth century.

Moving on to the first chapter, Super Black is a real compound developed at the National Physical Laboratory in Britain. The Eight Ball is a real structure at Fort Detrick (sorry for knocking it over), and liquid body armor is, amazingly enough, *real*, developed by the U.S. Army Research Laboratory.

I won't go into such specific detail with the rest of the novel. I just wanted to use the above examples to demonstrate how what might seem wild in this novel may have some basis in fact. For those interested in more specifics, please check out my website (jamesrollins.com).

The Imperial Dragon Court is an actual European organization that traces its roots back to the Middle Ages. It is a ceremonial and benevolent society of aristocrats of varying influence. The bloody subsect described in this book is of my own imagining and not meant to disparage anyone currently in the Court.

As to the heart of this novel, it would take volumes to

511

discuss the truth behind both m-state metals and the long trail they trace throughout history. Luckily, that volume has already been written, following in great detail the path from the Egyptians to modern times, including the strange effects of Meissner fields, superconductivity, and magnetism. I encourage anyone with even a slight interest in this topic to pick up *Lost Secrets of the Sacred Ark* by Sir Laurence Gardner. It was my own personal bible for this novel.

Speaking of bibles, if you were wondering about the conflict in the early Christian church between the followers of the apostles John and Thomas, a pair of great books on this topic were written by National Book Award-winning author Elaine Pagels: *Beyond Belief: The Secret Gospel of Thomas* and *The Gnostic Gospels*.

For those interested in more details of the Magi and a possible brotherhood that still exists today, I recommend *Magi: the Quest for a Secret Tradition* by Adrian Gilbert.

I also recommend and am indebted to Robert J. Hutchinson's *When in Rome, a Journal of Life in Vatican City*. It is a great and entertaining source of insight into the Vatican and its history.

Finally, I hope my own novel entertains but also raises some questions in the readers. In that vein, I'll end this discussion of fact and fiction by endorsing the primary adage of Gnostic tradition: to seek the truth . . . always and in all ways. It seems a fitting finish to this novel. So to quote Matthew 7:7,

'Seek, and you shall find.'

If you have enjoyed

# MAP OF BONES

don't miss James Rollins' latest
bestselling thriller

# ALTAR OF EDEN

Coming soon from Orion

Here's a taster...

April 2003
Baghdad, Iraq


The two boys stood outside the lion's cage.

"I don't want to go inside," the smaller one said. He kept close to his older brother and clasped tightly to his hand.

The two were bundled in jackets too large for their small forms, faces swathed in scarves, heads warmed by woolen caps. At this early hour, with the sun not yet up, the predawn chill had crept down to their bones.

They had to keep moving.

"Bari, the cage is empty. Stop being a *shakheef*. Look." Makeen, the older of the two, pushed the black iron gate wider and revealed the bare concrete walls inside. A few old gnawed bones lay piled in a dark corner. They would make a nice soup.

Makeen stared out at the ruins of the zoo. He remembered how it had once looked. Half a year ago, for his twelfth birthday, they had come here to picnic at the Al-Zawraa Gardens with its amusement-park rides and zoo. The family had spent a long warm afternoon wandering among the cages of monkeys, parrots, camels, wolves, bears. Makeen had even fed one of the camels an apple. He still remembered the rubbery lips on his palm.

Standing here now, he stared across the same park with older eyes, far older than half a year ago. The park sprawled

3

outward in a ruin of rubble and refuse. It was a haunted wasteland of fire-blackened walls, fetid pools of oily water, and blasted buildings.

A month ago, Makeen had watched from their apartment near the park as a firefight blazed across the lush gardens, waged by American forces and the Republican Guard. The fierce battle had begun at dusk, with the rattle of gunfire and the shriek of rockets continuing throughout the night.

But by the next morning, all had gone quiet. Smoke hung thickly and hid the sun for the entire day. From the balcony of their small apartment, Makeen had spotted a lion as it loped out of the park and into the city. It moved like a dusky shadow, then vanished into the streets. Other animals also escaped, but over the next two days hordes of people had swarmed back into the park.

*Looters*, his father had named them, and spat on the floor, cursing them in more foul language.

Cages were ripped open. Animals were stolen, many for food, but even more were sold on the black market across the river, opening a floodgate of exotic-animal smuggling to the West. Makeen's father had gone with a few other men to get help to protect their section of the city from the roving bands.

He had never returned. None of them had.

Over the next weeks, the burden had fallen upon Makeen to keep his family fed. His mother had taken to her bed, her forehead burning with fever, lost somewhere between terror and grief. All Makeen could get her to do was drink a few sips of water.

If he could make a nice soup for her, get her to eat something more . . .

He eyed the bones in the cage again. Each morning, he and his brother spent the hour before dawn searching the bombed-out park and zoo for anything they could scrounge to eat. He carried a burlap sack over his shoulder. All it held was a moldy orange and a handful of cracked seed swept up

4

off the floor of a birdcage. Little Bari had also found a dented can of beans in a rubbish bin. The discovery had brought tears to Makeen's eyes. He kept the treasure rolled up inside his little brother's thick sweater.

Yesterday, a larger boy with a long knife had stolen his sack, leaving Makeen empty-handed when he returned. They'd had nothing to eat that day.

But today they would eat well.

Even Mother, *inshallah*, he prayed.

Makeen entered the cage and dragged Bari with him. Distant gunfire crackled in short spurts, like the scolding claps of angry hands trying to warn them off.

Makeen took heed. He knew they had to hurry. He didn't want to be out when the sun was up. It would grow too dangerous. He hurried to the pile of bones, dropped his sack, and began shoving the gnawed knuckles and broken shafts inside.

Once finished, he tugged the sack closed and stood. Before he could take a step, a voice called in Arabic from nearby.

"*Yalla*! This way! Over here!"

Makeen ducked and pulled Bari down with him. They hid behind the knee-high cinderblock wall that fronted the lion's cage. He hugged his brother, urging him to remain silent, as two large shadows passed in front of the lion's cage.

Risking a peek, Makeen caught a glimpse of two men. One was tall in a khaki military uniform. The other was squat with a round belly, dressed in a dark suit.

"The entrance is hidden behind the zoo clinic," the fat man said as he passed the cage. He huffed and wheezed to keep up with the longer strides of the man in military fatigues. "I can only pray we are not too late."

Makeen spotted the holstered pistol on the taller man's belt and knew it would be death to be found eavesdropping.

Bari shivered in his embrace, sensing the danger, too.

Unfortunately the men did not go far. The clinic was directly across from their hiding spot. The fat man ignored the twisted main door. Days ago, crowbars had forced the way open. The facility had been cleaned out of drugs and medical supplies.

Instead, the heavy figure stepped to a blank wall framed by two columns. Makeen could not make out what the man did as he slipped his hand behind one of the columns, but a moment later a section of the wall swung open. It was a secret door.

Makeen shifted closer to the bars. Father had read them stories of Ali Baba, tales of secret caverns and vast stolen treasures hidden in the desert. All he and his brother had found at the zoo were bones and beans. Makeen's stomach churned as he imagined a feast fit for the Prince of Thieves that might wait below.

"Stay here," the fat man said, ducking through the entrance and down a dark set of stairs.

The military man took up a post by the doorway. His palm rested on his pistol. His gaze swung toward their hiding spot. Makeen ducked out of sight and held his breath. His heart pounded against his ribs.

Had he been spotted?

Footsteps approached the cage. Makeen clung tightly to his brother. But a moment later, he heard a match strike and smelled cigarette smoke. The man paced the front of the cage as if he were the one behind the bars, stalking back and forth like a bored tiger.

Bari shook within Makeen's embrace. His brother's fingers were clamped hard in his. What if the man should wander into the cage and find them huddled there?

It seemed an eternity when a familiar wheezing voice echoed out of the doorway. "I have them!"

The cigarette was dropped and ground out onto the cement just outside the cage door. The military man crossed back to join his companion.

The fat man gasped as he spoke. He must have run all the way back up. "The incubators were off-line," he said. "I

6

don't know how long the generators lasted after the power went out."

Makeen risked a peek through the bars of the cage door. The fat man carried a large metal briefcase in his hand.

"Are they secure?" the military man asked. He also spoke in Arabic, but his accent was not Iraqi.

The fat man dropped to one knee, balanced the case on his thick thigh, and thumbed open the lock. Makeen expected gold and diamonds, but instead the case held nothing but white eggs packed in molded black foam. They appeared no different from the chicken eggs his mother bought at the market.

Despite his terror, the sight of the eggs stirred Makeen's hunger.

The fat man counted them, inspecting them. "They're all intact," he said and let out a long rattling sigh of relief. "God willing, the embryos inside are still viable."

"And the rest of the lab?"

The fat man closed the case and stood up. "I'll leave it to your team to incinerate what lies below. No one must ever suspect what we've discovered. There can be no trace."

"I know my orders."

As the fat man stood, the military man raised his pistol and shot his companion in the face. The blast was a thunderclap. The back of the man's skull blew away in a cloud of bone and blood. The dead man stood for a moment longer, then flopped to the ground.

Makeen covered his mouth to stifle any sound.

"No trace," the murderer repeated and collected the case from the ground. He touched a radio on his shoulder. He switched to English.

"Bring in the trucks and prime the incendiary charges. Time to get out of this sandbox before any locals turn up."

Makeen had learned to speak a smattering of the American language. He couldn't pick out every word the man spoke, but he understood the message well enough.

*More men were coming. More guns.*

Makeen sought some means of escape, but they were trapped in the lion's cage. Perhaps his younger brother also recognized the growing danger. Bari's shaking had grown worse since the gunshot. Finally, his little brother's terror could no longer be held inside, and a quiet sob rattled out of his thin form.

Makeen squeezed his brother and prayed that the cry had not been heard.

Footsteps again approached. A sharp call barked toward them in Arabic. "Who's there? Show yourself! *Ta'aal hnaa!*"

Makeen pressed his lips to his brother's ear. "Stay hidden. Don't come out."

Makeen shoved Bari tighter into the corner, then stood up with his hands in the air. He backed up a step. "I was just looking for food!" Makeen said, stuttering, speaking fast.

The pistol stayed leveled at him. "Get out here, *walad*!"

Makeen obeyed. He moved to the cage door and slipped out. He kept his hands in the air. "Please, *ahki. Laa termi!*" He tried switching to English, to show he was on the man's side. "No shoot. I not see . . . I not know . . ."

He fought to find some argument, some words to save him. He read the expression on the other man's face—a mixture of sorrow and regret.

The pistol lifted higher with merciless intent.

Makeen felt hot tears flow down his cheeks.

Through the blur of his vision, he noted a shift of shadows. Behind the man, the secret door cracked open wider, pushed from inside. A large, dark shape slipped out and flowed toward the man's back. It ran low and stuck to the deeper shadows, as if fearing the light.

Makeen caught the barest glimpse of its oily form: muscular, lean, hairless, with eyes glinting with fury. His mind struggled to comprehend what he was seeing—but failed.

A scream of horror built inside his chest.

Though the beast made no noise, the man must have felt

a prickling of warning. He swung around as the creature leaped with a sharp cry. Gunshots blasted, eclipsed by a savage wail that raised the hairs on Makeen's body.

Makeen swung away and rushed back to the cage. "Bari!"

He grabbed his brother's arm and dragged him out of the lion's cage. He pushed Bari ahead of him. "*Yalla*! Run!"

Off to the side, man and beast fought on the ground.

More pistol shots fired.

Makeen heard the heavy tread of boots on pavement behind him. More men came running from the other side of the park. Shouts were punctuated by rifle blasts.

Ignoring them all, Makeen fled in raw terror across the bombed-out gardens, careless of who might see him. He kept running and running, chased by screams that would forever haunt his nightmares.

He understood nothing about what had happened. He knew only one thing for certain. He remembered the beast's ravenous eyes, shining with a cunning intelligence, aglow with a smokeless fire.

Makeen knew what he had seen.

The beast known as *Shaitan* in the Koran—he who was born of God's fire and cursed for not bowing down to Adam.

Makeen knew the truth.

At long last, the devil had come to Baghdad.

All Orion/Phoenix titles are available at your local bookshop or from the following address:

Mail Order Department
Littlehampton Book Services
FREEPOST BR535
Worthing, West Sussex, BN13 3BR
*telephone* 01903 828503, *facsimile* 01903 828802
*e-mail* MailOrders@lbsltd.co.uk
(Please ensure that you include full postal address details)

Payment can be made either by credit/debit card (Visa, Mastercard, Access and Switch accepted) or by sending a £ Sterling cheque or postal order made payable to *Littlehampton Book Services.*
DO NOT SEND CASH OR CURRENCY

**Please add the following to cover postage and packing**

*UK and BFPO:*
£1.50 for the first book, and 50p for each additional book to a maximum of £3.50

*Overseas and Eire:*
£2.50 for the first book plus £1.00 for the second book and 50p for each additional book ordered

---

BLOCK CAPITALS PLEASE

*name of cardholder* ........................

*delivery address
(if different from cardholder)*

*address of cardholder* ........................

........................

........................

........................

*postcode* ........................

*postcode* ........................

☐ I enclose my remittance for  £........................

☐ please debit my Mastercard/Visa/Access/Switch (delete as appropriate)

card number  ☐☐☐☐☐☐☐☐☐☐☐☐☐☐☐☐☐☐

expiry date  ☐☐☐☐     Switch issue no.  ☐☐

signature  ........................

*prices and availability are subject to change without notice*